COO 916 034X

D0334815

SPECIAL MESSAGE TO READERS

THE ULVERSCROFT FOUNDATION
(registered UK charity number 264873)

was established in 1972 to provide funds for research, diagnosis and treatment of eye diseases. Examples of major projects funded by the Ulverscroft Foundation are:-

- The Children's Eye Unit at Moorfields Eye Hospital, London
- The Ulverscroft Children's Eye Unit at Great Ormond Street Hospital for Sick Children
- Funding research into eye diseases and treatment at the Department of Ophthalmology, University of Leicester
- The Ulverscroft Vision Research Group, Institute of Child Health
- Twin operating theatres at the Western Ophthalmic Hospital, London
- The Chair of Ophthalmology at the Royal Australian College of Ophthalmologists

You can help further the work of the Foundation by making a donation or leaving a legacy. Every contribution is gratefully received. If you would like to help support the Foundation or require further information, please contact:

THE ULVERSCROFT FOUNDATION
The Green, Bradgate Road, Anstey Leicester LE7 7FU, England Tel: (0116) 236 4325

website: www.foundation.ulverscroft.com

Liz Trenow's family have been silk weavers for nearly three hundred years, and she grew up next to their mill in Sudbury, Suffolk, which is the oldest family-owned silk company in Britain. Liz worked in the mill for a few months but decided instead to become a journalist and spent fifteen years with regional and national newspapers, and on BBC radio and television news. *The Last Telegram* is her first novel.

THE LAST TELEGRAM

As the Nazis storm Europe, Lily Verner becomes an apprentice at her family's silk weaving factory. When they begin to weave parachute silk, there is no margin for error; one tiny fault could result in certain death for Allied soldiers. The war also brings Stefan, a German Jewish refugee, to Lily. Working on the looms, their love begins to grow — but there are suspicions that someone is tampering with the silk . . . Can their love survive the hardships of war? And will the Verners' silk stand the ultimate test?

LIZ TRENOW

THE LAST TELEGRAM

Complete and Unabridged

CHARNWOOD
Leicester

First published in Great Britain in 2012 by
Avon
London

First Charnwood Edition
published 2013
by arrangement with
Avon
A division of
HarperCollins*Publishers*
London

The moral right of the author has been asserted

This novel is entirely a work of fiction. The names, characters and incidents portrayed in it are the work of the author's imagination. Any resemblance to actual persons, living or dead, events or localities is entirely coincidental.

Copyright © 2012 by Liz Trenow
All rights reserved

A catalogue record for this book is available from the British Library.

ISBN 978–1–4448–1738–6

DUNDEE CITY
COUNCIL

LOCATION   LPR

COMMUNITY LIBS

ACCESSION NUMBER

COO 916 03LX

SUPPLIER   PRICE

ULV   £20·99

CLASS No.   DATE

823·91   9·12·2013

Published by
F. A. Thorpe (Publishing)
Anstey, Leicestershire

Set by Words & Graphics Ltd.
Anstey, Leicestershire
Printed and bound in Great Britain by
T. J. International Ltd., Padstow, Cornwall

This book is printed on acid-free paper

In memory of my father, Peter Walters (1919–2011), under whose directorship the mill produced many thousands of yards of wartime parachute silk.

All of it perfect.

Acknowledgements

The Last Telegram would probably never have been written without the encouragement, thoughtful reading and robust feedback of my tutor, Harriett Gilbert, on the MA in Creative Writing at City University in London and my fellow students, who continue to be a great support network. Simon Edge wisely encouraged me to write about my family background in silk weaving and my great friend Anne Sherer Broom was a constant source of inspiration, not to mention her knowledge of all things Jewish, and her brilliant suggestion that I should read Arthur Miller's play, *All My Sons*.

Although the plot and all of the characters are entirely fictional, parts of the story are based on real events and for this I owe a great debt to the memories of three remarkable men. From my father, the late Peter Walters, I learned how they kept the mill going during the Second World War, when most others closed, by weaving parachute silk. The family had become increasingly concerned about the plight of their many Jewish friends and business colleagues in Europe, which prompted them to sponsor five German boys to travel to England and work at the mill. One of them, Roger Lynton, fell in love with a local girl and, after internment in Australia and fighting for the Allies in North Africa, returned to work at the mill, married and had a family, and lived a long and happy life. Thirdly I am indebted to the late Anthony Gaddum, formerly Upper Bailiff of the Worshipful Company of Weavers, who told me about the extraordinary mission undertaken by his father, Peter, to source vital silk supplies from the Middle East at the height of the war.

I am grateful to David and Julius Walters for hosting a memorable tea party for former parachute weavers at the mill, and to Freda Baker for organising it. The memories I recorded that afternoon provided rich material. Richard Humphries, with his love of all things historic, marvellously produced an original wartime parachute burst testing machine and Andy Cowley, Engineering Manager of Airborne Systems Ltd, provided invaluable technical information about wartime parachute manufacture.

My daughters Becky and Polly, and my friend Mel Billowes, read early drafts and gave helpful feedback, and other good friends and family members have provided unwavering encouragement, especially my husband David, who has been consistently positive in believing that the book would, eventually, find a publisher.

Finally, huge thanks to the tireless work of Caroline Hardman and others at Christopher Little Literary Agency who recognised the early potential of the book and guided me towards developing it into fully-formed novel, and to Caroline Hogg of HarperCollins, who had a clear vision of what was needed to turn that dream of publication into a reality.

1

The history of silk owes much to the fairer sex. The Chinese Empress Hsi Ling is credited with its first discovery, in 2640 BC. It is said that a cocoon fell from the mulberry tree, under which she was sitting, into her cup of tea. As she sought to remove the cocoon its sticky threads started to unravel and cling to her fingers. Upon examining the thread more closely she immediately saw its potential and dedicated her life thereafter to the cultivation of the silkworm and production of silk for weaving and embroidery.
From *The History of Silk*, **by Harold Verner**

Perhaps because death leaves so little to say, funeral guests seem to take refuge in platitudes. 'He had a good innings . . . Splendid send-off . . . Very moving service . . . Such beautiful flowers . . . You are so wonderfully brave, Lily.'

It's not bravery: my squared shoulders, head held high, that careful expression of modesty and gratitude. Not bravery, just determination to survive today and, as soon as possible, get on with what remains of my life. The body in the expensive coffin, lined with Verners' silk and decorated with lilies, and now deep in the ground, is not the man I've loved and shared my life with for the past fifty-five years.

It is not the man who helped to put me back

1

together after the shattering events of the war, who held my hand and steadied my heart with his wise counsel, the man who took me as his own and became a loving father and grandfather. The joy of our lives together helped us both to bury the terrors of the past. No, that person disappeared months ago, when the illness took its final hold. His death was a blessed release and I have already done my grieving. Or at least, that's what I keep telling myself.

After the service the house fills with people wanting to 'pay their final respects'. But I long for them to go, and eventually they drift away, leaving behind the detritus of a remembered life along with the half-drunk glasses, the discarded morsels of food.

Around me, my son and his family are washing up, vacuuming, emptying the bins. In the harsh kitchen light I notice a shimmer of grey in Simon's hair (the rest of it is dark, like his father's) and realise with a jolt that he must be well into middle age. His wife Louise, once so slight, is rather rounder than before. No wonder, after two babies. They deserve to live in this house, I think, to have more room for their growing family. But today is not the right time to talk about moving.

I go to sit in the drawing room as they have bidden me, and watch for the first time the slide show that they have created for the guests at the wake. I am mesmerised as the TV screen flicks through familiar photographs, charting his life from sepia babyhood through monochrome middle years and into a technicolour old age,

2

each image occupying the screen for just a few brief seconds before blurring into the next.

At first I turn away, finding it annoying, even insulting. What a travesty, I think, a long, loving life bottled into a slide show. But as the carousel goes back to the beginning and the photographs start to repeat themselves, my relief that he is gone and will suffer no more is replaced, for the first time since his death, by a dawning realisation of my own loss.

It's no wonder I loved him so; such a good looking man, active and energetic. A man of unlimited selflessness, of many smiles and little guile. Who loved every part of me, infinitely. What a lucky woman. I find myself smiling back, with tears in my eyes.

My granddaughter brings a pot of tea. At seventeen, Emily is the oldest of her generation of Verners, a clever, sensitive girl growing up faster than I can bear. I see in her so much of myself at that age: not exactly pretty in the conventional way — her nose is slightly too long — but striking, with smooth cheeks and a creamy complexion that flushes at the slightest hint of discomfiture. Her hair, the colour of black coffee, grows thick and straight, and her dark inquisitive eyes shimmer with mischief or chill with disapproval. She has that determined Verner jawline that says, 'don't mess with me'. She's tall and lanky, all arms and legs, rarely out of the patched jeans and charity-shop jumpers which seem to be all the rage with her generation these days. Unsophisticated but self-confident, exhaustingly energetic — and always fun. Had

3

my own daughter lived, I sometimes think, she would have been like Emily.

At this afternoon's wake the streak of crimson she's emblazoned into the flick of her fringe was like an exotic bird darting among the dark suits and dresses. Soon she will fly, as they all do, these independent young women. But for the moment she indulges me with her company and conversation, and I cherish every moment.

She hands me a cup of weak tea with no milk, just how I like it, and then plonks herself down on the footstool next to me. We watch the slide show together for a few moments and she says, 'I miss Grandpa, you know. Such an amazing man. He was so full of ideas and enthusiasm — I loved the way he supported everything we did, even the crazy things.' She's right, I think to myself. I was a lucky woman.

'He always used to ask me about stuff,' she goes on. 'He was always interested in what I was doing with myself. Not many grownups do that. A great listener.'

As usual my smart girl goes straight to the heart of it. It's something I'm probably guilty of, not listening enough. 'You can talk to me, now that he's gone.' I say, a bit too quickly. 'Tell me what's new.'

'You really want to know?'

'Yes, I really do,' I say. Her legs, in heart-patterned black tights, seem to stretch for yards beyond her miniskirt and my heart swells with love for her, the way she gives me her undivided attention for these moments of proper talking time.

4

'Have I told you I'm going to India?' she says.

'My goodness, how wonderful,' I say. 'How long for?'

'Only a month,' she says airily.

I'm achingly envious of her youth, her energy, her freedom. I wanted to travel too, at her age, but war got in the way. My thoughts start to wander until I remember my commitment to listening. 'What are you going to do there?'

'We're going to an orphanage. In December, with a group from college. To dig the foundations for a cowshed,' she says triumphantly. I'm puzzled, and distracted by the idea of elegant Emily wielding a shovel in the heat, her slender hands calloused and dirty, hair dulled by dust.

'Why does an orphanage need a cowshed?'

'So they can give the children fresh milk. It doesn't get delivered to the doorstep like yours does, Gran,' she says, reprovingly. 'We're raising money to buy the cows.'

'How much do you need?'

'About two thousand. Didn't I tell you? I'm doing a sponsored parachute jump.' The thought of my precious Emily hanging from a parachute harness makes me feel giddy, as if capsized by some great gust of wind. 'Don't worry, it's perfectly safe,' she says. 'It's with a professional jump company, all above board. I'll show you.'

She returns with her handbag — an impractical affair covered in sequins — extracts a brochure and gives it to me. I pretend to read it, but the photographs of cheerful children preparing for their jumps seem to mock me and make me even more fearful. She takes the leaflet back. 'You should know all about parachutes, Gran. You used to make them, Dad said.'

'Well,' I start tentatively, 'weaving parachute silk was our contribution to the war effort. It kept us going when lots of other mills closed.' I can picture the weaving shed as if from above, each loom with its wide white spread, shuttles clacking back and forth, the rolls of woven silk growing almost imperceptibly thicker with each turn of the weighted cloth beam.

'But why did they use silk?'

'It's strong and light, packs into a small bag and unwraps quickly because it's so slippery.' My voice is steadying now and I can hear that old edge of pride. Silk seems still to be threaded through my veins. Even now I can smell its musty, nutty aroma, see the lustrous intensity of its colours — emerald, aquamarine, gold, crimson, purple — and recite the exotic names like a mantra: *brigandine, bombazine, brocatelle, douppion, organzine, pongee, schappe.*

She studies the leaflet again, peering through the long fringe that flops into her eyes. 'It says here the parachutes we're going to use are of high quality one-point-nine ounce, ripstop nylon. Why didn't they use nylon in those days? Wouldn't it have been cheaper?'

'They hadn't really invented nylon by then, not good enough for parachutes. You have to get it just right for parachutes,' I say and then, with a shiver, those pitiless words slip into my head after all these years. *Get it wrong and you've got dead pilots.*

She rubs my arm gently with her fingertips to smooth down the little hairs, looking at me anxiously. 'Are you cold, Gran?'

'No, my lovely, it's just the memories.' I send up a silent prayer that she will never know the dreary fear of war, when all normal life is suspended, the impossible becomes ordinary, when every decision seems to be a matter of life or death, when goodbyes are often for good.

It tends to take the shine off you.

A little later Emily's brother appears and loiters in his adolescent way, then comes and sits by me and holds my hand, in silence. I am touched to the core. Then her father comes in, looking weary. His filial duties complete, he hovers solicitously. 'Is there any more we can do, Mum?' I shake my head and mumble my gratitude for the nth time today.

'We'll probably be off in a few minutes. Sure you'll be all right?' he says. 'We can stay a little longer if you like.'

Finally they are persuaded to go. Though I love their company I long for peace, to stop being the brave widow, release my rictus smile. I make a fresh pot of tea, and there on the kitchen table is the leaflet Emily has left, presumably to prompt my sponsorship. I hide it under the newspaper and pour the tea, but my trembling hands cause a minor storm in the teacup. I decant the tea into a mug and carry it with two hands to my favourite chair.

In the drawing room, I am relieved to find that the slide show has been turned off, the TV screen returned to its innocuous blackness.

From the wide bay window looking westwards across the water meadows is an expanse of greenery and sky which always helps me to think more clearly.

The house is a fine, double-bayed Edwardian villa, built of mellow Suffolk bricks that look grey in the rain, but in sunlight take on the colour of golden honey. Not grand, just comfortable and well-proportioned, reflecting how my parents saw themselves, their place in the world. They built it on a piece of spare land next to the silk mill during a particularly prosperous period just after the Great War. 'It's silk umbrellas, satin facings and black mourning crêpe we have to thank for this place,' my father, always the merchant, would cheerfully and unselfconsciously inform visitors.

Stained-glass door panels throw kaleidoscope patterns of light into generous hallways, and the drawing room is sufficiently spacious to accommodate Mother's baby grand as well as three chintz sofas clustered companionably around a handsome marble fireplace.

To the mill side of the house, when I was a child, was a walled kitchen garden, lush with aromatic fruit bushes and deep green salads. On the other side, an ancient orchard provided an autumn abundance of apples and pears, so much treasured during the long years of rationing, and a grass tennis court in which worm casts ensured such an unpredictable bounce of the ball that our games could never be too competitive. The parade of horse chestnut trees along its lower edge still bloom each May with ostentatious

8

candelabra of flowers.

At the back of the house is the conservatory, restored after the doodlebug disaster but now much in need of repair. From the terrace, brick steps lead to a lawn that rolls out towards the water meadows. Through these meadows, yellow with cowslips in spring and buttercups in summer, meanders the river, lined with gnarled willows that appeared to my childhood eyes like processions of crook-backed witches. It is Constable country.

'Will you look at this view?' my mother would exclaim, stopping on the landing with a basket of laundry, resting it on the generous windowsill and stretching her back. 'People pay hundreds of guineas for paintings of this, but we see it from our windows every day. Never forget, little Lily, how lucky you are to live here.'

No, Mother, I have never forgotten.

I close my eyes and take a deep breath.

The room smells of old whisky and wood smoke and reverberates with long-ago conversations. Family secrets lurk in the skirting boards. This is where I grew up. I've never lived anywhere else, and after nearly eighty years it will be a wrench to leave. The place is full of memories, of my childhood, of him, of loving and losing.

As I walk ever more falteringly through the hallways, echoes of my life — mundane and strange, joyful and dreadful — are like shadows, always there, following my footsteps. Now that he is gone, I am determined to make a new start. No more guilt and heart-searching. No more 'what-ifs'. I need to make the most of the few more years that may be granted to me.

2

China maintained its monopoly of silk production for around 3,000 years. The secret was eventually released, it is said, by a Chinese princess. Given unhappily in marriage to an Indian prince, she was so distressed at the thought of forgoing her silken clothing that she hid some silkworm eggs in her headdress before travelling to India for the wedding ceremony. In this way they were secretly exported to her new country.

From *The History of Silk,* **by Harold Verner**

It's a week since the funeral and everyone remarks on how well I'm doing, but in the past couple of days I've been unaccountably out of sorts. Passing the hall mirror I catch a glimpse of a gaunt old woman, rather shorter than me, with sunken eyes and straggly grey hair, dressed in baggy beige. That can't be me, surely? Have I shrunk so much?

Of course I miss him, another human presence in the house; though the truth is that it's been hard the last few years, what with the care he needed and the worry I lived through. Now I can get on with the task in hand: sorting out this house, and my life.

Emily comes round after school. I'm usually delighted to see her and keep a special tin of her favourite biscuits for such occasions. But today

I'd rather not see anyone.

'What's up, Gran? You don't usually refuse tea.'

'I don't know. I'm just grumpy, for some reason.'

'What about?'

'I haven't a clue, perhaps just with the world.'

She looks at me too wisely for her years. 'I know what this is about, Gran.'

'It's a crotchety old woman having a bad day.'

'No, silly. It's part of the grieving process. It's quite natural.'

'What do you mean, the grieving *process*? You grieve, you get over it,' I snap. Why do young people today think they know it all?

She's unfazed by my irritation. 'The five stages of mourning. Now what were they?' She twists a stub of hair in her fingers and ponders for a moment. 'Some psychologist with a double-barrelled name described them. Okay, here we go. Are you paying attention? The five stages of grieving are,' she ticks them off on her long fingers, 'denial, anger, bargaining, depression and acceptance — something like that.'

'They've got lists for everything these days: ten steps to success, twenty ways to turn your life around, that kind of rubbish,' I grumble.

'She's really respected, honestly. Wish I could remember her name. We learned it in AS psychology. You should think about it. Perhaps you've reached the angry stage?'

She goes to make the tea, leaving me wondering. Why would I be angry? Our generation never even considered *how* we grieved, though heaven

11

knows we did enough of it. Perhaps there was too much to mourn. We just got on with it. Don't complain, make the best of a bad lot, keep on smiling. That's how we won the war, or so they told us.

Emily comes back with the tea tray. Along with knowing everything else she seems to have discovered where I hide the biscuits.

'No school today?'

'Revision week,' she says, airily. 'What are you up to?'

'Packing. Sorting out stuff for the charity shop.'

'Can I help?'

'There's nothing I'd like more.'

After tea we go upstairs to the spare room, where I've made a tentative start at turning out cupboards and wardrobes that have been untouched for years. Inside one of these mothball-scented mausoleums we find three of my suits hanging like empty carapaces. Why have I kept them for so long? Ridiculous to imagine that one day I might again wear a classic pencil skirt or a fitted jacket. It's been decades since I wore them but they still carry the imprint of my business self; skirts shiny-seated from office chairs, jacket elbows worn from resting on the table, chin in hand, through many a meeting.

'Now that's what you call power dressing,' Emily says, pulling on a jacket and admiring herself in the long mirror on the inside of the door. 'Look at those shoulder pads, and such tiny waists. You must have been a looker, Gran. Can I keep this one? Big shoulders are so cool.'

'Of course, my darling. I thought they went out in the eighties.'

'Back in again,' she says, moving the piles of clothes and black bin liners and sitting down on the bed, patting the empty space beside her. 'You really enjoyed your job, didn't you?'

'I suppose so,' I say, joining her. 'I never really thought about it before. We were too busy just getting on with it. But I suppose I did enjoy it.' I hear myself paraphrasing Gwen's analogy, 'It's a kind of alchemy, you know. Like turning dull metal into gold. But better because silk has such beautiful patterns and colours.'

'That's rather poetic,' Emily says. 'Dad never talks about it like that.'

'Neither did your grandfather,' I say. 'Men are never any good at showing their emotions. Besides, even with something as wonderful as silk, you tend to take it for granted when you work with it every day.'

'Didn't you ever get bored?'

I think for a moment. 'No, I don't believe I ever did.'

'You didn't seem especially happy when I asked you about parachute silk the other day.'

I wish the words would not grip my heart so painfully. 'It's only because I don't like the idea of you jumping out of a plane, dearest girl,' I say, trying to soothe myself as much as her.

'I'll be fine, Gran,' she says breezily. 'You mustn't worry. We're doing other stuff to raise money, too. If you find anything I could put in for our online auction when you're turning out your cupboards, that would be amazing.'

13

'Anything you like,' I say. She turns back to the wardrobe and seems to be rummaging on the floor.

'What's this, Gran?' comes her muffled voice.

'I don't know what you've found,' I say.

As she pulls out the brown leather briefcase my heart does a flip which feels more like a double cartwheel. It's battered and worn, but the embossed initials are still clear on the lid. Of course I knew it was there, but for the past sixty years it has been hidden in the darkest recesses of the wardrobe, and of my mind. Even though I haven't cast eyes on it for decades, those familiar twin aches of sorrow and guilt start to throb in my bones.

'What's in it, Gran?' she asks, impatiently fiddling with the catches. 'It seems to be jammed.'

It's locked, I now recall with relief, and the key is safely in my desk. Those old brass catches are sturdy enough to withstand even Emily's determined tugging. 'It's just old papers, probably rubbish,' I mutter, dazed by this unexpected discovery. I know every detail of what the case contains, of course, a package of memories so intense and so painful that I never want to confront them again. But I cannot bring myself to throw it away.

Perhaps I will retrieve it when she is gone and get rid of it once and for all, I think. Yes, that's what I'll do. 'Pop it back in the wardrobe, darling. I'll have a look later,' I say, as calmly as I can muster. 'Shall we have some lunch?'

★ ★ ★

14

After this little shock my enthusiasm for packing goes into a steep decline. I need to pop to the shop for more milk, but it's just started raining, so I am hunting in the cupboard under the stairs for my summer raincoat when something catches my eye: an old wooden tennis racket, still in its press, with a rusty wing nut at each corner. The catgut strings are baggy, the leather-wrapped handle frayed and greying with mould.

I pull it out of the cupboard, slip off the press and take a few tentative swings. The balance is still good. And then, without warning, I find myself back in that heat-wave day in 1938 — July, it must have been. Vera and I had played a desultory game of tennis — no shoes, just bare feet on the grass court. The only balls we could find were moth-eaten, and before long we had mis-hit all of them over the chain link fence into the long grass of the orchard. Tiptoeing carefully for fear of treading on the bees that were busily foraging in the flowering clover, we found two. The third was nowhere to be seen.

'Give up,' Vera sighed, flopping face down on the court, careless of grass stains, her tanned arms and legs splayed like a swimmer, her red-painted fingernails shouting freedom from school. I laid down beside her and breathed out slowly, allowing my thoughts to wander. The sun on my cheek became the touch of a warm hand, the gentle breeze in my hair his breath as he whispered that he loved me.

'Penny for them?' Vera said, after a bit.

'The usual. You know. Now shut up and let me get back to him.'

15

Vera had been my closest friend ever since I forgave her for pulling my pigtails at nursery school. In other words, for most of my life. By our teens we were an odd couple; I'd grown a good six inches taller than her, but despite doing all kinds of exercises my breasts refused to grow, while Vera was shaping up nicely, blooming into the hourglass figure of a Hollywood starlet.

I was no beauty, neither was I exactly plain, but I longed to look more feminine and made several embarrassing attempts to fix a permanent wave into my thick brown hair. Even today the smell of perm lotion leaves a bitter taste in my mouth, reminding me of the frizzy messes that were the catastrophic result of my bathroom experiments. So I'd opted instead for a new chin-length bob that made me feel tremendously bold and modern, while Vera bleached her hair a daring platinum blonde and shaped it into a Hollywood wave. Together we spent hours in front of the mirror practising our make-up, and Vera developed clever ways to emphasise her dimples and Clara Bow lips. She generously declared that she'd positively die for my cheekbones and long eyelashes.

In all other ways we were very alike — laughed at the same things, hankered after the same boys, loved the same music, felt strongly about the same injustices. We were both eighteen, just out of school and aching to fall in love.

'Do I hear you sighing in the arms of your lover?'

'*Mais oui, un très* sexy Frenchman.'

'You daft thing. Been reading too much *True Romance*.'

16

More silence, punctuated by the low comforting chug of a tractor on the road and cows on the water meadows calling for their calves. School seemed like another country. A mild anxiety about imminent exam results was the only blip in a future that otherwise stretched enticingly ahead. Then Vera said, 'What do you think's really going to happen?'

'What do you mean? I'm going to Geneva to learn French with the most handsome man on earth, and you're going to empty bed pans at Barts. That's what we planned, isn't it?'

She ignored the dig. 'I mean with the Germans. Hitler invading Austria and all that.'

'They're sorting it out, aren't they?' I said, watching wisps of cloud almost imperceptibly changing their shapes in the deepest of blue skies. That very morning at the breakfast table my father had sighed over *The Times* and muttered, 'Chamberlain had better get his skates on. Last thing we need is another ruddy war.' But here in the sunshine, I refused to imagine anything other than my perfect life.

'I flipping well hope so,' Vera said.

The branch-line train to Braintree whistled in the distance and the bruised smell of mown grass hung heavily in the air. It seemed impossible that armies of one country were marching into another, taking it over by force. And not so far away: Austria was just the other side of France. People we knew went on walking holidays there. My brother went skiing there, just last winter, and sent us a postcard of improbably-pointed mountains covered in snow.

The sun started to cool, slipping behind the poplars and casting long stripes of shade across the meadow. We got up and started looking again for the lost ball.

'We'd better get home,' I said, suddenly remembering. 'Mother said John might be on the boat train this afternoon.'

'Why didn't you say? He's been away months.'

'Nearly a year. I've missed him.'

'I thought you hated him,' she giggled, walking backwards in front of me, 'I certainly did. I've still got the scar from when he pushed me off the swing accidentally-on-purpose,' she said, pointing to her forehead.

'Teasing his little sister and her best friend was all part of the game.' The truth was that like most siblings John and I had spent our childhood tussling for parental attention, but to me he was always a golden boy; tall like a tennis ace, with a fashionable flick of dark blond hair at his forehead: Not intellectual, but an all-rounder, good at sports, musical like my mother and annoyingly confident of his attractiveness to girls. And yes, I had missed him while he'd been away studying in Switzerland.

★ ★ ★

Vera and I were helping to set the tea in the drawing room when the bell rang. I dashed to the front door.

'Hello Sis,' John boomed, his voice deeper than I remembered. Then to my surprise, he wrapped his arms round me and gave me a

18

powerful hug. He wouldn't have done that before, I thought. He stood back, looking me up and down. 'Golly, you've grown. Any moment now you'll be tall as me.'

'You've got taller, too,' I said. 'I'll never catch up.'

He laughed. 'You'd better not. Like the haircut.' Reeling from the unexpected compliment, surely the first I'd ever received from my brother, I saw his face go blank for a second and realised Vera was on the step behind me.

'Vera?' he said tentatively. She nodded, running fingers through her curls in a gesture I mistook for shyness. He recovered quickly. 'My goodness, you've grown up too,' he said, shaking her hand. She smiled demurely, looking up at him through her eyelashes. I'd seen that look before, but never directed at my brother. It felt uncomfortable.

'How did the exams go, you two?'

I winced at the unwanted memory. 'Don't ask. Truth will out in a couple of weeks' time.'

Mother appeared behind us and threw her arms round him with a joyful yelp. 'My dearest boy. Thank heavens you are home safely. Come in, come in.'

He took a deep breath as he came through the door into the hallway. 'Mmm. Home sweet home. Never thought I'd miss it so much. What's that wonderful smell?'

'I've baked your favourite lemon cake in your honour. You're just in time for tea,' Mother said. 'You'll stay too, Vera?'

'Have you ever known me turn down a slice of your cake, Mrs Verner?' she said.

Mother served tea and, as we talked, I noticed

how John had changed, how he had gained a new air of worldliness. Vera had certainly spotted it too. She smiled at him more than really necessary, and giggled at the feeblest of his jokes.

'Why are you back so soon?' Father asked. 'I hope you completed your course?'

'Don't worry, I finished all my exams,' John said cheerfully. 'Honestly. I've learned such a lot at the *Silkschüle*, Pa. Can't wait to get stuck in at the mill.' Father smiled indulgently, his face turning to a frown as John slurped his tea — his manners had slipped in his year away from home.

Then he said, 'What about your certificates?'

'They'll send them. I didn't fail or get kicked out, if that's what you are thinking. I was a star pupil, they said.'

'I still don't understand, John.' Father persisted. 'The course wasn't due to finish till the end of the month.' John shook his head, his mouth full of cake. 'So why did you leave early?'

'More tea, anyone?' Mother asked, to fill the silence. 'I'll put the kettle on.'

As she started to get up, John mumbled, almost to himself, 'To be honest, I wanted to get home.'

'That's nothing to be ashamed of, dear,' she said. 'We all get homesick sometimes.'

'That's not it,' he said, in a sombre voice. 'You don't understand what it was like. Things are happening over there. It's not comfortable, 'specially in Austria.'

'Things?' I said, with an involuntary shiver. 'What things?'

20

'Spit it out, lad,' Father said, gruffly. 'What's this is all about?'

John put down his cup and plate, and sat back in his chair, glancing out of the window towards the water meadows at that Constable view. Mother stopped, still holding the pot, and we all waited.

'It's like this,' he started, choosing his words with care. 'We'd been to Austria a few times — you know, we went skiing there. Did you get my postcard?'

Mother nodded. 'It's on the mantelpiece,' she said, 'pride of place.'

'It was fine that time. But then, a few weeks ago, we went back to Vienna to visit a loom factory. Fischers. The owner's son, a chap called Franz, showed us round.'

'I remember Herr Fischer, Franz's father. We bought looms from him once. A good man,' Father said. 'How are they doing?'

'It sounded as though business was a bit difficult. As he was showing us round, Franz dropped a few hints, and when we got outside away from the others I asked him directly what was happening. At first he shook his head and refused to say anything, but then he whispered to me that they'd been forced to sell the factory.'

'Forced?' I asked. 'Surely it's their choice?'

'They don't have any choice,' John said. 'The Nazis have passed a new law which makes it illegal for Jewish people to own businesses.'

'That's outrageous,' Father spluttered.

'His parents think that if they keep their heads down it will all go away,' John said as I struggled

21

to imagine how all of this could possibly be happening in Vienna, where they trained white horses to dance and played Strauss waltzes on New Year's Eve.

'Is there any way we can help them, do you think?' Mother said, sweetly. Her first concern was always to support anyone in trouble.

'I'm not sure. Franz says it feels unstoppable. It's pretty frightening. They don't know where the Nazis might go next,' John said solemnly. 'It's not just in business, you know. I saw yellow stars painted on homes and shops. Windows broken. Even people being jeered at in the street.' He turned to the window again with a faraway look, as if he could barely imagine what he'd seen. 'They're calling it a pogrom,' he almost whispered. I'd never heard the word before but it sounded menacing, making the air thick and hard to breathe.

Mother broke the silence. 'This is such gloomy talk,' she said brightly. 'I want to celebrate my son's return, not get depressed about what's happening in Europe. More cake, anyone?'

Later, Vera and I walked down the road to her home. She lived just a mile away and we usually kept each other company to the halfway point. 'What do you think?' I asked, when we were safely out of the house.

'Hasn't he changed? Grown up. Quite a looker these days.'

'Not about John,' I snapped irritably. 'I saw you fluttering your eyelashes, you little flirt. Lay off my brother.'

'Okay, okay. Don't lose your rag.'

'I meant, about what he *said*.'

'Oh that,' she said. 'It sounds grim.'

'Worse than grim for the Jews,' I said. 'I'm not sure what a pogrom is, exactly, but it sounds horrid.'

'Well there's not much we can do from here. Let's hope your father's right about Chamberlain sorting it out.'

'But what if he doesn't?'

She didn't reply at once, but we both knew what the answer was.

'Doesn't bear thinking about,' she said.

★   ★   ★

When I got back Father leaned out of his study door.

'Lily? A moment?'

It was a small room with a window facing out onto the mill yard, lined with books and heavy with the fusty fragrance of pipe tobacco. It was the warmest place in the house and in winter a coal fire burned constantly in the small grate. This was his sanctuary; the heavy panelled door was normally closed and even my mother knocked before entering.

It was one of my guilty pleasures to sneak in and look at his books when he wasn't there — *The Silk Weavers of Spitalfields; Sericulture in Japan; The Huguenots; So Spins the Silkworm*; and the history of a tape and label manufacturer innocently entitled *A Reputation in Ribbons* that always made me giggle. Most intriguing of all, inside a plain box file, were dozens of foolscap sheets filled with neat handwriting and, written on the front page in confident capitals: *A HISTORY OF SILK, by HAROLD VERNER*. I longed to ask whether he ever planned to publish it, but didn't dare admit knowing of its existence.

I perched uneasily on the desk. From his leather armchair by the window Father took a deep breath that was nearly, but not quite, a sigh.

'Mother and I have been having a chat,' he started, meaning he'd decided something and had told her what he thought. My mind raced. This was ominous. Whatever could it be? What had I done wrong recently?

'I won't beat around the bush, my darling. You've read the reports and now, with what John told us this afternoon . . . '

'About the pogrom?' The word was like a lump in my mouth.

He ran a hand distractedly through his thinning hair, pushing it over the balding patch at the back. 'Look, I know this will be disappointing, but you heard what he told us.'

I held my breath, dreading what he was about to say.

'In the circumstances Mother and I think it would be unwise for you to go to Geneva this September.'

A pulse started to thump painfully in my temple. 'Unwise? What do you mean? I'm not Jewish. Surely this pogrom thing won't make any difference to me?' He held my gaze, his expression fixed. He'd made up his mind. 'It isn't fair,' I heard myself whining. 'You didn't stop John going.'

'That was a year ago. Things have changed, my love.'

'The Nazis aren't in Switzerland.'

He shook his head. 'Not yet, perhaps. But Hitler is an ambitious man. We have absolutely no idea where he will go next.'

'But Chamberlain . . . ?' I was floundering, clinging to flotsam I knew wouldn't float.

'He's doing his best, poor man.' Father shook his head sadly. 'He believes in peace, and so do I. No one wants another war. But it's not looking too good.'

I couldn't comprehend what was happening. In the space of two minutes my future life, as far as I could see it, had slipped away and I was powerless to stop it. 'But I *have* to go. I've been planning it for months.'

'You don't need to make any quick decisions. We'll let Geneva know you won't be going in September, but other than that you can take your time.' Father's voice was still calm and reasonable. I felt anything but.

'I don't want to take my time. I want to go now,' I whined, like a petulant child. 'Besides, what would I do instead?'

He felt in his pocket for his tobacco pouch and favourite briar pipe. With infuriating precision he packed the pipe, deftly lit a match, held it to the bowl and puffed. After a moment he took it from his mouth and looked up, his face alight with certainty. 'How about a cookery course? Always comes in handy.'

I stared at him, a hot swell of anger erupting inside my head. 'You really don't understand, do you?' I registered his disapproving frown but the words spilled out anyway. 'Because I'm a girl you think my only ambition is to be a perfect little wife, cooking my husband wonderful meals and putting his slippers out every evening.'

'Watch your tone, Lily,' he warned.

To avoid meeting his eyes I started to pace the Persian rug by the desk. 'Times have changed, Father. I'm just as intelligent as any man and I'm not going to let my brain go soggy learning to be a wonderful cook or a perfect seamstress. I don't want to be a wife either, not yet anyway. I want to *do* something with my life.'

'And so you shall, Lily. We will find something for you. But not in Geneva, or anywhere else in Europe for that matter,' he said firmly. 'And now I think we should finish this discussion. It's time for bed.'

I nearly slammed the study door behind me, but thought better of it at the last minute and pulled it carefully closed. In my bedroom I cursed Father, Chamberlain and Hitler, in that order. I loved my room, with its pretty damask curtains and matching bedcover, but these treasured things now seemed to mock me, trapping me here in Westbury. After a while I caught sight of myself in the mirror and realised how wretched I looked. Self-pity would get me nowhere, and certainly not into a more interesting life. I needed to get away from home, perhaps to London, to be near Vera. But what could I do? I was qualified for nothing.

I remembered Aunt Phoebe. She was a rather distant figure, a maiden aunt who lived in

London with a lady companion, worked in an office somewhere, drove an Austin Seven all over Europe and cared little for what anyone else thought about her unconventional way of life. Perhaps I could train as a secretary, like her? Earn enough to rent a little flat? The idea started to seem quite attractive. It wasn't as romantic as Geneva, but at least I would get away and meet some interesting people.

Now all I had to do was convince Father that this was a reasonable plan.

At breakfast the next day I crossed my fingers behind my back and announced, 'I've decided to get a job in London. Vera and I are going to share a bedsit.' I hadn't asked her yet, but I was sure she would say yes.

'Lovely, dear.' Mother was distracted, serving breakfast eggs and bacon from the hotplate.

'Sounds fun,' John said, emptying most of the contents of the coffee jug into the giant cup he'd bought in France. 'Vera's a good laugh. What are you going to do?'

'Leave some coffee for me,' I said. 'I could do anything, but preferably something in an office. I'll need to get some experience first. I thought perhaps I could spend a few weeks helping Beryl at Cheapside?' Beryl managed Verners' London office. 'What do you think, Father?'

'Well now,' he said, carefully folding his newspaper and placing it beside his knife and fork. 'Another Verner in the firm? There's an idea.' He took the plate from Mother and started to butter his toast, neatly, right to the edges. 'A very good idea. But you'd have to work your way up like everyone else.'

'What do you mean, 'work my way up'?' Was he deliberately misinterpreting what I'd said?

'You'd have to start like John did, as a weaver,' he said, moving his fried egg onto the toast.

'That's not what I meant. I want *secretarial* experience, in an *office*. Not weaving,' I said, sharply. 'I don't need to know how to weave the stuff to type letters about it. Does Beryl have to weave?'

He gave me a fierce look and the room went quiet. Mother slipped out, muttering about more toast, and John studied the pattern on the tablecloth. Father put down his knife and fork with a small sigh, resigned to sacrificing his hot breakfast for the greater cause of instructing his wilful daughter.

'Let me explain, my dearest Lily, the basic principles of working life. Beryl came to us as a highly experienced administrator and you have no skills or experience. You know very well that I do not provide sinecures for my family and I will not give you a job just because you are a Verner. As I said, you need to learn the business from the bottom up to demonstrate that you are not just playing at it.'

He took a deep breath and then continued, 'But I'll make you an offer. Prove yourself here at Westbury and if, after six months, you are still determined to go to London and take up office work, I will pay for you to go to secretarial college. If that is what you really want. Otherwise, it's a cookery course. Take it or leave it.'

3

Weaving is the process of passing a 'weft' thread, normally in a shuttle, through 'warp' threads wound parallel to each other on a 'beam' of the total width of the cloth being woven. The structure of the weave is varied by raising or lowering selected warp threads each time the weft is passed through.
From *The History of Silk,* **by Harold Verner**

I never intended to become a silk weaver, but Herr Hitler and my Father had left me with little choice.

Of course I was already familiar with the mill, from living next door, carrying messages for Mother, or visiting to ask Father a favour. It held no romance for me — it was just a building full of noisy machinery, dusty paperwork and hard-edged commerce. The idea of spending six months there felt like a life sentence.

Then, as now, the original Old Mill could be seen clearly across the factory yard from the kitchen window of The Chestnuts: two symmetrical storeys of Victorian red brick, a wide low-pitched slate roof, green painted double front doors at the centre, two double sash windows on either side and three above. These days it's just a small part of the complex my son runs with impressive efficiency.

Behind Old Mill stretches an acre of modern

weaving sheds where the Rapier looms clash and clatter, producing cloth at a rate we could never have imagined in my day. Even now, in the heat of summer, when the doors are opened to allow a cooling breeze, I hear the distant looms like the low drone of bees. It reassures me that all is well.

The ebb and flow of work at the mill had always been part of our family life. In those days employees arrived and departed on foot or by bicycle for two shifts every weekday, except for a fortnight's closure at Christmas and the annual summer break. It's the same now, except they come by car and motorbike. Families have worked here for generations, ever since my great-great-grandfather moved the business out of London, away from its Spitalfields roots. In East Anglia they found water to power their mills and skilled weavers who had been made redundant by the declining wool trade.

Even today the weavers' faces seem familiar, though I no longer know them by name. I recognise family traits — heavy brows, cleft chins, tight curls, broad shoulders, unusual height or slightness — that have been handed down from father to son, from mother to daughter. They are loyal types, these weaving families, proud of their skills and the beauty of the fabrics they produce.

Then, as now, vans pulled into the yard several times a week to deliver bales of raw yarn and take away rolls of woven fabric. When not required at the London office, my father walked to work through the kitchen garden gate and across the yard, and came home for the cooked lunch that Mother had spent much of the morning preparing. She rarely stepped foot in the mill. Her place was in the home, she said, and that's how she liked it.

* * *

When I came in to breakfast that first day John looked me up and down and said smugly, 'You'd better change that skirt, Sis. You're better off in slacks for bending over looms. And you'll regret those heels after you've been on your feet for nine hours.'

'While you sit on your backside pushing papers around,' I grumbled, noticing his smart new suit and striped tie. It was bad enough that I had to start as a lowly apprentice weaver, but John had recently been promoted to the office, which made it worse.

I'd never envied what was in store for him: a lifelong commitment to the responsibility of running a silk mill in a rural town. As the eighth generation of male Verners it was unthinkable that he would do anything other than follow Father into the business, and take over as managing director when he retired. John was following the natural order of things.

'I bet you'll get the old battle-axe,' he said, crunching loudly on his toast.

'Language, and manners, please, John,' Mother muttered mildly.

'Who's that?' I asked.

'Gwen Collins. Assistant weaving floor manager. Does most of the training. Terrifying woman.'

'Thanks for the encouragement.'

'Don't listen to your brother, you'll get on splendidly,' Mother said encouragingly. 'You never know, you might even enjoy it.'

I was unconvinced. Setting off across the yard, the short trip I had seen my father and, more recently, John, take every morning, I felt depressed: this was far from the glamorous life I'd planned. But why were butterflies causing mayhem in my stomach — was I afraid of being ridiculed as the gaffer's daughter, I wondered, of letting him down? Or scared that I might not be able to learn fast enough, that people might laugh behind my back? Oh, get a grip Lily, I muttered to myself. This is a means to an end, remember? Besides, you haven't let anything beat you yet and you're not about to start now.

I took a deep breath and went through the big green double doors into the mill, and climbed the long wooden stairs to Father's office.

My first impressions of Gwen Collins were certainly not favourable. She wasn't exactly old — in her late twenties I judged — but otherwise John's description seemed pretty accurate. An unprepossessing woman, dumpy and shorter than me, in a shapeless brown overall and trousers with men's turn-ups, she had concealed her hair beneath an unflattering flowery scarf wrapped and knotted like a turban. There was something rather manly about her — a disregard for how others saw her, perhaps. Her expression was serious, even severe. But something softened it, gave her an air of vulnerability. Then I realised what it was: I had never seen anyone with so many freckles. They covered her face, merging into blobs which almost concealed the pale, nearly translucent skin beneath. She'd made no effort to hide them with make-up. Even her eyelids were speckled.

I returned the forceful handshake with what I hoped was a friendly smile. 'Pleased to meet you, Gwen. Father tells me you're going to teach me all you know. He says you're a mine of information.'

'Mr Harold is very kind, the regard is mutual,' she replied without returning the smile, and without even a glance at Father. Pale green eyes regarded me with unsettling intensity beneath her almost invisibly blonde eyelashes.

After an awkward pause she said briskly, 'Right, we'll make a start in the packing hall, so you can learn about what we produce, then we'll go round the mill to see how we weave it.' With no further pleasantries, she turned and led the way, striding down the corridor so purposefully I had to trot to keep up.

The packing hall was — still is today — a large room running the length of the first floor of Old Mill. Sun poured in through six tall windows along the southern wall, and the room was almost oppressively warm with that dry, sweet smell of raw silk that would soon become part of my very being. Along the opposite wall were deep wooden racks stacked from floor to ceiling with bolts of cloth.

In the centre, two workers stood at wide tables edged with shiny bronze yard-rules, expertly measuring, cutting, and rolling or folding bundles of material and wrapping them with sturdy brown paper and string. On the window side four others sat at tilted tables like architects' drawing boards, covered with cloth stretched between two rolls, one at the top and another at the bottom.

'These are pickers,' Gwen said, introducing me as 'Miss Lily, Mr Harold's daughter'. As we shook hands they lowered their eyes deferentially, probably cursing the fact that they would have to watch their language with another Verner hanging around.

'Just call me Lily, please,' I stuttered. 'It's my first day and I've got a lot to learn.' Naïvely, I imagined they might in time consider me one of them.

'They check the silk and mark each fault with a short red thread tied into the selvedge, that's the edge of the fabric,' Gwen said, pointing at the end of the roll. 'For every fault we supply an extra half yard — it's our reputation for quality.' I nodded frequently, trying to appear more enthusiastic than I felt. 'Now, how much do you know about silk?'

'Not much, I'm afraid,' I admitted, embarrassed. Surely a Verner should have silk in the blood?

I caught the first hint of a smile. 'I'll take that as a challenge, then.'

Gwen turned to a shelf and lifted a heavy roll onto the table, steadied an end with one hand and, in a single deft movement, grasped the loose end of the material and pulled out a cascade that unravelled like liquid gold.

'Wow,' I said, genuinely dazzled. She crumpled a bundle between her hands, lowering her ear to it. 'Listen.' I bent my head and she scrunched it again. It sounded like a footstep on dry snow, or cotton wool tearing. 'That's called *scroop*, a good test for real silk when it's been dyed in the yarn.' As I crumpled it the vibration ran through my hands, up my arms and into my ears, making me shiver.

She rolled up the gold with practised ease and pulled out a bolt of vivid scarlet, deep purple and green stripes, spread it across the table with that same skilled movement, then expertly folded a diagonal section into a necktie shape and held it beneath her chin. 'Tie materials are mostly rep stripes and Jacquard designs,' she said, 'woven to order for clubs and societies. Men so love their status symbols, don't they?' Again, I saw that puzzling crimp at the corner of her eyes.

'Jacquard?'

'Type of loom. Clever bit of kit for weaving patterns, brought here by your Huguenot ancestors. You'll see our looms when we go down to the weaving shed.'

She unravelled a third roll. This one had a navy background with a delicate gold *fleur-de-lys* pattern. She pulled a small brass object from her pocket, carefully unfolding it into a tiny magnifying glass hinged onto two plates, one of which had a square hole. She placed this on the silk and gestured for me to put my eye to the glass.

The motif was so enlarged that hair-like individual silk threads, almost invisible to the naked eye, looked like strands of wool so thick that I could measure them against the ruler markings along the inner square of the lower plate. 'I had no idea,' I murmured, fascinated by the miniature world under the glass. 'There's so much more to it than I ever imagined.' As I looked up, the glint of satisfaction that passed across Gwen's face reminded me of my Latin teacher when I'd finally managed to get those wretched declensions right.

She moved along the racking and pulled out a fat roll. 'This one's spun silk,' she said, unravelling the cloth and draping it over my hands. It was heavy, the texture of matt satin, the colour of clotted cream, and wonderfully sensuous. It felt deliciously soft and warm, like being stroked with eiderdown, and almost without thinking I lifted it to my cheek. Then I caught that knowing smile again, felt self-conscious and handed it back rather too hastily. Gwen's manner was unnerving; most of the time she was coolly professional and business-like, but sometimes her responses were disconcertingly intimate, as though she could read my thoughts.

She looked up at the clock. 'It's nearly coffee-break. Just time for the *pièce de résistance*.'

At first I thought the taffeta was aquamarine. But when its shimmering threads caught the light, the colour shifted to an intense royal blue. It was like a mirage, there one moment and gone the next. 'Beautiful, isn't it? It's shot silk. A blue weft shot through a green warp.' She held up a length, iridescent as a butterfly wing, into a shaft

36

of sunlight. I almost gasped.

As I took a piece of cloth and angled it to watch the colours change, I could feel Gwen's pale eyes interrogating my response. And in that moment I realised I'd never before properly appreciated silk, its brilliant, lustrous colours, the range of weaves and patterns. Father and John never talked about it this way.

That morning Gwen showed me how to use all my senses; not just seeing the colours and feeling its weave, but holding it up to the light, smelling it, folding to see how it loses or holds a crease, identifying the distinctive rustles and squeaks of each type of material, examining its weave under a magnifier, enjoying its variety. I was already hooked, like a trout on a fly-line, but I didn't know it yet. Only later did I come to understand how Gwen simply allowed the silk to seduce me.

* * *

The canteen, a large sunny room at the top of Old Mill that smelled not unpleasantly of cabbage and cigarette smoke, seemed to be the heart of the mill. A team of cheerful ladies provided morning coffee, hot midday meals and afternoon teas with homemade cakes and biscuits. Men and women sat at separate tables talking about football and politics, families and friendships. Weavers and warpers kept together, as did throwsters. Loom engineers — called tacklers — were a strong male clan in their oily overalls. The dyers, their aprons stained in many

37

colours, another. But a shared camaraderie crossed divides of gender and trade; old hands teased the newcomers, and if they responded with good humour they became part of the gang.

Gwen wasn't part of any gang, and seemed immune from canteen banter. We sat down at an empty table and she pulled off her turban, running her fingers through the ginger curls that corkscrewed round her head. Without her working woman's armour she seemed more approachable.

'Why haven't we met before, Gwen? Were you brought up in Westbury?'

She shook her head, stirring three teaspoons of sugar into chocolate-brown tea.

'How long have you lived here?'

'Six years. Six happy years, mostly,' she said, that rare smile lighting her face and giving me permission to ask more.

'Whatever made you want to become a weaver?' I said.

'I started out wanting to be an artist. Went to art school. One thing led to another . . . '

I was intrigued. I'd never met anyone who had been to art school and, from what I'd heard, they were full of Bohemians. But Gwen didn't seem the type. 'Golly. Art school? In London?'

'It's a long story,' she said, stacking her teacup and plate. 'Another time, perhaps.'

'So what brought you to Verners?' I persevered.

'Your father, Lily.' She paused, looked away, out of the canteen window towards the cricket willow plantation on the other side of the railway line. 'He's a very generous man. I owe him a lot.' I felt a prickle of shame for not having appreciated him much. He was my Father, strict but usually kindly, rather remote when he was wrapped up in work. I'd never considered how others might regard him.

The squawk of the klaxon signalled the end of break-time. Over the loud scraping of utility chairs — the stackable sort of metal piping with slung canvas seats and backs — Gwen shouted, 'Time to learn about the heart of the business, Miss Lily.'

After the peace of the packing hall, the weaving shed was a shock. As the door opened the noise was like running into a wall. Rows of grey-green looms stretched into the distance, great beasts, each in their own pool of light, a mass of complex oily iron in perpetual noisy motion — lifting, falling, sliding, striking, knocking, crashing, vibrating. How could anyone possibly work in this hellish metallic chaos?

The weavers seemed oblivious, moving un-hurriedly between their looms, pausing to watch the material slowly emerge from the incessant motion of the shuttle beam, or stooping over a stilled machine. I quickly realised that they were skilled lip-readers and could hold long conversations in spite of the noise. But much of the time their eyes were focused intently on the cloth.

★ ★ ★

That first evening, John mocked me for falling asleep on the sofa and had to wake me for supper. As I prepared for bed I wondered what I would have been doing in Geneva. Getting dressed for a party, perhaps, or having hot chocolate and pastries in a café? For the moment I was too tired for regrets. Ears ringing, eyes burning, legs aching, my head full of new information, I wondered how I would get up and do the same again tomorrow.

The following day I was relieved to discover that we were spending it in the relative peace of the winding mill. Here, the silk skeins shimmered and danced as they rotated on their spindles releasing threads to be doubled, twisted and wound onto bobbins, and from bobbins onto pirns that would go into the shuttles. I learned the difference between the warp — the lengthways threads held taut between two rollers at either side of the loom — and the weft, the cross-threads woven into the warp from the shuttle.

Gwen no longer seemed so formidable. I was quickly learning to respect her skill and deftness, and her encyclopaedic knowledge of silk in all aspects of its complex manufacture. But she was still an enigma. Why would an educated woman like her choose to come and live in Westbury, to work in a mill?

I would find out soon enough.

4

*Another outstanding property of silk is its resil-
ience, which can be demonstrated by crushing
a silk handkerchief in one hand and a cotton
handkerchief in the other. When released, the
silk version will spring or jump upwards, the cotton one will stay crushed for some time. It is
this property, along with its strength, tough-
ness, elasticity and resistance to fire and mildew
that makes silk so valuable for the manufacture
of parachutes.*
From *The History of Silk,* **by Harold Verner**

Long afterwards, John liked to embarrass me by
claiming, sometimes publicly, that eight generations of weaving history had been rescued by his
little sister's sex appeal.

It's true that Verners survived the catastrophe
of war because of our contracts to weave
parachute silk. While other mills folded or were
converted into armament or uniform factories,
we made it through, and came out the other
side. But the invitation that arrived for John just
a few months after I started work at the mill was
really the start of it all. 'It's from my old school
chum,' he said, ripping open the heavy bond
envelope with its impressively embossed crest.
He proudly placed the gilt-edged card next to
the carriage clock on the mantelpiece in the
drawing room.

Mr John Verner and partner. New Year's Eve, 1938. Black tie. Dinner and dancing 8 p.m., carriages 2 a.m. Overnight accommodation if desired, it read. Underneath was scrawled: *Do come, Johnnie. Would be good to see you again. Marcus.*

'His ma and pa have a pile near the coast,' he said. 'They're faded gentry but still not short of a bob or two. Should be a good bash.' I was green with envy, of course. Vera's latest bulletins from London had left me feeling very sorry for myself. She had discovered the 'local' next to the nurses' home, met lots of dishy doctors and went to the flicks at least once a week. Even with Christmas coming up, my social calendar was blank, and I was bored stiff.

So I didn't hesitate a single second when John said, a couple of days later, 'Want to come with me to that New Year's Eve bash, *Schwester?* Dig out the old glad rags,' he went on, 'we both deserve a break.' But I had no glad rags, at least nothing remotely passable for a sophisticated do. In the code language of formal invitations, 'black tie' meant women should wear ball gowns. Where would I find one of those in Westbury? And even if I could, how could I possibly afford it?

Then I remembered the blue-green shot silk that had so thrilled me on my first day at the mill, and asked Father if I could have a few yards as a Christmas present. I pored over fashion magazines, trying to imagine what style would make the most of my beanpole figure. It had to be modern, but formal enough to pass muster in 'black tie' company. At last I found the perfect pattern; the dress had a halterneck bodice that flowed into a wide full-length skirt to emphasise my waistline, and a bolero jacket for warmth.

In the days after Christmas Mother and I slaved over her old treadle sewing machine, and I endured countless pin-prickled fittings to get the dress just right. Now it was finished, and I barely recognised the elegant young woman looking back from the long mirror in my room. The cut of the gown and the shimmering silk made my figure, usually obscured in slacks and baggy jumpers at the factory, positively curvy.

My experiments with lipstick and mascara seemed to highlight interesting new features in a face I'd always considered plain. Even my straight brown bob seemed more sophisticated when I tucked the hair behind my ears to show off Mother's emerald drop-earrings. We had fashioned a little clutch bag from scraps of leftover silk, and my old white satin court shoes — with low heels, I didn't want to tower over any potential partner — had been tinted green by the dye works, to match the colour of the warp.

You'll do, I thought, observing myself sideways, sticking out my chest and practising a coy, leading-lady smile. You might even get asked for a dance or two.

★ ★ ★

As we drove up the mile-long drive through acres of parkland and caught sight of the manor, my excitement gave way to apprehension. It was a

43

red-brick Victorian gothic mansion with stone-arched windows, ornate chimneys and little turrets topping each corner of the building. Today I'd call it grandiose but at the time I was awestruck. The driveway was stuffed with smart motors: Jaguars, MG sports and Bentleys. John parked our modest Morris well out of view.

We were welcomed into a cavernous oak-panelled hallway by a real butler who led us upstairs to our rooms, carrying my case while I held the dress on its hanger before me like a shield. I feared I would never retrace our route as we trod endless gloomy corridors, taking frequent turns past dozens of identical doors.

My bedroom, when we finally reached it, seemed the size of a ballroom. It had once been very grand, I could see, but now the chintz curtains and bed coverlet were faded, and a miserly coal fire in a small grate made little impact on the overall chilliness. As I waited several minutes for a small stream of tepid water to emerge from the tap at the sink, I imagined the miles of piping it had to pass through to reach this distant room.

Shivering, I pulled on the dress and peered into the foxed glass of the mirror to apply my make-up, cursing as I dropped blobs of mascara onto my cheek. In the dim light of a single bulb hung from high in the ceiling I couldn't be sure whether I'd managed to scrub it off properly.

But it was ten past eight and I couldn't postpone the moment any longer. Tottering nervously through the maze of corridors, I lost my way several times. Eventually I found the top of the stairs and, having managed to negotiate these without tripping, followed the roar of voices to the drawing room. There, about forty people were knocking back champagne and talking at the tops of their voices, as if they had known each other for years.

I looked around urgently for John but he was nowhere to be seen. Instead, I found myself near a tall man holding court to three young women who waved their long cigarette holders ostentatiously and giggled a lot. With some alarm I noticed that the man was wearing what I at first took for a skirt but then realised was a Scottish kilt. I hugged myself into the corner against the wall, trying not to stare, and was greatly relieved when the gong sounded for dinner. Then, to my dismay, I noticed that the man in the skirt was smiling in my direction. The three girls glared as he walked over and offered his hand.

'Robert Cameron, pleased to meet you. Would you do me the pleasure of accompanying me to dinner?'

'Lily Verner, good evening.' I said, as I returned the hand-shake and noted his startlingly blue eyes.

'May I just say, Miss Verner, that dress is a stunner. Extraordinary colours. Silk, isn't it?' He took my arm and steered me firmly in the direction of the dining room. As we walked I stole a closer look; a kind of furry purse affair hung from his waist that I later learned was called a sporran. The kilt ended at the knees, and below that were hairy legs clad only in white socks, a small dagger stuffed into the top of one

45

of them. It felt uncomfortably intimate being so close to those bare legs, and I barely dared imagine what he might or might not be wearing beneath those swinging pleats.

By the precision of his courtesies I guessed Mr Cameron had once been in the forces but wasn't any more, not with those raffish sideburns. Slightly receding hair and deep smile lines suggested he was in his late twenties, and the high colour at his cheekbones and the small bulge above his crimson cummerbund seemed to evidence a life already well led.

'And where have they been hiding you, Miss Lily Verner?' he asked, helping me to be seated and then sitting himself beside me. I faltered, wishing I'd thought about this beforehand, planned what I would say. In this elevated company I could hardly admit I was an apprentice silk weaver.

'Oh, I've been around,' I answered airily, trying to sound sophisticated.

'Then tell me where you found this beautiful gown,' he persisted.

I tried to think of a posh London shop where they might sell ball gowns, but my mind went blank. Out of the blue, I decided to be completely honest. What did it matter, I'd never see any of these people again.

'From our family's silk mill,' I said, 'Verners, in Westbury. My father's the managing director.'

I'd anticipated a blank look, or at least a swift change of subject, but to my great surprise Mr Cameron leapt to his feet, clipped his heels in a military manner, bowed deeply, picked up my hand and kissed it.

'My goodness. Silk? How splendid. You look like a wee angel, but now here's proof you've been sent from heaven, Lily Verner.' Forty diners in the process of taking their places peered curiously at us between the silver candelabra, as I blushed to the tips of my ears. A few seats away on the opposite side, John raised his eyebrows: *Are you all right with that man?*

Mr Cameron sat down again. 'You could be the answer to my prayers. Let's get some wine and you can tell me all about it.'

'There's not such a great deal to tell,' I said, overwhelmed by his display of enthusiasm. I wasn't used to such effusive compliments.

'Rubbish,' he said robustly. 'I want to know everything, from start to finish. And you absolutely must call me Robbie.'

He clicked his fingers at a waiter and barked an order for wine, then listened with great attention as, between sips of nondescript soup, I told him about the mill, the silk, where it came from, how we wove it, the trade we supplied. Feeling bolder by the minute, I even admitted that I worked there, adding quickly, 'Just as a stopgap of course.'

'How charming,' he said, his face close to mine as he poured me another glass of wine, 'a beautiful girl like you, working in a silk mill. That's a new one on me.'

'But now you must tell me about you,' I said, feeling uncomfortable, 'and why you are so interested in silk.'

As we washed down the main course of rubbery grey meat with liberal quantities of red

47

wine, he explained that he had been born in Scotland — hence his entitlement to wearing a kilt — but had lived in England most of his life, was a cousin of our host, Johnnie's school friend Marcus, and had been a guards officer until quite recently. But now he was dedicating his life — and, I guessed, a private fortune — to his two great passions: flying, and parachute jumping. A glamorous girl I'd noticed earwigging from the other side of the table chimed in, 'Parachute jumping? Isn't that rather dangerous?'

'Of course, it used to be,' he said, becoming more expansive with the added attention. 'Those Montgolfiers and their French buddies back in the last century did a lot of experimenting with dogs. They didn't always survive.'

'Ooh, poor little poochies,' she simpered, 'that's awfully mean.'

Most of the guests at our end of the table were now listening to the conversation. 'Isn't a parachute dangerous if you jump out of a moving plane? Wouldn't it get tangled in the wings or the prop?' asked a military-looking chap opposite.

'Total myth, old man,' said Robbie, 'invented by the Air Ministry. They were dead scared that fliers might jump and dump expensive chunks of ironware before it was absolutely necessary. But they've finally accepted that parachutes save lives, if they're the right kind.'

'Is there a wrong kind?' I found myself genuinely curious.

'Lord, yes. Parachutes that collapse in the middle, that get pushed in by wind, lines that

48

tangle, packs that don't unfurl quickly enough. The design is critical.' He paused and took a long sip of wine, carefully wiping his lips with the napkin. His audience was waiting. 'But the most important thing is the silk. It has to be just right. Not too thick, not too thin, not too porous, not too impervious.' Then he turned to me and lowered his voice, 'Which is why, Miss Verner, I would like to have a serious conversation about silk with your father and brother — and you too of course — at some point very soon.'

'We'd be delighted,' I said, glowing in his attentiveness and flattered to be included, 'but if I am to call you Robbie, you must stop calling me Miss Verner. Call me Lily, please.'

'So, lovely Lily,' he said, refilling my glass, 'have you ever flown in a plane?'

'Er . . . no,' I stuttered nervously, 'I'm not sure it's my sort of thing.'

'Would you like to give it a try? We could go for a spin.'

'Perhaps, but can I finish my dinner first?'

He laughed generously, and as dessert was served I became vaguely aware of music coming from a distant room. 'Can you hear the band, Miss Lily Verner? I'll wager you're a good dancer. Hope you like Swing.'

I smiled and said nothing, to conceal my ignorance.

'Watch out for that one, Sis. Looks like a bit of a rogue and too old for you, anyway,' John whispered as we left the dining room. But I didn't care. The wine made me daring and confident, and I was determined to enjoy myself.

After a couple of rather sedate waltzes, Robbie went over and spoke to the bandleader. With broad smiles on their faces, the musicians switched pace and started to play a very fast jazzy number. He pulled me out onto the floor and started to dance like a wild thing, kicking his legs so high I barely dared look in case the skirt flew up too. He gestured to me to do the same, swinging me from side to side and twirling me around. It was exhilarating, dancing so freely, to such irresistible rhythms.

'It's the Lindy Hop,' he shouted over the music. 'Just come over from America. Named after Charlie Lindbergh. Fun, eh?'

I'd never heard of the man but it certainly was fun, if rather absurd, dancing like this in our formal gowns and dinner jackets, in a country house ballroom with its bright merciless light glittering from chandeliers and mirrors. It was impossible to keep still, and we Lindy Hopped right through until midnight, when the band reverted to Scottish tradition and we welcomed in the New Year with 'Auld Lang Syne.'

After champagne toasts to 'a peaceful 1939', Robbie proved equally accomplished at quick-steps and foxtrots, guiding me firmly across the floor and spinning me round at every opportunity. It felt so safe in his arms, and it was so easy to be graceful, that I was disappointed when the band stopped and the dancers started to drift away.

Robbie escorted me to the foot of the stairs with his arm fitted snugly around my waist.

'Goodnight, Miss Lily Verner.' He put a finger

to my chin, tipped my face upwards and pinned his lips to mine. My first kiss. I'd expected it to be more exciting, but it just felt a bit awkward, and after a polite pause I pulled away.

'I've had a lovely evening, but I must go to bed now,' I gabbled.

He was unabashed. 'You've already made it very special, you sweet thing. Sleep tight. See you in the morning.' He kissed my nose this time, and patted my backside as I turned to run up the stairs. As I climbed into my chilly bed, churning with champagne and confusion, I wondered if I might be falling in love.

★　★　★

Next day we were eating breakfast in proper country-house style — bacon, eggs, kedgeree and kippers served on ornate silver hotplates casually arrayed on the antique sideboard — when we heard the sound of an aircraft flying low over the house.

A small bi-plane came into view, circling twice, each time lower than before, and John said, 'Crikey. Look Lily, he's coming in.'

Sure enough, to our astonishment the plane flew even lower and then landed bumpily on the parkland between the trees, scattering the peacefully grazing flocks of deer.

'It's just Robbie showing off again,' said Miranda, our host's sister, to whom we'd been introduced the night before. Sure enough, as the plane drew to a halt, we saw his leather-clad figure emerging from the cockpit, jumping down and starting to lope towards the house. Before long he was helping himself to a hearty plateful of kedgeree and joining us at the table.

'Flying make you hungry?' John said casually, as if this kind of arrival at breakfast happened every day in our family.

'Ravenous.' Robbie shook clouds of pepper over his plate. 'I've been up since six.' We chatted for a while about last night, what fun it had been, and then he turned to John and said, almost offhand, 'Lovely day for a spin, old man. Care to join me? She can take a co-pilot and a passenger. Perhaps Lily would like to come too?'

'That'd be cracking,' John said, his face lighting up.

I panicked. 'Not for me, thank you. I haven't got anything warm to wear. Anyway, don't you think we should be getting home, John?'

'I'd really like to go,' he said. 'Come on, Sis. You're always moaning about life being boring. Have a bit of fun. When are you going to get a chance like this again?'

'I'll lend you my jacket, and a headscarf and gloves,' Miranda chipped in.

'See?' said Robbie triumphantly. 'No excuses now, Missy Lily.' It was pointless resisting. I swallowed my nerves, finished my coffee and went with Miranda to get togged up.

My terror as we took off was soon replaced with the enchantment of seeing a familiar landscape from an entirely new perspective. We flew southwards along the coast and then turned inland, following the river towards Westbury. From the air the town looked so small and insignificant, like a toy village. We buzzed low over the mill and The Chestnuts, but there was no sign of life. I imagined Father reading his newspaper by the drawing room fire, grumbling about irresponsible pilots interrupting the peace on his holiday.

★   ★   ★

Just a few days later John got a telephone call from Robbie, inviting himself to a meeting.

'He insists Lily must be there too,' he said, with a big wink in Father's direction. 'I couldn't possibly imagine why.'

'It's because he knows I understand about silk,' I snapped, but a bit of me hoped he was right. Since New Year's Eve I'd thought about nothing but Robbie Cameron, his confidence and perfect manners, the casual skill with which he manoeuvred that little plane, the strong arms lifting me down from its wing after we had landed, and how my legs had turned to jelly afterwards. In my head, I'd run through the events of that evening a hundred times, hoping it really was the start of something new, so the prospect of seeing him again was exciting and a little nerve-racking. Would he still like me, or was that just a one-night thing, I wondered?

★   ★   ★

Robbie arrived looking formal and business-like, in an expensive-looking pinstriped suit and public school tie. He shook hands with John

53

and me and then, as we waited for Father in the visitor's room at the mill, examined the framed certificates and photographs hanging on the walls. I saw his gaze linger on one of Father at Buckingham Palace proudly showing the King a piece of Verners silk woven for the coronation, and he made appreciative remarks as I showed him the leather-bound sample books containing every design Verners had woven in the past one hundred and fifty years.

When Father came in I watched him sizing up Robbie as they shook hands. 'Welcome to Verners, Mr Cameron,' he said, 'I've ordered coffee. Let's sit down and you can tell us why you are here.'

'Well, sir,' Robbie started, 'in a nutshell, I need a supplier of reliable quality parachute silk. I'm a parachute designer and manufacturer and I want to expand my company.'

'We don't weave parachute silk, as you probably know,' Father said cautiously, reminding me of the way he played whist and bridge. Even with us children, he would keep his cards close to his chest, his face giving nothing away.

'But we could do, Father,' John said. 'Let's not count anything out. But I want to know more. Why parachuting? I can see why flying is fun, but why would anyone want to jump out of a plane?'

'It's the thrill of it,' Robbie said. 'Nothing like it. I trained as a pilot, as you know, so I had to learn how to use a parachute. But when I took up parachute jumping as a hobby it soon became obvious that the 'chutes needed to be redesigned to make them safer. Last year I met an American

54

who had created some new designs along exactly the same lines as I'd envisaged, and he was already testing them. So we set up a company together to manufacture them. So far we haven't had any major orders, but we're working on it.'

'If it's just a hobby activity what makes you think there's going to be much call for them?' John asked.

'It won't just be a hobby, if we go to war,' Robbie said, suddenly serious. 'At the moment there's one major competitor producing parachutes for the Air Ministry, and though they say that's enough for their current requirements, they seem to be blind to what the Russians and Germans are up to.'

'And what are they up to, precisely?' Father asked.

'Testing parachutes for dropping ground troops and equipment into battle zones. Last year the Russians dropped twelve hundred men, a hundred and fifty machine guns and other armoury, and assembled them all within ten minutes. It was even reported in *Flight* magazine, so the government can't claim they don't know what's happening. But they don't seem to be taking any notice.'

'While they're talking there's still hope,' Father said. 'No one wants another war.'

'I totally agree, sir, but anyone who thinks we can avoid it is in cloud cuckoo land,' Robbie said, grimly. 'My uncle's just returned from Germany. He saw Nazi paratroops on exercise, and read a newspaper article by one of their generals about their plans for an airborne invasion of England.'

The atmosphere in the little room seemed to have become oppressive, reminding me of the day John arrived home with his talk of pogroms. I busied myself refilling the coffee cups. I hated people talking about war. It terrified me and I prayed it would never happen.

'We'll have to agree to disagree on this,' Father said, pulling out his pipe and lighting it, as we waited for his next move. And then he said, 'But in the meantime, Mr Cameron, how can Verners be of help to you?'

'We need to be ready to go into immediate parachute production when the demand comes, and believe me, it will,' Robbie said. 'If I were in your position, Mr Verner, I'd be starting test weaves of parachute silk and investing in finishing machinery. So you could do the whole job on the spot.'

Father puffed on his pipe, his expression non-committal.

'It's worth considering, Father,' John said. 'There won't be much demand for silk ties and facings if we do go to war.'

Father nodded thoughtfully. 'But it's an expensive investment. We would have to be certain there's really a demand before jumping into anything like that. We'd be putting all our chips on the chance of war.'

'I take your point, sir,' Robbie said, 'but the thing is, with parachute silk you have to get everything right. The quality of the yarn, the weave *and* the finishing. They're all critical to create the right porosity. Otherwise the parachutes are worse than useless. What we need is a company like yours, with a reputation for quality,' he gestured at the photographs on the wall, 'and generations of experience, who can get it right, from the start.'

You wily devil, I thought, you know exactly how to flatter my father into agreeing: heritage, quality, reputation. You're saying all the right things. But then he paused for a moment, and said those words that more than sixty years later still fill my heart with dread. 'Get it right and you save lives, sir. Get it wrong and you've got dead pilots.'

After that there wasn't much more discussion. Father agreed to consider his proposal, and John offered to take Robbie on a tour of the mill. I began to fear he might leave without even a moment's reference to New Year's Eve, but as he shook my hand to say goodbye, he pressed it warmly for a fraction longer than usual. 'It's been such a pleasure,' he said, his voice lowering to an intimate whisper. 'I will see you again very soon, Lily Verner, that's a promise.'

The intense blue gaze and colluding wink left me blushing and enchanted, all over again.

5

*The Revocation of the Edict of Nantes in 1685
resulted in a mass migration of French Protes-
tants, known as Huguenots, which has parallels
throughout the twentieth century. This change
in the law stripped non-Catholics of their civil
and religious rights, resulting in the flight of
around 250,000 skilled and wealthy refugees.
Many were silk weavers of great talent who
settled in England and particularly in Spitalfields,
East London.*
From *The History of Silk,* **by Harold Verner**

After four months my limbs were growing more
used to the physicality of weaving: the day-long
standing and walking between looms, bending
over the woven material to check for faults,
crouching under the warp to find lost threads,
heaving boxes of pirns to refill the shuttle. But at
the end of each shift my legs still felt heavy as
loom weights, my eyes stung from their constant
scrutiny of the fine Jacquard designs and my
eardrums were bruised by the constant noise.

It had been a bitter cold February and the
news was depressing. Hitler was war-mongering,
claiming that Jewish bankers were responsible for
leading Europe into a conflict that would result
in the annihilation of their race. As we waited for
John to return home from a meeting in London
one evening, the logs in the fire crackled so

alarmingly in the hearth that Father put the fireguard in place. 'More spit than heat, these willow logs,' he grumbled, sitting back down in his favourite armchair. 'Like that maniac Hitler.'

I didn't want to think about Hitler; my mind was focused on dinner — the delicious smell of baked potatoes was making my stomach rumble. But at long last John arrived with a metallic tang of wintry air as he headed for the fire. His suit was crumpled, a shirt button missing. Mother followed him into the room. 'Supper's ready, my dears,' she said.

'Can I have a moment to warm up, Ma?' John said. 'It was bloody cold on that train tonight. Got held up for ages just outside London.' He stood on the hearthrug with his back to the blaze, robustly rubbing his buttocks.

'Did you hear the news?' Father said.

'No,' John said, 'what is it this time?' Father summarised the bulletin.

'More excuses for his pogroms, and all of us powerless to stop it,' I said.

'Actually, I think I've found a way we can do something, just a small thing, to help,' John said, his face brightening.

'Go on then, spill it,' I said, impatiently.

'While the train was held up I got chatting to some chaps in my carriage,' John started. 'They were talking about Jewish children coming into England. Apparently there's been an agreement with the Germans. The Jews in Germany are allowed to send anyone eighteen or under out of the country, for a price, and only if they've got a sponsor.'

He began to pace restlessly in front of the fire. 'Things are getting really desperate,' he went on. 'They're being hounded. Not just closing businesses, but even synagogues too. Being sent off to work camps. Children being banned from their schools. It's no wonder the parents are trying to send them to safety.'

'So where are these children going to?' I asked.

'The trains are travelling to Holland and the children are being put onto boats to Harwich.'

'What happens when they get here?'

'Some of them have sponsor families who come to collect them. But the problem is,' John stopped pacing now and looked carefully at Father and Mother in turn, 'some of them have been let down by their sponsors and haven't got anywhere to go. They're stuck in a holiday camp somewhere in Essex.'

A vision of children, unwanted and in a foreign land, chased away my hunger. John's voice was firm now. 'I'd like to do something. What do you think?'

'Sherry, anyone?' Father said. He never liked to be rushed into decisions. No one responded but he walked slowly to the sideboard all the same, and poured four glasses from the decanter, arranged them neatly on a silver tray and handed them round.

'I'll come to the point,' John said, taking his glass and emptying it with a single gulp. 'We've got a big house and we can afford it. Why don't we take some of them in?'

Father returned the tray to the sideboard and set it down carefully before turning back to us.

'Just how do you think this is going to work?' he said in that low, reasonable tone he adopted when he needed more time to consider. 'The three of us are at the mill all day. We can't expect your mother to take on a bunch of children at the drop of a hat.'

'We can't ignore it, either,' John said, squaring his shoulders. 'I can't, anyway.'

As the alcohol travelled soothingly down my throat and warmed my stomach I wrestled with contradictory emotions. The last thing I wanted was a house full of noisy children, but it didn't feel right just to do nothing. 'How old did you say they are?' I asked.

'Five to seventeen,' John said.

An idea popped into my head. 'Then couldn't we take some older ones?'

'Go on,' John sat down on the sofa next to me.

'Find them somewhere nearby where they can live independently but keep an eye on them and help them?' I was struggling to form a plan. 'What about that cottage down the road? The one to let?'

'Aren't you getting carried away, Lily?' Father said, still in his reasonable voice. 'There are just a few things you perhaps haven't considered. Who would look after them? What would they do? What would they live on?'

I refused to be deterred. 'Why can't we give them jobs at the factory? Weavers start straight from school, at fifteen.' John nodded vigorously in support but Father finally cracked.

'You're in fantasy land, both of you,' he boomed, getting to his feet. 'Of course it's tough

61

for the Jews, but in case you hadn't noticed, business here is tough, too. We can't just create new jobs from nowhere. There's the cost of extra wages, and not just that, you have to consider our own staff. We can support the Jews in other ways, contribute financially if necessary, but we can't just take on a bunch of untrained boys at the mill. So you can stop trying to persuade me.'

He turned to Mother. 'Is dinner ready, dear?'

John scowled and we both stayed quiet. The conversation was closed, for the moment, but we could bring Father round, I knew, given time. He just needed to believe he was in control, so we just had to find a more subtle approach.

Two days later I ambushed him in his study. 'Can I have a word?'

'Come in,' he said, looking up from his newspaper.

Above the fireplace hung the Verner family tree, gilt-framed and written in ornamental script on yellowing parchment. I knew it almost by heart. At the very top was the founder of the family firm: *Joseph Verner, silk weaver (1662 — 1740) b. Spittle Fields, m. Mary (1684).* 'You know how proud we Verners are to be descended from Huguenots?' I said.

He frowned, puzzled at my sudden interest. 'Go on?'

'They were immigrants, weren't they? Fleeing from persecution by the Catholics?'

The frown smoothed into an indulgent smile. 'This is about those Jewish children, isn't it, my darling? I knew you wouldn't let it go.'

I smiled back, pushing home my advantage.

'So, what do you think?'

'You're right about the Verners,' he said, 'but that was then. It was different.'

'How different?' I was determined not to let him argue me out of it.

'The Huguenots were craftsmen, weavers and throwsters. England needed their skills. There was a good economic reason for letting them into our country.'

'But if we hadn't given them refuge, what would have happened to them? They'd have been killed like all the rest. Where would our family be now?'

'Look, Lily, I understand what you are saying. I still believe we can stop this trouble if we can only persuade the Germans to topple that madman. Then these children can go back to their families. Best place for them.'

'Of course you're right,' I conceded. 'But what happens to them in the meantime? Can you imagine what it must be like to be stuck in that holiday camp?'

He filled his pipe and puffed it into life. Finally he said, 'Leave it with me. I'll have another think. Perhaps I'll talk to Jim and Gwen and ask them to take soundings with the staff.'

'Thank you.' I hugged him, savouring his soothing smell of Old Virginia and hair oil.

'No guarantees, mind,' he said, turning back to his desk. 'Now run along and help your mother with supper. I've got work to do.'

The plan worked, just as I'd hoped. Over Sunday lunch Father announced with some triumph, as if it had been his very own idea, that the mill manager Jim Williams had agreed to take on three new apprentices as weavers, warpers or throwsters, depending on their skills.

John's forkful of food halted halfway to his mouth. 'How did this happen?' he mouthed across the table. 'Tell you later,' I mouthed back, smiling smugly.

'But we can't collect them yet,' Father was saying. 'I have to be up in town all next week.'

John had put his knife and fork down now. 'We could go instead,' he said, 'Lily and me can sort it out.'

'Please, Father,' I pleaded. 'I can't bear to think of those children waiting. They might even be sent back to Germany.'

He pondered for a few seconds and then said, 'I'll check with Jim. See if he wants to go, or if he's happy to delegate the job to you two.' Across the table, John was giving me a surreptitious thumbs-up. 'It's boys we want, remember,' Father said firmly. 'No more than three. Strong lads who'll really knuckle down to it.'

★ ★ ★

It was a dismal day as we drove in the rusty works van to the holiday camp. Clouds hung like damp sheets over the flat Essex fields and when we reached the coast, the marshy land dissolved into the North Sea in shades of sullen grey.

The road looked familiar. Surely this wasn't the same place I'd been as a child, on holiday with a friend's family? As we came closer the memories started to flood back. The holiday had been a disaster. I was horribly homesick, and to make things worse I was terrified of the flame-haired clown in a harlequin suit who had patrolled between the chalets each morning after breakfast, summoning us to the morning's entertainments. He reminded me of the Pied Piper illustration in my book of fairy tales and I was convinced that the children who followed him would never come back. So I refused to go with the clown, feigning all kinds of exotic ailments, and spent the rest of the holiday in my bunk bed, feeling humiliated and miserable.

'You're very quiet, Sis, what's on your mind?' John said. When I told him he laughed.

'Not too many clowns there these days, I don't suppose,' he said.

At the entrance, the words were still legible under peeling paint: *Welcome to Sunnyside Holiday Camp*. The gate was guarded, and spirals of barbed wire coiled along the top of the fence. We were ushered through and directed up a concrete driveway towards a group of buildings in the distance.

As we came closer we could see a gang of older boys kicking a football around on a patch of worn grass, and other children huddled against a chill wind on benches outside one of the pastel-painted chalets. Their faces were solemn and pale, like rows of white moons, turning to watch our van.

Pinned to each child's coat was a label. 'Like little parcels,' I said. John nodded, grim-faced.

We stopped and climbed out and the boys left their football game and ran over, crowding

65

round us, firing questions in their strange guttural tongue. They stopped in surprise when John started speaking in fluent German, and when he'd finished they began chattering even more excitedly than before.

'Don't worry,' he said to me. 'They're only asking who we are and why we are here. They want to know where we're from and if we can help. What they mostly seem to want to know is if we can take them to Piccadilly Circus,' he laughed. 'They're desperate for a bit of the high life, and who can blame them?'

At last an adult appeared, pushing his way through the gaggle. He was short, prematurely balding and scruffily dressed in workmen's jeans and a thick jacket, so different from the crisply intimidating holiday camp staff of my childhood memory. I warmed to him immediately.

'You must be John and Lily Verner? Welcome to Sunnyside. Name's a bit ironic on a day like today, don't you think? I'm Leo Samuels. They call me duty manager, though that's just a posh title for chief muggins.' He beamed as we shook hands. 'Now, what can we do for you, or rather, what can you do for us? Come into the office and let's keep warm while we talk.' To the boys he said, '*Geduldig Sein*, be patient.' As we walked he apologised for the way they had pestered us. 'You understand, they've been through terrible times, and being out here in the wilds of Essex isn't helping. They need to get settled as soon as possible.'

One of the larger chalets at the end of a row had a hastily-painted sign: *Kindertransport All*

Enquiries. Up two steps, a wooden balcony led through glazed double doors into a small living area next to a kitchenette, with what must have been bedrooms on either side. Leo gestured to a table covered in a chaos of papers and dirty mugs, and went to fill the kettle. 'Do sit down. Tea or coffee? How do you take it?'

He chattered cheerfully as he rinsed out three mugs in a cluttered basin, waiting for the kettle to boil. 'Sorry for the mess, but we're on a shoestring here,' he said, pushing aside untidy piles of papers and boxes on the table to make space for the tray.

'We're all volunteers and it's a bit hand-to-mouth, to say the least. Of course we're dead lucky they've let us have this place for free. You probably know that the boss is Jewish, that always helps. Otherwise we're totally dependent on charity and right now people have other things on their minds than helping a bunch of German children.'

He sighed. 'We're doing what we can for the poor little blighters. Most have sponsors, but this lot have been let down for one reason or another. So not only have they been through some terrible things and been sent away by their parents, but when they get here no one wants them. It's ruddy awful, if you'll excuse my French, Miss Verner.'

I cradled my cold fingers round the hot mug, struggling to imagine what it must feel like for these children, being so doubly rejected. No words, even coarse words, could come close to describing it.

'I was in Austria last year,' John said, 'and I saw what was happening.'

Leo shook his head sadly. 'It's so much worse, now.'

'I was afraid it would be,' John said. 'So when we heard about your work we had to do something.'

'It is very good of you,' Leo said simply, and took a sip of his coffee. 'So, how do you think you can you help us?'

'Our family runs a silk mill, in Westbury. Do you know it? About thirty miles from here,' John started.

'Silk, eh? How interesting,' Leo said, listening intently.

'We'd like to take on three new apprentices,' John went on. 'And we wondered if you had some older boys, sixteen, seventeen maybe. Preferably bright lads, who'd be capable of learning a skilled trade.'

'They've got to be mature and sensible types too,' I added. 'They'll be living in a rented house and will have to learn to look after themselves.'

Leo sat back, scratching the sparse hairs on his head. 'This is music to my ears, you know. Most people want younger ones, especially girls. They think the little 'uns are less trouble, though I'm not sure they're right. The older boys get overlooked and it's usually hard to place them.'

He thought for a moment and then said, 'Okay. I've got three in mind. First there's Stefan. He's obviously older than most of them. Between you and me I think he's over eighteen, the official limit. But his papers say he's seventeen and who are we to challenge it? He's obviously been through quite enough already without us interfering, poor lad. Don't know much about his background but he's clearly very bright.'

'Sounds just right,' I said.

Leo went on, 'Stefan's friendly with a couple of brothers, Kurt and Walter. Also nice lads. Kurt's seventeen but Walter's only fifteen. Is that too young?'

'Depends on the boy,' John said doubtfully. 'How mature he is.'

'Hard to tell, to be honest with you,' Leo said. 'But we obviously can't separate them and it's been almost impossible to find a double placement. Walter's just a little lad, but I reckon he'd soon shape up, especially with his brother Kurt looking after him. He's a pretty mature, level-headed boy. Why don't you meet them, see what you think?'

How could we refuse?

'Good,' said Leo, getting up. 'I'll get those three in here, explain what you're offering and we can see if they like the idea.' Halfway out of the door he turned back. 'All the lads are keen to see the bright lights of London, so you may have to persuade them Westbury's a good option. Not too far to the city by train, is it?'

As they came into the chalet I recognised the three boys as part of the football gang, but they were much more subdued than before. Leo introduced them: '*Stefan, Kurt, Walter, dies ist John Verner und seine Schwester Lily.*' They shook hands politely, barely meeting our eyes.

They seemed so different from English boys. Was it just the language barrier, or the way they looked — the pallor of their faces, the unfashionable haircuts, underfed frames and curious cut of their clothing? I found it impossible to fathom what was going on inside their heads.

As John started to talk they exchanged glances, their faces becoming more animated, even excited. When he finished, the boys started talking between themselves, words falling over each other, interrupting each other, all at once.

Stefan certainly seemed older than seventeen. He was skinny and taller than the others, dressed in a scruffy brown leather jacket and black trousers. He hadn't shaved for a couple of days and a dark shadow grew thickly on his slim face. His voice was more baritone than tenor and deep-set eyes peered out warily through his floppy fringe of untidy hair.

Kurt and Walter were very alike; in their tweed trousers, hand-knitted jumpers and woollen waistcoats they reminded me of the farm boys who came into Westbury on market days. Wiry kinks of mousy hair sprouted from their heads but their boyish cheeks showed little hint of growth. Kurt was chatty and confident, and Walter tended to repeat what his big brother said. Both of them appeared to defer to Stefan as their leader, turning to him if John or Leo said something they didn't understand.

Trying to gauge their personalities as they talked, I wondered how these boys would cope with the robust camaraderie among the men at the mill.

'They're all pretty keen,' John said, eventually turning to me. 'They're especially excited by the idea of earning their own money, and sharing a house.' He laughed. 'Though goodness knows whether they can cook and clean for themselves. What do you think?'

'We can worry about the housekeeping thing later. But can they learn quickly enough to be useful at the mill?' I said, recalling Father's strict instructions.

'Heaven knows.' John shrugged his shoulders. 'Only time will tell, I suppose.'

'If they're all good friends, perhaps they will support each other?'

He nodded, but his expression was still doubtful.

'One thing's clear. We can't leave them here,' I said, suddenly flooded with certainty, more convinced that this was the right decision than at any other time in my life. I wanted these boys to feel safe and be loved. I could not contemplate leaving them here.

'Let's go for it,' we both said at the same time, and then laughed at ourselves.

This time the handshakes were stronger and their smiles much more confident. There was formal paperwork to complete and signatures to be written and witnessed, then they collected their pitifully small suitcases before finally saying goodbye to Leo, promising to keep in touch and piling into the van. As we drove away they waved to their friends, then fell silent.

They must be glad to leave this grim place, I thought, but it is their last link with home.

They've suffered terribly and now they have no option but to follow the Pied Piper — two strangers in a battered old van — into an unknown future.

* * *

Over the next few days the German boys stayed at The Chestnuts and we spent time getting to know them. The fear started to leave their faces, their frames seemed to fill out and they gained confidence, trying out English phrases as we struggled to get our tongues around their strange German words.

We traipsed around Westbury finding kitchen equipment, bedding, rugs and curtains to make their cottage more homely. On the day they moved in, Mother and I pinned labels to everything around the house and led the boys through each room, saying the words. She made cartoon sketches of every item on their shopping list, and they took turns to ask the grocer and greengrocer for their purchases, laughing at each other's attempts, and gradually beginning to relax.

John took them to the tailors, buying each of them a couple of pairs of off-the-shelf trousers for smart and casual, a couple of shirts, fashionable Fair Isle jumpers and navy blazers for weekends. On Saturday they went with him to watch a local football match. Kurt and Walter were keen to play, and he promised to find a team for them.

But now it was time for them to earn their

keep. John and Jim Williams took them on a tour of the mill, then talked to them individually about the jobs we had planned for them. Walter and Kurt — still inseparable — would start as packers. Stefan was keen to be a weaver and Gwen agreed to take him as her new apprentice. It was a compliment, she told me, though it was barely recognisable as such. 'I reckon you can just about manage two looms on your own now, Lily,' was all she said. 'So I can concentrate on helping Stefan'.

I couldn't help smiling, watching them together on that first day. They made a curious pair — Gwen, short and dumpy, doing her best to communicate through hand gestures over the noise of the looms, or standing on tiptoe to shout into his ear; Stefan bending like a weeping willow over the loom, his fringe flopping in his eyes. She mimicked the way he constantly brushed the hair back from his forehead, offered him her flowery headscarf and made him laugh. His eyes followed her face intently, struggling to lip-read in a foreign language.

'That boy's a fast learner,' she said at the end of that first week. We were doing the Friday evening loom checks together, covering woven cloth and warps with dust sheets, ensuring that shuttle arms were securely docked, winding up loose threads and tucking away spare spools, turning off the power at each machine. Making everything safe for the weekend.

'He's got real aptitude,' she added. I could hear the warmth in her voice and even as I knew she was right — he already understood the elegant mechanics of the loom, how to balance the weights and tensions, and was deftly locating and retying lost warp threads — I felt a pinch of envy. She'd never praised me like that, not to my face at least.

'You'd better watch out. He'll soon be teaching you,' I laughed, trying to conceal my annoyance.

'I look forward to it. He's a very polite, charming young man. Deeper than the other two. Has an artistic touch. What do you think?'

'You'd know better than me,' I said, niggled she'd found something else to admire. 'With that art school background you said you'd tell me about.'

'You should come for tea some time, then maybe I will.'

'So you keep promising,' I said. I'd dropped so many hints over the past weeks, with no response, that I was starting to wonder why she was so reluctant. Did she just not like me enough to invite me into her personal life? Or was there something else, something she didn't want to reveal? Gwen was such an enigma.

As we finished our rounds and parted at the front door she touched me lightly on the shoulder, elusive as ever. 'Enjoy your weekend.'

★　★　★

Once the boys had moved into the cottage, we invited them to join us for lunch at The Chestnuts every Sunday.

'Help them learn proper manners. They'll turn

into savages in no time, living on their own,' Father said. 'We need to civilise them.' Mother enjoyed sharing her pleasure in English cooking, and it was usually a roast with all the trimmings that they appeared to relish.

Though homesickness still showed in their faces, Kurt and Walter were like other teenage boys — gawky, clumsy, fascinated by football and motorbikes. They struggled with English table etiquette, muddling their cutlery, slurping their drinks, leaning elbows on the table. At first, Father was lenient but after a few weeks he'd bark stern reminders: 'No talking with your mouth full.' They were slow to learn, and more than once he had to threaten them, 'If you don't take those elbows off the table at once, there will be no more lunch for you.' Walter giggled and Kurt — always the rebellious one — grimaced, but their hungry stomachs forced them into reluctant compliance.

Stefan needed no such prompting. His manners were already sophisticated and what he didn't already know of English etiquette he quickly picked up by watching. Now that he had abandoned the old leather jacket and black trousers for the cords, jumpers and jacket John had bought him, he looked almost like an English boy, apart from the hairstyle he insisted on keeping unfashionably long. But he was unlike any other boy I knew.

What I had mistaken for shyness, I slowly began to realise, was actually a confident stillness. While the others always needed to be active, Stefan seemed content to observe the world around him quietly, with an expression of mild curiosity and, I sensed, amusement simmering just below the surface. Little escapes those eyes, I thought, with a slight shiver.

That Sunday, Stefan handed back my copy of *The Hound of the Baskervilles* with one of his rare smiles.

'I enjoy very much, Miss Lily,' he said, his dark eyes sparkling. 'I would like to be a perfect English gentleman like your Sherlock Holmes.' He raised an imaginary bowler hat, pretended to twirl an umbrella and bowed deeply, making me laugh out loud. Stefan the clown was a side of his character he hadn't revealed till now.

In just two months his English improved so much I'd abandoned my intention to speak German. I was astonished by how quickly he learned; he could already read in another language. This was the second Conan Doyle book I'd lent him, and every time he visited he devoured Father's copy of *The Times*, urgently looking for news from Europe.

Over lunch, we encouraged them to talk about home. Of course, we got only the edited versions. Stefan told us about his parents, both schoolteachers in Hamburg, and his younger twin sisters. He hoped they would come to England once they'd saved or borrowed the money for permissions and transport. Kurt and Walter spoke longingly of the Bavarian hills and the family farm. The English countryside is so flat, they complained. As conversation flowed, I reflected with satisfaction that the boys were starting to feel more secure.

It was our usual custom to follow lunch with a walk on the water meadows, but that day it was pouring. 'Not a good day for a walk,' Father said, looking out of the drawing room window, 'it's raining cats and dogs.'

'Cats and dogs?' Walter said, frowning. 'Why do you say cats and dogs?' he asked, after we'd told him what it meant. We had no idea. Some English phrases were so hard to explain.

After coffee, Father suggested a game of cards. But I had a better idea.

'What about a song, Mother?' I said, pointing to the baby grand. It was rarely played these days, and generally served as a shelf for photographs and ornaments.

'I couldn't,' she said, blushing and nervously smoothing her skirt, 'haven't played for years.' She'd had a classical training and, though never a professional performer, she'd given piano lessons and played in local amateur concerts before marriage and children got in the way. When times at the mill had been hard and there was no extra cash for servants, her music had been sacrificed to housework and cooking.

'Come on, you can do it,' I said, going over to the piano stool and rifling through the piles of sheet music stored under its padded lid. I found what I was looking for; a score, now dog-eared and falling apart at the seams, *Music Hall Favourites*.

'Here we are,' I said. I moved the knick-knacks from the piano, propped it open, lifted out the music shelf, took her elbow and led her to the piano stool. 'Now all you have to do is play.'

'It's been so long.' She shook her head. 'My fingers won't know what to do.'

It was Stefan who finally persuaded her. He was sitting on the arm of the sofa, leaning forward, watching intently. 'Please, Mrs Verner. Please play for us,' he said. 'We like very much to hear the piano.'

As she started, everyone began to listen. Watching her fingers move over the keys with growing confidence, I remembered how she used to sit me on her knee as she played. With a child's selfishness it seemed then that her music was just for me. Now, hearing her again after so long, I realised what a sacrifice she had made, giving up her music to meet the demands of the family.

She stopped to look through the battered old score. 'Here's a good one. *My Old Man Said Follow the Van*.' As she started into the familiar tune, John and I got up and stood beside her, reading the words over her shoulder. After a couple of verses the boys came to join us, starting to hum along and sing the chorus with us.

When we sang the words '*dillied and dallied, dallied and dillied*', they started to giggle. 'What is '*dilly dally*', please?' Walter asked. I struggled to find a polite explanation.

'It means they spent a lot of time hanging around drinking, or talking, or . . . '

John interrupted, saying something in German, and they guffawed like schoolboys. Next time we repeated the chorus they made cheeky kissing noises and Father frowned in gentle reproach.

After three more numbers Mother declared she'd reached the end of her repertoire and went to make tea. As the others drifted back to the warmth of the fire, Stefan stayed by the piano, apparently lost in his own thoughts. Then he seemed to settle something in his mind and looked at me briefly with a slight smile before pulling out the stool and sitting down, tentatively spreading his hands over the keys. Something tugged in my heart as I noticed for the first time the perfect pink ovals of his nails at the end of each long, elegant finger.

He played a few scales and then, haltingly, started to pick out a tune I recognized as the opening bars of the *Moonlight Sonata*. Muttering at his mistakes and pausing to remember each following phrase, Stefan stumbled on, but his arpeggios sounded more like a doleful trudge than the calm moonlit landscape Beethoven had intended.

After a few minutes, he took his hands from the piano and sighed, lowering his head. The untrimmed wisps of dark hair curled down his neck and over his collar, and I felt a surge of sadness for this strange boy, so far from home.

'Play us the jazz,' Kurt said.

Stefan looked up at me.

'This is okay for you?' he asked. 'You like the jazz?'

'Very much,' I said, smiling encouragement.

Stefan turned back to the keyboard, took a deep breath, and launched into an exuberant ragtime piece. The solemn struggle with Beethoven was transformed into the joyful freedom of jazz. The fingers on Stefan's right hand moved so fast they became a blur as the left hand stretched into successions of complex chord sequences.

Everyone in the room started to move; heads nodding, feet tapping, even Father's knee was jiggling. The rhythm was irresistible.

'Remember those Swing steps, Lily?' John leapt up and took my hand as we clumsily tried to approximate the dance we'd learned on New Year's Eve. Kurt and Walter watched for a moment and then came to join us, doing their own wild version, waving arms and legs around without any regard for the rhythm.

From the piano, Stefan shouted, '*Swingjugend, swing. Swing heil!*' Kurt and Walter raised their arms in mock-Nazi salutes and repeated '*Swing heil! Swing heil!*'

Mother's eyebrows raised in alarm.

'What's that all about?' I shouted to Kurt.

'American jazz. Banned by the Nazis,' Kurt shouted back.

'Why is it banned?'

He shrugged. 'Stefan plays it for — what do you say?'

Stefan stopped playing and swivelled round. In the sudden stillness his voice was firm and clear, 'We play it because it is not allowed.'

'Who's we, Stefan?' John asked.

'*Swingjugend.*'

'Until they were arrested,' Kurt said, almost under his breath.

''Arrested'?' I repeated, failing for a moment to understand the full import of the word.

Stefan glowered at him. 'They just gave us a beating. As a warning.'

It was such a shocking image none of us knew

what to say next. My mind whirled, trying to understand. How could the police — or was it soldiers? — be so violent against young boys, just for playing music? The sense of menace seemed to seep into the room like a poison.

Mother spoke carefully, 'Are you saying that the police beat you and put you in prison, Stefan?'

Stefan nodded. 'The SS,' he said. 'But we were not in prison for long. It was just a warning.' He paused and then went on, 'That is why I had to leave Germany.'

'You poor boy,' she murmured. 'No wonder . . . '

'Were you all members . . . of this group?' I stuttered.

'Only Stefan,' Kurt said. 'We do not know about it till he tell us.'

'There is no *Jugend* where we live,' Walter added.

'Perhaps we make our own group, here in Westbury?' Kurt smiled, and the tension in the room started to settle. 'Can he play some more?'

Stefan looked at Father, who nodded.

This time we listened quietly. It didn't seem right to dance. Trying to make sense of what the boys had told us, I began to understand why this music was so important for Stefan. The baby grand had never known such spirited, emphatic playing. It was an act of protest and defiance, seeming to drive the menace out of the room.

After a few minutes he stopped, and we all applauded and cheered. As Stefan straightened up from a mock-formal bow, I saw for the first time his face fully illuminated with happiness.

6

Finishing is the final procedure in the long and complex process of transforming the silkworm's gossamer into a perfect piece of woven silk. Dependent on the type of fabric required, finishing can include dyeing, boiling, tentering, drying and pressing in a variety of ways to achieve an extraordinary range of characteristics: firmness, fullness, dullness, lustre, softness or draping quality. For certain technical applications, such as parachute silk, finishing is critical in determining the final porosity of the fabric.

From *The History of Silk*, **by Harold Verner**

I was sitting in a deckchair in the garden on that warm May evening, refreshing my tired feet in a bucket of cool water, a gin and tonic in my hand and reading the latest edition of *True Romance* while horned stag beetles bumbled around me in the dusk. I should have been content, but I wasn't. I was desperate for some romance of my own. Though fabled for having one pub for every thousand residents, Westbury offered few opportunities for meeting people, and John seemed to spend more and more time in London.

Robbie's intimately whispered promise to 'see you very soon' rang hollowly in my ears. He hadn't been in touch for three long months, not since the meeting at the mill. I'd stopped trying to be first to the telephone each time it rang, and had given up rushing to meet the postman. I was lonely and my social life was at a standstill.

So when I heard the raunchy toot-ti-toot of a car horn I didn't waste any time putting my shoes on, and sprinted round to the front of the house barefoot. John was already waiting on the front step.

'Nice motor,' I said, as a low-slung dark blue sports car drew up.

'It's a Morgan, spelled M-O-N-E-Y,' he whispered back.

The car scrunched to a halt on the gravel. Robbie looked just like a Hollywood leading man in his fur-lined flying jacket and a white scarf of what appeared to be parachute silk. His long absence was instantly forgiven. He pulled off his leather pilot's helmet, pushed himself up and swung his legs over the door.

'My new baby. What do you think?' He seemed extremely pleased with himself.

'Beautiful,' we chorused.

He pumped John's hand, 'How are you, old man? Long time no see.'

He lifted my fingers and kissed them with mock formality, eyes flirting, then looked down at my bare feet. My toes felt suddenly vulnerable.

'Hello Lily. Love the red nail polish, terribly erotic — I mean exotic.' He grinned with easy familiarity. 'How's tricks, one and all?'

'Not bad, not bad,' said John. 'Like the Morgan.'

'Little beauty, isn't she? Fancy a spin? There's

room for both of you, if Lily doesn't mind sitting sideways in the back.'

The smell of Castrol on the warm evening air promised adventure. As Robbie shimmied the car through the twisty lanes, each bend brought a new aroma; a greenstick bonfire, hay drying in the field, pungent piggeries, water mint, wild garlic and the sweeter notes of bluebells and cow parsley.

We pulled up at the pub and while Robbie went inside to get the drinks John and I sat on a bench by the river, watching an anxious mother duck shepherding her ducklings and listening to the calls of coots settling in the reed beds.

'I wonder why he's popped up just now?' John said. 'We're still waiting for him to sign that parachute silk contract, you know? It's been a while.'

'Are you going to ask him?'

'Watch and learn, Sis,' he said, tapping the side of his nose.

Robbie arrived with the drinks, and for a while we made small talk. 'Been doing much flying lately?' John asked.

'She is no more,' Robbie said, pulling a sorrowful face. 'Had a bit of a prang.'

'Golly. You crashed it?'

'I'd been out for a spin — lovely evening, bit like this. I was just coming into land when out of nowhere comes this ruddy great removal van toddling along the edge of the field,' he said smoothly. 'Managed to avoid it but the wheels clipped a hedge and next thing I knew we were doing a somersault. Fine in the air, that kind of thing, but not so clever at ground level. Ended up with her nose half buried in a ploughed field and me hanging upside down in the straps.'

He demonstrated leaning out of his seat, chest parallel to the ground, arms gripping an imaginary joystick, mock terror on his face, making us laugh. It seemed like a bit of a lark. We expected a jokey punch line.

'What did you do?' John asked.

'I felt this wet in my hair. It was petrol, dripping out of the tank onto the engine block. So my mind got made up sharpish. I jumped for it and ran away across the field. There was a ruddy great *whoomph* and the whole thing went up. Guy Fawkes would have been proud. That was the end of the plane, though. Miss her terribly.' He jerked his thumb towards the Morgan glistening in the twilight, engine ticking as it cooled. 'But the insurance paid for that little beauty.'

The story shocked me, much more than I'd expected. What if Robbie really had gone up in flames? I could imagine what John was thinking: we could have lost the contract, too.

Robbie took a swig of his pint. '*C'est la vie.* Anyway, what's been happening in Westbury? How's business?'

'Not bad, not bad, considering,' John said.

'Tough times for us all,' Robbie said. 'The harder old Chamberlain bargains for peace, the harder we seem to be working for war, don't you find?'

He offered us cigarettes from a slim monogrammed case and then, as he lit them for us with his gold Dunhill, added quite casually,

'By the way, how's the finishing going? The parachute contract's yours, you know, just as soon as you're ready to meet the specifications.'

John didn't miss a beat. 'The finishing plant's in and we're confident it'll be up and running in a week or so.' I sipped my shandy and smiled to myself at his bullishness. The truth, I knew, was less impressive.

For weeks now, John and Father had been preoccupied with installing the new equipment. By moving machinery around they had managed to clear a section of the winding mill to create a self-contained room next to the boiler house with its own double doors leading directly into the yard, convenient for the plumbing, drainage and hot water needed for the new plant. The equipment arrived from Switzerland on a lorry so long it had difficulty in negotiating the driveway. Each heavy section had to be lifted and rolled into the new finishing room before the machinery could be assembled. A team of engineers worked several days to construct it and link up the plumbing and wiring.

'You're very quiet, Lily,' Robbie said, turning to me. 'I gather you're in charge of weaving the stuff? How's that going?'

'It's going fine.' I caught John's eye. *Just watch me play the game too*. 'It's a plain taffeta in twelve *momme habotai*, and to be honest it's a doddle compared with some of the other things we have to weave. We should be able to get you some samples any day now, just as soon as the plant's up and running.'

Robbie nodded as if he knew what I was

talking about and John suppressed a smile. I surprised myself, too; it was a heady feeling, being an expert. Not what men usually expected of women, I thought, smugly.

What I said wasn't far from the truth. Weaving parachute silk *was* straightforward: thread of equal weight for both warp and weft, with no patterns or colour changes. Twist and tensions were clearly defined. The yarn we used was still 'in the gum' — the sticky sericin the caterpillar exudes to make its cocoon — which made it easier to handle. It would be 'de-gummed' by boiling the woven cloth as part of the finishing process.

Gwen had put me in charge of two looms weaving test runs with Stefan, so that he could take over two of his own once the contracts came in. As she predicted, he was already a good weaver and I found myself looking forward to working beside him each day. At first it was exciting to be developing a new material, but it was vital to be vigilant against broken threads, and these were tricky to detect against the blinding whiteness of the material. After hours of watching yards of plain white cloth emerging from the shuttle beam our eyes burned and we begged Gwen to let us weave stripes or Jacquard designs to relieve the boredom. But she was immovable. 'It's important work, has to be right. And you two are our experts now.'

After Robbie dropped us home John said, 'Very impressive, *Schwester*, the way you talked that up. You're turning into a right little businesswoman.'

'Thanks for the compliment,' I said, feeling quietly proud of myself, flattered that he'd noticed.

'Of course, it helps that he's pretty sweet on you. Better keep it that way, we're going to depend on him in the next little while.'

'He's not *sweet* on me, you're just imagining it,' I snapped. 'Besides, just because I'm a girl doesn't mean I have to simper at any chap with a chequebook.'

John backed away, palms up. 'Steady on, old thing. I just meant keep on the right side of him, nothing more or less. But mark my words, he'll ask you for a date within the week. I'd bet my hat on it.'

★ ★ ★

'It's that charming Mr Cameron on the blower. Wishes to speak to my beautiful daughter,' Father said, exchanging approving glances with Mother.

'I'll keep my hat then,' John said, making triumphant nudge-nudge gestures as I went to the telephone, cheeks burning.

The days till Saturday dragged slowly by. I was so excited at the prospect of my first proper date I could barely sit still. I emptied my wardrobe and chest of drawers trying on a dozen combinations of outfits, eventually settling on a tartan skirt and baby-blue cashmere twinset which felt both casual but also flatteringly feminine. My new silk stockings, fresh out of the pack, felt sleek and sexy. At last the evening arrived.

As I sat in the cinema with Robbie's arm around my shoulders I realised with a little thrill of excitement that he bore more than a passing resemblance to the star of the film, James Stewart. Being in the company of this handsome man felt deliciously glamorous.

Afterwards we went for a drink in the pub and it was past eleven by the time we returned home. Robbie offered his hand and I climbed with as much elegance as I could muster out of the low-slung car. He wrapped an arm around my waist, and with his other hand turned my face to his and kissed me. At first it was demure, like before, but then I felt him push my lips apart with his tongue, exploring my mouth with it. I felt myself in the hands of a skilled operator, closed my eyes and tried to lose myself in the moment.

But the sensation wasn't what I expected, not swoony, like in the movies. All I could think of was that he tasted of cigarettes and beer. I was glad when he stopped.

'You dear sweet thing,' he said, stroking my hair. 'We must do this again. We could have some serious fun together. Tell you what, I've got a friend who has a cottage in the Peaks. I could borrow a friend's plane and fly you there for a weekend. What do you think?'

'That sounds . . . cracking,' I stuttered. I could hardly concentrate as he kissed me goodbye, my head was in such a spin. Whatever did he mean? Was he really suggesting we should have a dirty weekend? That was a bit fast, even for James Stewart.

'You were back late last night. Have a nice time, dear?' Mother enquired as we cleared the breakfast dishes.

'Lovely. The film was a laugh,' I mumbled. 'James Stewart's a great actor.'

'Charming young man, isn't he? Your father's quite taken with him,' she said, distractedly.

Robbie was ideal boyfriend material. I was sure that I was falling in love. But how could I know for certain? What was I supposed to feel? Vera had been promised a weekend off soon, and I couldn't wait to tell her everything.

★ ★ ★

A few days later Mother, John and I were eating supper informally at the kitchen table. Father had stayed over in London. Out of the window I could see the mill in darkness, except for the lights of the new finishing plant casting bright stripes across the empty yard.

John pushed the ham and potato salad around his plate.

'Not hungry dear?' Mother asked.

'I'm fine,' he snapped.

'Sorry it's only a cold meal tonight, but I thought, with this weather.'

'I said I'm fine.' Like the slam of a shuttle.

Another silence, then he banged down his knife and fork. 'It's that ruddy vat in the finishing plant. I just can't get the thermostat and timer to work properly. I've tried and tried. We've wasted

God knows how much silk by over-boiling it. Now it's useless for parachutes and no one else is going to want it. We've spent thousands on this kit but unless we can get the silk right sharpish, we'll never get the contracts to pay off the debt.'

He sighed, rubbing his stubbly cheek. 'I'll just have to go back after supper and have another go.'

'Do you have to? You look all done in,' Mother murmured.

'Shall I come and help?' I said, surprising myself.

'Why should you? You've done a day's work already.'

'It's important to me too you know, the future of the mill and all that.' He raised his eyebrows. I barely understood how it had happened, but my apprenticeship no longer felt like filling in time until something better came along. I was starting to care.

'Come on then,' he said, pushing away his chair and getting up from the table. 'A pair of fresh eyes won't do any harm.'

Unlike the weaving shed, with its oily smells and dark looms, the finishing plant was dazzling — brightly lit and newly whitewashed, with shiny stainless steel vats and tubes, steamy and clean-smelling like a laundry.

Although I'd seen the machinery being installed I hadn't watched it working before. John showed me how the silk went through two large baths of boiling water to be de-gummed and rinsed, and how to lift the silk onto hooks called stenters which stretched it back to its previous width. After that it was hung in a hot air cupboard to dry, and run through yet more rollers to be pressed.

'Looks simple, doesn't it? But it's not. The silk has to go over the rollers at exactly the right speeds, and at the same time the temperature in the vats has to be exact.'

He wiped his brow. 'And even supposing we get all that right, we have to make sure the silk goes through the drier at the right speed and temperature so that it's just damp enough to be put through hot rollers to iron it — what we call calendering.'

Stacked on a rack were rolls of the untreated white silk Stefan and I had woven. 'I've had the vats heating and the thermostat says they're at the right temperature, so shall we have another go? Help me up with this roll, would you?'

'Hang on a sec,' I said. 'Didn't you say there was a problem with the thermostat?'

He frowned. Why was I asking difficult questions when I knew nothing about it? 'How am I supposed to know if we don't try it first?'

'Use a thermometer? Good old-fashioned kind?'

'Where on earth can we get one of those at this time of night?'

I had a moment of inspiration. 'Mother's jam thermometer, the brass one on the hook above the stove. I'll run back and get it.'

We lowered the thermometer into the vat on a piece of wire and, once the rolls were in place, John clicked a switch and the machinery started, pulling the silk through the first two vats. The steam ran in rivulets down our faces as we

92

worked side by side hooking the silk onto the stenters. John turned his attention to the control panel and checking the thermometer. I went outside to cool off.

When I came back he said, 'You were right, you know. The thermostat said two hundred and twelve degrees and cut out the heater, but the thermometer was only at a hundred and eighty-nine. I've had to adjust the thermostat higher still to get the water to boiling point. Bloody thing's obviously on the blink.' It was as though the machine had personally insulted him. Trying to conceal my smugness, I went to watch the silk emerge from the drier.

'Shouldn't this silk be rolling straight?' I called, over the growl of the machinery. He left the control panel and came to look.

'Oh blast, what the hell is wrong now?' he cursed, rushing to hit the off switch. The machinery sighed slightly as it came to a halt. 'If I run the rollers slowly in reverse, can you pull out the wrinkles?'

'I'll do my best.'

'Mind your fingers.'

'Will do, have a go.' As silk rewound it became clear what had caused the problem. 'I think this roller's slightly offset,' I called, 'that's why the silk's not rolling up straight.'

He stopped the machine and came back. 'By God you're right, Lily. Can't bloody trust anyone.' He went to a tool box and pulled out a large spanner. 'We'll have to adjust the axle.'

Finally we got started again and when I next looked the clock on the wall read half-past nine.

We'd been working for two hours, but I'd hardly noticed the time passing.

'Now we have to test it,' he said. 'Help me lift it over here. This thing's a burst tester, which checks how much strain the silk can take before it breaks. And then we have to put it through the porosity tester. That's the most important — it measures how quickly the air goes through the fabric.'

I hadn't noticed the two curious contraptions on the stainless steel table top. The smaller one looked rather like a sewing machine with a large dial attached to one side. John pulled out a few yards of material, laid it across the plate and lowered the lever, trapping the silk snugly over the hole below. 'Wind the handle, slowly.' As I turned the small wheel, the needle moved clockwise round its dial and the rubber expanded upwards into a dome, stretching the cloth till there was a slight 'whoof' as it broke.

'*Wundervoll*,' he said, releasing the leaver and inspecting the hole. 'Weft and warp broke together at eighty point three. That'll do nicely.' He wrote the result into a red-backed ledger.

With its orange rubber tubes and multiple dials, the porosity tester looked more like something out of science fiction. John positioned the silk and lowered the lever, compressing round rubber seals onto the material from both sides. When he pushed the button, the machine hissed and sighed for a few seconds. He scrutinised the needle as it leapt and settled on the dial, then threw his hands up into the air in triumph. 'Fourteen point four, the golden number. At last.' He did a little jig and gave me a hug.

'Fourteen point four what?'

'Cubic feet per second, that's how fast the air is supposed to go through a square foot of fabric. It's air permeability — the porosity index Robbie was going on about.'

'It has to be that exact?'

'Within a close range. We ought to repeat the test a couple of times to make sure it's consistent. But we can do that tomorrow.'

I was too excited to wait. 'We'll sleep better if we know it's right. Do a couple more now. It'll only take a few minutes.'

The next two came within the right range and we decided to call it a day. Walking back across the yard to the darkened house he said, 'Thanks for your help tonight, Sis.'

'I quite enjoyed it,' I said, glowing at the unexpected compliment.

'That thermometer was a stroke of genius, and I can't understand why no one spotted the wonky roller before.' He stopped. 'Want a smoke before we go in?'

We sat on the front step and lit up.

'Whatever happened to your plans to go to London?' he asked. 'Thought you couldn't wait to get away from here?'

'I'd like to some time,' I said, wondering whether this was still true. 'But working at the mill has turned out to be a lot more interesting than I imagined.'

'I hear good things about you from Gwen,' he said.

'She never says anything to me. What did she tell you?' I asked, quietly pleased.

'She says you've learned fast and you're a hard worker. Got an eye for detail,' he said, 'just what you need in a weaver.'

'That's good to hear,' I said. 'She goes on about how skilled Stefan is too, but she never tells him so he's always worrying whether she likes him. I wonder why she never praises anyone directly?'

'Nature of the beast,' John laughed. 'She's a funny old stick.'

We puffed in silence for a few moments.

'I don't want to be a weaver for ever, but it's quite important, what we are doing here, don't you think?' I said.

'We're preparing for war,' he said gloomily, 'war kills people.'

'Our parachutes will save lives, at least,' I said, not wanting to deflate my cheerful mood.

'That's one way of looking at it,' he said oddly, stubbing out the cigarette under his heel with surprising ferocity. I wondered what was on his mind, but forgot all about it until later, when Vera told me.

7

The silk we love for its softness and beauty is also one of the strongest and toughest fibres in the world. It has a strength of around five grams per denier compared with three grams per denier for a drawn wire of soft steel. It has much more elasticity than cotton or flax, and its resistance to shearing or twisting forces is considerably greater than that of the new rayons and nylons.
From *The History of Silk,* **by Harold Verner**

At last, Vera got a weekend off. She came home rarely these days.

I missed my best friend, our gossip and silliness, our shared sense of the ridiculous. She could only talk on the public telephone in a noisy corridor of the nurses' home, and at my end Father tended to hang around, muttering about the cost of the calls, so we couldn't speak for long. All I'd gathered was that her matron was a tyrant, and the pressure of studying as well as working long shifts was beginning to tell.

On Friday evening she arrived at the front door, still in her nurse's uniform, and pale with exhaustion.

'Just on my way home from the station,' she said. 'Caught the six o'clock from Liverpool Street.'

I hugged her. 'Are you here for the whole weekend?'

She nodded. 'Abso-bloody-lutely. I'm shattered,' she sighed.

'Got anything special planned?'

'Sleeping a lot. Catching up with the folks. Seeing you, of course. Can't wait for a proper chinwag.'

'I can't wait either, it's dull as dishwater round here,' I grimaced. 'Have you got time for a snifter?'

'I'd better get back to the folks soonish, but perhaps just a quick one,' she looked past me into the hall, in an odd sort of way. 'Where's John?'

'In the finishing room as usual, I expect. Why?' She ignored the question.

'Shall we go and sit by the tree?' she said. 'I really need some fresh air after London.'

'Take gee and tees with us?' I said.

'Now you're talking.'

The old Bramley apple tree had always been our favourite spot for our gossips, a place for sharing secrets about school or crushes on boys, where we could not be overheard. The sun was low in the sky, gleaming pinkly through the row of rustling poplars at the end of the orchard. The grass was tall, the clover still humming with bees, collared doves cooed calmingly as they settled for the night.

We sat on the wobbly wooden seat at the base of the tree, the ice in our glasses of gin and tonic tinkling cheerfully.

'It's so beautiful here, I never properly appreciated it before,' she sighed. 'All the apple blossom, and the candles on the horse chestnuts. You don't know how much I've missed green fields.'

'How's nursing?' I said. 'I want to hear everything.'

'Oh, okay,' she said wearily.

'You don't sound so sure. Is everything all right?'

'Yes,' she said more firmly. 'It's hard work. Great fun,' she tailed off, took a sip of her drink.

'But?' I said. 'Come on, Vera. Something's happened. You can't hide anything from me, I know you too well.'

To my relief, she was smiling now. 'I meant to save it for tomorrow. But I can't keep it in any more. Promise you won't be cross?'

'For heaven's sake, what's this all about?'

A pause, then she said quietly, 'It's John and me.'

I didn't get it. 'What about John and you?'

'We're dating.'

At first I didn't understand. 'What? John? You? I don't believe it. You're joking.' From the look on her face I could see she wasn't, and back-tracked quickly. 'Crikey . . . I mean . . . Oh, Vera.'

'We've been out for drinks in London. Twice. The second time, he kissed me.'

I forced a smile but my stomach started to churn with a disagreeable mixture of emotions; faint disgust coupled with an overriding sensation of raw, almost painful, jealousy. It felt like a slap in the face.

Whatever did she see in him? I thought of the times we'd ganged up against him, to trick him or get him into trouble. And the time she cracked her head when he pushed her off the swing. I felt sure she'd never forgive him. But now they seemed to be ganging up against me. It felt as though John had stolen my best friend.

She started to gabble, words pouring out as if

the dam had burst. 'I've fancied him for a while, since he got back last year. But I couldn't really believe he was interested in me. When he invited me out I thought he was just being kind. But we couldn't stop talking, he's so easy going, and he makes me laugh. Next time we went to the cinema, he kissed me and said he hoped I felt the same as him. I think I might be in love.'

As she rattled on I swigged my drink to quell the queasy feeling in my stomach. Yet I could see her happiness glowing through the weary pallor, returning roses to her cheeks, highlighting dimples flattened by tiredness. Why should I be so upset? My brother might be irritating but he was a decent chap, honest, and he had good prospects. Not a bad catch, and Vera was my best friend. Surely I should be happy for them both?

But there was something else in Vera's face, a guarded look I couldn't put my finger on. 'Have you told anyone else about it?'

'No one. He wants to keep it that way for the moment. Promise you won't spill the beans?'

'My best friend spoons my brother. How can I keep that a secret?'

'If you don't I may just have to keel you,' she said in that stagey piratical accent we used when we acted out the story of Peter Pan on the island. 'Walk zee plank. Beware zee crocodiles.'

Laughing made me feel a little better. 'When are you going to tell the world?'

'Soon I think. Probably. Depends on what happens . . . '

'What do you mean, 'what happens'? Are you planning to elope or something?' She sighed and put her face in her hands. 'Vera?' I said, putting my hand on her shoulder. 'I thought you were happy.'

'I am, of course,' she said, sitting up, 'but it's complicated.' She emptied her glass. 'There's something else I've got to tell you. I just can't keep it to myself any longer.'

'Put me out of my misery,' I said. Surely she wasn't pregnant?

'Oh, Lily,' she blurted out suddenly, with a sob in her voice, 'if there's a war, he says he's going to join up. Whatever am I going to do?'

The grass and the evening sky seemed to pale, like an overexposed photograph, and the persistent cooing of the collared doves became loud and irritating. 'I don't believe it. Why's he told you, but not us?' I squeaked.

She shook her head and, quite suddenly, I was overcome with anger. 'What a stupid, stupid selfish boy,' I found myself shouting. 'He never thinks of anyone else but himself. What about Mother and Father? They'll be devastated.'

'I shouldn't have told you,' she whispered, her voice cracked.

'He doesn't have to go. Father said he thought producing parachute silk would be a reserved occupation, like being a doctor or an engineer. They won't have to fight because they're needed here, at home.'

'I've already been through all that.' Her face was blotchy and wretched. 'But he says he can't stay at home while other people fight, and the Germans will invade unless we stop them.' She started to sob properly now, shoulders shaking, the tears leaving grimy streaks on her cheeks.

I pulled out an insubstantial lacy handkerchief, rather grubby.

'He doesn't have to stop them in person,' I said, as Vera tried to dry her eyes. I watched the ants running up and down the bark of the tree, busy in their miniature world, and envied their simple lives. 'How will we cope at the mill? Why hasn't he told us?'

'Because he knows your parents would try to dissuade him, that's why.' She gave a ragged sigh. 'Bloody, isn't it? Men feel it's their duty to go and fight, but . . . hell, I'm so terrified I'll lose him, just as we've found each other.' A new tear overflowed, trickled down her cheek and came to rest in a dimple.

'Let me talk to him.'

'Please don't. He'd be furious if he knew I'd told you.'

'Then *you'll* have to stop him.'

'You think I haven't tried?'

'This is so awful. Why do countries have to fight each other?'

We sat silently for a moment.

'Lord, is that the time?' she peered at the little watch pinned upside down to her breast pocket like a medal. 'I've got to go. The parents will worry. When John gets in would you mention that I'm back? Casually — you don't know about us, remember?'

'Shall I see you tomorrow, or have you got to see John instead?' I sounded like a jealous lover.

'Oh, Lily, don't be such an idiot. This won't stop us being best friends.' She jumped up, brushing the dust from her skirt. 'I'm sorry all of this has come as such a shock. I didn't mean to gab about his joining up, but I've been so worried. You're the only person I can talk to.'

* ★ *

I watched the sun setting behind the poplars and listened to the evening chorus of birds noisily staking their territories. An absurd thought crossed my mind — if birds could settle their differences by singing, why couldn't countries find some similarly peaceable way of doing it? Why did they have to fight each other?

Didn't John realise his misguided sense of duty could get him killed? I had to try to dissuade him. But what chance was there of changing his mind when Vera had already tried and failed? He seemed so absolute these days, so certain of his opinions. He railed against Chamberlain's peace-making — in his view nothing but brute force would stop the Nazis now. In any case, if I talked to him he'd be furious with Vera for breaking his confidence.

When I got back the house was empty and a cold supper was laid on the kitchen table, covered with muslin, a note propped against the water jug. *Gone to bed. Headache. Sorry. Mother.* I had no appetite, anyway. I pulled an armchair over to the sitting room window, poured myself another large gin and tonic, and sat with my head full of angry, miserable thoughts, as the air grew thick with dusk and the room went dark around me.

The following day, Vera and I went shopping in
Westbury for make-up, to cheer ourselves up. We
made a pact not to talk about war. Over strong
tea and stale cakes in Mary's Café, I told her
about my date with Robbie.

'Flying you away for the weekend, how
romantic,' Vera sighed. 'Sounds like something
out of Hollywood.'

'I won't go, of course.'

'You *must* go. When would you get a chance
like that again? To hell with your virginity, you've
got to lose it some time.' Vera might already have
lost hers, I thought, mildly disgusted at the
thought of her and my brother doing it. But it
wasn't the virginity thing that concerned me.

'To be honest, I'm not sure what I feel about
him. He's so gentlemanly and handsome and
he's got a beautiful car. Ma and Pa think he's the
bees knees. But . . . '

'But what?'

Why was I hesitating? I hardly knew myself.
I'd been desperate for a boyfriend and desolate
when Robbie had failed to follow up on his
promise. Now he seemed keen, I was having
doubts. And it wasn't just that I thought he was a
bit fast.

'What's up Lily?' A slow smile spread across
her face. 'There's someone else, isn't there?
Goodness, you are a dark horse. Go on, spill it.'

'No,' I said, firmly. 'No one else, nothing to
tell.'

There really was nothing, at least not that I

could make sense of. But something unexpected had happened that I couldn't get out of my mind.

* * *

All week the weather had been roasting, and so hot in the weaving shed that we had struggled to keep our hands dry to avoid staining the silk with sweat. The canteen, with its wide windows, was also sweltering and provided no respite at tea breaks. Stefan, Kurt and Walter had started to take their breaks outside to get some fresh air, and I was usually invited to join them.

That day I found Stefan on the bench behind the boiler house, on his own. It was cool there, shaded from direct sunshine by the overhang of the building.

'Where are the others?' I asked. Kurt and Walter had recently been promoted from the packing shed to work in the new finishing room with Bert.

'They have to finish a couple of rolls before they can stop, Bert said.'

Across the meadows a gentle breeze blew a blizzard of willow fluff. 'Is it snowing, in June?' he said, as we sat down with our glasses of orange squash.

'It's just the seed from the cricket bat willows, silly.'

'Cricket bat willows?'

'Those tall, straight trees.' I pointed. 'They use the wood for cricket bats.'

'All of those trees? That will make many bats.'

105

'Every English boy has to have one.'

'You and your cricket,' he laughed.

'It's like a religion,' I said.

'But why do they use that wood? Is it so special?'

'It is flexible and strong, and doesn't crack when you whack a cricket ball.'

'I know nothing about cricket, I'm a city boy,' he said, pulling out a packet of cigarettes, tapping the end, and taking out two. He lit them both and passed one to me. The intimacy of this gesture gave me a little jolt of pleasure. I found myself watching him without meaning to; no movement was superfluous. He reminded me of a sleek black cat.

'Tell me about your city,' I asked, trying unsuccessfully to blow smoke rings into the still air.

'Hamburg? It is a wonderful place. On a big river, the Elbe, a harbour, lots of ships. But most of all I like the music, it has many jazz clubs and bars.' The fingers on his left hand played silent notes on his knee.

'Where did you learn to play the piano?'

'From my mother. She taught me traditional music: Mozart, Bach, Beethoven, you know? She trained to be a concert pianist, but it was difficult to make money this way, so she became instead a teacher.'

'That's a coincidence. We both have mothers who are pianists,' I said.

'But I let my mother down. I was a rebel. My friends took me to a jazz club and I did not play Beethoven any more. Jazz was the only music for me. Bohemians, my father called us.' He took a drag of his cigarette and blew three perfectly-formed rings into the still air.

'Wow. Where did you learn to do that? In the jazz clubs?'

'Those clubs got me into trouble, too.'

I remembered that wet Sunday in the drawing room. 'What you told us about . . . *Swingjugend?* What were they? What happened?'

'Jazz is forbidden and the government is closing the clubs. The *Jugend* want to keep the clubs open. It is for . . . ' he struggled to find the right words.

'To protest?'

'Yes, that is it,' he said. 'To protest the Nazis.' I hadn't the heart to correct him. I was still struggling to understand why such joyful music should be banned in the first place. 'What is so bad about jazz?'

'It is negro music,' he said, bluntly. 'Not pure. Dirty. Like what they say about the Jews.'

I was shocked into silence. 'Dirty?' This quiet, sensitive boy slouched so elegantly against the wall, contemplating his feet, that gleaming mop of dark hair falling over his face? The notion would be laughable, if it weren't so sickening. 'Tell me what happened next.'

'When they arrested us they said if they caught us again, we'd be sent to work camps. We didn't care. The most important thing was to make a stand against them, against . . . It is horrible, living in fear, people shouting at you in the street, throwing things.'

He looked away across the field, almost talking to himself. 'When I got home, *Vati* told me they

107

had to get me out of Germany. People never came back from the camps, he said. I thought he was crazy. How can I leave my family? But he found a sponsor for me only, and they have the money for just my fare. They will come later, they said, but now they have no jobs they have no money to pay.' There was a break in his voice as it tailed away.

'You know my father is still trying very hard to get them work and visas?' I said. He had pulled all possible strings at the Rotary Club and the local Chamber of Commerce, but so far in vain. We all knew that if war came it would be too late.

Stefan lit another cigarette, raised it with a trembling hand, and exhaled slowly. No smoke rings this time. 'I will never forget that day. He would not let my mother and the girls come to the station in case she changed her mind. Everyone was crying, except for him. He was trying to be strong.'

His voice faltered and stopped. I put my hand gently onto his shoulder. Without warning, he threw down his cigarette, swivelled on the bench and wrapped his arms around me, burying his face in my neck. His hair smelled deliciously of sweat, shaving soap and cigarette smoke. We held each other for a long moment, listening to each other's heartbeats, matching the pace of our breathing.

Eventually he pulled away. I wanted to say something more but couldn't find the right words, and then the klaxon sounded the end of tea break. As we walked back into the mill we passed Bert returning to the finishing room. He was a short, bowed man getting on in years, who always wore the same grubby tweed jacket. I imagined him to be a widower, or more likely a bachelor who had never developed the social skills to attract a wife. He scowled and seemed barely to acknowledge us. I felt ridiculously guilty, as though I'd done something wrong just being seen with Stefan.

That night the heat was oppressive. I couldn't sleep. Even hours later I could feel the impression of that awkward embrace against me and it made my body feel heavy and hot. But what did it mean? Had he turned to me just for comfort? Or was there more to it? My thoughts were like a tangled skein. He was just a boy, nearly two years younger than me. Even if he really was older, as Leo had suggested at the camp, he could never admit it.

If Father found out he would be furious, might even send Stefan away. But nothing was going to happen.

And nothing did. Stefan and I continued to work closely at our looms, and often stood beside each other looking for lost warp threads, or checking the tension on the cloth beams. Occasionally a private smile passed between us, and once or twice I caught him watching me. As the weeks went by I wondered if that moment by the boiler house had meant anything at all.

Besides, Robbie was my ideal boyfriend: charming, rich, and fun. The perfect match. So why did my heart not leap when I thought of him?

8

Silk has a range of remarkable properties: it is rot-resistant, making it capable of being stored for many years without deterioration; it is non-allergenic, which makes it ideal for bandages; and it has very low conductivity and thus was widely used for insulation of electrical wiring before the advent of plastics.
From *The History of Silk,* **by Harold Verner**

For several weeks Father had been traipsing around the country meeting potential contractors, including Robbie's outfit in Hertfordshire.

Hitler had signed a non-aggression pact with Russia, which, the papers said, would effectively allow the Germans to invade Poland unhindered, so war seemed inevitable. All this was affecting our business terribly, it had never been worse. We'd had no new orders for weeks and faced the dismal prospect of having to lay workers off.

But that evening in late August, Father's face was bright with triumph. 'It's still hush-hush, but our test samples have been accepted,' he said, pouring sherry. 'Let's toast to that.'

'The ministry also wants a smallish quantity of fine white taffeta,' he went on after we'd all raised our glasses. 'Won't tell me what it's for, but one of the minions told me, on the QT, that it's for printing what they call escape and evasion maps. They're sewn inside airmen's uniforms so if they're downed in enemy territory they can find their way back.'

We sat down at the table and Mother brought out his favourite supper.

'I've made toad-in-the-hole to celebrate your success,' she said, starting to serve the sausages in their jackets of puffy Yorkshire batter. John was unusually quiet, I thought; he hadn't reacted with much excitement to Father's news. And then I remembered. It could be him, that airman downed behind the lines. Was he imagining what it would really be like; cold, hungry, frightened and possibly injured, not knowing who he could trust? A map might be some comfort, I supposed, but not much.

'I learned something else today,' Father said, pouring gravy liberally over his mashed potato. 'As of next week, the government's going to sequester all stocks of raw silk, so only mills with contracts for essential war uses will get any. Without these contracts we'd probably have had to close, at least for the duration. It could have been a disaster for us. As it is, we'll be busier than ever. Well done, everyone.'

As I watched John raise his glass to toast our success, the thought suddenly struck me. 'It's all very well for you,' I thought bitterly. 'You won't even be here to help.'

★   ★   ★

A couple of days later, I caught sight of Robbie at the top of the weaving-shed steps, scanning the rows of looms. He looked like some exotic creature among the weavers' dun overalls and headscarves, in his expensive pinstriped suit, a glossy black briefcase under his arm.

Gwen went to over to meet him and he bent to shout something in her ear. They came down the steps, and as they walked along the narrow aisle between the looms she fell a few steps behind and imitated his military gait; straight-backed, chin in the air. A dozen weavers looked up, amused by her gentle mimicry. Robbie grinned back, confident their smiles were for him.

'Great day,' he shouted. 'Just signed the parachute contract with your pa. Can you take a break?' He pointed towards the side door, opened to allow the breeze to circulate around the weaving shed. I nodded, untied my overall, pulled off my headscarf, tweaked my hair into shape and gestured to Stefan to ask him to watch my looms. As we walked away I caught his eyes following me, and Gwen watching Stefan.

'Phew, it's hot in there. Don't know how you stand it,' Robbie said, once we were outside. 'Who's the charmer?'

'Charmer?'

'Fellow at the loom next to you.'

'One of the German boys. What do you mean, charmer?'

'Never trust those sultry European types,' he said. There was a brittle edge to his voice.

While I was trying to think up a decent response without sounding defensive, he went on, 'Now look here, old thing. I wanted to say that I'm sorry I haven't organised that trip to the Peaks I promised. Problems borrowing a plane.'

112

Thank goodness, I thought. I'd dreaded the moment he'd suggest it again. 'But we're thinking of going to Cambridge on Sunday,' he went on. 'Take out a punt, have a picnic. The weather's wonderful and I need a bit of light relief. What do you say?'

'Sounds fun,' I said, relieved. 'Who's we?'

'A couple of friends. And you, I hope.'

Any misgivings I might have felt were immediately brushed aside. With a group of people nothing would get too heavy, I reasoned. I had visited Cambridge a few times before, and knew it to be a very beautiful, romantic city. I'd never been taken punting before. Robbie had promised champagne. How glamorous it sounded, and what an adventure.

★   ★   ★

The day dawned cloudlessly and by the time he arrived it had turned into a glorious morning. I felt like royalty, easing myself into the Morgan in a carefully-chosen strappy summer dress and sandals. The regiment of brass buttons on Robbie's blazer twinkled in the sun and my parents waved with approving smiles. John was nowhere to be seen. I wondered if he was piqued about not being invited, but hardly gave it a second thought.

When we reached the river, the punt looked so comfortable, with tartan rugs spread over the cushions and a large wicker picnic basket loaded in the front.

'Shouldn't we wait for the others?' I asked, as we prepared to climb on board.

'Others? Ah. Last minute decision. They can't

make it after all,' he said airily, taking my hand as I stepped onto the flat deck. 'Didn't I say? Never mind, we can have a good time together, can't we?'

I sat down on the soft warm cushions and watched him dealing efficiently with the ropes, casting off and pushing away from the bank. He must have planned it this way, I thought. It was not going to be the party I'd expected.

But it was impossible to be disappointed for long. From the Backs, the city seemed enchanted, the white filigree stonework of Kings' Chapel luminous against the unblemished blue of the sky. Robbie handled the unwieldy pole with great skill and as we glided along the river the swallows swooped close, dipping into the water and swirling into the air with shrill shrieks of warning.

Halfway to Grantchester we moored by a quiet bank shaded by weeping willows, and curious cows came over, huffing at us with their sweet grassy breath before wandering away. He poured champagne and we toasted the English country-side, to summertime, and even to the increasingly unlikely peace.

I drank too quickly and the bubbles went to my head. For a while we ate smoked salmon sandwiches and made silly conversation about nothing in particular. Robbie told stories and made me laugh. He refilled my glass several times and I didn't stop him. This must be what falling in love is like, I thought.

When we'd finished eating, he wedged his empty glass between the cushions and turned to

114

me, taking my hands, his expression suddenly serious.

'Lily, my dear, you must know by now what I feel about you?'

I nodded uncertainly, my heart starting to pound. Was he going to tell me he loved me? So soon?

'I've knocked around a bit, as you've probably gathered, but you're something special. Like the song says, I've got you under my skin.' I giggled nervously at the cliché, but he seemed unembarrassed.

'Why don't you come and give me a kiss?' he said, taking off his jacket, lying back and patting the cushions beside him. I hesitated a moment, feeling oddly reluctant. Kissing lying down seemed a little intimate, but what harm could come, out in the open air?

I lay down beside him and we cuddled and then kissed gently for a while. It was delicious, lying in his strong arms, safe and protected. He stroked my hair and said it smelled like apple blossom. He told me I was beautiful.

Then we started kissing again and it became more intense. Just relax and try to enjoy it, I said to myself, this is the way it is meant to be. But his tongue felt like an invasion, as if he was trying to capture me with his mouth. I found it difficult to breathe.

Then, when I was distracted by this, I felt his hand move to my breasts and start to squeeze them, each in turn. This is supposed to feel sexy, I thought, but it was just annoying and mildly uncomfortable. As it went on the pressure got stronger and started to hurt a bit, so I pushed his hand away. He didn't seem to take the hint. After a moment or two his hand moved back. I pushed it away again.

To my relief, his hand stayed away this time. But then, to my alarm, I realised that it had moved downwards, below his waist. The horrid thought flashed into my head that he was undoing his fly buttons. Surely not, I thought, not here? It scared me. I pulled away and started to sit up, but in a swift surprising movement that caught me unawares, his hand suddenly moved again, reaching up my skirt, almost to the top of my legs.

I squeaked with surprise and tried to push his hand away, but he took no notice, grabbing my arm and forcing it back over my head. He was so strong there was nothing I could do to resist. At the same time he moved his leg heavily over mine and pinned me down. I tried to sit up again, but he was holding my wrist almost painfully tight, and his chest was like a dead weight on top of me. I was trapped, terrified of what he might do next. I felt the warmth of bare flesh on my leg and panicked.

'No, Robbie. No.' My shout echoed across the water and an alarmed coot squawked in sympathy. 'Let me go!'

He held me a moment longer, as if considering his next move. Then I heard him mutter, 'Oh for Christ's sake.' He let go of my wrist and pushed me back roughly, almost violently, sat up, fumbled with his fly and rummaged in his jacket pocket for a cigarette. He was red in the face, panting as if he'd run a steeplechase.

'Whatever's the matter with you?' he said gruffly. 'You lead me on, then push me away.' He lit a cigarette and blew angry clouds of smoke across the water. I took deep breaths, trying to control the tears prickling the back of my throat.

'I'm sorry,' I said miserably, sitting up and straightening my clothes.

He was silent for a moment, then, 'But there *is* something between us, isn't there?'

'I think so. I mean, yes. But not that, not yet.' My head was spinning from the champagne and I couldn't think straight.

'Don't you feel the same way about me?' It felt like an interrogation.

'I just . . . ' I stuttered.

'Then what is it? Is there someone else? That Kraut boy?'

'No, not really.'

'No, not really,' he mimicked viciously. 'You owe me the truth, Lily.'

Now the shock was receding, my head was starting to ache and I started to feel irritated. 'It's just that I'm not sure about us.'

'You don't fancy me?'

'Yes, I mean no.'

'Is that a yes, you don't fancy me, or a no, you do?'

He took another long drag on his cigarette. As he turned away to exhale I noticed for the first time the hair thinning on the crown of his head, and felt a little sorry for him.

'I don't really know what I feel, if you want the honest truth,' I blurted. 'I like being with you. We have fun, don't we? This has been a lovely day and I'm sorry if I've spoiled it. I just don't think I'm ready for that. With anyone.'

I wiped my eyes with the back of my hand. He passed me a large white gentleman's handkerchief and I blew my nose as elegantly as possible.

'You should have thought about that before, shouldn't you?' His cigarette end hissed as it hit the water. 'You shouldn't promise what you don't intend to deliver.'

I hadn't promised anything, I thought angrily. But I didn't want to row with him any more, so I bit my tongue. He stood up and adjusted his trouser belt, walked to the end of the punt and took up the pole.

★　★　★

The drive back to Westbury was tense. I tried to lighten the mood by telling him the story of Gog Magog as we drove over the hills.

'They say giants sleep under here, did you know that?'

Robbie shook his head.

'King Gog led his Magog tribe of giants in a battle against the Romans. They found dozens of skeletons.'

'That's what you get with wars,' he muttered morosely.

When we got home I kissed him on the cheek, just to be courteous, and thanked him for the day. He didn't respond and said rather curtly, 'Better get off. Things to do, people to see. Be in touch soon.'

I knew he wouldn't, not this time, and realised that I didn't really care any more. When John asked, me, oh so breezily, how my 'big date' went, I told him everything except the bit after the picnic. But then he asked when I was seeing Robbie again, and when I said, as casually as possible, 'Probably not for a while,' he smelled a rat.

'I thought you were an item?' he said sharply. 'You haven't cheesed him off, have you?'

'Don't be an idiot,' I said. 'It's just I don't think we're really suited.'

'He's bloody keen on you. He pretty much admitted it to me, in so many words,' John said. 'For goodness sake, don't mess around with Robbie. You're playing with fire. Verners needs his contract.'

'He's signed it already,' I retorted.

'For an initial six months,' John said. 'We need to keep him on side so he'll renew it.'

I reassured him, of course, but his words troubled me. I hadn't known the contract was so short. Did I really have to pretend to be in love with someone, just to make sure we got it renewed? The idea made me feel grubby, and I tried to push it to the back of my mind.

At work I was becoming more confident, under Gwen's careful tutelage. Though I'd struggled to master the technique, with a few economical movements I could now knot threads as fine as a single hair. There was a round knot for normal use, or a more complex flat one for very fine material. The knot had to be trimmed closely, leaving no stray ends. Like all the

119

weavers I held concealed in my right palm a pair of tiny metal shears, like an extra set of finely sharpened fingers.

At first it had seemed an impossibility to fix a single broken warp thread among so many thousands but Gwen showed us how to find a tiny end, deftly re-thread and re-tie it, in a matter of seconds. She assured us that it would become second nature, in time.

I was nearing the end of my apprenticeship and proud of my new skills, feeling for the first time like a genuine weaver, not a fraud any more. My hands were smooth and soft, coated with microscopic filaments of silk that moulted from the fabrics we handled all day. And my lip-reading was fluent.

My unfavourable first impressions of Gwen were long forgotten, replaced by a deep admiration for her encyclopaedic knowledge of loom mechanics, her appreciation of the artistry of silk and its many woven designs and colours, and the dextrous way she handled its gossamer threads. I'd come to realise that her eccentric fashion sense was merely a proud disregard for convention, and that beneath the stern demeanour was a fiercely intelligent mind. Yet my attempts at moving towards a closer friendship had, until now, been rebuffed. That's not to say we'd been unfriendly, but we had not become pals in the way that I'd hoped; that girl-to-girl way I had with Vera. There was still something mysterious about Gwen that I couldn't fathom.

Then, at long last, she invited me to tea. I felt curiously nervous as I arrived at the large

Victorian house the other side of Westbury and rang the bell for the top floor flat, as instructed.

The Gwen who answered the door was very different from the one I knew at the mill. In a flowery shirt and casual, even stylish, slacks, her curls freed from the severe turban she always wore at work, she seemed relaxed and softer, more feminine.

'I'm afraid it's three flights,' she said, leading the way. 'My flat's in the old servants' quarters.'

As we reached the top of the stairs and she opened the door, a delicious smell of baking wafted out. 'Mmm. What's cooking, Gwen?' I asked. 'It's making my mouth water.'

'I've made scones, but they're not quite ready yet. Come in.'

The sloped ceilings of her little attic flat were so low I had to stoop my head. None of the furniture matched and it had a comfortable, lived-in atmosphere.

'It's so homely,' I said. 'How long have you lived here?'

'Six years or so. Ever since I came to Westbury,' she said. 'Have a seat.'

'So what brought you here?' I asked. 'You never did tell me.'

'It's a long story,' she sighed.

'You know almost everything about my family,' I said. 'And I know almost nothing about yours. It's only fair.'

'How long have you got?'

'Until the scones are ready.'

'Then it'll be the edited version,' she said, settling comfortably into the sofa. She seemed so much gentler and warmer at home, somehow more vulnerable. With her back to the window the sunlight blazed through her curls like a ginger halo, and she looked almost beautiful.

'My family are — were — a bit unusual,' she started with uncharacteristic hesitancy, and I found myself feeling mildly uneasy. What was she about to reveal, I wondered?

'Grandfather was a wealthy man, a silk merchant, and my father went into the business with him,' she went on. 'He got pretty rich playing the stock market. He was clever and successful, but he wasn't really happy. He'd always wanted to be an artist, so he took up art classes and fell in love with his tutor — my mother.'

'Throwing over the traces? I like him already.'

'His parents opposed it of course, but they married anyway and over the next few years he redeemed himself by making a fortune on the Stock Exchange. But then he defied them again. Quite suddenly, he threw in the towel and resigned from the company, sold some of his shares and bought a big rambling old house in Essex. Said he wanted to dedicate his life to art and love. That's when Grandfather officially disowned him. And that's where I was born.'

'Wow,' I said, 'what a romantic character.'

'You could call it that.' She sighed. 'He was certainly a charmer, very clever but totally feckless. When I was in my second year of textile design the stock market crashed and he lost all his — well, *our* — money. I had to leave art school and get a job as a waitress to support them. Over the next two or three years he

122

became more and more miserable and took to the bottle.' She paused again, distractedly twisting a curl in her finger, looking at something beyond me, beyond the walls of the attic room.

'Drink's a devil, Lily,' she said after a moment. I winced at the memory of what had happened in the punt, when I'd drunk too much.

'It gets people in its grip and sucks out their souls,' she said fiercely. 'In the end he was drunk most of the time and Mother threw him out of the house. We haven't heard from him since.' She glanced out of the window, as if he might just appear in view.

Best not to ask any more about him, I thought. 'You poor things. Where's your mother now?'

'She sold the house and rents a place near her sister in Dorset. I send cheques when I can. We were penniless, literally, but Grandfather took pity on us and offered to try to find me a job. He introduced me to Harold — they knew each other through the Weavers' Company. I went to see him at Cheapside and he offered me a job in the design room, here in Westbury.'

'A designer? So how come you ended up a weaver?'

'To be a designer, you need to know about weaving and the rest of the process, and I knew precious little. So Harold put me on a weaver's apprenticeship and I loved it. Loved the silk and the grease and the looms. Never looked back, thanks to him.'

'And look at you now, assistant factory manager.'

'I'm lucky. I still enjoy it, even after six years.'

'What happened to the art, though? Where are your masterpieces?' I gestured round the room.

'It's difficult to hang anything on these sloping walls,' she said in an offhand way.

The smell of baking wafted mouth-wateringly on the air. 'Hang on a tick, I think those scones are done.' She leapt to her feet and disappeared into the kitchen.

'Would you show them to me?' I shouted. She didn't reply, so when she came back I repeated the question. She put the plate of scones on the table, with butter and raspberry jam.

'Have one while they're still warm,' she said, pouring more tea.

'Thanks, they look delicious.' We helped ourselves and ate and talked about things at work for a while, and then I remembered. 'Really. I do want to see them, your paintings.'

'I don't show them to anyone, Lily.'

'We're friends, aren't we? That's what friends are for.' I mistook her reluctance for false modesty. 'I'm not just being polite.'

'I'm flattered,' she said, 'but they're life drawings, you know? Nudes. A bit personal, you might be shocked.'

'Try me,' I said, breezily, picturing the Rubens I'd seen in the Royal Academy. 'I'm unshockable.' How little I knew.

'You're very persistent,' she sighed, putting down her plate. She leaned behind the sofa to pull out a large cardboard portfolio and laid it on the hearthrug between us. Then she kneeled on the floor and I sat down beside her, now apprehensive about what she might be about to reveal. She untied the pink ribbons at either side of the portfolio. Then, as she turned the cardboard cover and the blank first page, it took all my self-control not to gasp with astonishment.

It was a drawing, in fluid and uncompromising charcoal lines, of a naked woman reclining sensuously on her back, with one knee bent and her arms relaxed above her head. The face was not fully drawn, but dark smudges around the eyes conveyed the same intensity I'd often seen in Gwen's. White chalk highlighted strong feminine curves, and dark bushes of underarm and pubic hair were fiercely scribbled in black.

I could feel myself blushing and Gwen's eyes on me, watching my face.

'She's very beautiful. Was she one of your models at art school?' I fumbled uncertainly.

'Not exactly.'

I hardly dared ask. 'Someone you knew?'

'Yes, she was a friend.'

'Why 'was'? Have you had a row?'

'Not really.' She paused again, and knelt back on her heels, brushing her fingers through her hair, still looking at the drawing. To ease the awkwardness I said, 'Would you rather not talk about her?'

'It feels like a long time ago now,' she said flatly. 'She was a fellow student in London. When I moved here it was impossible, just seeing her at weekends, all that pretence. It just fell apart.'

'Poor you. It's horrid when you argue with friends.'

She looked at me, oddly. 'We weren't just friends, Lily,' she said in a quiet voice, leaning

125

back against the sofa, uncrossing then recrossing her legs. 'Look, can I tell you something in confidence?'

'Of course,' I said, fearful of what she was going to say.

'There's something you need to know about me.' I felt like a leaf being reluctantly and inexorably drawn into a whirlpool. There was no going back.

'She was my lover.'

Her *lover?* I tried to take in what she'd said. 'You loved her?'

'We were lovers,' she said, to make sure I really understood.

Lovers. It meant they did 'it'. They were the real thing.

My face burned, my mind went blank. The air felt hot and heavy, compressed by the low ceilings. My brain skittered around the implication of the word and I had absolutely no idea how to respond.

'Oh my goodness. I knew you weren't married, but,' I pointed to her ringless finger, desperate not to sound shocked or blurt out something hurtful or stupid.

She turned back to the portfolio, pensively turning the loose leaves of heavy cartridge paper. Now there was nothing left to conceal. All the drawings were of the same woman; dressed and undressed, head and shoulder portraits, laughing, serious, coquettish. They felt so intimate, almost as if it were Gwen revealing herself.

There were loose charcoal sketches, tight pen and ink drawings and smaller studies of toes,

126

ears, hands — one showed fingers reaching into what looked like a tangle of wool. I was disturbed and fascinated, even a little excited, and way out of my depth.

She folded up the portfolio. 'So now you know. Have I shocked you?'

'Not at all,' I lied. 'I'm glad you trusted me enough to tell me.'

A taut smile. 'You will be discreet? Please? It's important in a small town like this. People don't understand.'

I nodded, my head in a spin. 'Of course. Does anyone else know? My father . . . ?'

'Good God, no,' Gwen interrupted emphatically, her eyes widening with alarm. 'Harold gave me a job because Grandfather once did him a favour over some silk supplies in the twenties, that's what I heard, and because he knew what dire straits we were in. He must never find out, Lily, promise me that.'

'My lips are sealed,' I said. 'I give you my word.'

She smiled wryly and we fell into an awkward silence. 'Another scone? I can make more tea.' I had no choice but to say yes. To leave now would be rude and far too pointed.

When she came back with the teapot Gwen said, 'Now it's your turn to tell me about you. I can't help but notice that you seem to be getting along rather well with Mr Cameron?'

'We've been on a few dates, nothing more,' I said, trying to sound casual. 'I don't think it's going any further.'

'Good,' she said. 'That's probably for the best.

He's a customer. And a tricky character to boot,' she said, buttering another scone.

'You hardly know him,' I said, feeling oddly defensive.

'I know the type,' she said. 'With his background and money, he'll think he owns the world,' she said, 'and girl-friends are just another possession.'

I said nothing, thinking that she had probably hit the nail on the head. But then she said, 'Besides, I suppose you know someone else is sweet on you?'

'What do you mean, 'sweet'? Who?'

'Young Herr Hoffmann.'

'Stefan?' My heart leapt. Stefan — sweet on me? The very thought made me suddenly giddy, a blast of heat flushed my cheeks and my stomach fizzled. I tried to sound dismissive. 'Don't be silly. He hasn't said anything to me.'

'It's so bloody obvious,' she shook her head. 'I can't believe you haven't noticed. You must be the only person in the mill who hasn't.' She put down her cup and looked directly into my face, her pale eyes piercing. 'Lily, please be careful.'

'Careful of what, for goodness sake?' I said. Why was she interfering like this?

'He's just a boy. Don't lead him on,' she said, more gently.

Now my stomach felt queasy, recalling what Robbie had said that day in the punt. 'I'm not doing anything of the sort. Anyway, if you don't mind my saying, it really is none of your business, Gwen,' I retorted, a little too sharply.

'Hear me out, Lily. Please. It's more

complicated than you think. He's German, and Jewish, there's a war in the offing. And you're the boss's daughter. Things get round. Just be careful,' she repeated.

'Is this why you invited me here? To warn me off Stefan?' I asked, rattled now.

'No . . . Well yes, a bit,' she admitted, with an apologetic smile. 'I thought, if the opportunity arose it might be best to tell you before Harold hears about it. But it wasn't just that, silly, I wanted to get to know you better. I thought we could be friends, now you're going to stick around for a while?'

Unsure how to respond, I nodded and said that yes, it would be good to be friends, but that it was probably time for me to head back.

★   ★   ★

I walked the long route home to try and clear the turmoil my head. Thinking about Stefan made me light-headed, I felt like skipping with joy. Gwen was probably right about being careful but, now that I knew, the idea of doing nothing seemed almost unbearable. She was right about Robbie as well. He was a selfish man, used to getting his own way. I needed to treat him with care, too. Why did life have to be so complicated?

And then there was Gwen's own revelation, which I barely dared to contemplate. I decided to put it to the back of my mind and pretend that she had never told me. That afternoon she had also shown me a side of herself that I liked very much: a warm, relaxed, funny Gwen. She seemed so normal, so clever, wise and honest. I really did want her as a friend.

When I got home, all these petty worries were instantly forgotten, paled into unimportance by the report on the six o-clock news.

Chamberlain had issued Hitler an ultimatum.

9

Silk has frequently featured in wars. The Silk Wars of 1514 resulted in a blockade of the East — West silk route from China to the Mediterranean by the Mongol King Selim 1 (1512–20). The Persians diverted their caravans via Aleppo, but Selim confiscated all Persian goods passing through the Ottoman Empire. The resultant shortages served to heighten the value of pure silk in the West.
From *The History of Silk,* **by Harold Verner**

'It is evil things that we shall be fighting against — brute force, bad faith, injustice, oppression and persecution — and against them I am certain that right will prevail.'

Towards the end of his speech Chamberlain's voice, coming through the mahogany fretwork of the wireless in our drawing room, sounded increasingly querulous, as though he were going to break down in tears. That's certainly how I felt. Father and John sat on the two easy chairs, with matching fixed expressions. Mother and I were on cushions at their feet and during the speech she had quietly taken my hand, making me feel even more wobbly.

The German boys, who had come early for the occasion, sat in a row on the sofa, their bodies held tight. Stefan leaned forward with his face in

131

his hands, next to him Kurt sat rigidly, his jaw working. As the final phrases crackled out, I could see Walter flushing with the effort of fighting back tears. The words hung in the room, like a cloud of poisonous gas. Father turned off the wireless and the green light behind the tuning dial faded slowly and disappeared.

Kurt broke the silence. 'So, our countries are now at war,' he said in a low voice.

'We mustn't have that kind of talk, Kurt,' Father said firmly.

''Brute force and bad faith'. That is what your prime minister says.' Kurt stood up and started to pace like a caged tiger.

'It is a fight for justice and human rights,' John said, quietly. 'Remember what Hitler is doing to your people, Kurt.'

'Anyone for sherry?' Father said. 'Or something stronger?'

'It is our only hope,' Stefan said quietly, his face even paler than usual. 'I will fight, if I am allowed.'

'Fight your own people?' Kurt said with a mirthless laugh. He pointed two fingers at his own temple. 'Shall I kill myself now, to save you the trouble?'

'Don't be a bloody idiot.' Stefan leapt to his feet and grabbed Kurt's arm. 'It's the Nazis we need to fight, not the people.'

'But people will get killed, our family and friends too,' Kurt shouted back.

'Why don't you stop, both of you!' Walter yelled, putting his hands over his ears.

'Calm down, boys,' Father said. 'Have a drink

132

and let us talk sensibly.'

Stefan took a glass and sat down again but Kurt refused, and remained standing. 'They won't let you join the army,' he said, bitterly. 'You're the enemy, remember?'

'No, it's not like that,' I started, shaken by Kurt's outburst.

'They'll probably send us home, anyway,' he went on. 'Or lock us up.'

'Kurt, please,' I said, feeling sick and slightly panicky at the thought. He might be right. I remembered hearing how Germans got rounded up during the last war. Enemy aliens, they called them.

Mother stood up. 'Oh, Kurt, my dear, I'm sure they wouldn't do that,' she said, as he wrenched the door open and slammed it behind him. Walter got up quietly and let himself out, and shortly afterwards we heard the front door close.

'Shall I go and get them back?' I asked.

'He'll cool down,' Stefan said calmly. 'They'll come back when they are ready.'

Father went round with the sherry bottle again. 'Let's drink to a speedy resolution,' he said and we all raised our glasses except for John, who was standing at the window apparently absorbed by the view. After a few moments, still with his back to us, he said quietly, 'If you'd like me to find out whether Germans can join up, Stefan, I'll ask at the recruiting office in Cambridge. I'm going there tomorrow.'

So Vera had failed to change his mind. Mother let out a whimper, like a wounded puppy. Father took a sharp intake of breath and held it for a moment, his hand clenched around the slender stem of his glass as if clutching onto his own emotions. When he finally spoke, his voice was tightly controlled, 'I hope you're not going to do anything rash, Son.'

John turned round, standing stiff and tall, as if he was already in uniform. 'It's not rash, Father. I've been considering it for months now. It's the only thing to do.'

The usually measured tock-tick, tock-tick of the grandfather clock in the hallway sounded hurried and uneven. Stefan was pale and still as a statue. Mother looked as though she'd been crumpled by a huge hand.

'My dearest boy,' she whispered, 'you must do what you believe is right.' She took out a lace-edged handkerchief and blew her nose.

'You and I need to have a talk about this.' Father took John by the arm and steered him towards the door. 'How long will lunch be, Grace?'

She didn't reply. As they left the room I caught John's eye. *How could you?* I mouthed at him.

★   ★   ★

It was just as well we'd planned a cold dish for luncheon, because it was more than an hour before Father and John emerged, their faces flushed. Stefan had gone to the cottage to find the others, and Mother and I got into the sherry bottle again. Judging by the raised voices it had clearly been what they used to call a 'robust debate'.

'So?' we said, simultaneously.

'I'm afraid his mind's made up,' Father said. 'I can't dissuade him, so I think we have to support his decision. In fact, it is very courageous and I am proud of him.'

John sat on the side of Mother's chair and put his arm round her shoulders.

'I know it's hard, but I have to go. I couldn't stay behind in Westbury watching my friends and the chaps from the mill going off to war without me.'

Her voice was wobbly. 'Of course you must do what feels right. But just promise me you won't go to the front line.'

'I'll have to do whatever I'm best suited to. I'm a pretty handy engineer now, and Robbie's given me a taste for flying, so I fancy the RAF. If they won't have me, the army. But I promise I won't take any silly risks.'

She nodded and got up unsteadily, clutching her handkerchief in a tight fist, and left the room muttering about making tea. John started towards the door but Father shook his head, 'Best to leave her now. When you've got children of your own you'll understand what she's going through.'

He turned to me. 'Lily, my darling, go and see if she's all right, would you?'

★   ★   ★

Much later, when Mother had sobbed herself into a fitful sleep and the sun was low in the sky, there was a knock at the front door. It was

135

Stefan, alone. This was unusual: the boys usually let themselves in through the back door. And they usually came together.

'Will you talk with me?' he said, almost under his breath, and as I looked back into his eyes I felt a tremor of anxiety. What was he going to say? Something about going to join up with John? Had something happened with Kurt? The evening light streamed through the hallway behind me and illuminated his pale, serious face. Long eyelashes cast shadows over his high cheekbones and gentle licks of hair framed his brow. How beautiful he is, I thought, my heart doing jazz steps in my chest. Why have I never properly noticed this before?

'Would you like to come in?'

'No, I would like to walk.' There was an unusual urgency in his voice.

'Wait a mo, I'll let them know I'm going out for some air,' I said shakily, trying to sound calm. 'We can go over to the meadow.'

We walked in silence along paths we'd both walked many times but never, until now, alone with each other. The evening was still and warm, with enough clouds in an otherwise clear sky to promise a fine sunset. After a hot summer the grass was unusually dry and the sun's horizontal beams shimmered through the seed heads like *moiré* silk.

When we got to the river we stopped, standing side by side and peering down into the water running sluggishly beneath steep banks overhung with skeleton stalks of cow parsley. Turquoise damselflies skimmed close over its glassy surface.

The leaves on the willow trees on the other bank were starting, even now, to turn yellow. Autumn was not far away.

I forced myself to wait for him to speak first. Finally he said, 'This is a big day.'

'It's frightening for us all,' I said, choosing my words carefully.

'I am worried to think of what is happening for my family.'

'Perhaps,' I struggled to find something consoling to say, when we knew there was little hope, 'perhaps they have managed to get over the border?'

He shook his head. 'It is not so easy.'

'But even if they haven't, war will sort things out and life will be better when it is over.'

We stood without speaking for a few moments.

'We cannot let that man do so many evils,' he said, suddenly angry, spitting out the words like gunfire. 'We must stop him.'

It was no time to correct his English. 'Would you really try to join up?'

'Yes, if it will get rid of Hitler.'

Something drove me to say it, to force out the truth. 'They won't let you sign up till you're eighteen, you know.'

He took a deep breath and looked away towards the hills on the other side of the meadows. Had I gone too far this time? Warblers chattered quietly in the reeds. After a long pause he said, quite calmly, 'I am not the age on my papers. This is what we had to write so I could come out of Germany. But I think you know this, don't you?'

I nodded.

He turned and looked me directly in the eyes. 'Can I trust you, Lily?'

I met his gaze. 'So how old are you, really?'

'I am twenty-one years. Today.'

'Today?' I gasped, slow to grasp this unexpected extra twist.

'It is my birthday,' he said simply.

'Oh, Stefan. What a day for a birthday,' I squeaked. And without a second thought, I stood on tiptoe and hugged him. In an instant his arms wrapped so tightly around me I could barely breathe. After a moment our faces turned, our cheeks touched and our lips met, lightly at first, then stronger and deeper. Every part of my consciousness became concentrated into that kiss, the meadows and the rest of the world around us receded and time was suspended.

We barely noticed when a large Golden Retriever bustled out of the long grass and pushed past, but as the dog's owner appeared we jumped apart.

'Pleasant evening for a terrible day.' The man walked briskly by us without waiting for a reply. Though I didn't see his face, the hunched back and baggy jacket were familiar.

'Bert?' I mouthed to Stefan, and we giggled like naughty children.

I grabbed Stefan's hand and pulled him, half running, along the riverbank towards the lock. It had once been used by barges bringing coal to power the mill but river traffic had long since ceased and their hulks had rotted in the mud. Vera and I used to dare each other to walk across

138

the narrow beam of the heavy gates. It was the only way to reach 'our' island, but the slightest slip could mean a sheer drop into the still depths of the basin or the turbulent water on the downstream side. The island was our secret playground, where we built camps, pretended to be pirates or Indians, used thorns to prick fingers, mixed our blood and swore lifetime allegiance.

The beams looked rotten and dangerous now, but I felt daring and fearless and Stefan followed me across without a second's hesitation, agile as a cat. Pushing aside brambles and climbing over fallen willows, I led him through the shrubby undergrowth to the other side of the island, where Vera and I had made our main camp. There was still a clearing here, under elder bushes weighed with heavy clusters of purple berries.

We kissed again now, more boldly, all doubts gone. I held my breath till I felt faint as his fingers moved slowly over my breasts and down to my waist. He pressed his hips against me and as I felt his hardness my body seemed to melt like butter in the sun, all on its own, without having to think about it. So different from how it had been with Robbie.

He cradled my face between his hands, breathing hard. 'I've wanted this for so long.'

'Me too,' I murmured, swallowed up in his gaze.

His eyes glittered with pleasure. 'You wanted this too?'

I nodded, wordless and lightheaded with happiness.

'Then what have we been waiting for?' We

laughed and kissed again, longer and deeper this time. I didn't care what was happening in the world — my entire being focused on the joy of his lips, his tongue, the heat of his body against mine.

After a long time we stopped, exhausted by the intensity of our discovery. He took my hand and led me over to a log where we sat and lit up cigarettes. As we watched the sun starting to set across the water I stole a glance at him, saw a frown fleeting across his brow.

'You've gone quiet. What is it, Stefan?'

'It is nothing,' he shook his head. Then a longer pause, and he started, 'But . . . '

'What is it?' I said again.

'You say you want me, but . . . '

'But what? Tell me, please.'

He whispered, 'People say Mr Cameron is your boyfriend.'

'No, he's not,' I almost shouted with relief. 'Robbie *wanted* me to be his girlfriend. We had a few dates. But there's nothing — really nothing — between us. Please believe me.'

'I saw you together. He is so confident, like you belong to him.'

I stopped his words with a kiss.

'But there is another thing . . . ' he started, afterward. My heart plummeted again as he searched for the words.

'Mr Harold? What will he think?'

'Shhh,' I put a finger to his lips. 'Let's not worry about that now.'

'But his daughter? He might not be pleased . . . '

'It would be best to keep it quiet, for a while,' I said.

'They think I am only seventeen. They must not know my real age.'

'It's our secret. Just between the two of us. Please don't worry,' I said, hugging him again. 'We have found each other now, that's the most important thing. We will find a way.'

I was worried too, of course. Gwen's words echoed round my head. But, as the rays of evening sun illuminated our little grove with a rosy tint, it all seemed a long way away. I was determined not to ruin this precious moment. I wanted nothing else but to hold Stefan's hand and watch the pinks and purples in the sky reflected in the wide, still water above the weir.

But then a horrible wail started up, a rising and falling across the water meadow: an air raid siren. Stefan's eyes were wide, full of panic. 'What is it, Lily? Is it an attack?'

I grabbed his hand and started running towards the copse. 'It's probably just a test, but we'd better take cover, just in case.'

We pushed our way through the undergrowth and into the shelter of the trees, holding each other, hearts thumping, till the siren stopped. Time passed and nothing happened, but the spell was broken. War had arrived, whether we liked it or not.

10

The invention of the Jacquard machine at the end of the eighteenth century, and its introduction to Great Britain early in the nineteenth, had the effect of vastly increasing the demand for textile designs for both women's and men's wear as well as for furnishing fabrics, and led to rising prosperity for those manufacturers who embraced the new technology.
From *The History of Silk*, **by Harold Verner**

Despite the newspapers' gloomy predictions, the war made hardly made any difference at first. John went off to the recruiting office and we held our breath. They told him he would hear from them soon, but the weeks went by and no letter arrived. He said nothing more, and I began to harbour absurd hopes that they had lost his address, or just forgotten him.

At work we were busier than ever. We took on extra weavers and set up extra shifts to meet ever increasing demands for parachute silk from Camerons and the other customers. In our 'spare' time we had to keep up with the instructions and precautions that the War Office issued on an almost daily basis; gas masks, blackouts, taping windows, filling fire buckets, reporting for local defence volunteers and fire watch duties. It seemed never ending.

We had some leftover rolls of the thick black

double-satin facing usually used for dinner jacket lapels that we'd never be able to sell in wartime, so this made excellent blackout blinds. We used all the packing room's supplies of parcel tape to criss-cross three hundred and twenty individual panes of glass in the mill, and more in the house. The tacklers put up long rows of hooks in each area of the mill, to hang up the fearsome-looking gas masks everyone had been issued with.

Yet tucked away in East Anglia those weeks truly did feel like a phoney war. Air raid sirens wailed mournfully from time to time but each time it turned out to be a practice drill or a false alarm — very jumpy fingers in the control rooms, we assumed. Other than that, life went on as normal.

Except that nothing was normal for me any more.

Stefan had become the axis of my world. No need to consult Vera; I was in no doubt this time, and I knew with absolute certainty that he felt the same. All those *True Romance* clichés I'd scoffed at were actually happening to me. I thought about him constantly, and found myself saying his name under my breath for the sheer pleasure of it. I started taking more care of my appearance, being careful, of course, not to make this too obvious.

When I saw him for the first time each morning, my heart really did beat faster. Embarrassing places in my body would experience sudden hotnesses at inappropriate moments. I lost my appetite, prompting Mother to speculate out loud that I might be mooning over Robbie. I didn't correct

her — it was convenient to let them misunder-
stand.

Every day was delicious agony, working so
close together yet unable to show any sign of
affection towards each other. It was so difficult
to be circumspect when even whispers could be
understood by our lip-reading fellow weavers. We
were especially careful when Gwen was around
— which was most of the time.

But we found other ways. When he walked
past me, in the gaps between our looms, he
would pause, oh so briefly, so that we could feel
the heat of each other's bodies, drink in the
smell of each other's skin. When we thought no
one else was watching we mouthed sweet
nothings over the rage of the looms. Rather, in
our case, sweet everythings.

He left little messages tucked under my shuttle
or hidden in other places that only I would
discover when I checked my looms at the start of
each morning. He was a deft cartoonist and
could portray with a few simple strokes a manic
Hitler growing several heads, or Kurt and Walter
having a pillow fight. Sometimes they were
soppy, stick figures of couples kissing or holding
hands that melted my heart.

Work filled most of our days, and finding a
time or place to meet without being discovered
was almost impossible. I never asked what stories
Stefan told to Kurt and Walter, but at home I
became a master of what I hoped were plausible
excuses. Before the nights started to draw in I
took to taking walks after supper to 'clear my
head'. On Saturday mornings, a breezy 'Just

popping out to the chemist' worked well for a while. No one would dare to pry into personal matters.

Whenever the weather promised to be dry we met on the island, arriving separately so that we were less likely to be rumbled. We rebuilt the den from fallen branches and evergreen fronds to keep off the worst of the weather. He found an old tarpaulin and laid it over the peaty, sweet-smelling earth, and his long camel coat served as a blanket.

We laughed and learned about each other, unpeeling layers of understanding about our languages, our cultures and how we saw the world; finding out how alike we were, and how different. One evening we dallied so long we didn't notice how dark it had become. Feeling our way across the damp slippery wooden beam of the lock gates, with the water roaring beneath us, was terrifying.

We had to find another place, a dry, warm, undisturbed place, not too far from home, that we could both reach without being observed. But where?

The idea came to me one cold morning when I was rummaging in the hall cupboard for my scarf and gloves. I dislodged a net of tennis balls which fell open and rolled everywhere. As I collected them up, fretting because I was already late for work, I remembered the tennis hut. It was just at the end of the court, beyond the orchard. I could be there in minutes and in winter it was locked up. No one went there. I knew where the key was hidden. I scribbled a

145

hasty note for Stefan, with a map, and slipped it to him at tea break.

That first evening I remembered too late that I should have brought a torch. I fumbled for the key in its usual hiding place under the eave of the shed, and knocked it to the ground. By the time I'd scrabbled around to find it my knees were muddy and hands covered in leaf mould, but I was triumphant. The lock was rusty and the key difficult to turn but it finally gave, and I opened the door.

Inside it was pitch black, dry and dusty, with a strong disinfectant smell from the tarry twine of the tennis netting. There was no electricity, of course, and any light would be too risky until we'd had a chance to black out the small window in the door. I stumbled over the rolled up bundle of netting and then cracked my elbow on something tall and wooden blocking the centre of the room. The umpire's chair.

I was cursing under my breath when Stefan arrived and I felt instantly better. He laughed at my misadventures, and we kissed hungrily; it had been a week since we had last met.

After a while we started to explore the darkness together, pushing aside sticky filaments of spiders' webs and feeling our way towards the back of the shed where we discovered, against the back wall, a small garden table, a broken-down bench and some lumpy cushions.

'It's like our own little house,' he said, cupping the flame with his hand as he lit cigarettes for us both.

It was perfect.

The next time, he brought blackout fabric and thumb tacks so that we could close the door and light a candle. With his coat laid over the prickly sisal matting we held each other and kissed and tasted and smelled, discovering each other more daringly. Each time we met, our desire grew stronger, our exploration bolder. I loved the way his long, slim limbs wrapped themselves around me, and counted five newly-sprouted black hairs on his otherwise smooth chest. He marvelled at the softness of my skin — silken Lily, he called me — and discovered the birthmark on the back of my thigh I'd almost forgotten. 'The shape of a mouse,' he said, kissing it, '*meine Lilymaus*.'

'I've brought something to show you,' he said one evening, pulling a small buff envelope from his pocket. Inside were three small, dog-eared black and white photographs of his family and, handling them like precious objects, he passed them to me, one by one. There was his father Isaak, tall and serious looking, with a full head of dark hair, so like Stefan. His mother Hannah, much shorter, had curly lighter-coloured hair, with her arms protectively round two identical little girls, Anna and Else, like blonde angels.

As we looked at the photographs he started to talk more freely than ever before about his family and his childhood. It sounded idyllic; lots of friends, visits to the theatre, opera, swimming in the lakes in summer. But when I asked about the music, his mood seemed to chill. He reflected ruefully on the trouble he'd caused when he turned seventeen and started refusing to play his mother's beloved classical composers, learning

147

jazz instead, hanging out with what he called a wild crowd, and wearing bohemian clothes.

As life became more difficult Stefan started to reject his Jewishness. He had no strong belief in God and, to his mother's great distress, announced that he wasn't going to synagogue any more. He declared himself to be an atheist.

Then he met the *Swingjugend*. Atheist or not, he realised that he would always be a Jew in the eyes of the government. As he was forced to change schools, endured the daily fear of walking the streets, of insults shouted and stones thrown, playing jazz became an act of defiance. Just as his parents were fearfully attempting to play down their heritage he rediscovered it, openly defended it, and was arrested and beaten by the secret police for it.

As we met in the tennis hut over several weeks, the memories emerged slowly and painfully. At times he would be racked with anxiety about what had happened to his family, now that their letters had stopped. And he was terrified that his false papers might be discovered, of being deported. There was little I could say to comfort him. All I could offer was the present moment, and us.

'If none of this had happened, we would not have met,' I said. 'I planned to travel and meet a dark, handsome stranger. But the war has brought him to me instead.' To distract ourselves we made plans for the future. We would go to Geneva and then on to Hamburg. He would take me to meet his family and show me his country, the foods he liked to eat, the music we would

148

dance to. He would teach me how to play the piano.

That hut was our little heaven, an oasis of happiness in a bleak time. But it couldn't last.

★   ★   ★

Father pulled down the blinds over the glazed partition that separated his office from the secretaries' area. From his grave expression I knew it must be bad news — had we lost a contract? Or perhaps John had heard from the RAF?

'Take a seat,' he said. I waited anxiously as he filled and lit his pipe. 'How are you getting on?' he said eventually.

'Fine. Working hard. We all are,' I said, wondering what he was coming to.

'You look weary, my darling. Time for a bit of R&R don't you think? Seen much of Robbie Cameron lately?' he asked, puzzlingly. Why was he making small talk about my love life? Here at the mill?

'Not much,' I muttered, 'what with one thing and another.'

'Pity,' he murmured through his teeth, clamped on the stem of his pipe. 'Your mother and I think he's a topping chap. Lovely manners.'

If only you knew, I thought, still puzzled. And what he said next caught me completely off guard. 'Now the thing is, Lily. This is a bit tricky old girl,' he stumbled, frowning. 'You see, Bert came to see me this morning.'

'Go on,' I said, more bravely than I felt, as the hairs on my neck started to bristle.

'He's seen you and young Stefan Hoffmann together. Several times. He didn't say exactly what he'd seen, but he suggested there's something between you. More than just friendship. Is he right?'

Bloody Bert, I thought. A nosy parker and a sneak. 'What business is it of his?' I nearly shouted.

'Before you go off the deep end, just consider for a moment, would you?' Father said, calmly.

'How dare he? I don't go round telling people what he's up to,' I muttered, furious now.

'In case you hadn't noticed, we are at war with Germany. Do you think it is very sensible, being seen out after dark, alone with a German boy?' Father said, more firmly now, 'What do you expect people to think?'

I snapped. 'That's ridiculous. Stefan might be German, but he is no threat. You know that. I know that. Why's everyone getting so aerated?'

He interrupted sharply. 'Watch your tone, Lily.'

'Or is it his Jewishness you object to?' I persisted. The implication would infuriate him, but I didn't care.

'Of course not,' he said, getting riled now. 'In normal times . . . '

I interrupted him, 'So what's the problem?'

Father stood up and turned to look out of the window behind the desk. I watched his shoulders slump as he took a deep, silent sigh.

'Listen to me, my darling. You have to

understand. Stefan is a nice lad. But he's younger than you,' he said in a low tone. 'Even in peacetime it might be considered unusual.'

'What do a couple of years matter?' I said, tempted to tell him the truth. 'Anyway I love him. Don't you remember what that feels like?'

'He's handsome, I grant you, different from the local boys,' he said. 'Right now you may think you are in love but in the longer term you'll choose someone more suitable.'

'Someone like Robbie, I suppose? Well, I'm sorry to disappoint you. I hate that man, and nothing you say will ever change my mind.'

Father raised his eyebrows, but he didn't pursue it.

'It's not just that,' he said calmly, sitting down again and fiddling with the pens in the mahogany rack beside the blotter on his desk. 'It's what people *think*. We cannot afford to have suspicions and rumours flying around the mill.'

' 'Suspicions'? Whatever are we supposed to be doing?'

His face was severe. 'Do I really have to spell it out?'

I nodded, my mouth dry, half knowing what he was going to say.

'People think you are collaborating with the enemy.'

The bluntness of his words shocked me and I nearly laughed at the absurdity. Stefan, the enemy? The Jewish boy who wants to be a perfect English gentleman? And me, collaborating?

'The two of us acting as agents for the Hun?

That's ridiculous, you know it is,' I burst out, more bravely than I felt. 'You should just tell Bert and the rest — whoever they are — that they've got totally the wrong end of the stick.'

He put his finger to his lips. 'Shhh. Do you want everyone in the office to hear?'

'I don't care if the whole bloody world knows. We're doing nothing wrong. This is not puppy love, Father. And it won't go away just because of some stupid spy theory.'

'Now, listen to me, please, Lily.' He walked around his desk and stood close, his voice low and dangerous. 'This is not a silly game, it is real life in a country at war. I won't accept any further argument. You are in a position of responsibility and, whether you like it or not, this relationship must end. Otherwise I will be forced to tell Stefan that he must find another sponsor.'

I gasped, winded by the finality of his words. 'That's not fair.'

He walked past me and opened the door. 'War's not fair,' he said, firmly. 'If you haven't discovered that yet, you soon will.'

I ran out of the office and lurched down the long stairs two at a time, blinded by tears. I swung round the banister at the bottom and crashed into Gwen. We both fell over and the box she was carrying broke open as it tumbled onto the floor. Dozens of wooden pirns clattered out, rolling in all directions across the hallway.

'Woah,' she said, trying to grab the box. 'Look where you're going.'

It was all too much. I started to sob.

'Oh, Lily, have you hurt yourself?' she said,

tenderly, pulling out a handkerchief. I shook my head. 'Then what's wrong?' She moved closer, trying to put her arm round my shoulder.

'Don't ask,' I said, refusing the hanky and getting up shakily.

'Do you want to talk?' she said as we collected the wooden reels, putting them back in the box.

'Nothing to talk about,' I sniffed, wiping my nose on my sleeve. 'Something I need to sort out for myself.'

She stopped and straightened up, looking me in the eye with that intense gaze. 'Look, I won't interfere if you don't want me to,' she said. 'But I'm always here if you need me.' How could someone like her ever understand, I thought, as I started back to the weaving floor.

Stefan knew something was wrong, as soon as he caught sight of me.

'Are you all right?' he mouthed. I shook my head as the tears started again.

He glanced at the factory clock hanging on the wall above the looms, visible from every corner of the weaving shed. Its foot-long hands were often our enemy, as they crept around the hours, but this time they were generous, it was nearly tea break.

'Bench?' he mouthed.

I nodded. It was chilly outside, we could probably be alone.

'Father knows,' I blurted as soon as we were sitting down. 'Bert sneaked on us.'

''Sneaked'?' he said, puzzled.

'He's seen us together. Told Father.'

The colour drained from Stefan's face. 'What

153

did Mr Harold say?'

I shook my head, unwilling to tell him about Father's ultimatum.

'*Scheisse*,' he swore, under his breath. Then he lit cigarettes for both of us and took a long drag.

'Does he say we must not see each other, Lily?'

I felt sick and panicky at the thought. 'I won't give you up. I love you.'

He looked up at the sky in the way boys do when they want their eyes to swallow back tears. 'But Mr Harold is my sponsor,' he said, his voice cracking, 'I cannot disobey him.'

I put my hand on his. 'Let me work on him.'

'He might send me away.'

'I won't let that happen. I promise.'

'How can you stop it?'

'We have to be even more careful.'

'Here? At the mill? In Westbury?' He stubbed out his cigarette furiously into the gravel. 'It is impossible. Someone will always see us.' I knew in my heart that he was right, but I wasn't ready to admit defeat.

'Let's talk? I'll come to the cottage after work.'

'No Lily,' his voice was tight and fearful now. 'It is too much to risk. You must not come. We have to wait.'

'Wait? Till when?' I felt like crying again.

'Until it's all over.'

'That might be months — years even.'

He nodded. The tears overflowed down my cheeks and I couldn't think of anything to say. We sat in silence, feeling powerless and desperate.

'I must go now,' he said suddenly, standing up. I tried to grab his hand but he pulled away and strode off up the yard, stiff-backed and resolute. I sat on the bench and hid my face in my hands, surrendering to the sobs that rasped my chest.

★　★　★

When the klaxon sounded at the end of tea break I went to the cloakroom to splash my face with cold water and make myself look more respectable before heading back to the weaving shed. Stefan was nowhere to be seen and another weaver was working at his looms. Gwen intercepted me and led me to the side door, her face tense and pale.

'What the hell's going on?' I spluttered.

'I've sent Stefan home for the rest of the shift,' she said. 'And you're to go home too. Harold's orders.'

'No,' I shouted, disbelieving. This was all happening too fast.

'Tomorrow you'll be on the Jacquards,' she went on. 'Helen's going to take over your work. I'm so sorry, Lily. Nothing I could do.'

The Jacquard looms — weaving motifs for military ties — were on the far side of the weaving shed. It was obvious what Father intended, and Gwen was acting as his henchman. My carefully gathered composure crumbled.

'You're not sorry,' I yelled into her shocked face. 'You could have persuaded him. We are adults, you know. You don't have to separate us like naughty children.'

She started to say something but my anger boiled up again.

'Don't deny it. You've got what you wanted all along, haven't you? You don't want anyone else to be happy, to be in love like normal people.'

Her eyes widened with shock, her face went ashen. I'd crossed the line, but I didn't care.

'For goodness sake, Lily, it's not like that,' she began, but I didn't want to listen.

'Oh, never bloody mind,' I started to walk away, then run, along the side path.

'Don't forget your gas mask,' she called behind me.

'To hell with the bloody gas mask!' I shouted back, almost hysterical now. 'I don't care if I die!'

I didn't stop running till I'd crossed the railway line onto the water meadows. The grey drizzle quickly soaked through my overalls and mingled with the tears still running unchecked down my face. Mud squelched into my lightweight shoes, but I barely noticed. Furious, bitter thoughts raged around my head. She pretends to be my friend, takes me into her confidence and then sides with the enemy. Why does everyone treat us like children? Can't they see Stefan is just an ordinary boy — how could we possibly be doing any harm? And anyway, what right have they to dictate what we should do — it's up to me and Stefan. It's our lives.

As I trudged the muddy paths, I started to calm down and think more rationally. To be together, we had to get away from Westbury. But how, and where? We could run away to Scotland perhaps, or America, until the war was over. Get odd jobs to pay for our living costs. Or perhaps we could both volunteer for the ambulance corps and go to the front line together? I imagined the glow of selfless courage: helping our brave boys, careless of our own safety.

It felt better to have plans, even wild ones that would be difficult, if not impossible, to achieve. With each step my optimism grew, and after a while the grey drizzle seemed to lift and a glimmer of late afternoon sun lit the low hills beyond the meadows. I started back with new resolve. I would find a way of seeing him, tell him what I had been thinking. We would plan our escape together. They'd regret it when we were gone.

When I got back to the house I found Mother at the kitchen table with an unopened letter addressed to John in one hand. In the other was a crumpled handkerchief.

She looked at me, red-eyed. 'This is it, Lily. His call-up papers.'

I pulled up a chair and put my arms around her.

'Whatever are we going to do without him?' she croaked.

'We'll cope, Mother. People do, you know.' I said quietly, trying to convince myself.

'But what if he's killed? It was terrible, last time,' she said. 'Thousands died.'

Not thousands, millions, I thought. There were no words of consolation. We held each other and sobbed. Finally she sat up, wiped her eyes and took a deep breath.

'Sorry, Lily, I must get a grip,' she sniffed. 'It's

no good falling apart, worrying about what might happen. Got to just get on with it, haven't we? Keep ourselves busy. Keep the home fires burning, and all that.'

She stood up unsteadily, starting to lay the table for supper. I dried my eyes and put the unopened envelope back on the hall table. A few moments later John arrived home and came into the kitchen with the envelope, now opened. He was smiling.

'It's good news, Mother,' he said. 'I'll be in training for a few months in Canada. So you mustn't worry.'

She looked unconvinced.

'I'll be safe as houses,' he said, 'but we're off next Monday. I'd better telephone Vera.'

After several minutes of hushed conversation he came back into the kitchen.

'She wants to talk to you, Lily,' he said. 'Tell her it'll be okay, there's a love.'

'I'm so terrified that he'll never come back,' Vera sobbed down the crackly line, her voice echoing in the hospital hallways.

'Don't be silly, he's only on training. I know he won't be with us for Christmas, but he'll be back in March.'

'But after that? He'll be on bombing raids. It's so dangerous, Lily.'

As I tried to comfort her, my own miseries slipped into perspective. What had I been thinking? Even if we couldn't be together, at least Stefan was safe here in Westbury. At the right moment, I would talk to Father — or perhaps Mother first, she might be more sympathetic — and make them understand how much he

158

meant to me. How much we loved each other. If our relationship could be out in the open with my parents' approval, any stupid suspicions would be scotched. There was still the small matter of his official age — but we both knew the truth and anyway, in the eyes of the world, what did a couple of years matter?

I started to think more rationally. For the moment I would put on a brave front, endure our enforced separation with dignity. When everything had calmed down we would talk, and work out what to do.

11

In 1773 Spitalfields weavers petitioned for better labour rates, resulting in the Spitalfields Act setting payment terms for the surrounding three miles. Merchants soon discovered an alternative source of labour in the skilled and willing hands of East Anglian wool weavers, whose trade was at that time in decline. Verners was one of those firms who settled there, and prospered as a result.
From *The History of Silk,* **by Harold Verner**

John was not the only one joining up. Twenty other men — some of our very best tacklers and weavers — had been called up at the same time and it was Father's idea to have a leaving party at the mill.

'Demonstrate support for our brave boys,' he said, and no one disagreed. We needed to put aside our own fears and celebrate their courage. The canteen was strung with bunting and union flags painstakingly sewn from strips of scrap silk. Kathleen and her staff baked sausage rolls and gaudily-iced cupcakes, Father had ordered a barrel of beer and Mother brought a demijohn of home-made lemonade. Families were invited too, and everyone had put on their Sunday best.

I looked around for Stefan and the boys but couldn't see them in the crowd. Had Father told them not to come, I wondered? It was probably good advice. Anti-German feelings might be running high.

It was a muted affair at first. Everyone was sombre, speaking in hushed voices, queuing quietly for food and drink, politely muttering, 'After you. No, after you.' But the beer did its magic, conversation started to flow and the noise levels rose. After a while Father asked John to bring the others to the front of the room. As I helped Father onto a chair beside them, everyone fell silent.

'I'm not going to make a long speech,' he started, ignoring the cheers, 'but I'd like to say a few words to thank our boys, and their families of course, for so bravely . . . '

I watched John and the others, all of them under twenty-five years old, standing awkwardly, with painfully fixed smiles, embarrassed by the attention. A handsome bunch, I thought, they should be spending their energies in loving and working, and playing football, not going off to fight and kill. I shivered at the thought that all over Britain similar speeches were being made. How many of them would return?

My eyes wandered to the hatch where Mother stood, lemonade jug still in hand, struggling to maintain her composure. I watched a tear escape and slip down her face, followed by several more. Kathleen moved over and put a hand on her shoulder, gently taking the jug from her hand. Around the room other mothers, sisters and girlfriends discreetly dabbed eyes with handkerchiefs that had been carefully concealed in cuffs, while the men stood expressionless, their jaws tight.

But I didn't feel like crying. I was angry. With the men responsible for this war. With the madman Hitler and the other politicians, and the Germans who seemed to follow him without question. For the way they persecuted Jews and invaded countries. For giving even the gentlest of our young men, however ill-suited for combat, no choice but to fight. My jaw was clenched and my whole body tense with the effort of containing my fury. I felt helpless. At least John and the others were able to take action, but what could I do?

Then I realised. The idea energised me like a lungful of oxygen. I took a deep breath and made a silent promise; I would dedicate myself to helping Father make the mill work more efficiently, produce everything the War Ministry required of us on time and to the best possible quality. I owed this to John and the rest, as well as to the German boys and their Jewish families, to help win this horrible war. I would prove to him that I was worthy of being trusted and then perhaps he would realise that my love for Stefan was real and important. He and Mother would welcome Stefan into their family.

Loud hurrahs jolted me from my reverie. 'Three cheers for our brave boys!'

I went over to John and whispered in his ear, 'Just make sure you come back in one piece. I'll do everything I can to help Father while you're away.'

'I will, Sis, I will,' he whispered back. 'You're a good kid. Look after the folks for me.'

He left the following day, first to see Vera in

London, and then on to Canada. Father had managed to remain steadfastly cheerful but now, two days later, the strain was starting to show and there were dark shadows round his eyes. Already we felt John's absence like an empty space, at home and at the mill.

'These are tough times, Lily,' he said, and then stalled, studying the ink patterns on his office blotter. I could see he needed time to compose himself. As I waited, I looked up at the portrait of my ancestor hanging beside the desk.

Joseph, the company's founder, had been sufficiently prosperous to commission the local artist Thomas Gainsborough to paint his portrait, but had been too mean — or just not wealthy enough — to pay for a full-length composition, or even to include the hands, for which he would have had to pay extra. An expert had described it as 'a minor example likely to have been commissioned from the lower end of the master's price range.' But it was — and still is — nonetheless prized by the family, fittingly framed in ornate gilt.

Father followed my gaze. 'It's a heavy responsibility, keeping this place going, carrying on the work he started, and all those generations of Verners. But it's a duty we have, war or no war.'

'I know I'm no replacement for John, but I'll do all I can to help.'

'Good, good.' He opened a brown foolscap folder on his desk and distractedly shuffled the papers inside. 'I've been thinking we need to sort out our systems here in the office. We also need to look at our staffing now that all those chaps are going off to war. So,' he looked up as if seeing me for the first time, 'how would you like to come and work in the office after Christmas? Help me sort it out?'

'Of course, just tell me, whatever you want me to do,' I said, my excitement rising. This wasn't what I'd expected when he'd called me into the office this morning.

'How about becoming 'Assistant to the Managing Director'?'

My first instinct was to lean over the desk and kiss him, but I restrained myself and tried hard not to giggle as he stood up and shook my hand, firmly and formally.

'Welcome on board,' he said, as if I'd joined the crew of a ship. 'I don't think I've said this before, but I am very proud of you, Lily. You've applied yourself to this business in a way I never expected, and you've shown great maturity over that business with Stefan. I'm sorry it has to be this way, but you clearly understand why.'

He clapped me on the shoulder, man-to-man. 'I'm pleased to have you with us.'

'I'll do my best,' I said. 'I owe it to John and the boys.'

'The first job is to recruit and train more weavers, probably women. Can I put you and Gwen in charge of that?'

'Aye, aye Captain,' I said, with a clip of the heels and a mock salute that made him smile for the first time.

As I turned to leave there was a knock on the door. It was Jim Williams, our factory manager, in his shirt sleeves and waistcoat, cap in hand. 'May I have a word, Mr Harold?'

'Of course, come in. Let me introduce my new assistant.'

'Congratulations Miss Lily,' he said with a smile, shaking my hand. 'I'm sure you will do very well.'

'Shall I go now?' I asked.

'Not unless Jim wants you to?'

He shook his head. 'Miss Lily may want to hear this too.'

'Then sit down, both of you please. Now, Jim?'

'It's like this, Mr Harold,' he started, 'I've been wrestling with me conscience since the do at the weekend. Seeing the boys so brave. And even though the wife's set against it I've decided to sign up too. My old man died at Ypres, and I can hear his voice telling me we mustn't let the Hun get away with it. Not after so many lives were lost stopping them last time.'

Father sighed and shook his head sadly. 'I understand. Of course you must do what your conscience tells you. I can only wish you good luck and a safe return.'

Jim knew all the workers by name, could fix any piece of machinery, and recite the denier, twist, warp and weave specifications for every type of cloth we wove. I knew how hard it would be to replace him. He'd also taken charge of all our war arrangements: blackout blinds, storage for gas masks, extra fire precautions, and an evening shift to fulfil the increasing demand for parachute silk.

After he'd gone Father said, 'He'll be a great

loss, you know. But thankfully we have someone else who is very well equipped to step into his shoes,' he smiled up at me. 'Verners is going to have a female factory manager for the first time in its history. Can you ask Gwen to come up?'

★ ★ ★

It was probably the quietest and most solemn Christmas we had ever had, just like a normal Sunday really, with a few presents to share with the boys around the tree afterwards. It was agonising being in the same room as Stefan yet unable to touch him, or even talk to him privately. The homesickness in the boys' eyes was heart breaking, and no one felt like celebrating.

In January I went to work proudly wearing a new blue serge office suit, rustled up on the sewing machine by Mother. I took some small consolation in the fact that my working career was moving forward, at last.

I was still learning how to use the office switchboard when his call came in. 'Hello, er . . . Verners and Sons, umm, good morning,' I stuttered.

'Lily, is that you?'

The cultured vowels were horribly familiar, but I quickly recovered myself. 'Indeed it is Miss Verner, Assistant to the Director. How can I help you, Mr Cameron?' I should have known better than to be clever with Robbie.

'A promotion? Congratulations, Miss Verner. It never suited you, you know, working on the shop floor — you're too classy. At least you won't have to wear that gruesome turban affair any more.' His gall was breathtaking. I nearly threw down the receiver in disgust. 'Would the Assistant to the Director be able to consider a request?'

'Only if you ask very politely,' I managed.

'I'm passing your way next week. Thought you might like to jolly along your troops with a gander at what they're producing. Only take half an hour or so. What do you say?'

★ ★ ★

I tried to melt into the background as Father welcomed Robbie with a vigorous handshake. 'Jolly good show old man. Good to see you again.'

Robbie was ebullient as usual. 'Mr Verner, Miss Verner,' he smirked, 'the pleasure is entirely mine. I am most grateful for the opportunity. Show the chaps our appreciation for the terrific work they've been doing here, eh?'

'There'll be plenty of women soon, and not so many chaps,' I said quietly, but he ignored me.

'Where would you like to do your demonstration?' Father said. 'Canteen?'

Robbie glanced out of the office window. 'How's about outside, in the yard? It's not too windy, and I'd like room to pull this thing out of its pack.' He held up a small khaki canvas bag, and I realised that it held a parachute. I'd no idea that amount of silk could be folded into something so compact.

Gwen and Robbie organised 'the troops'. He

stood at the mill door holding open the bag. As each person came out he handed them a piece of canopy, instructing them to hold it tight as they walked away slowly, keeping the roped edge as taut as possible. A great expanse of silk began to emerge from the bag, rippling like white horses on a blustery sea, so that the people holding it had to lean outwards and grip with both hands to prevent themselves being lifted off the ground. By the time the canopy was completely freed, nearly forty people were holding it and standing around its perimeter.

Stefan was among the last to emerge, purposely avoiding my eyes. I watched his expression lift as he saw the dazzling white dome that almost filled the yard. It was certainly an impressive sight.

When everyone else had gathered round, Robbie started. 'Thought you'd like to see what your hard work is for,' he shouted against the snapping of the silk in the breeze. 'We'll need many thousands more like this in the months to come. And I don't need to tell you,' he went on, his parade-ground voice ringing off the brick walls of the mill, 'how important this work is — every bit as vital as producing guns, ammunition or warships. The difference is that these beautiful bits of kit,' he gestured to the parachute, rippling more gently now in a brief glint of wintry sun, 'are designed to *save* lives.'

The parachute was indeed beautiful. People gazed at it silently, absorbed and intrigued, even a little in awe. They leaned across, looked underneath, felt the fine weave of the silk and gestured to each other, pointing out the elegant complexity of the canopy's construction, the angled sections sewn with treble-turned seams, hems at its edges and the hole in the centre neatly rolled around tough rope reinforcements. And the fabric had probably been woven by me or Stefan, I thought, understanding for the first time the reality of our work, how important it was, and feeling suddenly proud.

'So my final message is,' Robbie's voice took on a Churchillian resonance, 'keep up the good work. Never forget how vital it is, and how important to get it right. Together we can help win this wretched war.' As he finished, everyone cheered 'hear, hear' or clapped, and Father shook Robbie's hand.

I was helping to stuff the parachute back into its bag, surrounded by a crowd of people queuing to get back into the mill, when I felt something being slipped into the pocket of my overalls. I couldn't let go of the ends I was holding but caught a view of Stefan's head disappearing into the doorway. My heart danced — it was a note, surely? I couldn't wait to read it. But before I could slip away, I heard Father approaching with Robbie.

'Great stuff old chap,' he said. 'Terrific boost for morale. How's about a quick snifter at the house before you go? Sun will soon be below the yard arm. Grace would love to see you.'

Robbie looked up at the sky, then at his watch. I was sure he would say he needed to get home before dark because of the blackout, but he smiled at me smugly and said, 'It would be an absolute pleasure to meet the charming Mrs Verner again and spend a little more time with your lovely daughter.'

'I'll be over at the house shortly,' I said, squeezing out a smile. 'Just a few things to tie up in the office.' Stefan's message read, *Can we meet? Same place. Midnight?*

My heart started to pound. Why did he want to meet now? Was it just that he was missing me, or something more worrying? Perhaps he was making plans to leave Westbury, or find another job. Maybe he had gone to enlist, and they had accepted him. My imagination ran riot and waiting was agonising. The 'snifter' turned into two, then three, as Robbie and Father talked about silk and moved on to politics. I pretended to listen politely, itching for Robbie to leave. Then, as her casserole threatened to burn in the oven, Mother invited him to stay for supper.

'I really should be on my way, Mrs Verner,' he said, standing up and putting down his glass. 'Before it's completely dark. Get back before the blackout.'

'Oh my dear,' she said, peering out of the window. 'You can't drive out there without lights. It's far too late. Why don't you stay for supper and we can find you a bed for the night?'

No! I shouted inside my head. The thought of Robbie sleeping in our house made me feel deeply uneasy. With all my strength of concentration, I willed him to refuse.

'Your cooking smells so delicious that I'll accept your kind invitation for dinner but I couldn't possibly impose further on your hospitality, Mrs V,' he said, and I tried not to sigh audibly with relief. 'I'll take myself off afterwards to the Anchor. I've stayed there before — it's very comfortable. It'll do me perfectly well,' he said.

Dinner became an endurance test. I was desperate to get Robbie out of the house but he seemed to be settling in nicely, heaping excessive compliments on Mother's culinary skills and, to her obvious delight, accepting seconds of each course to prove his point. How dare he cosy up to my family? I made a few attempts at conversation but it always dried up. I couldn't focus, with my head full of anxiety about the night ahead.

The grandfather clock struck ten, just as mother was offering coffee. At half past ten I excused myself and went up to my bedroom. I lay on the bed, willing the time to pass, exhausted by the events and emotions of the day and almost paralysed with anticipation. I woke with a jolt at two minutes to twelve.

When I slipped out of the back door the night was coal black. No moonlight, no stars, no street lights. Waiting for my eyes to adjust, I caught a slight movement to the side of the terrace, the red end of a lit cigarette and a tendril of smoke rising into the air. My heart leapt.

'Stefan?' I called, in a whisper.

There was no reply. Then, out of the shadows came a tall figure.

'Robbie? What the hell are you doing here?' I said, shaky with the shock.

'I could very well ask the same of you,' he said smoothly.

'But you were going to the Anchor.'

'Grace and Harold most kindly insisted I stay,' he said. Grace and Harold. The intimacy made me shudder. 'And I was just turning in when I remembered I hadn't put the top up on the Morgan. Still, this is rather jolly, meeting you here. Turn up for the books. Have a cigarette,' he said, clicking open his slim silver case.

'No thanks,' I said, trying to sound unfazed as my brain whirred frantically. 'I just came out for some air.' I needed to end this conversation as quickly as possible and get Robbie to go inside, or find some excuse to get away myself, perhaps to go back into the house and leave by the front door. I hoped Stefan would wait for me. 'Anyway,' I said as casually as possible, 'it's a bit cold out here. Think I'll head off to bed.' He wasn't stupid. He would know I was lying, but I didn't care.

'Before you go,' he said, stepping between me and the doorway, 'I've a little question you might be able to help me with.'

'Try me,' I said, trying to keep calm, 'but make it quick. I don't want to catch my death.'

'Have you had any problems with burglars round here?'

'Not that I know of,' I said, wondering what the hell he was getting at.

'So would you consider it rather unusual,' he said, slick as oil, 'to see a man lurking in your orchard at the dead of night?'

My stomach lurched. 'Yes, very, unusual,' I managed, fearing the worst.

His tone was low and menacing. 'Unless, I

172

suppose, this was the German lad, the Stefan character you mistook me for?'

There was no escape. I had to brazen this one out, deny everything, to make him go away. There was little hope now of getting to the tennis hut. I drew myself up and straightened my shoulders. 'I really don't know what you are talking about, Robbie. And I don't like your tone of voice. Now, I am getting cold and want to go to bed. Will you please step aside and let me come by?'

He didn't move. He took a drag on his cigarette and in the flare I could see the triumphant smile on his face. 'Chilly Miss Lily,' he sneered, throwing down the butt and reaching out towards me. 'Would you like me to warm you up?'

'No, I would not.' I pushed his arm away. 'Now let me past, please.'

He grabbed hold of my shoulders, and I nearly screamed. I tried to wriggle out of his grasp but he tightened his grip. He was too strong. I stopped struggling, stiffening myself against whatever was going to happen next, a forced kiss, a hand between my legs, or something worse. My heart banged so hard in my chest I thought it might explode.

But he made no further move, just holding me, his whisky breath blowing in my face.

'Now listen carefully,' he said, in a hoarse whisper. 'I am going to say this only once. I know what your game is, you little flirt.' I made another attempt to get out of his grasp, but he held me firm. 'What would Harold do if he knew that creepy little Kraut was lurking around his garden at the dead of night?'

He knew I wouldn't answer.

'Or that his beloved daughter was having a little dalliance with a Jew boy?'

'How dare you . . . ' I spat, but he talked over me.

'Any sensible man would report him for spying, wouldn't he? Get him locked up as an enemy alien, or get him sent back to his good friends, the Nazis. That's what would happen.'

'My father would do no such thing,' I said, wrenching myself out of his grip. 'And this is none of your business, anyway.'

'Ah, but it is,' he said menacingly, 'very much my business. If someone was stealing parachute production secrets I would be duty bound to report it.'

'That's bloody ridiculous,' I said, 'and you know it.' But we both knew he'd played the trump card.

'And now,' he said, 'I think you owe me a little something.' Two hands clamped firmly each side of my head and pulled my face upwards, his lips pressed against mine, a hard tongue prising them open and pushing into my mouth. It tasted disgusting. I struggled and tried to pull away but he held me too tightly. I was helpless, hating every moment of it. Finally he let me go, though keeping his arm round my shoulders.

'My sweet little Lily,' he whispered in my ear, 'you are quite irresistible you know, especially when you're playing hard to get. But don't think I am going to leave it at this. You'll come round.

Who knows, you might even make marriage material when you grow up a bit.'

I felt invaded and contaminated, needed to rinse my mouth and spit out the taste of him.

'I've enjoyed our little talk,' he was saying, stroking my cheek. 'A very nice surprise. But it's time to hit the sack now, don't you think?' He stood aside, ushering me through the door.

* * *

I ran upstairs and into the bathroom, desperate to wash Robbie Cameron off my skin. Even though I cleaned my teeth twice, I could still taste his breath and spent the rest of the night in a ferment of fury and fear. I was frantic about Stefan. What had he been planning to tell me? What had he thought when I failed to turn up? Would Robbie really tell Father that he had seen me going out to meet Stefan, I wondered. Or did he just want to leave the threat hanging over my head? It was such a ruddy mess.

* * *

Next morning I went in to work early to miss breakfast and avoid any chance of meeting Robbie.

The weaving shed was for once still and silent, the rows of looms like giant angular beasts, slumbering peacefully, ready to be woken for the day's work ahead. I left a note on Stefan's loom: *Sorry I couldn't meet you. Need to explain. When?*

There was no response, all day, and I told myself to keep calm. He would contact me when he was ready. Besides, I would see him in two days' time when he came for Sunday lunch with the others, and could try to catch him alone then.

But on Sunday only Kurt and Walter arrived on the doorstep.

'Sorry, Mrs Grace,' Kurt said, looking embarrassed. 'Stefan says he is not well.'

While Mother twittered about whether she should take him some medicine, a hot water bottle, or some lunch, I mouthed at Kurt, 'What's wrong?'

He shrugged his shoulders.

'Let me pop down and see him, Mother, while you finish the vegetables. Just check that he's okay, whether he needs anything, aspirin or something,' I said, seizing this unexpected opportunity. 'Then you could go after lunch.'

I waited for Father to intervene, but he just raised his eyebrows. If this was intended as a warning, I decided to ignore it.

Stefan answered the door, fully dressed. He didn't look the slightest bit unwell.

'Why are you here?' he said, sharply, glancing up the road in either direction.

'Kurt said you were ill.'

He didn't reply. And didn't move.

'Let me in, it's cold out here,' I said. 'I need to explain about the other night.'

His face was pinched and expressionless, his voice steely. 'Do not come again. We cannot meet any more.'

'You said in your note we had to talk? What

did you want to talk about?'

He shook his head. 'Nothing. It does not matter any more.'

'It does matter, or you wouldn't have sent me a note,' I said, feeling desperate now.

Stefan stood squarely in the doorway. '*Scheisse*, Lily. Just go,' he hissed.

'Please, let me explain,' I pleaded. It felt like my last chance.

He turned and closed the door in my face. I hammered on it but he refused to answer. I slunk home, utterly confused and dejected.

12

As with every generation of immigrants, the Huguenots faced prejudice: accusations of stealing jobs, of low standards of housing and hygiene, of creating public disorder and having low morals. It was even reported in London that Huguenots had smaller heads than the English, implying that they were less intelligent. A newspaper likened them to a 'swarm of frogs' and urged that they be kicked out of the country.
From *The History of Silk*, **by Harold Verner**

Gwen came into my office first thing on Monday morning, and caught me looking out of the window hoping to catch a glimpse of Stefan on his way into work.

'I need a big favour,' she said.

'What's that,' I said, distracted, trying to see the boys in the crowd of workers milling down the yard.

'I've got to go to the warehouse today,' she said, 'and Peter was supposed to go with me, but he's just rung in sick. I need someone to share the driving and help with the lifting.' Requisitions of raw silk were distributed from a depot north of Huntingdon — well away from bombing targets — but it was a good three hours from Westbury in the works van. Collections had always been Jim's job, now it was Gwen's. Peter, our new warehouse manager, was frequently off

178

work. He'd served in the Expeditionary Force and his nerves were shattered.

'I've got such a lot to do here,' I lied. 'I can't drive anyway, so I wouldn't be much help.' The truth was I desperately hoped to find Stefan, on his own, today, to explain. I really didn't want to be out for the whole day.

'Now's your chance to learn,' she said, ignoring my surliness. 'Please, Lily. It's the only day we can go, and we really need that raw, now.'

I had no choice. 'Okay then, since you ask so nicely,' I said, 'Give me half an hour to get ready.'

'You're a brick,' she said.

★ ★ ★

Once we were clear of Westbury and onto the open road, she pulled over.

'Your turn,' she said.

'What? I can't drive.'

'Don't worry, I'll teach you. There's no traffic, the road's straight-ish here,' she said. We switched places and she showed me how to adjust the seat for my longer legs, and then calmly talked me through the controls, putting her hand over mine to demonstrate the movement of the gear lever.

'I can do it,' I said impatiently, shaking her hand off.

'Okay,' she said, 'turn her on.'

I started the engine and tried to move off, stalled several times, kangaroo-hopped in first and then crunched my way up through the gears.

As we got under way I soon got the hang of it and, as the miles ran by, even started to enjoy myself. I could see why men were so besotted with driving. Such power and freedom — anything seemed possible. I could follow the road anywhere I wanted. Take unplanned turnings, discover new places, forget my responsibilities.

Gwen seemed to sense my mood lifting. 'Great feeling, isn't it?' she said, and then, in a sing-song voice, ''The open road, the dusty highway, the heath, the common, the hedgerows.''

''Here to-day, up and off to somewhere else to-morrow!'' I quoted back, forgetting to be grumpy.

''The whole world before you, and a horizon that's always changing!'' she finished, laughing. 'Poor old Toad. He came to such a sticky end.'

'True. But now I understand why he thought it was worth it.'

We drove in silence again for a while.

'Lily?' she said.

'Yes?'

'I'm sorry about that business over Stefan.'

'Me too.' I wasn't going to forgive her that easily.

'I didn't have any option, Harold gave the order and he's the boss.'

'Well, it doesn't matter any more. Stefan's not speaking to me,' I said.

I negotiated the junction onto the Great North Road, and crunched my way through the gears to an exhilarating top speed of forty-five miles an hour.

'It's hardly surprising,' she said, out of the blue.

'What's hardly surprising?'

180

'Stefan. Not speaking to you. After Thursday.'

'Stop talking in riddles please. What about Thursday?'

'Robbie. Staying the night at The Chestnuts.'

The realisation hit me like a slap in the face. What an idiot I had been. I'd assumed Stefan was furious with me because I failed to turn up for our assignation, but now I understood: he would have seen the Morgan in the driveway or, even worse, might even have seen me with Robbie that night. How could he have known that Robbie had threatened me, had forced that kiss on me?

It all became horribly, bitterly clear. His coldness wasn't anger or fear, it was jealousy. He thought I had betrayed him. And now, every mile was taking us further from Westbury. I wanted to turn the van around immediately, speed back and explain what had happened, to hug and kiss him, reassure him of my love.

The road blurred, and then the tears started to spill down my cheeks. Gwen glanced over anxiously. 'Pull over, Lily, now. That lay-by,' she ordered.

I swerved off the road and skidded to a stop, failing to take the van out of gear, and we jerked and stalled. She leaned over and turned off the engine.

I leaned my head on the steering wheel. 'Robbie stayed because of the blackout, not for me,' I sobbed.

'That's not what it looked like,' she said unsympathetically. 'I assumed it was a date.'

'Why does everyone jump to conclusions? It's not fair.'

'You tell me,' Gwen said quietly, 'about unfairness. About people jumping to conclusions.'

I wondered for a moment what she was referring to. No one had been unfair to Gwen, surely? She was well respected by everyone. And then I remembered, with a flush of shame, how I'd taunted her about 'normal people' falling in love.

'What I said that day, Gwen. I was just angry, it came out without thinking.'

'Most prejudice is unthinking,' she said, flatly.

'Look, I am really sorry,' I said. 'Please forgive me, it was a stupid thing to say. I've been under such strain over all this.'

Lorries whooshed by, rocking the van. 'Come on,' she said. 'Time to get moving or we won't get back before dark. Let me drive for a while.'

'Why is life so complicated?' I said, as we pulled back on to the road. She shook her head but didn't reply.

I had no idea how much more complicated it would soon become.

*   *   *

Cradling my morning cup of coffee, weary and bleary eyed from our long drive the day before, I stood on tiptoe once more looking out through my office window hoping for a glance of Stefan. I was still racked with anxiety about the misunderstanding, and determined to find an excuse to have a few moments with him, to explain what had happened.

Then I saw him, walking into the yard with the

others. At first I didn't recognise him. I'd never seen him wear a hat before. Sure, it was cold, but why was he wearing it pulled so strangely low over his forehead?

At elevenses I went to the canteen to get the office coffees and when Stefan came in it was clear what the hat had been hiding: a dark purple bruise spreading from his right eye towards the temple, already discolouring into an ugly yellow and black.

I joined him in the queue and whispered, 'What happened to your face?'

'Nothing,' he said under his breath.

'It's not nothing. It looks dreadful. Tell me,' I said. It looked as though he had been punched, but Stefan was the last person I'd expect to get into a fight. Were the tensions starting to tell? I wondered.

'I fell against a door,' he said curtly, not meeting my eye. He refused to say anything further, and I couldn't press him any more in public.

As the day went on I became convinced there was more to it. Should I intervene and risk Father's anger, or just let it go? Stefan was an adult, he could look after himself. Then I realised; this provided me with the perfect excuse to visit him — I was concerned for his welfare, that was all.

Walter answered the door.

'I've been sent to find out how Stefan is,' I lied. 'Can I come in?'

He let me into the front room and called up the stairs, 'Miss Lily to see you, Stef.'

When he finally appeared, his face was even more shockingly discoloured. The bruise had spread right across his temple with deep purple canyons appearing above and below his eyelids.

'I came to see if you are okay.'

'I am okay,' he said, flatly.

'Where did you really get that shiner?'

'Shiner?'

I pointed to his eye.

'I told you,' he said. 'It was a door.'

'Yes,' said Kurt, coming into the room. 'We were wrestling and he fell.'

'I don't believe either of you,' I said. 'Why don't you make me a cup of tea and tell me what really happened?'

'We haven't got any milk,' Walter called from the kitchen. Even he was in cahoots.

'I'll have it without.'

The four of us sat on their threadbare chairs, sipping black tea from saucer-less cups. I tried again. 'Now I want the truth.' They exchanged glances. No one said a word. 'It obviously wasn't a door,' I said. 'There's no sharp edge on that bruise. It looks as though you've been in a fight.'

'No!' Stefan almost shouted. 'You know I do not fight.'

'Then what really happened?'

Finally Kurt spoke, in a quiet voice. 'Last night we went into Westbury for fish and chips.' Stefan scowled into his cup as Kurt continued, 'On the way home we passed the Kings Arms and went inside for a beer.'

'Bitter,' Walter screwed up his face. 'It is not nice beer.'

'Have brown ale next time, it's sweeter,' Kurt said gently, then went on with the story. 'Anyway, there is a piano and Stefan tried a few notes. People asked him to go on so he played some jazz tunes.'

'They loved it,' said Walter.

'Especially those girls.' Kurt grinned slyly and Stefan tapped a cigarette from a crumpled packet, pretending not to notice.

'What girls?'

'They were all over him.'

Stefan finally snapped. 'Just shut up, both of you.' He lit the cigarette and sucked on it fiercely.

'I was playing ragtime, that sort of thing,' he said, blowing out with a sharp sigh. 'The landlord was pleased. He said it would bring in customers and gave us free beer.'

Kurt chimed in. 'There were some girls by the piano, dancing.'

'Go on,' I said, dreading what was coming.

'Walter was *betrunken* . . . ?' Kurt said.

'Drunk? Tipsy?'

'That is not fair. It was not only me,' Walter whined.

'We decided to leave,' Stefan went on. 'When I stopped playing everyone clapped and thanked us and we said good-night and they said see you next week. But the men were waiting outside. They shouted at us.'

'What did they say?'

No one spoke. I repeated the question.

Then Walter whispered, with his eyes to the floor, 'They said, 'keep off our women, German scum.'' The coarse violence of the words was like a grenade exploding in the little room.

'Stefan tried to explain but one of them just punched him,' Kurt went on.

I started to tremble. I could hardly believe it, these were Westbury folk, neighbours, perhaps workers at the mill. I'd never heard of anything like this happening in our town before.

'We have to tell Father,' I said, getting up to leave. 'He can talk to the police.'

Stefan blocked my way. 'No, Lily,' he said firmly. 'You must not tell anyone else.'

'It's serious, Stefan. We have to do something.'

'No,' he said again, even more determinedly.

'Okay,' I said, feeling like a coward. I had little option but to agree. 'If anything else happens you must promise to tell me immediately.'

They nodded and there seemed to be nothing more to say. I felt unwelcome. 'I'll be going then,' I said, beckoning Stefan to follow me to the front door. 'We've got to talk,' I whispered, 'Please. I need to explain.'

He shook his head. 'There is nothing to talk about,' he said icily.

But when the boys arrived for Sunday lunch two days later he handed me a book. 'Thank you for lending this, Miss Lily,' he said formally, as if we were strangers. 'I liked the chapter where they find the man who was lost.' I thanked him and my heart hammered in my chest as I replaced the book on the shelf. There was no lost man in the story.

After everyone had gone to bed that evening I retrieved the note from the pages of the book.

Thursday 10 o'clock. S.

Waiting was almost unbearable. When we met by chance at the mill he avoided my eyes. I could read nothing into his expression, but every sight of him made me sick with apprehension. After being so cool, why had he asked to meet me? Would he offer me an opportunity to explain, or did he just want a showdown?

When Thursday evening finally arrived I crept quickly downstairs, avoiding the squeaky floorboards, and silently let myself out of the back door. It was the middle of February and perishingly cold outside, there was no moon, and the stars were brilliant in a cloudless sky. I was through the orchard in seconds and slipped around the side of the tennis hut, my eyes trying to adjust to the blackness. It was the cloud of cigarette smoke that I saw first.

He was waiting for me outside, sitting on an old orange crate, huddled in his camel overcoat and a scarf. When he looked up, his pale face was like a half moon in the darkness. I unlocked the door and we went inside, lit a candle and sat, not touching, on the old garden bench.

'Smoke?' he said.

He avoided meeting my eyes in the flare of the match, and for a few moments we sat side by side, smoking and exhaling silently into the dusty air.

'Stefan,' I said quietly, 'are you okay?'

'What do *you* think?' he muttered through his teeth.

'I think you have misunderstood something. About Robbie being at The Chestnuts that night,' I said, carefully, still unsure what he might or might not have seen.

He took a deep drag, sighed it out. 'I think you have lied to me,' he said, bitterly.

'No,' I almost shouted. 'Look at me,' I whispered, waiting till he finally raised his eyes. 'There is nothing between me and Robbie. Nothing. My parents invited him to stay. Because of the blackout.'

Stefan turned away, took another drag.

'That night, he caught me on my way out to see you. He had gone to check his car, he said. He was standing at the back door and he told me he had seen you. He threatened me. Said he would tell Father. I couldn't get away. I am *not* lying to you. I promise.'

More silence. I felt like shaking him.

'Stefan? Say something.'

Eventually, he whispered, 'I saw you kissing. It made me sick to see.'

So now the truth was out. How could I persuade him what had really happened?

'Listen to me, Stefan. You must believe what I am going to tell you.'

'How can I believe, when you lie to me?' he hissed.

'I am going to tell you, and then it is your choice whether you want to believe me. Robbie threatened me, and then he forced me to kiss him. It was disgusting. It made me feel sick too. But I couldn't get away.'

There was a long silence. Stefan finished his cigarette and stubbed it out defiantly into the floor. We had always agreed to take care with

188

cigarette ends, to clear up any evidence behind us.

'How can I know if you are telling the truth?' he said at last, his eyes glittering with anger, or was it tears? I didn't stop to check. I decided to risk it, turned his face to mine and kissed him lightly on the mouth. At first, his lips stayed hard and unyielding, but he didn't pull away. Then, at last, he started to kiss me back.

'I love you,' I said, when we stopped. 'You believe me, don't you?'

'I think so,' he said, kissing me again.

Quite a bit later he said, 'I wanted to meet you that night because I missed you so much. But when I saw you with Mr Cameron I felt like killing him. I was so angry it frightened me.'

'That won't help, you know. He's paying our wages at the moment.'

He snorted mirthlessly. 'Does this allow him to threaten you?'

'Of course not,' I sighed, 'but it's complicated.'

'Will he tell Mr Harold, as he said?'

'I don't think so. I think it's just a threat. He likes to have power over people.'

'It is still dangerous for us to meet, I think,' he said sadly.

'But Robbie is not usually here. It's only Father we have to worry about.'

Stefan pulled me to my feet, kissing me again, on my forehead, nose and chin, behind my ears, down the back of my neck, and pressing his body into mine as if we could just become one. I felt giddy and reckless with relief and desire.

'I can't live without this,' I breathed. 'Perhaps

189

we could just ration ourselves?'

'Ration what?' he said.

'How often we meet?'

'Like chocolate,' he laughed. 'You're so much sweeter.'

'And you are much more addictive,' I said, stroking his cheek.

'We just have to be very, very, very careful,' he said, solemnly. We sealed our agreement with a final kiss, and as I picked my way home in the dark and sneaked back into the silent house, my cheeks ached from smiling to myself. I was happier than I'd been for months.

The next time, Stefan brought bottles of pale ale and I'd stolen some biscuits from Mother's store cupboard, but we didn't really need peace offerings. For two blissful hours we talked and kissed, drunk on the joy of being together again, as though we'd been separated for years, not just a couple of months. All the mistrust and confusion cleared like clouds on a summer's day.

We kept strictly to our agreement, being very careful at all times, and meeting only once a fortnight. At least we now knew, with a certainty like a warm blanket, that we would always love each other, whatever happened. The tennis hut was hardly the most romantic trysting place, but despite the constant concern about being discovered, those stolen hours were some of the happiest in my life. Even now, the smell of tar instantly evokes their heady joy.

Spring arrived at last. Bees hummed in the apple blossom, the birds were courting and baby calves cavorted on the water meadows. When you are in love, romance seems to be everywhere and, sure enough, when John and Vera turned up for supper together I'd never seen her looking so pretty before: she positively glowed. He was back from Canada for five days' leave before joining his squadron. They were holding hands and looking so pleased with themselves I knew at once what they were about to tell us. She wore a new, shapely floral dress, her hair was elegantly waved, with a silver clasp on one side. The ring glistened on her finger.

Once we were all together in the drawing room John said, rather formally, 'Mother, Father, Lily. We've got something to tell you. I've proposed to Vera, and I'm glad to say she has accepted.'

Vera blushed gratifyingly as he kissed her on the cheek. 'Last night her parents gave us their blessing.'

Mother threw her arms round them both. 'Oh, my lovely children, this is such wonderful news,' she said through her tears. 'I hope you will both be very happy.'

Father slapped John on the back and shook his hand. 'Excellent choice, old man, jolly good show. You'll make a lovely couple.'

'You little minx, seducing my brother like that,' I said, hugging her.

'He's a pushover,' she giggled, looking up at John. 'What do you think?'

'I'm thrilled. Don't tell me he got down on one knee?'

'C'mon Lily, you know your brother. It was over a pint, in some squalid London pub.'

'The very best beer,' John said, cheerfully. 'No expense spared.'

'Let's see the ring.' Vera held up her finger. It was a simple elegant silver setting with a single diamond. 'I never knew you had such good taste, John.'

'We men have hidden depths,' he said, winking at Vera.

'Where will you get married?' Mother asked. 'Church or registry office?'

'Not sure where or when yet,' John said. 'I'm just overjoyed she's agreed to be my wife.'

It was so good to have him back home. His squadron was stationed in Cambridgeshire — just a couple of hours away from Westbury or London — so he would be able to visit whenever he had a few days off. We all tried not to think about the dangers he would face with each bombing raid. Only after several glasses of champagne did Vera's mask slip. I found her in the toilet, trying to remove mascara that had run down her cheeks.

'I just want to lock him up and throw away the key,' she sobbed.

'That's the only thing that would stop him,' I agreed. Now he had graduated with top marks as a bomber pilot, John was keener than ever. 'But he's obviously very good at this flying business. He'll be fine,' I said, convincing neither of us.

13

Legend has it that silk was brought to the West by two Persian monks who in AD 552 penetrated into China as Christian missionaries, and amidst their pious occupations, viewed with a curious eye the manufacture of silk. Indignant zeal, excited by seeing unbelievers engrossed in a lucrative branch of commerce, prompted them to conceal some silk-worm eggs in a hollow cane, coming thence to Constantinople and presenting them to the Emperor Justinian for a handsome reward.
From *The History of Silk*, **by Harold Verner**

By May 1940 the news from Europe was grim.

German troops were in Holland and Belgium, just the other side of the North Sea, and rapidly moving forward into Northern France. In East Anglia we felt perilously close to the front line, with only a narrow strip of North Sea between us and their apparently unstoppable forces. Our holiday beaches became off-limit fortresses, with roads barricaded and coastal bridges blown up to impede the progress of any invading force. Even Churchill's bullish speeches failed to lift our optimism, and a sense of gloomy inevitability seemed to settle over our lives.

In this febrile atmosphere spy fever became an epidemic, and official posters everywhere warning that CARELESS TALK COSTS LIVES only helped to heighten people's fears. One evening in the tennis hut, Stefan pulled out a torn-out page from a tabloid newspaper and pointed to the headline. It read: GERMAN SPIES HELD IN SABOTAGE PLOT. I quickly scanned the story. It was a lurid and unlikely tale, ending with the exhortation: *'It is every Briton's duty to protect our noble country: report all suspicious behaviour to your local police station, NOW.'*

'What if someone reports me, Lily? About my papers? About my age? Could they send me back to Germany?'

'Your papers were good enough to get you here, weren't they? No one's going to check them again now. Don't worry, my darling,' I said, trying to distract him with a kiss.

But my reassurances soon began to sound increasingly hollow. Soon enough, newspapers were reporting that new laws were being prepared, requiring all German and Austrian men over twenty years old to register as 'enemy aliens'. Kurt and Walter were too young to qualify and so, officially, was Stefan. But that didn't stop him being consumed with anxiety. His memories of being arrested and imprisoned in Germany seemed to replay themselves in his mind. I pressed him to talk about it, but he refused.

It got worse. As large-scale casualties were reported from fighting in France, anti-German sentiment seemed to spread like a rash. I tried to put it to the back of my mind: the boys had been working at the mill for over a year now, and seemed to be well liked by everyone. I was so convinced that no one who knew them could possibly dislike or mistrust them that I failed to notice what was really happening.

I was collecting the office tea tray from the canteen when I noticed that Kurt and Walter were not sitting, as usual, with Bert and the tacklers. Stefan was not with his usual group of weavers. Instead, the three of them sat at a table on their own. It struck me as odd, but I didn't give it a further thought.

Then, a few days later, I was washing my hands when, through the open door into the toilet area, I overheard two women talking to each other between the cubicles.

'Only stands to reason,' one said, 'shouldn't trust any of 'em.'

The response was inaudible over the sound of the flush, except for the words 'parachute silk'. I couldn't be absolutely sure what they were talking about, but whatever it was sent prickles up the back of my neck. I crept away and lurked behind some shelves, waiting for them. After a while the women emerged; two older weavers who had worked for Verners all of their lives and had always appeared motherly, even protective towards Stefan. I'd jumped to silly conclusions. They must have been talking about something else.

Perhaps we were all deluding ourselves, like the Fischer family in Vienna. We'd had no news of them since the outbreak of war and I remembered what John had said about their attitude to the Nazis: 'if they keep their heads down it will all go away.'

But just two weeks later, the red paint splashed over the front door of the boys' cottage brought us face-to-face with the shocking reality. It was so crudely daubed that the words were hard to read, but as Father and I got closer the obscene words became plain: FUCK OFF JEWBOYS.

We called the police and soon afterwards a stout man arrived on a bicycle altogether too flimsy for him. 'Constable Kilby, Westbury police,' he said, puffing as he leaned the bike against the wall and took off his helmet. He looked at the door, mouthing the words as he read them, twice. He shook his head, 'This is a bad old business, sir. I understand these lads are your employees at the mill?'

Father nodded, 'That is correct, Constable. Now, shall we go inside?'

The six of us crowded awkwardly in the tiny front room. 'Now, lads, who's going to tell me what's been going on?' he said, gravely.

Kurt and Walter nudged Stefan simultaneously.

'Begin at the beginning then, laddie. Don't miss anything out.'

'A few nights ago there was a crash,' Stefan started, studying his feet. 'A stone through our window. With a piece of paper.'

'A stone? A piece of paper?' I struggled to understand. Why hadn't he mentioned this?

'With writing on it.'

'What did it say, laddie? Speak up now,' the policeman frowned and wiped his brow.

'It said,' Stefan cleared his throat, 'it said 'Krauts go home'.'

I heard a moan and realised it was me.

196

'Then, this morning,' Stefan gestured towards the front door. 'That.'

'Have you still got the piece of paper?' Constable Kilby asked.

'We burned it,' Kurt said.

'Don't worry, laddie. Any idea who wrote it?'

They shook their heads.

'What about those men from the pub?' I said.

'What men are these, exactly?' asked the policeman.

Father's face reddened as Stefan recounted the story about the attack outside the pub. 'Why didn't you tell me about this before?' he growled. 'This is not just casual prejudice, it's anti-Semitism. It must not be tolerated.'

Stefan shook his head. 'We did not want to bother you, Mr Harold.'

The constable sighed. 'I'm afraid it'll be tricky to prove who did it, sir. I could go to the King's Arms and have a word with the landlord. See if he can identify the men.'

'But they might come and find us again,' Walter said, in a small voice.

'Can't deny that's a possibility, laddie,' Constable Kilby said, shaking his head sadly. 'On balance, it might be best to keep your heads down, stay out of harm's way. In my experience, if you don't react they'll get bored with the idea soon enough.'

*　*　*

When Gwen called in on her way home from work a week later, she found us huddled around the radio once more, listening to the six o'clock bulletin. The news about the Expeditionary Force was devastating, but at least they were now being rescued.

'All those little ships. Incredible what they're doing at Dunkirk,' I said.

'Yes, I've heard,' she said rather curtly, her face drawn and sombre. 'It's hard to imagine what they're going through. But I need to speak to you and Harold, in private please. It's more bad news, I'm afraid, only closer to home.'

Instinctively I knew it was something to do with the boys, and it felt as though a stone had dropped into the pit of my stomach. 'Come in,' I said. 'Would you like a drink? Sherry?'

'Any chance of something stronger?'

'Gee and tee? They haven't rationed that yet. Or whisky and water?'

'Whisky please, straight.'

We went into the drawing room and I turned off the radio as Father poured and handed her a glass. She took a long slug.

'I'm afraid I have unwelcome news, Mr Harold. There are rumours going round the mill.'

'Rumours? What about?' Father said, frowning.

'They say parachute silk is being deliberately sabotaged.'

I thought for a moment this was just a repeat of the gossip I'd overheard a few weeks before. Then I quickly realised it had escalated into something much more dangerous; these rumours were malicious, intended to get the boys into trouble, perhaps get them sacked or worse. It wasn't just aimed at Stefan either. He wove

198

parachute silk, but Kurt and Walter also worked on it, in the finishing plant.

'What utter tosh,' Father exploded. 'We test every roll. I've not been told of any problems.'

'I'm just reporting what I've heard, sir.' Gwen crossed her arms defensively.

'Quite right, quite right,' he muttered, pulling the pipe out of his pocket. 'And thank you for bringing it to my attention. Do you have any clues who it is?'

Gwen shook her head. 'I've tried to find out, believe me. I have suspicions but couldn't pin it on anyone in particular.' Should I tell them what I'd heard in the toilets, I wondered. I had no proof that the conversation was anything to do with the boys.

And while I was wondering, a more treacherous thought occurred. Could Gwen have heard similar gossip, and be exaggerating it deliberately to stir things up against Stefan because she disapproved of my relationship with him? Surely not? That was several months ago, she hadn't said anything about it since then and I knew she valued him very highly as a weaver.

I was grateful when Father stood up, purposefully knocking out his pipe in the hearth. 'We need to put a stop to this, right now. We'll call a meeting tomorrow, for all staff,' he said, reassuringly decisive. 'Tell them it is mandatory, Gwen. The day shift folk must come to the canteen at five o'clock sharp after work — and make sure the evening shift know so they can get there in time, too.'

After seeing her out, he came back into the

room and sat down beside me on the sofa. 'I know what you're thinking — someone's trying to discredit those boys. Leave it to me. We'll scotch these rumours. Don't you worry, my darling. Time for supper.'

His words did little to reassure me. The truth was slippery and increasingly treacherous, I thought, like walking on marbles. I had no idea who to trust any more.

★ ★ ★

The canteen was packed. Chairs and tables had been stacked against the walls to make room for more than a hundred workers — both shifts — gathered in their usual groups. A buzz of expectant chatter filled the room. Stefan, Kurt and Walter were in the corner, looking cheerful enough. I hoped they were unaware of the rumours. Squeezing through the crowd I checked each face, hoping the culprits might somehow reveal themselves. Gwen held out her hand to steady Father as he stepped up onto a chair.

He cleared his throat and held up his hand. The room went quiet.

'Thank you for coming at short notice.' He composed his features into a genial expression and modulated his voice into that combination of authority and amiability that earned him such respect. 'It's the end of a working day for some of you, and the start for others, so I won't keep you long. First, I want to thank everyone for putting your backs into the essential war production we have delivered with such success so far, in what are difficult times for all of us, both personally and professionally.' He paused, smiling around as if we were all his children.

'I've called this meeting so that everyone who works for Verners and Sons can be reassured that there are no — I repeat NO — problems whatsoever with the production of parachute silk in this mill. You have my word. Every roll is rigorously tested, and we sample test again to double check. Every single one has come well within the ministry's specifications and we have absolutely no complaints from our major clients, Camerons Ltd.'

He paused again, scanning the crowd, and his voice became louder and more deliberate. 'I would like to add that anyone spreading rumours suggesting otherwise will be severely disciplined. Any suggestion that would reduce confidence in our products could seriously affect our contribution to the war effort and the viability of our business, not to mention the jobs of everyone who works here.'

'And finally,' he raised his voice further still, 'I would like to remind you, as if you needed reminding, that careless talk can cost lives — and that means the lives of any one of us or our families.' He looked around again at the silent faces.

'Well, that's all for now. For the day shift it's time to go home for a well-earned rest, or back to work for the rest of you. Thank you and good evening.'

There was a short burst of applause as he

climbed down from the chair. He shook dozens of hands as people offered thanks and support, saying a few friendly words to each one. I looked back towards where the boys had been standing, but they'd disappeared.

14

There is no fabric more sensuous than silk. Its use for nightwear and bed sheets has been popular for centuries and, recently, finely powdered silk fibre has been adopted for the preparation of luxury unguents for the skin. It is remarkable that a thread so loved for its beauty and sensuality comes from the simple caterpillar of the moth Bombyx Mori.
From *The History of Silk,* **by Harold Verner**

Stefan's note broke all the rules. It said, *Come to the cottage tonight, seven o'clock, if you can.*

It was difficult to get away at this early hour but I concocted an outrageous lie and arrived only half an hour late.

'What's all this?' I said, breathless from running, and scared of more bad news.

'I'm so happy you can come,' he said, letting me in with a quick glance up the road in each direction. He closed the door and pulled me into his arms, but I pushed him away.

'Hang on. Where are Kurt and Walter?'

'At the cinema.' A sweet, shy smile spread across his face. 'They won't be back till half past ten. We have three hours alone. What do you think? Can you stay?'

No more words were needed. The moment we'd longed for had arrived. He took my hand and led me up the narrow staircase to his room.

It was sparsely furnished with just a bed, chair and chest of drawers, but he'd lit a couple of candles and it looked cosy in their gentle glow. A bunch of wild flowers stood in a jam jar on the bedside table.

I started to tremble even more as he unbuttoned my blouse and unhooked my bra. We kissed again, and my legs turned to jelly but I somehow remained standing. I could hear the blood pulsing in my ears, pounding through my body.

As I tried to help him take off his jumper he moved backwards to pull it over his head, stumbled on the rug and fell onto the bed, pulling me on top of him. The tension was broken; we rolled around half naked, giggling like children.

He drew back the candlewick bedspread and eiderdown and we sat down.

'You crazy, lovely boy,' I whispered, kissing him again.

Hurriedly now, we pulled off the rest of our clothes and climbed between the sheets. We were both shaking, pushed awkwardly together in the narrow single bed. But as we turned to each other, tentatively stroking and kissing, the warmth enveloped us and after a while our bodies seemed to melt and merge into one.

He lifted himself onto his arms and pulled back the cover. My nipples were hard as pebbles and, as he bent to kiss them, darts of electricity fizzed deliciously through my body. I tangled my fingers in the familiar thicket of his hair, dark against my pale skin, and moaned with pleasure.

After a while he gently pushed one leg over mine, pushing them apart, and pulled himself on to me, heavy and hot, resting on his elbows. For a moment he gazed deep into my eyes as if trying to penetrate my mind. Then he closed his eyes and, with a guttural groan, pushed into me. I was so ready I felt barely any pain, just surprise at the extraordinary sensation and the utter joy of abandoning myself, opening up to him. It felt like the most natural thing on earth, to hold him inside me. As he started to move, faster and faster, I lost myself in the urgency and heard myself calling his name, over and over, as if my life depended on it.

Afterwards we lay tangled in each other's limbs, amazed and relieved that we'd finally joined our bodies in the way we'd longed for. Eventually he got up to make tea.

As we sat in bed with our cups I said, 'I'm glad we waited. This is the way it's meant to be. In bed, not in a grubby old tennis hut.'

He turned to look into my eyes. 'It was better than I ever imagined,' he whispered. 'Now I know why you English call it making love.'

'Have we got time to try it again?' I said coyly, putting down my cup and reaching beneath the covers.

★ ★ ★

The next morning, my skin still tingling, I watched again out of the office window to catch a glimpse of my lover — just thinking the word made me quiver with joy — as he arrived for

205

work. I couldn't stop smiling and I expected him to be the same.

But when the three of them turned the corner into the yard, I could see they were walking in silence, heads down, bodies bowed, feet slouching across the gravel. Stefan's face looked drawn and pale, more like the solemn anxious boy I'd met at the Kindertransport camp. Under his arm was a folded newspaper. Perhaps they had stayed up drinking after Kurt and Walter got back, I tried to reassure myself, and were feeling a bit worse for wear. That was the obvious explanation. I didn't give it much thought, as the morning passed in the usual frenzy of telephone calls and paperwork.

Just before tea break Gwen appeared, knocked and came into the office, pulling the door closed behind her.

'Stefan's not himself today. Has anything happened to him, do you know?'

My heart jumped and I tried to keep the smile from my face. Oh yes, something momentous had happened — to us both.

'What do you mean?' I said, as calmly as possible.

'He's made five mistakes already — we'll have to deduct three yards from just twenty he's woven. He seems to be in a dream.'

I was finding it hard to concentrate, too. No wonder, when hot flushes swelled secret parts of my body without warning. 'Perhaps he's had a bad night,' I said. 'He's pretty anxious after that paint incident. They're really going through it, those boys.'

She interrupted, irritably. 'Would I bother you if I thought he'd just had a bad night? There's something else about him today, can't put my finger on it.'

There was something about her persistent, over-solicitous manner I started to find irritating. Was Gwen testing me? Or even trying to stir things up again?

I forced a smile. 'Don't worry. I'll try to have a word with him at lunchtime. See if anything's troubling him.'

'You'll tell me, won't you, if there's something I should know?'

'Of course,' I lied, to get her out of my office as quickly as possible.

When the lunch klaxon sounded I went to the canteen. Unusually, none of the boys were there, but I assumed perhaps they'd gone into town for something. At afternoon break I walked around the building, past the smoking bench behind the boiler room. They were nowhere to be seen.

Then, as I made my way back to the office I saw them in the distance, walking back across the water meadows, deep in conversation. I was instantly reassured; they'd been out for some fresh air — what an obvious thing to do on such a fine day.

As the day shift clocked off I watched once more out of the office window but the boys did not appear. I went down to the weaving floor. The evening weaver was now at Stefan's looms, so he must have slipped out of the side door and the back gate. I would go to the cottage after dark, and we would talk through anything that was worrying him. All would be well. If the other boys were out, we might even make love again. The thought made my body hot and heavy, and I had to prevent my hand straying down to what Stefan called my *Mäuseloch*. I shivered with pleasure at the memory of his touch, recalling his shy attempts to translate, 'Where the mouse lives, you know, a small dark secret place. So warm.' He still pronounced Ws like Vs.

★ ★ ★

The Chestnuts was quiet as I went through the hallway into the kitchen and I found my parents sitting together at the table. In front of them was a copy of *The Times*. The front page headline read: FRANCE SURRENDERS.

'Terrible news, my dear,' Father said. 'We're all alone in this, now.'

As I leaned over their shoulders to find out more, my eye was caught by another, smaller headline further down the page. MORE ENEMY ALIENS INTERNED — BIG ROUND-UP BY POLICE. It took a moment to sink in.

'Oh no, the boys,' I croaked, starting to run.

When I got to the cottage, a dark blue van was already parked outside and two large men filled the front room: Constable Kilby and another man in plain clothes, with a thin face and eyes like a weasel.

'Remember me? I'm Lily Verner,' I panted, out of breath from running. 'Where are they?'

The constable pointed, and I sprinted up the narrow staircase Stefan and I had climbed just the previous evening. Walter sat on the top step with his head in his hands and Kurt was in their bedroom, in a similar pose. I ran into Stefan's room. On the bed were neatly arrayed his few possessions, and the small leather suitcase with his initials on the lid. The wild flowers in the jam jar were already starting to wilt.

'What's going on?'

His face was dark. 'We're under arrest.'

'What? They're taking you now? Where?'

I tried to hug him but he pushed me away. 'They say we've got to go with them. They won't tell us where.'

'But that's not right. You're category C, aren't you, a refugee? You're no danger.' My head was spinning. Surely it couldn't be allowed?

'They won't listen. They've got orders to take us.'

'All three of you?'

He nodded bleakly.

I couldn't understand. 'Kurt and Walter too?'

'Yes.'

'But Walter's too young.'

'He's sixteen. Already an adult, they said.'

'But where are they taking you?'

'I expect we'll find out.' The same flat tone.

'Let me talk to them.'

'We've tried. But they might listen to you. You're English,' he said, bitterly.

As I ran downstairs Father arrived at the front door. 'What's happening, Lily?' he said.

I pointed towards the back door where the two men now stood outside smoking.

'They're being arrested, all of them,' I said,

trying to keep my voice from trembling. 'We've got to stop it.'

'Leave this to me my love,' he said, straightening his shoulders and walking through the kitchen and through the back door. I followed close behind.

'Now look here, my good fellows,' he said firmly. 'I'd be obliged if you could tell me exactly what's going on.'

Constable Kilby was the first to respond. 'Good afternoon Mr Verner. Sorry we have to meet again in such circumstances. We've got orders to arrest all adult male enemy aliens, sixteen and over. All categories, sir, for internment.' Weasel-face stayed silent. I wondered who he was.

'But they're just boys, Jewish refugees,' I almost shouted. 'What possible harm could they do?' I suddenly remembered Robbie's threat and gave an involuntary shiver. 'Are you acting on some kind of information?'

'Not for us to say, miss. We're just obeying orders.'

'I never heard anything so preposterous,' Father said. 'These lads are skilled workers carrying out essential war work. I can't spare them I'm afraid.'

'Don't matter what they do, sir,' said the constable. 'They're enemy aliens and I've got orders to arrest them.'

'What if I say no?'

'Then I would have to arrest you too, sir, for preventing me from carrying out my duty.'

Father drew himself up so that his eyes were

nearly level with the policeman's chin. 'I have to inform you that I'm personally acquainted with several local magistrates. They will not be impressed with this behaviour.'

Weasel-face now stepped forward and took Father's arm, leading him aside. I moved with them. His voice was like oil. 'Excuse me, sir. But could I ask you to describe exactly what is your relationship with these Germans?'

'I am their employer. My name is Harold Verner and this is my daughter Lily. She also works for me. The boys arrived on the Kindertransport and I have given them a home and jobs in my silk mill just along the road. All above board. We've got papers to prove it.'

'I see. And is it your habit to befriend Germans?' he said, looking across to include me in the question.

'Now look here, this is bloody impertinent.' I'd never heard my father swear before. 'It is absolutely none of your business who we employ.'

'There you are wrong, Mr Verner,' said the man smoothly. 'It is *absolutely* my business. I am charged by the War Ministry to ensure that Constable Kilby carries out the government's new emergency measures regarding the internment of male enemy aliens. I am sure you will understand the sensitivity of the issue, in the current heightened levels of concern about a potential invasion.'

'I understand of course,' Father tempered his voice a little, 'but that won't stop me appealing against this absurd heavy handedness. These are

211

innocent boys and I can vouch for their good character.'

I turned to see that Constable Kilby had gone inside and heard him shouting, 'Get a move on, lads.' The realisation hit me. Not even Father could stop this. They were going to be taken away. We had only a few minutes left. I pushed past the policeman, ran up the stairs into Stefan's room and slammed the door behind me. His suitcase was closed. I sat down on the bed beside him.

'It's so unfair.' I put my arm around his shoulders but he didn't respond, and his body felt cold and ungiving. We sat in silence for a few moments.

He sighed and rubbed his eyes roughly. 'I don't know what we have done wrong.'

'It's just a government precaution. It won't be for long.' My words sounded hollow — I wasn't even convincing myself. 'I might even be able to come and visit you.'

I could feel the seconds ticking away.

He turned and took my face in his hands, looking into my eyes. '*Ich liebe Dich, Lilymaus, vergiss mich nicht.*' It sounded like a sigh.

'I love you too. I'll wait as long as it takes.'

'Will you look after this for me?' He handed me a small black leather writing case.

'What's in it?'

'My photographs and some other precious things my mother gave me. They will be safer with you.'

'I'll guard them with my life,' I said, trying to stop my voice wobbling, to be strong for him.

'Now I know you'll have to come back for them.'

As we kissed, the policeman shouted again. 'Come on lads. Two minutes, or I'll have to come and get you.'

I clutched at him, willing time to stop, trying to capture the feel of his lips, the warmth of his body, the touch of his fingers, the sweet smell of his hair.

'Write to me soon,' I whispered.

'Every day,' he promised.

And then we were downstairs and all of us embracing, and the boys were ushered through the front door by the policeman, each carrying the small suitcases they had arrived with all those months ago. Weasel-face shepherded them towards the van. There was the sound of doors opening, slamming shut. Kurt waving, tears streaking Walter's cheeks, and Stefan's pale face at the window, his eyes soft and sad.

The policeman got into the driver's seat and, as Weasel-face got in beside him, I started towards the front of the van as if by some desperate force of strength I could stop it driving off. Father shouted, 'No, Lily', grabbing my arm and pulling me back. He held me, both arms around me, and we watched in silence as the van accelerated away and disappeared as it turned the corner at the end of the road.

I gripped his hand and leaned on him to prevent myself falling, as if the world had just stopped and I was still turning.

* * *

It was nearly Christmas by the time we heard any more. Six long months during which, alone in my room each night, I tried to relive every moment, every sensation and gesture, every word of our precious last evening together. Six months of wondering where Stefan was and what he was doing, of looking up at the stars and moon, hoping he too could see them and was thinking of me. Six months of half lived days, tearful nights and dreary, painful emptiness, like losing a limb. I avoided going past the cottage. We'd given up the tenancy and its empty windows looked like blank eyes, keeping their sad secrets. I hid Stefan's writing case safely at the back of the drawer in my bedside table.

Father and I tried to find out where they had been sent, but each time we met with a wall of official secrecy. In my worst moments I wondered whether Robbie had told the authorities about the boys, and contemplated the idea of challenging him. But each time, I flunked it. He would deny any involvement, of course, and the last thing I wanted was to give him any cause to feel vindicated or triumphant, or any reason to visit me again. And of course, our contract with Camerons was due for renewal any time now.

But, as the months went by, my conspiracy theories seemed increasingly unlikely. The weary truth was, of course that, like all the Kindertransport children, the boys' names and those of their sponsors were already on some government paperwork somewhere. It was inevitable they would be traced, and it was far too late to change anything now.

Small planes fought in the summer skies, there were desperate battles and devastating air raids, but I felt oddly detached from it all. Churchill tried valiantly to raise our spirits with his speeches. But nothing raised mine, until I received that first small blue aerogramme tightly packed with Stefan's neat, curlicued handwriting.

Hay Camp, Australia   *7th October 1940*

My Dearest Lilymaus
   I hope you are well and this letter reaches you safely. You may be surprised to hear that I am in Australia. How we got here is too long to write. Many trains and buses, then on a dreadful overcrowded ship called Dunera for two months. It was very hard, but we survived and landed here three weeks ago.
   We are in a camp locked up like criminals — kosher butchers, Italian waiters, Austrian accordion players and boys like us! But we have enough to eat and are treated well. After the journey Australia is like heaven.
   Have you ever been in a desert? It is hot and the sand blows into everything but I did not expect it to be beautiful. Every morning flocks of green parrots fly over our camp, and the sunsets are like the colours of silk — gold, red, purple and blue. Last night the sky shimmered like shot silk. When the stars come out, they are upside down!
   The worst thing is being so far away from

you, my lovely Lily. I think of us on our island together, watching the sky. Or in 'our' tennis hut! It is hard to bear, especially at night. I pray you are safe and well. Please write if you can.

Ich liebe Dich, Dien Stefan x x x x

15

The medieval age of chivalry was an age of silk. Epic poems of gallantry and heroic deeds were circulated by wandering troubadours, tournaments were bedecked with silk-hung tents and banners, and rich silks caparisoned the horses. Knights received a silken sleeve or veil as a 'gage', a token of honour from the lady symbolically defended in the joust.
From *The History of Silk,* **by Harold Verner**

Christmas 1940 was only enlivened by the arrival of John, who had been given a few days leave, and Vera, who caught the last train out of London on Christmas Eve and had to stand all the way. They were both exhausted, and when we asked John about the bombing raids he clammed up. When Vera wasn't with us at The Chestnuts he spent most of the time sleeping.

I spent much of the time in bed too, wrapped up against the cold, reading and re-reading the three precious aerogrammes that had arrived from Stefan, my few tenuous links with the boy who consumed my thoughts. At least he was safe, tucked away in the Australian desert and well away from war, I reasoned, even though his absence made an aching gap in my life. We were all glad when Christmas was over so that we could stop pretending that we were enjoying ourselves and get back to work. But we should have treasured every moment.

It was just a few days later, and early morning, when the measured rings sounded insistently through our sleepy house. I met Father on the landing, still in his pyjamas. 'Go back to bed, I'll get it,' I said, heading downstairs, wrapping my dressing gown tight against the winter chill.

The woman at the other end of the phone was flustered. 'Is that Grace?'

'No, it's Lily. Who's this?'

'Beryl. From the London office.'

'Beryl. Of course. Good morning,' I said, taken aback. She usually sounded so calm and efficient.

'Have you been listening to the news?'

'No, not yet.' I glanced at the grandfather clock. It was ten past seven.

'Is Harold awake? I need to speak to him. There's been a hell of a raid. They say Cheapside's been hit.' I sat down heavily on the hall chair to catch my breath. This could be a disaster. The London office housed not only hundreds of precious customer files and accounts ledgers, but also the Verners archive of silk samples, dating back two hundred years.

Father was coming downstairs in his red paisley dressing gown. 'Who is it?'

'Beryl. She says the office might have been bombed.'

He took the receiver and spoke calmly into it. 'Beryl, good morning. Harold here.' As he listened his face, already shadowed with morning stubble, turned greyer still.

'Have you rung anyone else? The police?' I

couldn't hear her reply.

'There's nothing else for it, then. I'm on my way.' Then, more firmly. 'No Beryl, you are absolutely not to go. I can handle it. Stay at home and I'll telephone you as soon as I know anything further.'

He put the receiver carefully into its cradle and turned to Mother and me, steadying himself with a hand on the telephone table. 'It doesn't look good,' he said. 'All Beryl knows is the radio report of a huge raid — the biggest yet, they're saying — and direct hits on the City. They mentioned Cheapside and a dozen other streets. She's tried the police but no one's answering.' He glanced at the clock. 'If I hurry I can catch the eight thirty.'

'You must have a cooked breakfast before you go, my darling.'

'Don't fuss, Grace. Tea and toast will do.' As he turned to climb the stairs his shoulders sagged and his usually firm step seemed tentative and weary. Something inside me clicked.

'I'm coming with you,' I said.

'I'm not sure, Lily, it could be unpleasant.'

'You'll need me even more if that's the case.'

He paused, then nodded his assent. 'Wrap up warm then, my darling.'

At breakfast we listened to Alvar Liddell's portentous news: '*More than thirty German aircraft were destroyed in last night's raids over London. The raids lasted several hours and incendiary bombs caused over a thousand fires. Many are still burning despite the valiant efforts of our fire services, whose work has been hampered by broken water mains and an unusually low tide in the River Thames.'*

* * *

The railway carriage was packed with business-people, and servicemen returning to their units after the Christmas break. There was an air of almost ghoulish excitement as they exchanged stories.

'Literally hundreds of the buggers this time, they said.'

'The ack-acks didn't stand a chance.'

'Don't seem to be able to stop them, do we?'

'Did you hear about the food storage warehouses that were hit the other night?' one said.

'Apparently all the little urchins were out collecting peanuts that had been roasted in the fire,' the other replied, and they both laughed, mirthlessly.

'And what about all those butter rations that got melted? There were rivers of the stuff, they said. The housewives were out scraping it off the roads.'

'Don't blame them, must be grim.'

'There's not enough rescue workers. People are dying under the rubble.'

'Any news on casualties?'

As their conversation ebbed and flowed I watched the morning mist slowly lifting over small villages, farms, fields and woodland, all so calm and apparently unaffected by war, and wondered gloomily how long we could hold out.

Would the landscape look different under German control? Would they straighten out the roads and hedges, make everything symmetrical for greater efficiency? I missed Stefan, but for the moment I was glad that he and the other boys were safely interned, away from the threat.

Father looked up from his newspaper. 'I should have moved them out of London sooner,' he said quietly.

'You mustn't blame yourself,' I whispered back. 'No one's been hurt, as far as we know.'

The head office of Verners and Sons, Silk Merchants, had operated in London since 1740: first in Spitalfields and for the past fifty years in the City, dealing with customers at home and overseas, buying and selling raw and woven silk, and managing the financial controls and audit. To the London staff, Westbury was merely the manufacturing end of the business. When the bombing started, Father had suggested they leave London, but they had been reluctant to move out to 'the sticks'. As the air raids became more devastating, he had insisted. Just before Christmas they had packed up the office ready to move in January, just a few days' time. And now this.

The sun started to break through, but towards London the sky became dulled with a yellowish haze of smoke. The train edged into Liverpool Street Station even more tentatively than usual and, as we arrived, we could see why. The station was in complete confusion. The platforms were so jammed with people trying to get on trains leaving London that it was almost impossible to

221

get off the train. We pressed on through the crowds towards the tube station, but when we got there we could see at the entrance a hastily handwritten sign: *Closed due to Bombing*. At the bus depot, a dozen red double-deckers were parked, going nowhere. The taxi rank was empty.

'Looks like we're on Shanks's pony,' Father said. 'Are you up for it?'

I nodded. I'd walked the route to Cheapside with him just a couple of months ago, it was just a few streets away. 'Only takes ten minutes, doesn't it?'

But as we came out of the station we stopped in our tracks. The streets were unrecognisable, transformed into piles of rubble, punctured by craters and broken buildings. Our eyes searched for familiar landmarks, but there were none. It looked like a foreign place. The city had been remodelled. It was chaotic, reminding me of the terrifying Old Testament depictions of hell in the colour plates of our ancient family Bible.

Father took my hand and squeezed it. I squeezed his back, too stunned for words.

My thoughts could barely keep up with the horrors my eyes were witnessing. In some places, the interiors of what had once been offices were exposed where external walls had been ripped away, some of them strangely untouched, with desks and cabinets, curtains and carpets still in place.

On the top floor of a building to our left there was a kitchen, complete with cooker and fridge, chairs set in their places around the table still laid with blue and white striped plates and a matching fruit bowl, as though its occupants had just left the room. Next door was a bathroom with the mirror hanging above the basin, towels on their rails, bizarrely undisturbed.

On the other side of the road a bus had been thrown, like a toy discarded by a careless giant, coming to rest on its side against a wall. Through its crazed, charred windows we could see the rows of seats still in place. I prayed no one had been on board.

After several moments Father cleared his throat.

'Ruddy hell,' he said. 'Do you think we can find our way through this mess?'

I wanted to run away, to pretend we had never witnessed these terrifying scenes, but heard myself saying, 'We've got to get to Cheapside somehow.'

We started to walk again, and the sheer effort of concentration needed to pick our way among the debris helped push the fear to the back of my mind. The air was filled with cloying, suffocating mortar dust and the acrid, choking smoke of fires still burning among the rubble, like some kind of infernal underworld. In places I had to hold my coat sleeve to my nose because of the sickening stench of raw sewage from broken drains. We became covered, like everything and everyone else, in black smuts and grey dust.

At almost every corner were roadblocks. When Father approached a policeman to ask which route we should take, he answered with weary resignation.

'Your guess is as good as mine, sir. It's a

bugger's muddle just about everywhere.' He regarded us with sad eyes. 'I wouldn't bother, if I were you, with the young lady and all.'

Father turned to me. 'Do you want to turn back?'

I shook my head. 'Not now we've come this far. What about you?'

'I'd never have brought you if I'd known. I can't believe the office can have escaped damage in this lot,' he said.

'We're here to find out, aren't we?' I said, trying to keep my spirits up. 'It can't be far now. Let's carry on.'

In one place — it must have been Threadneedle Street — dozens of people, children and adults, swarmed over the ruins of a destroyed building, apparently unafraid of collapses and unexploded bombs. The police and air raid wardens were trying to keep order, but it was an impossible task. As they shooed one group away others clambered onto the wreckage behind them.

'What are they looking for?' I asked a warden.

'Money,' he said, with a resigned sigh. 'Happens every time a bank gets hit. We can't control them. But the vaults are safe under the rubble, there's not usually much to be had.'

A small boy ran past triumphantly waving a bent coin, heading towards a caravan with a blackboard advertising, *Tea ½d, toast with butter 1d*.

'Let's have a cuppa,' Father said, 'I'll get them.'

I sat on a broken wall and, as I waited, my eye

was caught by a rescue worker who crouched down to pick up something that looked like part of a shop dummy. With rising revulsion I realised that that it was in fact a human hand, a very pale, slender hand with rings on the fingers, stopping abruptly at the wrist, cleanly, with no blood. I wanted to turn away but my gaze seemed unwillingly fixed. The man appeared almost unmoved. Still crouching, he gently eased the rings from the fingers, put them into a brown envelope, wrote something on it with a stub of pencil, and put it into his pocket. He wrapped the hand in a strip of white sheeting and carefully placed it into his shoulder bag before standing up to continue his search.

All this he executed in the most matter-of-fact way. No one else seemed to have noticed, and I could barely believe what I'd seen. This was the hand of a real woman, whose body was probably buried in the rubble, I thought, with a shiver. Till last night she had been going about her daily life, working, eating, sleeping, trying to have a bit of fun in spite of the war. Now, in an instant, all that was wiped out. Her family had lost a sister, wife or mother. They would learn this from the rings, I supposed, but what was left of her body might never be identified. How many other dead or dying people lay concealed under these anonymous piles of bricks and mortar? I found myself scanning the wreckage, gruesomely fascinated, afraid to see other body parts.

Father returned with two steaming mugs. 'Are you all right my dear?' he asked anxiously. 'You look as though you've seen a ghost.'

225

'I think I have,' I said, standing to take the cup from him. The hot sweet tea burning my throat was a welcome reminder that I was still alive, still capable of feeling. Father pressed me to tell him what was wrong, and as I described what I'd seen, my legs started to tremble uncontrollably. He sat me down again, gave me his handkerchief and held me against his solid, reassuring bulk until the sobs stopped.

'I wish I could protect you from this, my darling.' With my head against his chest his voice was a deep, comforting rumble. 'But it won't last forever, and we'll see it through together, you and me.'

'I love you, Father,' I said, raising my head to kiss his cheek and realising that it was the first time, as an adult, that I'd told him.

He squeezed me tighter. 'My precious girl. I love you too. It means so much, having you working with me. Couldn't do it without you. It's the only good thing about this bloody war.'

'I wish it was over.' I said, feeling tearful again.

'We'll get through it together, my darling,' he said. 'John will come home safely and we'll all get back to normal. You'll see.'

I wished that I could believe him, that these weren't just empty words to comfort me. We had to cling on to some kind of hope, I supposed, even in the middle of this desperate hopelessness.

We fell into silence as we finished our tea.

'Okay to carry on?' he asked.

I nodded.

'Onwards and upwards then?' he said. 'Let's see what the Huns have done to our office.'

226

* ★ *

At first, Cheapside seemed to have escaped the worst of the bombing. As we rounded the Mansion House corner and peered down Poultry, only a few buildings appeared to be damaged. In the distance, shrouded in smoke, we could see the outline of St Paul's Cathedral dome, like a mirage. It was hard to believe it could still be intact.

'Look at that,' I said, pointing at the dome, 'must be a good sign, surely?'

Father nodded. 'Let's hope and pray so.'

We skirted heaps of debris and picked our way down the road. We negotiated the King Street junction, counting the door numbers as we walked: fifteen, seventeen, nineteen, twenty-one. That block was intact. We passed Bread Street and Milk Street. Twenty-three, twenty-five, twenty-seven, twenty-nine, thirty-one. I stopped walking to peer ahead through the dusty air and my heart sank. Where numbers thirty-nine to forty-three should have been was a great gap, like a missing tooth.

'It's forty-one.' Father's voice was thick with shock. We stumbled forward and then stopped, dumbstruck, at the base of a pyramid of brick, timber and stone that for the past fifty years had been the head office of Verners and Sons. The back wall towered perilously over the ruins. There were jagged holes in the adjoining walls of the buildings still standing on either side.

I looked at Father. He seemed hollowed out and unsteady, as if a gust of wind could blow him over. I took his hand but he said nothing, distracted and unresponsive. I wondered what to do next — surely we should call for help? And then I realised there was nothing to be done. The building was utterly demolished, and everything with it. We could only be grateful that because the raid had been at night, it was unlikely anyone had been inside. Had they been, they would never have survived.

Just at that moment I caught a flash of colour out of the corner of my eye. Someone in a red coat was clambering over the ruins. Father saw it too, and jumped as if he'd been given an electric shock. He pulled away from my hand, and started to run towards the pile of rubble, shouting 'Beryl!' then, more desperately, 'Get off there, Beryl, it's not safe.'

The woman turned, her face grey with dust, and called back. 'I can see the boxes, Harold. They're just here.' She pointed and started to scrabble frantically in the rubble.

Just then there was a quiet, almost imperceptible rumble, like distant thunder. A few lumps of mortar toppled from the high wall of the next door building, crashing like hammer blows onto the rubble below, sending up a new cloud of choking mortar dust.

Father stopped at the base of the mound, coughing and trying to fan the dust away with his hands. I ran to his side, holding my sleeve over my arm.

As the air cleared we could see Beryl, apparently undeterred, still on her knees, pulling up bricks and throwing them to one side, careless of her own discomfort and danger. We both knew that it was hopeless, but she was like a woman possessed. She seemed transfixed by some vain, desperate hope of excavating the precious boxes she had so carefully packed just a few days before.

'For heaven's sake, come down Beryl,' Father shouted again. 'Leave them. It's too dangerous.'

I looked around for anyone who could help, but the nearest people were many yards away, well out of yelling distance. There was a short moment of silence, and then another heart-sinking rumble. We all looked up as one or two more bricks fell down, landing in an apparently random way. Beryl at last seemed to have regained her senses and started scrambling back down towards us.

There was a sudden, deafening thunder crack as more bricks came smashing down.

'Watch out!' My scream echoed off the walls of the buildings. For a second, Beryl looked towards us, her face pale and expressionless.

I thought they had landed well away from her but then to our horror she started to topple, in a lingering, unhurried way, as if in a slow-motion movie. For a moment I thought she'd just missed her footing, but then she was lying horribly still, sprawled face down. Her coat was like a sickening splash of blood across the greyness, reminding me of the red paint daubed on the door of the boys' cottage so many months ago.

It was a second before either of us could comprehend what had happened.

'Bloody hell, she's been hit.' Father bellowed,

stumbling forward to the base of the mound of rubble, starting to clamber upwards towards her still form. I ran after him, trying to grab his hand and stop him. But he was powered with the strength of a desperate man, and easily pulled away from me.

'Stop, Father. It's not safe. For God's sake. Stop.' I looked around, panicky, for anyone, a policeman or a warden. 'Help, we need help,' I screamed, again, but the street seemed to be completely deserted.

My mind went blank and, by some kind of reflex, without instruction from my brain or any conscious awareness of the danger I was in, my legs started to run towards him again. My only thought was to pull him away to safety.

The rubble was jagged and vicious. Pausing for a second to catch my breath I noticed in a detached way, as if observing someone else, that my hands and knees were bleeding. But I felt no pain.

Ahead of me, at the top of the mountain, I saw Father reach Beryl's prostrate form. He crouched down and turned her over gently. He lifted her head and cradled it on his knees, brushing strands of dark hair from her dust-covered face. Her arms fell limply by her side, like a rag doll.

He looked up and shouted, 'Get help, Lily. She's injured. She needs medical attention.'

'It's too dangerous to stay there, Father. Come down, please,' I shouted back.

'I can't leave her here,' he said. 'Help me get her down.'

I was just starting to climb again when we

both heard a much louder and longer rumble than before. It shook the ground like an earthquake.

'Get down, Father. Now. Come away,' I screamed, but my words were lost in the roar. Instinctively recoiling and squinting up between my hands I could see another slab of the back wall starting to move. I closed my eyes and held my breath as it crashed, like a great clap of thunder, onto the rubble below, throwing up another cloud of impenetrable, choking dust.

When I could see again Father was still several yards away, crouched over Beryl, straining to lift her, apparently oblivious to the mortal danger he had just escaped.

'Come away, Father. Please. Come down,' I yelled again, coughing in the dust. He took no notice, still struggling to pick up Beryl's floppy, lifeless body. I started to scramble towards him again. There was nothing else to do. I had to grab him and physically manhandle him to safety.

Then I heard the loudest noise of all, like the deep, guttural growl of an angered creature. Above us, a crack appeared in the back wall and grew wider. I screamed again at Father and then cowered and covered my head with my arms. It went quiet for a few seconds and I turned my head sideways to look upwards. Almost silently now, the crack grew bigger still and I could see the sky starting to show through it like jagged blue lightning.

I watched in horror as a huge slab of wall gradually detached itself in slow motion, pivoting ninety degrees from the vertical to the horizontal. Then it started to fall, flat and intact, like the floor of a giant lift speeding down towards us, and blotting out the sky.

I heard myself calling out again. Even now I imagined that we could both escape. My head told my limbs to run but my body felt like a lump of concrete. For a long, agonising moment the world went still. Nothing moved.

I was pinioned to the ground by a massive blast of air.

And then the world went black.

★ ★ ★

When I opened my eyes I was in a white bed, in a white room. My head hurt horribly, and I closed my eyes again. Someone touched my shoulder and a familiar voice whispered, 'Lily. Wake up. Open your eyes. It's me, Vera.'

I tried to say hello, but it came out as a groan. My head felt like a lump of lead, heavy and numb.

'You're in hospital. Gave me such a shock, just came on duty and there you were, being wheeled in. You're safe now. If you count being nursed by me as safe.'

She shook my shoulder again, gently, coaxing, 'Come on, open your eyes. It's me, Vera.'

Time seemed to pass, and when I looked again, she was still there.

'Thank goodness. We thought you'd gone again,' she said, confusingly.

'Mm schtill hrr.' I couldn't open my mouth.

Moving my jaw felt as though hot needles were piercing the side of my face and poking into my brain.

'Yes, you're still here,' she said, stroking my hand. 'You've got concussion and your face is a bit battered, but otherwise you're not seriously injured, thank heavens.'

A little later someone helped me drink sweet tea through a straw. It tasted delicious.

'Whrs Vra?'

'She's coming to see you soon, Lily,' said a soothing voice.

The next time I regained consciousness, I was propped up against the pillows looking at the dark bulky forms of two men standing at the end of my bed. Vera was holding my hand, talking softly.

'Lily?'

'Mmm.'

'Can you remember anything?'

'Nhnh.'

'There was a collapse, at Cheapside. Remember? Your father was there, and Beryl, you know, from the London office.'

'Huh?' The wall, the wall was tumbling down. Oh god, now I remembered it falling, the blackness. 'Fthr?' I whimpered.

'I'm afraid they didn't make it,' said Vera's gentle voice.

Then a man's deep intonation, 'Your father was very brave. He died a hero, Miss Verner. He was trying to save Mrs Madeley, the warden told us.'

I closed my eyes. If I can keep breathing,

in-out, in-out, in-out, in-out, this moment will go away, I will not have heard these words, these things will not have happened.

'I'm sure he didn't suffer,' Vera said softly. 'There was nothing the ambulance men could do. He was dead when they reached him. Beryl too.'

They must have sedated me at this point, because I recall nothing more until I woke up again.

'Whrs fther?' I asked the nurse who was offering me more tea. My face still ached horribly and talking properly was impossible. She looked at me oddly. 'Can't you remember the policemen who came yesterday? What they told you?'

I was baffled. How did she know what my nightmare was about?

'Vera will be back in a bit, she'll come and have a word with you,' she said calmingly.

Vera sat by my bedside and explained it all again. I closed my eyes and listened, but couldn't bring myself to believe her. Eventually I opened my eyes, and the sight of her drawn, anxious face made me understand that what she was saying was true. The realisation welled up with a rushing sound in my ears, my body started to shake and my head filled with pain. Then the tears came. I couldn't stop. She sat on the bed and held me, rocked me in her arms for hours, it seemed. When she had to leave, the void opened and the agony flooded back. Eventually, exhausted and wrung dry with weeping I slept, only to wake and face the nightmare all over again.

Each day she found time between her busy

shifts to visit me on the ward. She talked to me, trying to distract me from my misery. I could not imagine a world without my father, but she told me again and again that people loved me and I would come through it. Life has to carry on, she said. I didn't believe her.

I couldn't understand why Mother hadn't come to see me, when I needed her most. Her gentle touch had healed many a childhood hurt. Each day at visiting time, I was disappointed.

'Hws mther?' I asked Vera.

'She's a bit poorly to travel,' she said. 'Gwen's staying with her.'

Gwen? 'Where's John?'

'We've sent a message to his squadron. He'll be home as soon as he can.'

She told me a brick must have hit the side of my head. It had broken my jaw, which they'd wired together. They fed me soup and flavoured milk through a straw.

On the fourth day she asked if I was ready to look at myself, and when I nodded, she got out her powder compact and opened the small mirror. I barely recognised the face peering back, it was so grotesquely swollen and purple and yellow with bruises.

'Will I ever look human again?' I muttered, close to tears. She hugged me. 'You'll heal, Lily. Inside and out. I promise.'

★ ★ ★

As Gwen approached down the long ward and drew nearer, I could see her adjusting her expression, trying to control her reaction to my disfigurement. But her embrace was warm, and her smell familiar and comforting.

'Thanks for coming,' I mumbled.

'Oh, you poor dear thing, does it hurt to talk?' She sat down on the bed, defying the notice on the wall.

I nodded. 'How's Mother?'

'Taking it hard, stays in bed mostly. Says she's too exhausted to get up,' she said, taking my hand in hers. We might not have been the best of friends of late, but I realised now how much I'd missed her. 'When I told her I was coming to see you, she said to give you a hug, send you all her love, hopes you'll understand.'

Imagining Mother struggling to cope, not even able to get out of bed, I slowly started to comprehend the devastation she too must be suffering. She was usually so active, enthusiastic, full of life. I had been so wrapped up in my own tragedy I hadn't stopped to think about how it would affect others. At least I'd been there, witnessed Father's heroism, and that was some kind of consolation. For everyone else, it would feel as though he'd just walked out of their lives. That strong constant presence, on whom so many relied, had simply evaporated into thin air.

'I'm trying to get her involved in planning the funeral,' Gwen said carefully. 'Give her something to think about, that she can do for him.'

A funeral. The word was a shock. My father's funeral.

'We're just hoping John will get back soon,' she went on. 'Latest is that he could be home in a week. But I'm afraid you may not be mended in time.'

His body would be buried. The very idea hurt so much I'd shut it out. It felt surreal, so far removed from the cocoon of this hospital ward.

Vera arrived with cups of tea she'd wheedled from the kitchen. 'Gwen's been a tower of strength,' she said. 'Looking after your mum, running the mill, sorting out the accounts that were destroyed. A Trojan.'

'It's what anyone would do,' said Gwen quietly. 'Harold and Grace gave me a second chance. Time to return the favour.'

She reached into her handbag. 'Nearly forgot,' and pulled out four blue aerogrammes. My heart leapt. 'Presents from Australia,' she said, smiling.

Throughout these weeks of misery my single, constant consolation had been the thought of Stefan, safe in his Australian desert, away from the mayhem. Holding these precious letters, seeing his curly handwriting, the surge of relief brought tears swelling up and overflowing down my cheeks. Wiping them away, gingerly, with the back of my hand, I checked the postmark dates and ripped open the most recent, quickly scanned the words and the sign-off: *Ich liebe Dich, meine Lilymaus, S.* With a row of crosses for kisses.

'How are they getting on? Are they okay?' Vera asked.

'Looks like it,' I said, sniffing, trying to smile. 'Still behind wire, in the desert.'

'Poor things,' she said quietly. I put the letters under my pillow for savouring later, when I could be alone.

As Gwen and Vera sat beside my bed and chatted about everyday things, the mill and the workers, Robbie's recent renewal of the Camerons contract and the pressure he was putting on them, the latest news of the war, I realised Vera was right: life would carry on. I just had to get better and try to be strong for my mother.

★　★　★

It was five weeks before they finally agreed that I was well enough to leave hospital. Gwen came to help me home; I was too wobbly to manage it on my own. As we took a cab back to the station — a luxury she insisted on paying for — I could hardly bear to look out of the window at the devastated city. It was like revisiting a nightmare. Every pile of rubble in every street reminded me of the one Father had died in, like ancient burial mounds for countless anonymous innocent people who had been trying to get on with their everyday lives.

Eventually the sight and the memories overwhelmed me and I collapsed, weeping, in Gwen's arms in the back of the cab. The driver sighed sympathetically. He'd seen it all before, a hundred times.

When we arrived home the weather was gloomy and cold and the atmosphere at The Chestnuts deeply sombre. On the train Gwen told me that though Mother had got out of bed for the funeral she had, since then, literally 'turned her face to the wall' as Gwen put it.

I didn't fully comprehend what she meant

until I saw it for myself,

'Mother? It's me, Lily. I'm here.' The bedroom curtains were closed. Through the gloom I could just make out her figure, curled up in a foetal position with her back to the room.

'Look at me, Mother.' I sat on the bed and rubbed her bony shoulders, stroked her greying unkempt hair. Her eyes were open and the tears fell silently, wetting the pillow. I leaned over and kissed her.

'Mother?' I said again. But she would not, or could not, respond. I wiped away her tears and for half an hour I simply talked; about the accident, about how brave Father had been trying to save Beryl, about my jaw, and my scar, and my good fortune in ending up at Vera's hospital.

I cried too, then pulled myself together. I asked about the funeral, about the hundreds of people who attended, so many it was standing room only. But nothing seemed to register. Eventually I went downstairs to make tea.

'Is she like this all the time?' I asked. 'Has the doctor been?'

'Yes, Dr Fairweather came and prescribed something called Mist. Pot. Brom., but she refused to take it,' John said. 'We're at our wit's end.'

'He said it would take a while,' Gwen said, pouring the tea. 'He advised us to just talk to her as much as possible, and make sure she eats well. But she's hardly got any appetite, and making anything tasty is almost impossible on these miserable rations. There's nothing in the kitchen garden.'

'Gwen's been wonderful, but it's not fair to expect her to carry on like this,' John said. 'I've been thinking we might have to hire a nurse. Do you mind staying just a little longer, Gwen?'

'It's the least I can do for Grace,' Gwen said, smiling in her calm, reassuring way, the freckles crinkling around her eyes.

'Let's leave it a day or two, John. I can't think straight right now,' I said. I was sure Mother would come around, now that I was home to look after her, but I was wrong. A week passed, and there was little change. She still refused to leave her bed. The doctor came again, described it as 'nervous exhaustion resultant from extreme shock'. He wasn't optimistic. 'We must give it time, perhaps quite a long time. She's going to need all the love and support you can give.'

I wrote to Stefan twice a week, describing the minutiae of my life — in the hospital, and now at home. I hoped it would keep his spirits up, to hear that life was going on, even if he was stuck in his desert isolation. He wrote back when he could. There was only a weekly collection from Hay Camp, writing paper was in scarce supply, and post frequently went missing, unaccounted for.

But twelve treasured blue aerogrammes were now carefully stored in my bedside drawer, alongside the black writing case he'd entrusted to me. I was frequently tempted to look inside but something stopped me from prying. Apart from the photos he'd showed me, I knew it contained other small mementoes from his family. Keeping the bag safe was my way of helping to protect them, safe for the time when they might all meet again. I didn't want to break the spell by opening it.

I so wanted to see him and hold him, and hated the idea of those thousands of miles between us. The longing made my bones ache. Each night before going to sleep I would read his letters, repeating my favourite sentences over and over again like a mantra, and they comforted me.

16

Experiments with artificial fibres before and during the Second World War led to the production of nylon parachute fabrics which eventually became more widely used, especially for paratroops and drops of cargo. However, silk remained the fabric of choice among pilots and crews of fighter planes because of its ability to compact into small spaces and to recover its shape instantly.
From *The History of Silk*, **by Harold Verner**

We hired a daily help to keep an eye on Mother so that I could go back to work for a few hours each day. She remained in her room, refusing to get dressed, come down for meals, or even open the curtains.

When I suggested that sunlight would make her feel better she said, 'What is there to see? More reminders. I can't face it.'

Perhaps giving in to sadness is the best way for her, I wondered. Allowing herself to grieve properly. But for me, the distraction of going into the mill each day seemed to help. My strength was returning and it was a relief to go back to something like normal life. But it felt strange without Father. His office remained untouched. By avoiding going into it, I could almost persuade myself that he'd just gone away for a few weeks.

'Snifter hour,' John announced one afternoon after work. 'Come into the sitting room, both of you, we need a confab.' Gwen and I sat on the sofa as he fixed the drinks. As he approached, holding the drinks tray, my stomach lurched. For a fleeting, disturbing moment, something about the set of his shoulders made me think he was Father.

'Lily?' he said, handing me a glass. 'You okay?'

'I'm fine,' I said, taking a long swig. Gin and tonic reminded me of sunnier times. Of times when I felt safe. When I assumed that both of my parents would live into comfortable old age. Of times without war.

'Cheers,' John said. 'It's good to see you looking better, Sis. You seem nearly back to normal.'

'Thanks to the two of you,' I said. As we raised our glasses I was totally unprepared for what came next.

'Look chaps, I need to talk to you about something,' John said, sitting down in Father's easy chair opposite us. He fumbled in his jacket pocket and pulled out an envelope. 'I got this from my squadron leader today,' he said. 'They want to know when I plan to return.'

I was horrified. 'You're not going back to flying? Not after everything that's happened?'

He nodded, avoiding my eyes.

'You can't,' I said firmly. 'That's just ridiculous. We need you here. How are we going to run the place without you?'

'You'd be fine,' he said. 'You're more than capable.'

'And have you told Vera? I don't suppose she's

very happy about the idea either.'

'She doesn't want me to go, of course,' he said. 'But I tried to explain. They need me. Planning a big push, apparently,' he said casually.

He turned to Gwen. 'You and Lily can run the mill between you, don't you think?'

I looked at her, checking her reaction, but her expression was non-committal. 'Don't get me involved,' she said, 'this is between you two.'

'Don't try to make Gwen take sides,' I said, angrily. 'You're crazy even to consider the idea. Can't you see how selfish you're being?' I pointed at the ceiling. 'Anyway, who's going to look after Mother?'

John smiled wryly. 'I mentioned it to Vera the other day but she snapped my head off.'

'You asked her to give up nursing to come and look after your mother?' I could hardly believe the nerve of him.

'Yup. Told her I'd be happier if she was out of London, away from the bombs. Boy, was she cross.' He mimicked an angry Vera, ' 'Don't you have any idea about what we do, how important it is? Patching up your boys and sending them back to fight your bloody war? Without us you'd have no army, no air force, no navy.' I was duly reprimanded.'

'What if you get killed? Mother couldn't take any more. It would destroy her.'

'Steady on, old girl,' he said calmly. 'Of course it's dangerous, but it doesn't mean I don't intend on coming home in one piece. I'm a good pilot. I've flown two dozen raids already. I don't take risks.'

'No one can guarantee that, and you know it. Anyway, it's completely unfair of you even to think about leaving us to manage here, after all that's happened,' I said, standing up and starting to stomp out of the room. 'I'm going to check on the supper.'

Later, we ate in virtual silence and I went to my bedroom immediately afterwards. I needed time to myself, to clear my head. Was John being totally unreasonable, or was it me, expecting more than he could give?

There was a gentle tap on the door. 'Lily? Are you awake?'

Before I had time to respond, Gwen was in the room. She sat on the side of my bed and sighed slightly.

'If John's determined to go, I think we can manage, don't you?'

'I suppose he's sent you to persuade me?' I said, tetchily.

'Give me more credit,' she snapped.

'It's quite simple,' I said. 'I don't want him killed. Don't you know the bomber casualty figures? They're horrendous.'

She nodded. 'I do know. But in the end it's his choice. He wants to go. Says it's his duty, feels guilty his crew's flying raids without him. We shouldn't make him feel guilty the other way, for leaving us.'

'What about Mother?'

'You and I can care for her. Between us. I want to help. I owe so much to Harold; to both of them.'

'I can't cope here on my own,' I said. 'I really

can't. It makes me panicky just thinking about it.'

'What if I stay in the house, for a while?' she said, gently.

'You wouldn't mind? What about your lovely little flat?'

'There's nothing I'd like more,' she said, 'I love this place.'

'It's not only that. I don't feel confident about running the mill. I've only been there eighteen months and I've never been in charge. It's too much responsibility.'

'C'mon Lily. You're perfectly capable. You know that. I don't want John to go back either but, if he has to, we'll manage just fine. Besides, weaving parachute silk's hardly difficult.'

Why was she so confident, I wondered? Then it dawned on me; she'd already managed single-handedly while I was in hospital, before John came home. So perhaps, just perhaps, it would be possible. If we did it together.

'What about those meetings and committees? The Silk Association, Ministry of Supply?' I'd looked at Father's diary, seen all the dates coming up, assumed John would attend them.

'You'll just have to go instead, won't you?' she said. 'Shake 'em up a bit to have a woman attending. You might even enjoy it.'

'But what would I call myself?'

'Acting Managing Director, silly,' she said, smiling.

'Crikey.' Acting Managing Director. It sounded alarming, but exciting too. And then I remembered my promise to Father, the day after John left. It was my side of the bargain, to do whatever he asked of me, to help win this horrible war and bring back John, Stefan and all the others home safely. My mind was made up.

'We'll have to change the company name,' Gwen said.

'What do you mean?'

'How does Verners and Sons and Daughter sound?'

'That's just loopy,' I said, laughing, and then I realised it wasn't quite so ridiculous after all. 'Come to think of it, why not?'

'We'll get the sign writers onto it right away.' She hugged me. 'It'll be all right, you know. We can do this.' For the first time, I started to believe her.

★　★　★

I was nervous about the meeting, but summer had arrived and in spite of terrible news from Russia and the Far East, the bombings on London had almost ceased and I couldn't help feeling cheerful. That morning in my bedroom mirror I'd seen a businesswoman, young but determined in her navy blue jacket and pencil skirt, with a newly pressed white blouse — all bought with my saved-up clothing coupons. Make-up almost concealed the scar on my jaw and I'd grown my hair longer to cover it.

I took out Father's Silk Association tie pin and fixed it to my lapel. He would be proud of me, I thought. We were producing everything the Ministry of Supply wanted us to, playing our

247

small part in saving airmen's lives. In the past six months I had grown in confidence, learned so much.

Now I was about to test myself again.

'How do I look?'

Gwen leaned forward and plucked a loose thread of silk from my sleeve that I must have picked up from brushing past a loom. 'Very smart, Miss Verner. You'll wow those stuffy old businessmen.' She sniffed the air. 'You smell nice, too. Chanel No 5?'

'Stole a dab of Mother's. Will you be all right with her today?' Six months on from Father's death, Mother still rarely left her room. In my darker moments I wondered if she would ever fully recover.

'We'll be fine,' Gwen said. 'Make sure you're back for supper. We've got meat pie tonight, as a special treat. Make a change from carrots and turnips. And don't forget the new series of *It's That Man Again* on the radio. I'll have another go at getting Grace to come downstairs and listen with us. Tommy Handley will cheer us all up. He's such a funny guy.'

'You're a real pal,' I told Gwen. 'If I survive the stuffy old businessmen I'll deserve a drink too. Let's crack open a bottle of Frank's cider, shall we?'

'Sounds good. Now off you go and don't worry about us,' Gwen said, with a brush of her lips on my cheek.

I hadn't been to London since the accident so it was a difficult moment, arriving at Liverpool Street Station. I had to steel myself to get out of the train and walk along the platform, trying not to think about that day. Father and I had given each other the courage to carry on. Now I had to do it on my own.

The devastation in the streets was still horribly evident but the piles of rubble had been pushed aside to clear the roads, filling the gaps where buildings used to be. I was grateful to find the buses running, and managed to get a seat on the top deck.

As we came to the West End the sun came out. The plane trees were in leaf and hundreds of people were out enjoying the parks; men working on newly dug allotments, families playing, soldiers with their girls, and office workers sunning themselves in the lunch break. Silver barrage balloons glinted in the sunlight like giant abstract sculptures. It gave me hope, seeing that London could go on living and people could go on enjoying themselves in spite of the bombs and the great losses.

The Ministry of Supply was based in Shell Mex House on the north bank of the Thames. Even with sandbags stacked at the entrance and criss-crossed tape on every window, to my country mouse eyes it looked more like an Art Deco palace than an office building. A soldier on guard smiled appreciatively at me. I smiled back, showed my business card, and he let me inside.

In the entrance hall, enormous columns of multi-coloured marble stretched upwards to support the intricately decorated plaster ceiling. Hanging from its centre was a huge chandelier, larger even than the one at the Manor, with a thousand crystals that shimmered spangles of light into the whole space, including the highly polished buttons on the doorman's uniform. He directed me up the sweeping staircase. The brass banister was so beautifully polished I avoided using it for fear of leaving fingerprints, and I tried not to gawp too obviously at the portraits of pompous men rising up along the stairway in their ostentatious gilt frames.

The top of the stairs led into an empty rectangular room the size of half a tennis court, carpeted in an expanse of deep claret patterned with yellow cockleshells. Dusty sunshine streamed through five tall windows opposite, and I wandered over to look out across Embankment to the river, flowing so calmly, so unaware of the utter disruption of war.

The curtains were Jacquard woven with a delicate shell motif and I'd just started to examine the design when a voice barked across the room, 'We need tea and coffee please, Miss. Pronto.' I looked up to see a balding gentleman in an over-tight three-piece suit gesturing towards the long table on the other side of the room, set with green utility china cups and saucers on a white tablecloth.

Caught off guard, I stuttered, 'I'm sorry. I really don't know where it's got to.'

'Well go and find out, they'll be arriving soon,' he commanded imperiously. Without waiting for an answer, he turned and went into another doorway.

I was about to follow him to clear up the misunderstanding when a lady with a trolley arrived, and started to set out the tea. She was followed shortly by a number of large, confident men, all greeting each other in self-important voices.

As they gathered round the tea table I could see they were grouping themselves into clans. The businessmen, even in their expensive pinstriped suits, appeared positively dowdy beside RAF officers with their flocks of epaulette wings, and even these were outshone by the galaxies of stars glittering on the army men's khaki.

I straightened my skirt and walked as casually as possible across the wide stretch of carpet, poured a cup of grey coffee, moved towards the pinstripers and insinuated myself into a gap in their circle. They were so engaged in animated conversation most of them hardly seemed to notice me, but a younger man with a brightly striped tie smiled sweetly.

'Hello,' he said. 'I don't think we've met before?'

'I'm Lily Verner.' I said, returning the smile. 'Verner and Sons.'

'Ah, Verners,' he said, a little distractedly. 'I think we supply you with yarn. Michael Merrison. How do you do.' His hand was large and warm.

The others peered at me, mumbled hellos, shook my hand in turn and, after an awkward pause, resumed their discussion.

'Don't know about you lot but conscription's causing us all kind of problems,' said one. 'All I've got left is women and old boys.'

'Bloody difficult to find good people these days,' another agreed.

The conversation continued in this vein. I couldn't let the implied criticism of women workers go unchallenged.

'Actually, I find it's a good combination,' I found myself saying, hardly believing this authoritative voice was coming from me. 'The old boys have plenty of experience and women make excellent weavers, quick to learn and very dextrous, don't you think?'

They stopped and looked at each other, apparently disconcerted by my intervention, wondering how to react. The younger man was grinning again, and he had just started to say something when a loud voice summoned us into the meeting room and the group broke up.

The army and Air Force chaps moved first, filing confidently into what appeared to be their usual seats along either side of a long oval mahogany table with a dazzling sheen. The businessmen courteously stood aside for me and as I entered the room, I could see five khaki uniforms seating themselves on the far side and on the nearside, six grey-blue uniforms taking their chairs. By the time I could see past the crowd of large backs, the only place untaken was next to the stout man who had shouted at me earlier.

'I thought Marilyn was clerking?' he said, peering at me with a puzzled expression as I sat down.

'My name is Lily Verner, how do you do,' I replied, with what I hoped was a forgiving smile.

At that moment, he was distracted by something behind me, and I twisted round to see a young woman standing beside my chair, her notebook in hand. With a sinking feeling in my stomach I realised that she was Marilyn, the clerk, and I was sitting in her seat.

The room fell silent and every face turned towards me. I could see, at the other end of the table, the young businessman collecting an extra chair and placing it next to his.

'Miss Verner, would you like to sit here?' he called.

I walked the length of the room, cheeks burning, and sat down murmuring my gratitude. He slid a piece of paper towards me and I studied it carefully. It read: *Agenda. Minutes of previous meeting. Item 1: Parachute Silk Supplies. Item 2: Insulation Silk Supplies. Any Other Business. Date of Next Meeting.*

The stout person turned out to be the chairman, Sir George Markham, head of the silk section of the Ministry of Supply. He called the meeting to order and introduced himself, though no one else was invited to do so. Perhaps they all knew each other already. After my *faux pas* with the seating I was not about to pipe up.

People were distributing more pieces of paper entitled *Minutes of the Meeting 29th November 1939*. I took a copy and passed the others on.

The name at the top, among the list of attendees, was like a slap in the face: Mr Harold Verner. I was so busy being nervous that I'd completely forgotten he would have been here the last time this meeting was held. Father had

253

sat in this same room, probably with the same people in their same seats, less than a month before he died. And not just then, but many times before.

I could almost feel his solid presence, see him at this table, sitting with back straight, his face fully engaged with the proceedings, his voice, calm and reasonable, making sure his points were always fully understood. Which chair had he sat on? What contributions had he made? Who were his allies, or even his friends? It should be you here today Father, not me, I thought, but you will never sit here again. The sadness was dizzying, threatening to overwhelm me.

There was a hand on my shoulder, and I heard the nice young man's voice asking 'Miss Verner, are you all right?'

I nodded and took a few deep breaths. Tell me what to do, I asked Father silently, how shall I react to these people, in these surroundings that are so familiar to you? But there was no reply.

'Agenda Item One,' the chairman announced firmly. 'Raw silk supplies. You all know the problem, and the minister wants it sorted, sharpish. Put plainly, if we're going to win this war we need more parachutes, and we're perilously short of raw silk. Japan is siding with the Axis powers, and controls trade routes to China. It goes without saying that European silk is unobtainable. Over to you, gentlemen.'

Within moments the two sides were sniping at each other across the table.

'Why can't you use cotton like our paratroopers — or are your fliers too grand for that?'

254

The Air Force returned fire. 'You try fitting one of those bulky cotton jobs into the cockpit of a fighter plane, old man, you'd soon see why.'

'Gentlemen, please,' the chairman said wearily. 'We have a mutual enemy to fight, remember?'

One of the business types raised his hand like a school-child. It struck me as a silly gesture for a grown man, and I thought of Vera. She'd have been sitting here, shoulders shaking, trying to stifle her giggles.

'Yes, Johnson?' asked the chairman.

'How are those R&D men getting on with nylon?'

'They're working hard on it, but they can't get the strength-to-bulk ratios right,' said the chairman. 'We're pushing them hard, and hope to have a result soon.'

An RAF man sniped again, 'Our chaps won't accept nylon 'chutes, even if you get the other things sorted. Anywhere near fire and it melts like candle wax. You feel what it's like to have a load of molten nylon running down your back and you'll realise why they're not keen.' His troops muttered support and the khaki side held their fire.

'I can see it's not going to be an easy one, but we can defer our decision until we've got the R&D results, if you're all agreed,' the chairman said, and there were nods round the table as they moved on to the next item on the agenda: insulation silk.

The room was airless and smelled of undisturbed dust. Through the windows, past the military haircuts, I watched the plane trees glittering green and silver in the sunshine and for a moment lost the thread of the discussion. Turning my gaze back into the room, I caught the young man looking at me again, his eyes so dark blue they seemed almost violet. A nice face, honest and dependable, I thought, failing to notice that the chairman was addressing me.

'Miss Verner, are you with us?'

I nodded, blushing again.

'I assume you are here because your father has another engagement? Do you have anything to contribute to this debate on his behalf?'

I cleared my throat. 'I am sorry to tell you that my father passed away in December.' Everyone's eyes turned towards me. 'So I am attending this meeting as acting managing director of Verner and Sons.'

Since no one responded, I took a deep breath and forced myself to carry on. 'However, I am pleased to report that Verners is weaving more than three thousand yards of parachute silk every week, all of which has been accepted by your ministry as being of correct weight and porosity.' I could hear Father's voice now, leading my words. 'We have also experimented, on behalf of the ministry, with cotton-silk mix using fine cotton for the warp, which is currently under testing.'

The chairman nodded encouragement, Marilyn was scribbling busily in her notebook, and suddenly everyone was paying attention. I could sense the young man beside me, urging me on.

'I am new to this committee,' I said, growing in confidence now. Father's voice had disappeared, I was speaking for myself. Perhaps Gwen was right; they might be more likely to listen to a woman. 'But I hope to be able to contribute fully and will do whatever I can to support the sourcing of additional raw silk stocks or the development of new fibres.'

'Thank you Miss Verner, for that helpful contribution. And please accept the condolences of myself and the committee for the sad loss of your father. He was a stalwart member of this committee.' There was a new warmth in the chairman's voice and mutterings of 'hear, hear' around the table.

When the meeting finally ended we filed back downstairs into the lobby and as I headed straight for the door, longing for fresh air, the young businessman caught up with me.

'I am so sorry to hear about Mr Verner. I only met him once but he seemed very knowledgeable, and a real gentleman,' he said. 'Please let me introduce myself properly. I am Michael Merrison, of Merrisons Silk Merchants. We deserve a cup of tea after all that. There's a Lyons nearby, would you care to join me? They may even have something other than carrot cake — what a treat that would be.'

Over tea and Battenberg (a treat indeed) in the crowded, noisy Corner House he told me about his family business, which sourced silk yarn from round the world. The company was based in Macclesfield, the centre of the weaving industry. His northern vowels sounded mildly exotic to me.

'Do you supply Verners?'

'Of course. Since way back.'

'No wonder your name's familiar.'

We clicked at once, Michael and I, though at the time I thought little of it. He was self-assured without being arrogant, funny without being silly. Not handsome, but good-looking, with his brown curly hair and eyes that seemed never far from a smile. And he had perfect manners.

I felt a sense of kinship; his family and mine had known each other and worked together, perhaps for generations.

'Do you enjoy working for the family business?' I asked.

'Frankly, it was the last thing I imagined myself doing. I was going to be an explorer and find the source of the Nile.'

'Dr Merrison, I presume?' People at neighbouring tables turned and smiled at his generous guffaw.

'When Father finally persuaded me to hang up my pith helmet and join the yarn trade, I discovered it was surprisingly interesting. We all consider what we grow up with to be much more mundane than it really is.'

'It was like that for me. I was going to travel the world and learn languages till the war came along. Then I fell in love with silk.'

'Well, there's a silver lining,' he said. 'Otherwise we might not have met.' The flirtatious smile reminded me of Stefan's, made me ache for him. I must be careful not to lead Michael on, I thought. But I would like him to be a friend.

'Is yours a reserved occupation too?'

'It is, but I joined up anyway, after Dunkirk.'

'What happened? Were you injured?'

He nodded, his mouth full of Battenberg. 'But it shames me to say I never saw active service. Hurt my back during training, and they couldn't fix it, so they paid me off.'

'Why's that so shameful?'

'They were such a great bunch. Now they're in North Africa in the heat and the sand, dying by the dozen, while I'm just swanning round in my pinstripes. It's hard to bear.'

'Hardly swanning. I'd have thought that making sure we have enough supplies of silk is pretty critical.'

'It's certainly a struggle at the moment, what with the Japanese blockade.' He paused, then leaned over the table and lowered his voice. 'Can I trust you with a secret, Lily?'

'Of course.'

'It's so exciting I can hardly keep it to myself. This morning, before the committee, I went to a meeting with Sir George's people in the ministry. We've submitted a proposal for sourcing silk in the Middle East — in Syria and the Lebanon — and they've agreed it. My father went a few years ago and he knows some people. They've asked me to go and get things moving, just as soon as it can be arranged.'

'My goodness. How exciting.'

'The hill farmers there have grown silk worms for centuries, but only for local use. They're not commercial. That's going to be my job. Get them producing more cocoons and set up filatures to reel it.'

'How on earth will you get there? You can't fly over France, or the Med. Or North Africa, surely.'

'It's going to be tricky.' He tapped the side of his nose. 'They're working it out for me. There's talk of a flying boat up the Nile to Cairo.'

'Wow, you might find the source after all. When do you go?'

'Soon, I think. They're also organising me a crash course in Arabic.' The violet-blue eyes beamed. 'Sounds terrific, doesn't it?'

'Sounds terrifying. But if that's what you want to do.'

'Can we keep in touch?'

'Of course. But,' I started.

'No buts,' he put a finger to his lips. 'No one can promise anything to anyone in this bloody war. All we can do is hope.'

On the train home I reflected, with a warm glow, that it had been a very successful day. I had survived my first serious business meeting, held my own against the old hands and had tea with a very agreeable young man.

My cheery 'hello, I'm home' met with no reply, but I thought nothing of it and started up the stairs to get changed. Then I heard Gwen calling from the kitchen. 'Lily, we're in here.' Her voice was urgent. I hurried in. She and Vera were sitting at the table.

'Vera, how lovely. Have you got the day off?' No sooner were the words out of my mouth than I saw the telegram in her hand. She looked up with red eyes.

'John's missing in action.'

17

The silk moth caterpillar can lower itself to the ground by the silk thread it spins. In the 1920s Leslie Irvin, of the Irvin Parachute Company, created an informal but elite international association called the 'Caterpillar Club' for all those who have successfully used a parachute to bail out of a disabled aircraft. After authentication by the parachute maker, applicants receive a membership certificate and a distinctive lapel pin.
From *The History of Silk,* **by Harold Verner**

A long, fearful fortnight passed till the day I came home from work to find Mother up and dressed, sitting at the kitchen table.

'Are you all right?' I said, trying not to sound too shocked. Since the telegram about John, she had taken to her bed again.

'I've had a call from John's squadron leader, dear,' she said in a small voice, spots of pink appearing on her pale cheeks with the effort of giving me her news. 'He's alive. A prisoner of war.'

'Oh, Mum. How wonderful.' I hugged her wasted frame and sat down, holding her two hands in mine. The late afternoon sun reflected off the mill walls opposite, filling the room with a peachy glow. Now John was alive perhaps she would start to live again too.

'Did he tell you any more?'

'He said their bomber was badly damaged by flak but they managed to get halfway home before they had to bail out over the North Sea. Oh my darling, God must have been with thcm.' She paused to wipe her eyes and went on, 'They were rescued by a German patrol boat and taken to hospital in Belgium. Can you believe it? They got him well enough to travel to a camp in Germany.'

She waved a piece of paper with a hastily scribbled address, her eyes begging me for affirmation. 'He must be all right now, don't you think?'

I couldn't imagine what prisoner of war camp could be like, but at least he was alive. 'It's a miracle. Have you phoned Vera?'

'Oh yes,' she said, with a frail smile. 'I should think the whole hospital knows by now. She said it was like every Christmas and birthday all rolled into one.' She gestured to a pile of books. 'What do you think he'd like to read? I'm making up a parcel.'

After three long and anxious weeks his first letter arrived. A pink aerogramme crammed with tiny writing in pencil, addressed from Stalag Luft Two, one of the camps for airmen.

Dearest People,

I am sure the past weeks have been difficult for you but I hope this letter will put your fears at rest. I am alive and well, and with the company of the other fellows in the camp life is perfectly good. I was lucky enough to be rescued and given excellent medical treatment for minor injuries. We have most of what we need, but what would be most welcome would be books, cigarettes and a pair of warm pyjamas . . .

And so he went on — as he would in future — in a determinedly cheerful tone. We only learned after the war that his injuries had been serious: his leg broken in several places, not to mention losing most of his teeth.

His letters came irregularly, sometimes several at once, and some with black censor marks through words or even whole sentences. The way he told it, camp life sounded positively jolly, what with the plays and concerts they put on, the football matches they won and lost. He'd also made himself useful as an interpreter between the prisoners and the guards, he said.

But it was impossible to divine what his existence was really like. I imagined that in reality he was frightened and homesick, bored, cold and hungry, suffering from deprivation and uncertainty, possibly even cruelty. But he never once let on.

Knowing John was safe gave Mother a new reason to live. As he and his fellow PoWs became her exclusive focus, she gradually gained in strength. The dining room table became her centre of operations, piled with items for the next Red Cross parcel: carefully chosen books, knitted hats, scarves and gloves, precious bars of chocolate, even gramophone records.

Packages arrived too — scripts of plays he'd requested for the camp drama society that had to be ordered from a special publisher, and extra-warm clothing from a London supplier

263

that we couldn't buy locally. Every weekend was busy with fundraising; making cakes and jam for bring-and-buy events, turning out clothes for jumble sales.

Arriving home one evening I heard the faint tinkle of the piano in the drawing room. I listened closer — it was a cheerful, jazzy tune. It sounded so much like Stefan's touch that my heart jumped, recalling that Sunday he'd played after lunch. How long ago that seemed. I turned the handle and edged the door open. My initial disappointment — of course it couldn't have been Stefan — was immediately replaced with delight.

It was Mother, head bent over the keyboard, feeling her way through a ragtime number. I crept away, leaving the door ajar. When Gwen arrived home she found me sitting on the stairs listening to Mother rehearse her old favourites: Debussy, Vaughan Williams and, finally, some old music hall songs.

'Shhh,' I gestured, finger to lips.

'God bless her.' Gwen's face lit up. She sat beside me, putting an arm round my shoulders.

At supper I broached the subject. 'Lovely to hear you playing, Mother.'

She flushed with embarrassment. 'I'm so rusty, my fingers just won't do what I want them to.'

'Sounded fine to us,' Gwen said.

'It'll come back quickly if you practise. When you're more confident, why don't you do a small concert to raise funds for the Red Cross?' I suggested, ignoring her horrified expression. 'We could serve tea and cake, charge a small entrance fee. Invite Vera and her family and the other PoW families. It'd give them a tonic to hear some cheerful music.'

'I'm nothing like good enough to play in public yet,' she said firmly.

But she continued to practise every day, and after just a few weeks we managed to convince her, set a date for the concert, put up posters, and made cakes. Vera persuaded matron to allow her the weekend off. We lugged thirty canteen chairs across the yard from the mill and squeezed them into the drawing room and hallway. When the afternoon arrived people queued to get in through the door, and in the house it was standing room only.

The concert started and I posted myself at the door to greet latecomers. When I heard the familiar rumble of the Morgan's exhaust, my heart sank.

'Your ma wrote to tell me about her concert,' Robbie shouted cheerfully as he parked the car and bounded up the steps, as if nothing had passed between us the last time we met. 'I wanted to support her, especially after the shock of losing your father, and with your bro in PoW camp. It must be tough for you all.'

Hardly trusting myself to be civil, I said nothing, but submitted to a kiss on the cheek out of politeness and showed him straight into the drawing room. The last time I had seen him was on that fateful evening in the garden, and I still wondered whether he'd had anything to do with the boys' internment. He had sent a rather formal letter of condolence following my father's death, but other than that we'd heard little from him.

Mother played beautifully. Vera, Gwen and I watched from the back, all of us close to tears, as the audience applauded and called for an encore. At the tea after the concert I steered clear of Robbie, but out of the corner of my eye could see how he was on his very best behaviour, being charming and courteous to everyone, especially Mother, causing her to blush crimson with his copious compliments. At last he left, and I felt able to behave and breathe normally once more.

Mother was completely buoyed up by all the accolades she'd received, and that day I began to believe we might all recover from Father's death, after all. If only John and Stefan would come home safely.

★   ★   ★

Then, one bright July morning, I was glancing quickly through the newspaper before leaving for work when my eye was caught by a headline.

'Do you have to read that gloomy stuff?' Gwen called through the kitchen door, brushing her hair in the hall mirror. 'It's so depressing.'

It was such a tiny, discreet paragraph at the bottom of page five I could so easily have missed it. 'Come and look at this,' I shouted through the doorway.

'Must I? Have you seen the time? We're late for work.'

'Yes, you must. Come and tell me what it means.'

266

She gave a stagey groan and put her hand on my shoulder as she leaned over to read:

INTERNEES MAY JOIN UP

BRITAIN'S internees in Australia have been informed that they may be released if they apply and are accepted for enlistment in the British Pioneer Corps, the Department of the Army has confirmed today.

The words skittered with unanswered questions. Was the offer for all internees, regardless of their nationality? Would he apply?

If sufficient applications are received, a training programme will be funded and delivered in Australia before their deployment overseas.

Would enough applications be received? If Stefan joined up, where would he be sent to fight? Would he come to England first? How would they travel? Would ships be able to get through?

With characteristic lack of sentiment, Gwen said, 'Looks like your boy could be coming home.'

I studied the terse newspaper report again and again, trying to make sense of it, praying he would be safe, muttering under my breath like a mantra: *please let it be you, come home soon, oh please, stay safe and come home soon.* His letters continued to arrive but he didn't mention any opportunities for release — I realised that the two month time-delay meant that they would have been written long before the news reached him. In September he wrote to say he was hopeful of coming home soon, but then his letters stopped and I began to wonder, even dared to hope, that this silence meant he was already in transit. I tried to ring the Department but no one was prepared to talk to me. There was nothing for it but to wait.

Christmas came and went again, and I began to lose hope. But in January I had only been back at work a few days when my secretary peered tentatively round the office door. She looked nervous. I'd told her not to put any calls through this morning.

'Miss Lily, sorry to interrupt, but there's a Mr Stephen Holmes on the telephone. He's very persistent.'

'Can't you find out what he wants?' I said distractedly, trying not to sound cross. The annual accounts were overdue. They were pretty straightforward: the cost of incoming raw silk, plus labour, plus overheads, equals the price of parachute silk going out. But I needed to understand them before I could sign them off, and accounts were probably my least favourite part of the job.

A moment later she was back. 'The gentleman wouldn't say. Personal, he said.'

'I don't know a Mr Holmes, personally or otherwise. Tell him I'll phone back.' I said, becoming irritated.

She came back again, smiling as if she knew something I didn't.

'Yes, what is it now?' I snapped.

'Miss Lily, the gentleman says to ask whether the name Stefan means anything to you.'

The world seemed to stop for second. She said, still smiling, 'Miss Lily? Are you all right?'

'Sorry, yes, I'm fine. I'll take it,' I said. The breath seemed to have stopped in my chest. 'Thank you. Please put him through.'

My hand shook as I picked up the receiver. 'Stefan? Is it really you? Where are you?'

'Stephen now, I'll explain later. In Liverpool. Just got off the ship.' His voice was just the same, warm and deep, but much more English. Only the tiniest hint of a German inflection remained. 'We have to be quick, I've put in my last sixpence.'

'Can you come home?' I gasped. The ache to hold him was so fierce it seemed to stifle me.

'I'll be in London the day after tomorrow. Can you come?'

'Of course, where?' The pips started.

'Waterloo, midday,' he said, as the line cut off. I held the receiver, unwilling to let go of it, until the dialling tone sounded loudly in my ear. As I replaced it into the cradle fat tears of relief welled over and dripped onto the ledger, smudging the figures. For some reason this made me laugh out loud. To hell with accounts, I thought, drying my face and blotting the inky puddles with my hanky. What does anything matter now he's home?

The next two days were a seesaw of high elation and deep anxiety. With some trepidation I sat Mother and Gwen down that evening, and explained what was happening. They were full of questions I couldn't answer: 'What about Kurt and Walter?' and, 'Is he going to join up, like *The Times* said?' But, most important of all, both of them were supportive.

'You've waited so long for the lad, he obviously means a lot to you,' was what Mother said. 'We have to take our happiness when we can find it these days.'

I was desperate to see him again, hold him and keep him safe. It had been eighteen long, tough months; would he still find me attractive? I scrutinised myself in the mirror and could see the strains of war etched in my face. Almost without noticing, our lives had become drab and workaday and I had stopped worrying about my appearance. I'd lost weight from hard work and unappetising rations, my skin was dingy from too little sunshine, my hair lacklustre and the style strictly utilitarian. My scar, though fading well, still showed as a pink line from temple to chin. I couldn't remember the last time I'd used make-up.

Then it occurred to me that Stefan would certainly also have changed, after his terrible experiences on the ship and in the desert. Would he look different? Would he be hardened, even embittered, I wondered? Why couldn't he come home, to Westbury? If he'd joined the Pioneer

Corps, what did they do, where would he be posted?

The night before, my anxieties focused into a panic about practicalities. What should I wear? Most of my clothes were threadbare and dowdy, and of course I had no ladder-free nylons. There was a smart dress and matching coat I kept for special occasions, but that might be overdoing it. Or would the casual trousers and the jacket, even with its patched elbows, look more like the Lily he'd known before? After much fretting and consultation with Gwen, I opted for slacks with a pink cardigan borrowed from Mother. The colour flattered my complexion and the mock pearl buttons gave a touch of glamour. I'd have to wear my old duffel for warmth but I could sling it off as I went to meet him, I thought, smiling as I allowed myself to imagine the moment.

It turned out to be a good choice: the train to London was unheated on that chilly January day. On the bus between Liverpool Street and Waterloo Station I used my powder compact mirror to apply lipstick, thought it looked too brazen, rubbed it off with a handkerchief, then applied it again, like a nervous schoolgirl. Now, breathless and sick with anticipation, I barely recognised him, disguised beneath bulky army fatigues, brown lace-up boots and a brutal military haircut. He was standing under the station clock along with a dozen or so other servicemen anxiously casting their eyes over the crowds, looking for their sweethearts.

'Stefan? Is it you?'

'Stephen now, remember?' he whispered, kissing my cheek and running his hand over my hair. In person, he sounded entirely English. All trace of an accent had disappeared.

I touched the rough fabric of his sleeve. 'This feels like a dream.'

He grinned, his teeth brilliant white in the desert-tanned face, new smile lines at the corner of his eyes. 'Wait till I kiss you properly,' he whispered. 'Then you'll know it's real.'

'Where are Kurt and Walter?'

'It's a long story.'

'We've so much to catch up. How long have you got?'

'Till tomorrow morning.'

Just a handful of hours, after so long. I took his hand. 'Come on then. Let's find a hotel and make the most of it.'

* * *

He smelled of unknown places, musty train carriages and stale cigarette smoke, like a stranger. When he took off the ugly, scratchy uniform his body was unfamiliar too: where it had once been pale and slender it was now muscular and tanned, his narrow shoulders and thighs had thickened, his voice was more bass than baritone and the once sparse hairs on his chest were now too many to count. But when we kissed, the taste of him and the feel of his lips were just as I remembered and, when our bodies met, every sensation appeared to have been amplified by our long absence.

272

'I've been dreaming about this for so long,' he said afterwards, rolling onto his back, looking up at the stains on the ceiling. 'And the real thing was even better than in my dreams.'

We cuddled against the chill air under the frayed spread. The bed that had creaked so embarrassingly a few moments before now felt like a warm cocoon protecting us from the world, reminding me of the last time, at the cottage. That was more than a year ago, yet now we were together again it seemed like only yesterday. No candles this time, of course, no wild flowers in a jam jar. But despite the fusty smells, the cheap ply furniture and fussy ornaments, the tap dripping steadily into a stained sink, the handwritten sign, *hot water between six and seven p.m. only*, the room felt like a little corner of heaven.

He was studying the ceiling.

'What are you looking at up there?'

He reached an arm from under the covers and pointed at the damp stains in the plaster. 'Over there, a shuttle. Next to it's a pirn, and there, a skein of raw silk. Is that a warping crccl? Scc, I remember it all.'

He propped himself on one elbow, looking into my face. 'Because of you, Lilymouse, this no-good Jewish rebel became a silk weaver, and now I'm a proper English gentleman and a soldier.'

And after he kissed me, he asked, 'So, what can you see?'

'I see,' I said, looking into his eyes, 'the man I love. Jewish, German or English. Stephen, Stefan, it doesn't matter a jot to me who you are.'

As dusk drew in we pulled down the blackouts

but the light from the single bulb above the bed was so harsh we turned it off again, and raised the blinds. With no streetlights or car headlamps, London at night was like the countryside, and the room filled with the gentle light of the evening sky.

We couldn't bear to waste precious moments going to a café, so we chain-smoked to ward off our hunger. He asked me how things were going in Westbury and, tentatively, stroking the scar on my cheek, about the accident in Cheapside. It was the first time in months that I'd talked about it and the horror came back, of course, but in Stefan's arms it felt just a little less painful.

'I'll miss him too,' he said. 'Mr Harold would do anything to protect us boys. He was like a father to us.'

When I finally ran out of words, I said, 'And now, your story please. Don't leave anything out.'

Along with thousands of other internees Kurt, Walter and Stefan — or Stephen as he insisted I must now call him — had endured a nightmare two-month voyage on the *Dunera*.

'They crammed in three thousand of us, when it was meant to hold only sixteen hundred,' he said. 'Germans and Italians mostly, some people had lived in England for years but they got interned all the same because they were classed as enemy aliens. It was horrible, cramped, smelly, airless, disgusting. The second night there was a terrible crash — we were hit by a torpedo but not badly damaged. After that we changed direction, started going south instead of west.

274

But they never told us where we were going.

'We lived in the cargo holds. Some had hammocks, but most of us slept on the floor. There wasn't enough food and water, people fought over it. They let us out on deck for exercise just a few minutes a day, if we were lucky. Like prison. The guards treated us like prisoners, stole stuff from our suitcases. They were genuine crooks — can you believe it? Yes, really. They'd let them out of gaol so they could guard us. Crazy.'

What a bitter twist, I thought, criminals guarding innocent people. But there was a silver lining, Stefan said. Later, some of the internees wrote to the British newspapers and Government ministers, complaining about the way they had been treated. There were questions in Parliament and an official enquiry, which resulted in them being freed and allowed to come home.

'What about your things, were they stolen too?' I asked.

'Some, yes, but nothing valuable. I'm glad I left my writing case with you and the photos. You still have it safe?'

'Yes, my darling. Of course, I'm sorry, I should have brought it with me.'

'Don't worry, I will come to Westbury soon. Keep it safe for me a little longer.'

When they finally arrived in the Australian desert there was no camp; they had to build their own huts. Stefan spoke without bitterness, apparently sanguine about his experiences, about their incarceration behind barbed wire with a thousand others, in scorching heat with not enough to eat.

'At least the Aussies weren't cruel,' he said. 'And I had Kurt and Walter. We were a family.'

He pulled out a wallet from his jacket pocket and gave me a paper note. 'We even had our own money.' I could make out the roughly printed words: *Hay Camp One Pound*. 'To earn money I taught piano lessons. I brought this note back as a souvenir for you. It won't buy much here I'm afraid,' he said wryly.

'Wherever did you get a piano, in the desert?' I asked.

'I don't know,' he said. 'I think the local town gave it to us. They called it Joanna but I never found out why. Isn't that an English girl's name?'

'It's rhyming slang for pianna,' I said, laughing. 'They must have been Cockneys.'

He frowned, not understanding, and went on, 'My most talented student was a German Jew who'd lived for years in France and got out just before the invasion. In exchange for my music lessons he taught me French. Good bloke. We talked all the time and I got fairly fluent.'

He took my face in his hands, '*Lilymouse, tu es la plus jolie fille la de tout Londres. Je t'aime, ma petite souris.*'

'*Je t'aime aussi. Tu es un très* sexy Frenchman,' I replied, in my schoolgirl accent, and we lost ourselves in kisses once more.

'What about Kurt and Walter? Why aren't they with you?' I asked, a little later.

'They told us we could come back if we agreed to enlist with the Allies. So we had to have a long talk about this. Kurt does not want to fight Germans, and Walter is too young to join up. So when we heard that they could get Australian visas instead, they decided to stay.' He went quiet. 'It was hard for us to be separated, but I had to get back to my Lily.'

'I love you,' I whispered.

'And I love you, Lilymouse,' he said, leaning over to kiss my nose. Then he lay back and, after a thoughtful pause, 'It is also . . . for my family . . . you know?'

I nodded, only half understanding. 'Did the army make you change your name when you enlisted?'

'No, but they suggested it would be a good idea,' he said, almost whispering. 'Coming back here.'

'I see why you chose Stephen. But Holmes? After your friend Sherlock?' I asked gently.

'Elementary, my dear Watson,' he said, smiling now. I remembered that deep bow, the twirl of that imaginary umbrella. Stefan the clown. The boy I first fell in love with.

'So what happens next?' I asked, praying he would not tell me he was going to the front line.

'This,' he said, handing me his beret. The metal badge glistened. 'All of us internees, we've been signed up to the Pioneer Corps. They seem like a good bunch, Italians, Germans, all kinds. The King's Own Enemy Aliens, we call ourselves.'

'Why the pick and shovel?'

'We do the things front-line troops don't want to; digging, building, fetching and carrying, cleaning. The dirty jobs brigade,' he said cheerfully, sitting up to light a cigarette.

'Where will you be you based?'

'Ilfracombe,' he said, struggling to pronounce the unfamiliar syllables. 'I go there tomorrow.'

'In Devon? That's a seaside resort.' At least it's in England, I thought, and he won't be going to the front line. But then he added, 'With a bit of luck I won't have to dig latrines for long. I plan to transfer to a fighting regiment, as soon as they'll have me.'

After he drifted off I listened to his gentle breathing, wishing that my every night could be filled with it. I thought about the choice he had made, coming back to this war-torn country to join up and possibly to fight, instead of staying in Australia, all for me. I heard again the sadness in his voice as he talked about having to change his name, about what his parents would think, and wondering how they were faring. What would the next few months bring? I lay unsleeping, partly from excitement, partly full of dread, till the sound of the landlady going downstairs, the crashings in the kitchen and the smell of frying bread signalled that our precious night was over.

Once dressed, we became shy of each other again.

'Keep yourself safe,' I said, as he picked up his kit bag, 'and come home to Westbury soon.'

'Home. That sounds good,' he said, kissing my cheek. 'I'll telephone as soon as I can.'

Then he was gone.

I sat on the crumpled bed and lifted the pillow

to my face, but his smell was already fading. I checked my lipstick in the mirror, picked up the Hay Camp pound note from the bedside table, snapped shut my handbag and prepared to meet the world again.

18

While China has been the world's main producer of raw silk for many centuries, during the nineteenth and twentieth centuries the Japanese introduced mechanisation and quality control to produce yarns of a new and remarkable consistency. During wartime, raw silk was sourced from the Middle East, but this never matched up to Japanese quality.
From *The History of Silk*, **by Harold Verner**

Compared with many, we considered ourselves fortunate. Stefan served with the Pioneers for more than a year, being posted all over the country. So although we didn't get much opportunity to see each other, and he never had long enough on leave to come home to Westbury, at least there were telephone calls, and the luxury of letters that took just a week to arrive.

There was little time for moping. Although it seemed as though the tide of war was at last turning, at the mill work was frenetic and in the past few weeks things had been going horribly wrong.

As I unlocked the heavy green door and let myself into the mill that morning I could hear the phone echoing through the empty offices. Sprinting up the stairs two at a time, I missed my footing and stumbled, smashing my shin on the top step. Cursing, I pulled myself up and fumbled to find the right key for the office door.

The insistent ringing continued but when I lifted the receiver there was only a dialling tone. Damn and blast. Who the hell was ringing so early? If it wasn't a wrong number it was probably bad news. I tried to catch my breath, rubbing my bruised shin.

Usually I loved being in the mill in the morning, before everyone else arrived. The sweet smell of silk hanging in the still, silent air, mixed with the sharp tang of engine oil, was familiar and comforting. And yet, that day, it reminded me of the trouble we were in.

With the heavy bunch of master keys clinking from my belt I could let myself into every part of the mill, click on the lights at the main switchboard and wander freely down the aisles of grey-green looms, along the rows of spindly winding machines, past the warping creel with thousands of threads hanging limply, their tension released.

Without the eyes of the weavers and throwsters on me, I was free to examine their work without fearing they'd think I was finding fault. The machines were stilled but not sleeping, crouched in readiness for the day's action. Once or twice I found myself talking to them, even stroking them, as if they were alive.

At this hour the canteen, normally the carefully guarded domain of Kathleen and her team, was also mine. That morning I treated myself to an extra ration of evaporated milk, hoping its sweetness would disguise the bitter aftertaste of chicory in the coffee concentrate. I savoured it, looking across the weaving shed roof where the morning sun slanted through the rows of cricket bat willows, and remembered Stefan's curiosity about them, that day by the boiler shed. So long ago. A tint of green washed through their wintry branches and, for a moment, lifted my spirits.

But walking back through the packing hall this fleeting moment of optimism disappeared. Stacked on the shelving beside the door were several rolls of pure white parachute silk. The weavers had warned us, but we'd been under such pressure to produce more and more, we told them to carry on weaving in hopes they would produce enough yards of fault-free cloth to satisfy Camerons' demands. Now, the pickers had scrutinised each roll, and loops of red thread knotted into the selvedge marked every imperfection.

They were festooned with what looked like drips of blood.

With this number of faults the silk was unusable for parachutes. We hadn't even bothered to send it for finishing. We'd wasted two bales of precious raw yarn. We might find another use for it later, but with the parachute manufacturers desperate for more supplies, this was a disaster.

Back in the office the telephone was ringing again.

'Lily?'

I felt slightly sick at the sound of his voice. These days our usual dealings with Camerons were through his manager. 'Robbie? What's the problem? It's half past seven in the morning.'

'Listen, we've got a real panic on. The ministry's on my back about parachute supplies — I reckon they've got a big push in the offing. Promised them we'd double it this week but we're well off target. What happened to your delivery yesterday? Why did you send our van away?'

'I told you on Wednesday about the problems we've been having,' I said, trying not to sound defensive.

'But you didn't say you couldn't deliver even a yard of the stuff. Don't you realise there's petrol rationing, Lily?'

Of course I did. 'I'm sorry. They didn't tell me till it was too late.'

'You're the ruddy manager. You've got to keep on top of these things.' He was right of course, his driver had had a wasted journey. It had been my mistake. 'And to cap it all,' he went on, 'I had a call from Cartwright himself last night.'

'Cartwright?'

'Head honcho at the ministry. Bloody man phoned me at home, would you believe? He's not happy, threatening all kinds of things.'

'The finishing plant's playing up again,' I said, keeping my voice as steady as possible. 'And you know we've been having to use that Syrian raw for the past few weeks. It's a nightmare to weave.'

'He knows. Your mate Michael's in for a bollocking.'

'That's not fair. At least he's getting us something. It's hardly his fault it isn't up to

Japanese quality.' Poor Michael, he was doing his best. But Robbie neither knew nor cared.

'Look, it's very simple. How many rolls can you get to me next week?'

'Hard to say, Robbie,' I said, panicking slightly. I was playing for time, trying to placate him but also being realistic. I couldn't let him down again.

'Thirty?' he said.

'That'd be a stretch.'

'Twenty then. At least. End of Tuesday latest. And they'd better be up to scratch.'

'Don't worry, we test every roll.' Dancing before my eyes were Bert's figures, the erratic porosity results we'd been having this past week.

'Seems to be a problem with you, Lily, promising what you can't deliver. And if you can't deliver this time we really will have to reconsider Verners' contract. Okay?'

He hung up without saying goodbye. I shouted into the receiver, slammed it down, ran into Father's office and banged the door so hard the glass rattled in its frame. Robbie's jibe hurt more than his threats. How dare he bring that up again? I was tempted to run home and weep in Gwen's arms, but she'd still be getting up and having breakfast. No, I must sort this out myself, be strong, display real leadership. I'll bloody well show the bastard, I thought.

It wasn't just the poor quality raw. We also had problems in the finishing plant. The thermostat and timing mechanisms were on the blink again but our engineers were unable to fix them, baffled by the Swiss technology. We'd searched for replacement parts without success, and importing new kit was impossible.

After Father died I'd shut the door to this office, leaving everything untouched, unable to accept that he would never again sit at his desk. Finally, at Gwen's insistence I'd moved in. 'It's symbolic,' she said. 'Feels like a ship without a captain.' I wished now, more than anything, that I could hand the ship back.

I looked out of the office window, trying to quieten my jangling heart. In the yard below the morning shift workers were starting to arrive, some on foot and others by bike, some alone with the sleep still in their faces, others in groups animated by chat and laughter, encouraging each other at the end of a long week. In all the chaos of wartime, these steadfast, decent people were depending on me.

I picked up the framed photograph of our family from Father's desk. We are posed formally in Sunday best. Mother is smiling, seated on an elaborate cast-iron garden chair with three-year-old me on her lap and John, aged five, at her other side. Father, every inch the confident successful businessman in his prime, stands behind us.

I scrutinised his face. 'Now, what would you do?' I said out loud, trying to hear his voice. Then I sat at his desk, on the wooden chair I knew so well from spinning on as a child. Before long the ideas began to flow, and I started to write. When Gwen arrived for our usual morning catch-up I handed her a piece of foolscap paper. On it I had written:

Problem 1: *Syrian Raw. Variable quality leading to unacceptable level of faults in woven piece. But is all we can get, so have to use.*

Solution: greater care in preparation. Need to run twisting & throwing at slower pace. To increase output add extra half-shift from next Monday. Pay overtime &/or recruit more throwsters — internally? Fred re: numbers & training existing & new workers — must understand importance of extra care. Get him to calculate additional costs. Where to make savings to cover this? ASAP. Believe he can be entrusted with this.

Problem 2: *Thermostat in finishing plant. Unreliable, cannot be repaired.*

Solution: Need to override vat control on manual & monitor with stand-alone thermometer and stopwatch. Talk to Bert, task to implement & train Ruby in use of same. ASAP.

N.B. Is he capable of this? Can he be relied on?

Gwen read in silence, then looked at me curiously. 'Have you been communing with the gaffer this morning?'

'Kind of,' I gestured to the photograph. 'I thought about what he would do, and how irritating it was when he insisted on going back to basics.'

She laughed affectionately. 'I remember it well.'

'Seemed to work for me this morning though

— I feel a lot better than I did after Robbie's phone call.'

'Robbie? What was that about?' she said, raising her eyebrows suspiciously.

Her face flushed as I repeated the conversation. 'That's outrageous. How dare he threaten you? So what if he's got the ministry on his back? It's no excuse for that kind of behaviour. I always said he was a bully.'

'You're right, but he's pulling the purse strings, I'm afraid.' I stood up and stretched. 'Come on, time for action. We'll show him we can deliver on our promises. If we get the throwsters sorted out today we could have enough yarn for a weekend weaving shift, what do you think? We might even have enough to start finishing on Monday evening. We'll have to pay overtime and say goodbye to our weekend, but with a bit of luck we could have the delivery ready by late Tuesday.'

She nodded. 'With a bit of luck and a following wind, perhaps.'

'Can you get hold of Fred and Bert? My diary's free most of today. Say ten o'clock?'

'Your word is my command.'

'Thanks for being such a brick, Gwen. I owe you,' I called as she bustled out of the office.

She turned with a half-smile. 'You bet. I'll call it in one day.'

Fred said he was up for the challenge if we'd pay the throwsters overtime. But in Bert's weathered face the rheumy eyes were sceptical. He listened morosely as I told him how we planned to bypass the thermostat and run the finishing plant on manual.

'That's all very well, Miss Lily, but how're we supposed to know the water temperature's even?' he grumbled. 'And I don't know about them stopwatches. It'll pretty much be guesswork, whatever. We'd have been better off without this new-fangled machinery in the first place, I reckon.'

I'd never trusted him since he sneaked to Father about me and Stefan. Watching his departing back I imagined what he was thinking: *Wouldn't have happened if Mr Harold had been around. See what you get when you have a chit of a girl running the place. And she consorted with that German lot.*

'C'mon Lily,' Gwen said after he'd gone. 'We'll just have to prove it *can* be done. Present him with a *fait accompli*.'

'We can't just waltz in and take over his machinery.'

'You're the boss, Lily. You can do whatever you like, whatever you need to do.' She came round the desk and gave me a hug. 'We'll do it together.'

★   ★   ★

By Sunday Fred's team had managed, by scrutinising every inch and dumping some of the worst sections of Syrian raw, to throw two thousand bobbins of almost perfect yarn. It was slow work but it paid off. The parachute looms were weaving again.

On Tuesday morning my alarm rang at half past five. I reluctantly dragged myself out of bed,

288

feeling sick with sleeplessness and apprehension. A thousand square yards of silk had to be finished and tested perfect by five o'clock that evening. Without stopping for breakfast I crossed the kitchen garden, let myself out of the gate into the yard and walked down the slope. I could see the lit end of Gwen's cigarette in the grey dawn as she waited by the finishing room door.

She was right, we made a good team, working side by side. The bright lights, gleaming steel and steamy warmth perked us up, and by half past seven we had boiled, dried and stentered a whole roll of parachute silk, using a manual vat thermometer and two stopwatches.

My hands shook as I tried to thread the end of the roll into the porosity tester.

'Let me have a go.' She pushed me aside and took over, pulling a few yards of material and laying it flat on the base of the machine, lowering the lever and pressing the button. Our eyes were fixed on the dial as the machine hissed and sighed, and as the needle settled we shouted simultaneously, 'Fourteen cubic feet per second!'

As we measured and tested, I wrote the results in Bert's red-backed ledger with the stubby pencil tied to it with string: 14; 14.6; 14.2; 14.8. With each hiss and sigh of the machine we held our breath. With each settling of the needle we whooped like schoolgirls, as each result came in within the required porosity tolerance.

The clock on the wall read eight o'clock. 'The final test,' she announced. 'If this is okay we're in business.' When the result came in on the nail we jumped up and down, laughing triumphantly.

'We did it!' I shouted.

'We're brilliant.' She stopped jumping and looked into my eyes. Her hands cradled my cheeks and for a brief, surreal moment I thought she might be about to kiss me. Just then the door opened and Bert shuffled in, looking surprised, clearly wondering what we were doing in his finishing room.

He stood uncomfortably in his coat and scarf, shifting his weight and contemplating the floor as I explained we'd come in early to check what silk had been delivered from the weaving shed, and then ended up trialling the plant on manual. I made it sound like a spontaneous decision, not a planned takeover of his domain. Gwen nodded support.

'This morning's test results. They show it can be done on manual,' she said, pointing to the ledger. He scrutinised my scribbled figures in silence.

'I see.' He cleared his throat. 'S'pose you want the rest of them rolls done?'

'Yes, we need all twenty finished by this afternoon,' I said. 'Perfectly. There's a van coming from Cameron's around five. Gwen will stay and help you and Ruby do the rest.'

* * *

It was early afternoon when Camerons' factory manager phoned to confirm their driver would arrive at half past five. Would the twenty rolls be ready by then, he politely enquired. With fingers crossed, I said we were on track and promised to

290

let them know of any delays. Then I headed to the finishing room. Bert was standing hunched outside the door, smoking. Hearing my feet on the gravel he looked up, his gnarled face expressionless.

'How's it going, Bert?'

'Okay. A couple of problems.'

Dread dragged at my feet as we went inside. I looked round. 'Where's Gwen?'

'Someone from the warping mill came and asked for her. Emergency, they said,' he mumbled. ''Bout an hour ago. We've been pushing on without her.'

'What results are you getting?' He gestured to the ledger. Beside my scribbles was a column in his old-fashioned handwriting:

March 2nd 1942
Roll 1 Avg 14.3 variation +/− 0.5
Roll 2 Avg 14.2 variation +/− 2.3
Roll 3 Avg 14.3 variation +/− 0.7
Roll 4 Avg 14.6 variation +/− 0.5
Roll 5 Avg 14.2 variation +/− 3.8
Roll 6 Avg 14.0 variation +/− 4.2

'Does this mean that some parts of Roll 6 could be only 9.8?'

He nodded.

'And others up to 18.2?'

I began to pace, trying to quell my rising anger. 'This just won't do, Bert. Unless we can get at least twenty rolls finished within proper tolerances by five this afternoon, we could lose the contract. Gwen showed you how to do it.

Whatever have you been doing differently with these last couple of rolls?'

I looked him in the eye. He shook his head, dumbly, infuriatingly.

'For goodness sake. Stop the machine. Stop what you're doing, Ruby. Go and find Gwen. I need her in my office, at once.' I stormed back to the main building.

As I heard Gwen's footsteps on the stairs I willed myself to stay calm.

'What's up, Lily?'

'You left Bert and Ruby on their own to finish those rolls? Unsupervised?'

'There was an emergency in the warping room. I was only gone half an hour. They can cope.' Her defensiveness just riled me more.

'For Christ's sake! This is a far worse emergency. In that time they've managed to make a mess of two rolls. Haven't you been down to check?'

'Bloody hell,' she said. 'It was going fine when I left. I showed them how to do it, and the results were perfect.'

'Well they aren't now. Get back down there and sort it out. Don't leave them for a second, till you've got twenty rolls perfect,' I shouted.

Her face went ashen. She turned and left without a word.

The afternoon dragged on. I felt shamefaced for shouting and anxious about what was happening in the finishing room, but resisted the temptation to check on their progress. Around four o'clock I was returning from the canteen with my tea when I met Gwen climbing the stairs. She was pale with exhaustion, her curls lank. We went into my office and shut the door.

'I'm sorry about being so horrible earlier, Gwen. I just lost it. The tension, all that.'

'I didn't take it personally.' She smiled weakly.

'How's it going?'

'Not so bad,' she said, sitting down. 'We've finished. All but those two rolls you saw are now within an acceptable variation. We can give Camerons eighteen — that's worth a journey.'

'We promised him twenty.' My anger simmered, but I held it back.

'We've done our very best. We can get a further ten to him by the day after tomorrow.'

'I'd better get on the blower and warn him,' I said, dreading the response. *Seems to be a problem with you, Lily.*

'I've sent Bert and Ruby home early. They were shattered. Hope you don't mind.'

'Why don't you go home too? I'll deal with the delivery.' Anything to get her out of the office. I needed to think about what to do.

'Sure?'

I nodded. 'I'll see you later. Don't wait for me. I'll grab something when I get in.'

With a touch on my shoulder, she was gone.

* * *

I was deeply asleep with my head on the desk when a horn sounded loudly in the yard, jolting me awake. The office clock read ten to seven. I was confused. It was dark outside and silent inside: no voices from the office, no rumble of looms from the weaving shed. It must still be evening. The horn went again, then a pause, followed by an impatient knocking. I stood up, fuzzy with sleep, brushed my fingers through my hair, went downstairs yawning, and opened the door.

'Robbie?' My heart sank, after such a difficult day he was the last person I wanted to see.

'Sorry I'm so late. My driver had bad news and there was no one else,' he said quietly.

'Poor man.'

'His son. Caught it. In the desert. Bloody awful.'

We stood there on the doorstep in a pool of porch light and the cows on the water meadows mooed to each other as they settled for the night. I thought of how Stefan described his desert and tried to imagine a battle being fought in that sand and heat, flies and dust. How far away it felt.

'I wanted to come anyway. To say sorry. I was a cad on Friday. That phone call.'

He reached his hand towards my face. Instinctively I recoiled, taking a step back.

'Woah,' he raised both hands, palms towards me. 'You think I'm still tempted? Oh no. I got over you, Lily, a long while ago,' he said, with a sneer in his voice.

'Sorry. I just thought . . . ' I stuttered. Why did he always catch me off guard?

'I was only pointing — is that a bruise?' he said, gesturing at my cheek.

I put my hand up and felt the trace of Father's blotter indented into my skin, where I'd slept on it.

'It's nothing,' I said, rubbing it.

'Good. So, have you got the twenty rolls you promised?' For a few seconds I hesitated, still befuddled with sleep. 'I tried to phone, but there wasn't any answer,' I lied.

As he loomed above me, the overhead light shadowed furrows in his brow. 'Lily, you *promised*. You said you'd bloody well deliver this time.' His body tensed and for a second I was terrified that he might really hit me. 'For Christ's sake, I haven't come all this way . . . ' he shouted.

Confused and alarmed by his sudden anger. I stuttered, 'Yes, it's fine, fine. There's . . . '

'Twenty rolls? That was the deal, Lily. That's what you promised.' His words were like machine gun fire. 'So? So what's it to be?'

There was no other answer I could give.

'Yes.' I said. 'Twenty. Take twenty.'

19

Westbury silk has been worn by generations of royal brides in gowns of satin, with its luxurious feel and draping qualities, or of crisp taffeta which holds its shape for a 'fairytale' ballerina-style dress. And not just for princesses. A gown of white or cream silk is the dream choice of every bride.
From *The History of Silk*, **by Harold Verner**

I covered up my deception well.

Early next morning I moved rolls about in the finishing room so no one would notice I'd let the faulty ones go. I was especially pleasant to Gwen and even to Bert, to make up for yesterday's behaviour. No one would ever find out, I reasoned, even smugly deceiving myself that my lie had saved the firm from losing the Cameron contract. I buried it deep and eventually stopped thinking about it. We were busier than ever and now Stefan was back in the country, my conscience was easily distracted.

I hadn't seen Stefan for nearly a year, and then, in June, I received an exciting invitation. *I'm at the caravan this weekend*, the telegram read, *Can you make it? Valley Farm, Coombe Martin.*

It took all day to cross the country by train to Bristol, then by bus to Ilfracombe, and an hour's wait for a taxi. We drove through the village and finally stopped at the entrance to a narrow lane with high hedges either side, a raised grassy mound running between its deep muddy tracks.

'Allroight if I leaves yew here?' the driver said. 'Gew down the end, through the gate, ther'it'll be.' For much of the ride I'd been trying to fathom his West County accent, but this was clear enough. I'd caught glimpses of Exmoor through gaps in the cloud, but now it had closed in properly and started to drizzle. With only a light jacket, no umbrella, no raincoat and stupidly lightweight shoes, I was soon soaked and covered in mud to my ankles. We haven't seen each other for ages, I thought gloomily, and here I am looking like a drowned rat.

But when I saw Stefan, all six feet of him stooping in the doorway of the caravan with that sweet sultry smile, I no longer cared how bedraggled I looked.

The van, a tiny, dirty-cream blob the shape of a squashed egg nestled into the green fold of a bumpy field, belonged to a friend of Stefan's, a chap in the Corps who rented it out for just a few shillings. Despite the unpromising outward appearance it was reasonably well supplied with basic equipment, and spacious enough for a tiny kitchen and a dining table. The bench seats were already converted into a double bed and we were soon cosily wrapped in blankets smelling only mildly of mildew, listening to the rain splattering on the roof, and buffeted by the wind.

Later, when the weather cleared, we strolled along the lane to the village, with the foothills of the moor looming darkly ahead of us against the evening sky. 'We could walk up there tomorrow,' he said.

'No boots,' I said, smiling. 'What a shame. We might just have to stay in bed all day.' It felt deliciously carefree. No demands, nobody watching or judging us, nothing to conceal. We could do exactly what we wanted — for two whole days.

The pub was cheerless and almost empty, but the beer was plentiful and after a couple of pints we stopped noticing its sour taste. This is like normal life at last, I thought, watching him hungrily devour a plateful of cheese and potato pie. Just time to be ourselves, to get to know each other properly. No separations, no uniforms, no rationing, no war.

Over the weekend we spent many more hours wrapped up in our blankets in the fug of the van. 'It's like heaven on wheels,' I said.

'Perhaps we could run away, towing our house behind us?' he said, laughing. I quoted the passage about Toad and the open road from *The Wind in the Willows*, promising to lend him the book next time he came to Westbury.

'Make it soon,' I whispered into his ear.

'Very soon, I promise,' he murmured, kissing the back of my neck.

★   ★   ★

There were plenty of other distractions at work. I was even enjoying it, feeling more comfortable in my role as Acting Managing Director, learning about being a boss, when to be decisive and when to hold my tongue, that it was always better to listen carefully and consider before responding to questions, how to chair meetings that allowed people to have their say but didn't overrun, and how to be sympathetic but firm with tricky staff.

Even attending national committees held few fears for me, these days. I was greeted warmly and respectfully — no longer the new girl. But I did miss the friendly face of Michael Merrison. We'd been receiving supplies of 'his' Syrian raw but I hadn't heard anything from him personally for over a year. Then his letter arrived.

Beirut 2nd July 1943

Dearest Lily,

Sorry it has taken so long to write. It's been jolly busy but I know that's no real excuse. Anyway here I am, after an exciting journey and getting stuck into the job. Up until now I've been completely on my tod but at last they've sent me some help.

And what a title they have given him — Assistant to the Chief Assistant, Ministry of Supply, Near and Middle East! This suggests that I am Chief Assistant, but who I am supposed to be assisting is more of a mystery.

But it does mean I can finally get some leave. It's back via Cairo again but it will be worth it — a whole six weeks! I can't wait to see the folks, and hope we can meet up, too. Not sure if you will be in London at any point. What do you think?

Can't say much in a letter but we've been

doing the rounds of people who oil the wheels: the President's aides & Ministers, key bods in the ex-pat fraternity and the Archbishop, who's now a friend — who'd have thought it! Visiting hill farms & filatures here in the city.

I expect you are weaving 'my' raw by now? It seems the ministry is also at last starting to appreciate what we've done out here. The raw might not be up to Japanese standards, but hopefully it's bringing our pilots down safely.

Time for bed. I hope to see you very soon.

Dear, sweet Michael. How he little knew about the problems his silk yarn had caused us. But I wasn't going to tell him. He was doing his best, and it was better than nothing.

A few weeks later he telephoned. He was back in the country. 'Can we meet?' he said. 'I'm down in London on Thursday.'

'It's a bit tricky for me to get away that day,' I said, flicking through the diary.

'I could come to Westbury instead, around teatime? Call it a business trip and charge it to the Ministry? I'd have a couple of hours before I have to get back.'

'Cracking idea,' I said. 'It's been ages. We'll go for tea. But there won't be any Battenberg this time, I'm afraid.'

'Just seeing you will be treat enough for me,' he said, sweetly.

As I waited for him at the station I found myself curiously nervous and eager to see Michael again, with his big open smile and easy humour. So much had happened since then, and

I looked forward to hearing about his Middle East adventures.

Even though we had only met once we'd had such good fun together it felt as though I already knew him well, but when he climbed off the train at Westbury Station he looked so stiff and serious I began to think my memory had deceived me. As we walked into town, making faltering small talk, I wondered whether the afternoon was going to be heavy going.

The Chantry Tea Room was run by a couple of elderly spinster sisters who had kitted out their front room with dark oak furniture and faded frilly chintz. Their teacakes and scones were legendary, though rumour had it that their wartime jam was disgusting.

We were the only customers that afternoon and, once we had been shown to our table, I opened my handbag and revealed the jar of Mother's homemade raspberry jam I'd sneaked from home.

'You cheeky little devil,' he whispered, laughing at last. 'We can't use that. The old dears would be so insulted.'

'I don't see why not. We don't have to tell them,' I said.

When the scones and teacakes arrived he tried the carrot jam and made a face. So I opened my jar under the table, and we giggled like schoolchildren as I made a sticky mess trying to sneak a dollop onto each of our plates. It broke the ice and, as we ate, he relaxed into the Michael I remembered.

'What we'd give for a slice of Battenberg these days,' he said, trying one of the dried-up pastries the ladies had proudly presented on a tiered porcelain cake stand. 'The Arabs are hot on honey pastries, which are delicious, but I do yearn for a good old sponge.'

After that, our two hours rushed by as he entertained me with stories of his extraordinary journey out to Beirut via the Nile and Cairo then by flying boat across the Med, about the Lebanon and the filatures he'd been busy setting up in Beirut to process the cocoons into raw silk.

'Where do the cocoons come from?' I asked.

'I've been dead lucky getting introductions to dozens of old silk farmers living in the hills,' he said. 'They usually only produce enough for their own use, or for their village, but I persuaded most of them to double their quantities. They'd do anything for a bit of extra cash at the moment,' he said. 'But listen to this, Lily. Most of the big import/export merchants in Beirut were sending all their Iranian and Turkish raw to Italy, on a big contract from Mussolini. I couldn't think how to get my hands on it.'

'How did you get your hands on it?' I said.

'I went to see them and noticed most of the men were wearing skullcaps. They were Jewish,' he laughed.

I was astonished. 'They didn't realise who Mussolini was supporting?'

He shook his head. 'But once I told them, and they went away and checked out my story, all their stocks were mine. For a good price, too. Stroke of genius, though I say it myself.' So confident and kind, so solid and dependable. Not Hollywood handsome, but good looking, with that exotic combination of dark hair and deep violet eyes.

When we came to say goodbye at the station he held my hands, then awkwardly tried to kiss me on the mouth. I turned my face and his lips ended up on my earlobe.

'I'm so sorry,' he blustered. 'I'm such an idiot.'

'There's nothing to apologise for,' I said, blushing foolishly.

'I didn't even think to ask whether you have a boyfriend.'

It felt brutal, but I had to be honest. 'Actually I do. His name's Stephen.'

He looked abashed, struggling to find something to say. 'Is he serving abroad?' he finally blurted out.

'He's with the Pioneer Corps,' I said quietly. It was not prestigious, I knew. Michael would wonder what kind of person this boyfriend was. But it was the truth.

'Lucky fellow,' he said wistfully, then frowned. 'Oh no, I don't mean lucky being in the Pioneer Corps.' He faltered, and added, 'Not that there's anything wrong with that.' Confusion flooded his face again. 'Oh goodness. I'm digging myself into a hole here. Can't get anything right.'

The whistle went, there were only a few seconds left.

'Please don't worry. I like you very much as you are,' I tried to reassure him. There was a longer blast on the whistle, and he climbed into the carriage and opened the window. As the train started to puff away he shouted, 'And you're a wonderful girl.'

A few months later I received a Christmas card. Michael had made it himself — they were not widely available in the Lebanon, I assumed — a pen and ink drawing of him in swimming trunks on a beach, standing by a fir tree, and wearing a Father Christmas hat. Inside he wrote: *Hope Christmas is as happy as possible. I had such a lovely time seeing you in Westbury that day, and thank you for the delicious jam! Sorry for being such a dolt. But I will always be your friend and if you ever change your mind . . .*

★　★　★

It turned out to be the most memorable Christmas of my life.

We'd made a determined effort to be jolly, put in an early order for a goose from a local farmer, and had carefully saved carrots and potatoes from last year's crop. There were carrots in the pudding too, to make it a bit sweeter and cover up the shortage of sugar, but we made a brandy cream to improve the taste. We set aside four bottles of Frank's famously powerful turnip wine, and when Vera popped in on Christmas Eve it was time to start celebrating.

She was bursting with excitement, eyes sparkling in her weary face.

'Look,' she said, pressing a copy of the Red Cross magazine, *Prisoner of War*, into Mother's hand. 'It's a photo of John. He's dressed up as Nanki Poo. In *The Mikado*, would you believe it?'

We gathered round, eager to see. The small

grainy photo showed a group of grinning men in bedsheet kimonos and fake Mandarin moustaches, like a bunch of lads in the village pantomime.

'They look cheerful enough,' Mother said.

'Who was Nanki Poo?' I asked, feeling painfully ignorant.

'A wandering minstrel, it's one of the lead roles. Look at his cardboard guitar,' Vera said, laughing. 'John won't be doing much wandering this Christmas, but at least he's safer there than being in the thick of it.'

Mother peered more closely at the photograph, then kissed it. 'This is a lovely Christmas present. Just knowing he's alive is enough for me.'

'With a bit of luck the Allies'll crack on through Italy this year and get the Germans on the run,' Gwen said, popping the cork she'd been wrestling with. 'Then they can all come home.'

I was barely listening, my head full of thoughts of Stefan. I hadn't seen him since our weekend in the caravan, though we'd spoken on the telephone every week or so. He'd hoped to get leave over Christmas but I'd had no word, and as the evening drew on I resigned myself to not seeing him.

Sitting down for dinner, we toasted to absent friends, and Mother said, 'To Harold, my dear husband.' The room went quiet — it was the first time in many months that she had referred to him by name. 'I thought I'd never recover,' she went on, 'but I'm still here, thanks to you girls. I know he's up there watching, pleased to see us

305

all getting on with it in spite of everything.'

'To Harold, my mentor and my friend,' Gwen said, lifting her glass, and we all did the same. In the sombre silence that followed, the telephone made us jump. I ran out into the hall, my heart banging in my chest.

'Stefan?'

'Stephen. I'm just about to catch a train to London and if I can make it I'll get a connection from Liverpool Street and be there eleven-ish. Is it okay to arrive so late? Sorry I couldn't let you know before, but they've only just released us.'

'Of course it's okay. It's wonderful. We've got a feast lined up.'

'Is there enough? I don't want to make you short.'

'There's loads. And you will stay here with us, of course?'

'What about Grace?' The pips started.

'I don't care what Mother thinks. I'm a big girl now. And I love you.'

'I love you too,' he said just before the line went dead.

* * *

Vera had gone home and Mother and Gwen had giggled their way to bed by the time Stefan arrived, shortly before midnight. He was already in mufti, carrying his small brown suitcase and an army-issue kit bag, his face streaked with railway soot and grey with exhaustion. I made cocoa and we sat at the kitchen table holding hands, just looking at each other, drinking in the

306

joy of being together. Then, faintly, I heard church bells. I raised the sash, and the peal was clear now, echoing off the wall of the mill opposite.

'What's that for?' he asked, looking alarmed.

'This is the first Christmas eve for four years they've been allowed to ring the church bells,' I said. 'Now there's no fear they'd have to use them to warn about an invasion.'

'Bells or no bells, it's enough for me to be back here with you,' he hugged me from behind, nuzzling my neck. 'It's two and a half years since I left Westbury. In that police van. Remember?'

I nodded, barely able to speak with happiness. In the warmth of each other's arms we welcomed the chill night air, listening to the peals ebbing and flowing in the breeze. As they ended I closed the window. When I turned round his face registered something.

'Have you got my writing case? The one I left with you?'

I tiptoed upstairs to get it.

He unzipped it, took out a buff envelope from one of the pockets and set it aside on the table. 'Photos of my family — you've seen them before.' From another pocket he pulled out a small piece of blue and white silk, with two tassels threaded into it. 'This is a part of my prayer shawl.' I felt the weave: good quality twenty-twenty-four rep. 'You know I don't pray. But every English boy has a cricket bat, and every Jewish boy has a tallith. Mother insisted I bring it, to remind me.'

Finally he pulled out a small, red felt

drawstring bag and put it on the table in front of me. 'This was my Mother's. I want you to have it.'

Hands shaking, I pulled it open. Inside was a silver band, set with small pearls and sapphires. Stefan, church bells, and now a ring, I thought, a perfect Christmas.

He took it from me, slipped it onto my wedding finger, then looked up with a huge smile.

'Let's get married. Soon,' he said.

That night we barely slept. We seemed to have been elevated to another plane, beyond the clinging desperation and anxiety of imminent parting that wartime so often brought. Exhaustion made our lovemaking lazy and languid, climbing slowly till we balanced on a pinhead of intensity before falling in a torrent of relief and joy.

Afterwards I lay awake for hours, my whole body glowing.

★ ★ ★

I spent the morning of my wedding day — St Valentine's 1944 — with my head in the toilet. Gwen brought a cup of weak tea and rested it on the side of the sink.

'I feel dreadful,' I groaned. 'I haven't eaten anything different from the rest of you. Do you think it's just nerves?'

'Everyone's nervous on their wedding day,' she said, then added mysteriously, 'but could it be something else?'

I couldn't think what she was talking about. But then, as I retched into the bowl once more, it dawned on me. 'I haven't been counting,' I said wiping my mouth. 'But it does seem a while. Oh hell, I can't be, can I? I thought I'd been careful.'

'It's just as well you're getting married today,' she said, laughing unsympathetically. 'Otherwise you might have some explaining to do.'

The rest of the day went by in such a spin I barely gave it another thought, till later. It was a plain ceremony in Westbury Registry Office with just Mother, Gwen and Vera as witnesses. I wished so much that Father could have seen us — any concerns he'd had about Stefan would have melted away as soon as he knew he had joined up to fight for the Allies.

Mother had spent days at the sewing machine: a simple knee-length dress and jacket in cream Shantung silk for me, and pale green silk blouses for Vera and Gwen as my 'matrons of honour'. She ran out of time to make anything for herself, so wore her best tweed suit.

Stefan, of course, wore his Pioneer Corps dress uniform. It made him look taller and more handsome, but at the same time rather formal and remote, not part of our world. Was it the uniform, I wondered, or just the natural nerves of a young man on his wedding day? Even after the ceremony and a couple of glasses of sparkling wine at the White Hart, he seemed tense and quieter than usual. Never mind, I thought, just wait till we get to our hotel. I know how to make him smile.

We had only one night together before he had to return to the Pioneers. In the almost deserted hotel, the honeymoon suite was dominated by an imposing four-poster bed. From the window was the perfect Suffolk view; a village street lined with wood-beamed houses sloping down to a ford complete with Muscovy ducks and, in the distance, an imposing flint church. In the bay were two Lloyd loom chairs. He sat down and lit a cigarette, apparently oblivious to the view.

'Come and give Mrs Holmes a cuddle,' I said, jumping up onto the bed, admiring the soft white quilt and lace-trimmed linen. 'I've got something to tell you.'

He turned, but his face seemed hardly to register that I'd spoken. He did not move.

'Stefan?'

'For Christ's sake, it's *Stephen*,' he snapped. 'Don't you realise how important it is?' He went to the basin, straightened the mirror, wetted his hands and ran them through his hair.

'I'm so sorry,' I said gently. 'It's hard to think of you as anything other than the Stefan I love so much. I thought it would be okay when we are alone?'

He shook his head, stony faced. 'Not even then,' he said, through his teeth.

'Okay, you'll be Stephen from now on, I promise, even in private. Or do you prefer Steve?' My stomach knotted with confusion and disquiet.

'Whatever you like. Just not Stefan.' His voice was taut as a warp.

'But it's not just that, is it?' I climbed off the

310

high bed and sat in a chair. Whatever was biting him?

He stayed at the basin with his head bent, knuckles white from gripping the sides of the porcelain. I waited, rigid in the uncomfortable chair, hardly daring to breathe.

What was it he couldn't tell me? What could the worst thing be? He didn't love me any more? He'd found out I was pregnant and didn't want the baby? Bad news about his family? He'd committed some terrible crime and was about to be court-martialled?

'Lily?' his head was still down, his voice muffled.

'Yes? What is it? Tell me.' My thoughts ran wild, but the one thing I failed to imagine was what he now said.

'When I wore that uniform today it was,' he hesitated, 'not right.'

'Not right? What was wrong with it?'

He loosened his grip on the basin, straightened his back and came to sit down opposite me. 'Me wearing it was wrong.'

'Why? You're in the Pioneer Corps, aren't you?'

'Not any longer. I've been transferred.' His eyes still refused to meet mine.

'Where to?'

'This is the problem. I am not allowed to tell you.'

I struggled to understand. 'Why is it so secret? Where are you going, what are you going to do?'

'I don't know any of these things yet. But even if I did, I couldn't tell you.'

311

'But I am your wife.' He'd disappeared inside himself again. 'Stef . . . Stephen?'

In the silence I could hear my heart hammering.

'I'm sorry Lily. I cannot tell you any more. Please do not ask me. You just have to accept it.'

Shock was turning to fear. 'Is it dangerous? Are you going to the front line?' Another terrifying thought. 'Behind the lines?'

He shook his head. 'I cannot answer, Lily. Please understand.'

His secrecy was exasperating. 'But why? Did you choose this?' He shook his head again. 'No, they asked me. I could not refuse.'

'*Could* not?'

'Did not *want* to refuse.'

'But why you?'

'My languages, I think, German, French, English.'

'So you said yes to this, this . . . thing. Even though you know it is dangerous?'

'I do not know it is dangerous. All I know is . . . it is very important. We have to push them back, to liberate France, Holland, Belgium, Germany and . . . '

I began to get a glimmer of understanding. 'And your family?' I said, gently.

He nodded. 'And the others. So we can be ourselves again.'

'What about the danger to you? Being . . . '

He put his finger to his lips. 'I am not Jewish,' he said firmly, emphasising each word. 'Not any more, remember? Not for the moment.'

There was something about the simple way he

said this, his tone of absolute resolve, that made it suddenly, perfectly clear. Now I understood. Everything he had done since coming back from Australia was about avenging his country, his race, his family. This was the most important thing for him, so vital that it was worth completely reinventing himself, denying his heritage. So that he could, perhaps, one day, recover it.

For the first time I started to appreciate how hard that must have been. And now, I assumed from what he refused to say, he was planning something even more difficult and dangerous: to go among the very people who would certainly kill him if they discovered his true origins.

I broke the long silence. 'I'm starting to understand. But you must also understand this: you are the most important person in the world to me. Whatever you do, you must promise me you will come home safely.'

He sighed deeply, the tension in his neck and shoulders visibly melting as he slumped back in the chair.

'I will do my best. Thank you for understanding,' he said simply, closing his eyes, overcome with weariness.

'Shall I order some tea?' I said.

Later, when I told him about my missed period and morning sickness, he reacted at first with disbelief and then with utter joy. I lay in bed suffused with love as he pranced crazily round the room stark naked, grinning insanely, whisper-shouting for fear of disturbing the rest of the hotel, 'I'm going to be a father, an oh-so-English father.' The image stayed in my head for weeks, long after he had gone.

★ ★ ★

Mother was over the moon when the doctor confirmed my news. She was back to normal, thankfully, running the house and cooking with great ingenuity on scarce rations. Last year's carefully stored fruit and vegetables had run out or rotted in the cellar but in the kitchen garden the new seedlings were already a few inches high and our fruit trees were in flower.

'My goodness, how exciting. I'm going to be a grandmother. I'll write to John immediately and tell him he's going to be an uncle.' Then she added, a little wistfully, 'I do wish Harold were here to enjoy it, too. What a world to bring a poor little mite into.'

'Come on Mother, it'll all be over by the time he's old enough to know anything different,' I said, cheerfully.

Gwen congratulated me too, and said all the right things, but her eyes weren't smiling. I tried to reassure her life would continue as normal when the baby arrived. With the naïve optimism of every first-time mother I imagined my child gurgling happily in his cradle as I took phone calls, scrutinised accounts and made rounds of the mill floor.

Pressure from Camerons and the ministry was more intense than ever. All the looms were weaving non-stop for eighteen hours a day, and I was grateful when Gwen offered to manage the

314

evening shift. Struggling with morning sickness and the exhaustion of early pregnancy, I usually crept up to bed immediately after supper.

The lengthening days of that spring brought with them an air of anticipation and excitement, even optimism. We really believed the end was in sight. Something was going to happen, soon, though we didn't know precisely what. Robbie intimated we were weaving parachute silk not only for our own airmen but for the Allied fliers too. The country was gearing up for a big push into Europe.

And then, at the end of March, came the telephone call I dreaded.

'It's been confirmed. I've finished training. I am on my way,' Stefan said.

I sat down on the hall floor, feeling dizzy, trying to understand what he was saying.

'What do you mean, 'on your way'? Where to? When?'

'You know I can't say, silly, but soon. Can you come to London tomorrow?'

My head whirred, trying to picture that page of my diary. And then I realised, nothing was more important than this. Everything else could wait.

'Of course. What time?'

'Four? Same place?'

'Perfect. See you there, my darling. I love you.'

'Me too. See you tomorrow.'

* * *

We met at 'our' boarding house, knowing that we had just a few hours together, precious moments to cherish, to keep us going through the separation we knew was ahead.

We were lying blissfully in each other's arms when the moan of air raid sirens started, and there was an urgent knocking on our bedroom door. 'Everyone out,' the landlady called. 'Shelter over the road. Tube station.'

'When will they ever give up?' he groaned. 'It's just their last gasp. Won't amount to much.' We held each other tight under the covers, trying to block out the noise. But when the crackle of the ack-acks began and the explosions came close enough to rattle the windowpanes he got out of bed, pulling on his trousers.

'Come on, we're going to the shelter,' he said.

We dressed hurriedly and ran out of the now-empty boarding house into the street. A warden was shepherding people towards the station down the road. My legs felt like dead weights and he grabbed my hand to pull me along. There were two more thunderous explosions even closer by, and I felt sure we'd be hit before we could get there.

Just as we reached the entrance, a deafening blast knocked us to the floor. Stefan shielded me with his body, covering my head with his arms, his face buried in my hair. Broken glass fell round us like an orchestra of tinkling triangles. For a few moments I lay there, my heart pounding, fearing the worst. He was heavy and I struggled to breathe.

'Lily? Are you okay?' His voice seemed muted — it was only later I realised I'd been temporarily deafened.

316

'I think so,' I gasped back.

When the sound of falling glass stopped we sat up and gingerly started to brush ourselves down. 'Don't move a moment,' he said, getting out a handkerchief to pick the shards from my hair. I could just make out, through clouds of dust, two or three others carefully brushing themselves down, but no one seemed seriously hurt. The explosions had stopped. Perhaps that was the pilot's last bomb, I thought, and he was even now dodging the ack-acks on his way back to Germany.

'That was a close shave.' My voice came out more shakily than I felt.

'Are you okay?' he said. 'How's the baby?'

'Fine, I think,' I said, feeling my tummy. It wasn't even starting to show yet, so how could I tell whether any harm had been done? 'What about you?'

'Nothing serious,' he said. We got to our feet slowly, checking each other for cuts. As the dust started to clear we stood, arm in arm, looking back across the street. The bomb had landed just forty yards away outside our boarding house, and from the crater were leaping dark flames and choking smoke like a giant witches' cauldron. The front wall of the building had sheared away, exposing the rooms above. In the light of the fire we could just make out the bedroom we'd left minutes earlier, the bed probably still warm from our bodies.

We ducked as another bomb dropped close by. 'Come on,' he said, taking my hand. 'It's not safe here. Let's go down and see if anyone's making tea.'

The few remaining hours of our precious night together were spent with several thousand other people squeezed onto the platform like sardines, drinking sweet tea and singing to keep up our spirits.

When they started on 'My Old Man', we both joined in, singing gustily.

'Remember when Grace taught us this song,' he shouted over the hubbub. 'And you told us what 'dilly dally' meant?'

'It was the first time I heard you play the piano,' I shouted back, recalling the little things I'd noticed that day, his long elegant fingers, the wisps of dark hair on the back of his neck.

'That was the day I first fell in love with you,' I whispered, 'though I didn't know it at the time.'

'Oh, I knew it long before then,' he replied, kissing me. 'From the moment I first saw you, at that camp.'

'You're making it up, you soppy thing,' I laughed. 'You were just a boy, just off the boat.'

'Being just off the boat didn't stop me falling in love,' he said. 'I had never met anyone so beautiful in my life.'

Such extremes of sadness and joy, I mused later, stroking his hair as we lay in each other's arms on the hard concrete platform. He left his family in desperate circumstances, but met me. And now I could not imagine life without him.

The next morning he eluded the wardens and braved the shattered boarding house to retrieve his army kit bag and my smaller holdall.

'That bomb was a good omen,' he said, wiping

away my dusty tears. 'We survived that, so we can survive the rest of the war. Look after yourself and little Stevie.' He patted my stomach, and kissed me again. Then he was gone.

By the time my train reached Westbury I could barely stand and had to be helped out of the train. I had never known such agony, overwhelming my whole body in surges of increasing intensity.

The station master hailed a taxi. 'Take Miss Verner to The Chestnuts, quickly,' I heard him say, 'I'll phone for a doctor.'

Dr Fairweather arrived at the same time as me. He opened the door of the taxi, took my pulse, placed his hand on my forehead, asked me where it hurt, felt my belly and said, 'We need to get you inside.' He wrapped my arm around his shoulders and heaved me up the front steps.

As Mother opened the door her face fell slack with shock. 'Lily? What's happened? Is she going to be okay?'

'She's losing the baby,' he said, bluntly. 'Get old towels and a rubber sheet if you've got one. Some newspapers and some hot water would be good, too.'

This can't be happening, I thought through the haze of pain, I'm not ready yet.

They told me that she was a girl, a miniature human being the size of a baby's hand, with all her features starting to form; ten fingers, ten toes, two ears and two firmly closed eyes. Dead, of course. I named her Hannah, after Stefan's mother. He'd like that, I thought.

When it was all over, and the house was quiet

319

and dark, despair hit me like a black tidal wave. As I tried to stifle my wails into the pillow, I heard a quiet knock on the door.

'Lily? Can I come in?'

Gwen knew words wouldn't help. She lay down beside me and held me until I stopped shuddering and eventually slept. When I woke in the early hours she was still there, the soft brushed cotton of her Viyella pyjamas and the smell of her talcum powder wrapped warmly round me. And even as the misery of the past twenty-four hours reasserted its clangour in my head, the gentle rhythm of her breathing soothed me, and I slept again.

20

Silk is often associated with mourning. During Victorian times, black clothing was de rigeur for funeral guests. 'Widow's weeds', black, concealing clothes often of silk bombazine, and heavy veils of silk crêpe, were usually worn for more than a year. Black silk was also used for mourning accessories like handkerchiefs, umbrellas, hats and shoes.
From *The History of Silk,* **by Harold Verner**

There was no news for weeks.

At first I didn't worry. Stefan was brave and smart, and he had promised me faithfully that he would avoid danger wherever he could. There were so many reminders of him that I felt he was still with me. Gwen and I took Mother for a walk in the bluebell woods and we gasped at the shimmering display that nature provided, year after year, in defiance of everything happening around us. The same blue as the sapphires in my ring, I thought, twisting it on my finger and recalling Stefan's proposal. Was it just five months ago? A lifetime had passed since then.

June brought the willow fluff which always reminded me of that day on the bench, when Stefan and I first held each other. At night I would cuddle my pillow and try to summon his presence, the love in his seal-black eyes, the warmth of his body, his slow smile, our wordless understanding.

They told us to listen for an announcement, and as the three of us gathered around Father's old radio to listen to John Snagge, I couldn't help remembering the day war was declared, our first kiss, on Stefan's twenty-first birthday.

D-Day has come. Early this morning the Allies began the assault on the north western face of Hitler's European fortress. The first official news came just after half past nine, when Supreme Headquarters of the Allied Expeditionary Force issued Communiqué Number One. This said, 'Under the command of General Eisenhower, Allied naval forces, supported by strong air forces, began landing Allied armies this morning on the northern coast of France.'

The news was thrilling and terrifying, all at once. Each day we rushed out to buy the newspapers, each evening we stayed glued to the six o'clock news on the radio. Churchill called it 'the beginning of the end'.

Stefan had warned me not to expect any kind of communication, I assumed because he would be behind enemy lines. I couldn't write to him either. In some ways, I thought at the time, this was a blessing. My heart still ached from the loss of our baby but I would not have told him about it when he was so far from home. I consoled myself with the thought that once he was back, we would have plenty of chances to try again.

I read and re-read his letters, kissed his photograph each night before sleeping, and tried to imagine him safe in the care of a French resistance group, growing fat on the fruits of the countryside. He had been taken from me once and returned safely. It would be the same this time. There would be plenty of time for making more babies. My body felt hot and heavy just thinking about it.

But with each passing week my sense of foreboding grew. One night I dreamed I was back on Christmas Day 1938, when Stefan arrived on the porch asking to see me. The low sunlight streaming through the house illuminating his face, his long eyelashes casting shadows on his cheeks. And then I noticed the figure was wearing the uniform of a telegram boy, he was holding an envelope. I woke in a ferment of fear. After that, the possibility that I might never see him again would prowl my thoughts and sometimes pounce, paralysing me with anxiety.

In August came news of the liberation of Paris. Everyone went out to celebrate but I hid in my room, finding it impossible to share their joy. If the Allies were making such good progress, why couldn't letters get through? Stefan must have known how desperate I was for some kind of news. I scanned every newspaper photograph of celebrating Parisians crowding the boulevards and cracking open bottles of champagne, desperately looking for his face among them. It was absurd, I knew, but I couldn't help hoping. Once the hangovers cleared they would be on their way home.

A few more days passed, and the surge of optimism flooding the news reports only helped to deepen my fears.

Then the telegram arrived.

*   *   *

Out of politeness, and to spare the feelings of the painfully young delivery boy, I took the small brown envelope, said 'thank you' and closed the front door. Even without opening the envelope I knew what it would say. With John in a PoW camp, it must be Stefan. *Missing in action, presumed dead.* They always hedged their bets until it had been confirmed.

I did not scream or drop to the floor hysterically, as they did in the movies. My brain went blank, I was frozen to the spot and I appeared to stop breathing. The world went icy cold. If I stayed perfectly still, my subconscious seemed to be telling me, perhaps I could turn back time, to prevent this from happening?

But the grandfather clock tick-tocked steadily. Seconds passed, then minutes. When it started to chime the hour with ten long, clamorous gongs, I was jolted from my paralysis. The world had not stopped.

Numbed of all emotion, I leaned my cheek against the coolness of the stained glass and wondered, in a detached sort of way, what would happen next.

'Who was it?' Gwen said, coming out into the hall. She saw the envelope in my hand and her face bleached white. 'Oh God, Lily, no.'

I tried to speak, to say something brave but no words would come out. She took the envelope,

324

turned it over. 'You haven't opened it.'

I shook my head, numbly.

'Do you want me to?'

I nodded.

★ ★ ★

Mourning is like sleepwalking through deep snow. Its landscape is endless and unchanging. Every step is painful and exhausting. The world becomes monochrome; colours lose their hue, music is muffled and distorted.

Not knowing, that was the most terrible thing. At least that's what I believed then.

Like a drowning soul clinging to driftwood I sometimes allowed myself to imagine that I would open the door and find him on the doorstep, weary but unharmed, and we would fall into each other's arms. But, with dreary inevitability, the chill reality of those words always intervened: *Missing, presumed dead*. I knew what they really meant, and it was easier not to torment myself, not to hope.

Gwen and Mother tiptoed around me. I became expert at suppressing my emotions, and despite their protestations I insisted on going into work, where I applied myself with a single-minded focus I'd never experienced before. Like an automaton. It replaced thinking.

Except at night. When I closed my eyes or even lay in the dark with them open, his face came to me. Sometimes calm and sad, sometimes weeping, troubled and angry, or screaming with fear. Scenarios of his death played out through my head in pitiless variety. He lay in agony, clutching a stomach wound (Vera once told me these were the worst), writhing in the slime of a trench, on a beach with crimson blood pumping onto yellow sand, his face blackening as he burned in a blazing tank, his body flung apart through the air by the violence of a plane crash. I didn't even know when it had happened. I'd been carrying on as normal for days and perhaps weeks, in casual ignorance. The guilt cut like a knife.

The visions denied me the blessed oblivion of sleep. When I dropped off, even for the briefest of moments, I dreamed of terrifying things and had to force myself awake to escape them. Or, worse, would dream that I was in his arms, rolled in our warm, silky cocoon, irradiated with happiness. And then I would wake with a start to the icy, bitter reality. I would never again stroke his skin, smell his hair, taste his lips, hear the deep tones of his voice.

A few desperate nights later, I crawled downstairs to the drawing room drinks cabinet and without guilt drank two large glasses of whisky. In the morning I woke with a throbbing head realising, with grim satisfaction, that for the first time in weeks I'd slept without dreaming.

I did the same the next time, and the next. One night, as I poured the drink, my hands shook so much that I dropped the tumbler. In the half darkness, the sound of the shattering glass was like an explosion reverberating through the silent house. I held my breath, praying that Gwen and Mother were so soundly asleep they would not hear it. Tiptoeing to the kitchen to find a dustpan, I met Gwen coming down the stairs in her pyjamas, holding a hairbrush in front of her like a weapon.

'Christ, Lily, I thought you were a burglar.'

I gestured vaguely towards the kitchen hoping to make her think I was on my way to make tea or cocoa. I could clean up the mess in the drawing room later.

'What are you doing up at this time of night?' she said. 'You smell like a distillery.' Slowly, her sleepy face registered understanding. 'Oh, Lily. I'm such an idiot. I thought you were being so strong. But you're not, are you?'

'I'm fine, honestly.' If only she would go back to bed and let me get on with clearing up.

'Except at night?'

I nodded, not trusting my voice. The sympathy in those pale green eyes was weakening my armour.

'Come on, let's clear up the glass and pour ourselves another one,' she said firmly. She went to the kitchen and came back carrying a cloth and a dustpan and brush, as I stood in the hall, unable to move.

In those few moments, Gwen had understood what had been happening to me, even before I dared admit it to myself. And she realised that ticking me off would only induce more self-denial. How did she manage to be so strong, so intuitive, so generous? She had become the warp to my weft. How had I been so absorbed in my own woes that I'd utterly failed to appreciate this, before now?

It was this realisation, rather than my own

misery, which finally undermined me. Abandoning any attempt to hold back the tears now, I leaned against the wall, my knees crumpled and I slid, snivelling, down to the floor. I was wiping my nose on the sleeve of my nightdress when Gwen pulled me up and led me into the moonlit drawing room, sat me on the sofa, took a handkerchief from her pyjama pocket and put a fresh tumbler of whisky in my hand. She wrapped a blanket round my knees, tucking me in like a child.

'So, talk to me,' she said.

'There's nothing to say.'

'Tell me how much you loved him.'

And so I started, often incoherent, weeping with wretchedness or roaring with rage. How he was my life. No one would ever replace him. About my misery, and my nightmares. 'I just want to die, too,' I moaned, finally running out of words and tears.

Gwen leaned back and stretched. 'You are not going to die, Lily,' she said firmly. 'You will get by somehow. Life goes on. It always does. But now we both need some sleep.'

I nodded, sniffing.

'And you're putting off going back to bed?'

I nodded again.

'Would it help if I stayed with you tonight?' I must have looked disconcerted. She squeezed my hand. 'Just that, stupid. Nothing more.'

That night I slept better than at any time in the past weeks. Each time I woke, Gwen's solid, reassuring presence and gentle breathing soothed me back to sleep again.

I had long since stopped reading the 'killed in

action' columns but the deaths must have been announced in the newspaper, because around that time came a flurry of condolence letters — from cousins and aunts, employees at the mill, some of his former Pioneer pals. Michael, now back in the country, telephoned and promised to visit when petrol rationing allowed. All this I found comforting, even heart-warming. But when the envelope arrived with Robbie's handwriting on the front, my heart sank and I put it aside for opening later.

When I finally plucked up the courage to read it I realised that I need not have worried after all.

Dearest Lily,

We may have had our differences in the past, but please believe me when I say how sincerely sorry I was to hear about the death of your husband Stephen. I am sure he was an extremely brave man and this must be a terrible blow.

I know just a little of what you must be suffering: I too have family members and friends who will never return, and it is hard to imagine the world continuing without them. My only consolation is that their deaths have been in a good cause; what we fervently hope is the defeat of evil. I firmly believe it is now the bounden duty of all of us remaining to appreciate what we have, enjoy every day and work hard to fulfil the promise of the better world that they died for.

I hope to be in Westbury before long and

if so, may I call in to offer my condolences in person?
Affectionately yours,
Robbie

I had to read the signature twice to confirm that its author really was Robbie Cameron. The letter was certainly pompous but the sentiment was surprisingly sympathetic, considering how malicious he'd been about Stefan in the past. Where was the arrogant Robbie I'd first met nearly five years ago? The bully who had threatened me and pushed me into such a disastrous decision? War had changed us all; had it perhaps softened him, made him more compassionate and sensitive? It certainly sounded so, and though I was still suspicious, a part of me rather hoped that he might prove to be a reformed man.

Vera got special leave to come home and see me. We sat on the drawing room sofa for hours as I talked about Stefan, the same words pouring out once more, like the tears, the unstoppable, painful stream. She wept with me, and then took me for a gentle walk around the garden and the orchard, to clear our heads, she said, till it was time for supper.

I had no appetite, hadn't eaten properly for days, but felt obliged to retain some kind of normality by turning up for meals, even though sitting through them was purgatory. This time was no different. The four of us sat in the dining room — with all its memories of Father and the boys — while Mother served the meal she had summoned from our still scarce rations.

Gwen served turnip wine and Vera chatted with Mother about rationing, lavishing compliments about the wonderful culinary results she seemed to achieve with so little, as I pushed morsels guiltily around my plate. Then a long, tense silence fell over the four of us. There really was nothing more to say.

'I must show you my latest letter from John,' Vera said.

'Oh, yes please,' Mother responded eagerly, 'I haven't heard anything for a few weeks. What does he say?'

'He's been moved, to some other camp, Stalag Luft V. He doesn't say why, but reading between the lines he's not that pleased about it.'

' 'Not pleased'?' Mother chipped in quickly. 'He's all right, isn't he?'

'There are whole sentences blacked out by the censor in his last couple of letters, so I wondered if he'd been caught trying to send out information? Perhaps moving him was some kind of punishment.'

'Have others been moved too?' Mother's voice was spiky with worry.

'No, I think it's just him, and that's part of the problem, why he's unhappy,' Vera said.

'Poor boy, that's terrible.' Mother went on, 'I know how important it is for those boys to have their friends, people they can trust.'

Gwen started to chip in and, as the conversation continued, I could feel myself becoming itchy and irritated. Such petty inanities, such minor, miserable little details. Rehearsed over and over again. The compression started to build

331

behind my eyes until it felt as though my head would explode. Why couldn't they talk about something else, something important, for once? John was my brother, and I was worried about him too, but he was alive, for heaven's sake, and relatively safe. While thousands of others were getting themselves killed.

'Oh, I do hope he is safe, Vera, what do you think?' Mother was wittering on. 'Shall we ask the Red Cross to check for us?'

I tried to suppress it, but my anger started rising like a red surge that I couldn't control. For heaven's sake, I thought, John sleeps in a bed every night with blankets and food and a roof over his head. He will come home to us, when it's all over. Unlike Stefan and the others, their bodies scattered in the dirt, discarded like so many pieces of rubbish.

Vera had just started to reply when the dam in my head burst open. 'Oh for Christ's sake,' I barked. 'Can't you just stop talking about John, for once?'

The three of them looked up, their shocked faces as if seeing me for the first time, forks frozen halfway to their mouths.

'It's John this, John that. All the ruddy time. The way you three are going on, anyone would think there was nobody else in the world, nothing else more interesting or important to talk about.'

'Oh, my dear, I am so sorry,' Mother said, 'It must be dreadful for you.'

There was a moment's silence. I glared around the table, daring someone to speak. Then I'd give them both barrels, I thought.

'But John's your brother, Lily, and he's my fiancé,' Vera started.

That was it.

'Yes, and your bloody fiancé is safe and sound, and he will come back to you,' I roared, watching with satisfaction as the blood drained from her face. 'While Stefan — my husband, Stefan, remember him? He's never coming back. Never. Never.'

I threw down my knife and fork with a clatter onto the plate, pushed back my chair and stood up. Mother stood up too.

'No, don't mind about me,' I said. 'You just stay and enjoy your meal, have your little chats about John. I'm going to bed.'

I slammed the door, and didn't care how childish it was.

A little later Gwen came, knocking quietly on my door.

'Go away,' I shouted. But she didn't. She came into my room and said nothing. I held myself stiff, my back to her as she lifted the covers and climbed into my bed. I stayed unmoving, miserable and unyielding, angry with myself for breaking down and being so horrid to my friends and family, to the people who loved and supported me.

But as her warmth started to envelop me, the desire to be held in the arms of another human being became irresistible. I turned around and she pulled me close as the tears came, racking my body once more. Finally we slept, curled like nestled spoons, her breath on the back of my neck, her hand gently stroking my hair, my shoulder, enveloped in the smell of her talcum powder and the regular rhythm of her breath, slowly in-out, in-out.

The next night she did the same, and each night after that. I loved the comforting solidity of her presence, the strength in her arms, the way she listened, in silence, and then said just the right things. Before sleeping, we would whisper like schoolgirls sharing secrets, and I even learned to giggle again. I began to look forward to night times. There was nothing more to it, I told myself, just the consolation of being close.

21

In its natural state Bombyx Mori will turn into a moth after about three weeks inside its pupa, and will exude a substance which dissolves the gummy sericin so that it can push its way out of the cocoon. For commercial silk production, however, it is a sad fact that the moth must be killed before it emerges so that a continuous filament of silk can be recovered undamaged.
From *The History of Silk*, **by Harold Verner**

Normal life, of a sort, slowly resumed. We had no choice. After our great hopes for D-Day, the fighting in Europe was still relentless. At home, bombs — the worst kind yet — were still falling, fire watches to be manned, ration queues to be endured. But there were small glimmers of hope: our boys were starting to win battles, most of the time, and the blackout had been lifted.

Orders from the Ministry of Supply for parachute silk had been steadily reducing to the point that it was hard to justify keeping two shifts going at the mill. I began to worry whether we might have to lay people off, or have enough business to carry us through to peacetime. And after the war, then what? The business world would have changed completely, we would need to find new markets and customers, but who would have the money, or even the desire, to buy luxury items at a time like this? It was hard to imagine, but I began to wonder whether the long and venerable history of the mill might end with me.

At home, the three of us — Mother, Gwen and me — fell into a predictable routine. It was easier to cope that way and I came to resent any change, or any visitors, which might threaten to disrupt the pattern of our days. I tolerated their determined cheerfulness when we were together and was grateful when they allowed me to be alone with my sadness. A world of women, that's what we had become at home, and largely at the mill too, except for the men who were too old or too ill to go to the front line. A comforting, comfortable world of women, loving, supportive and unthreatening.

Gwen and I became inseparable, at work and at home. I couldn't imagine life without her. She read my thoughts and understood my moods, always knew what to say, or what not to say. She taught me how to laugh again and how to drink moderately without getting drunk.

'Five years of war,' she said, raising her glass as we sat on the terrace in the golden light of that late September evening. 'Doesn't it feel like a lifetime?'

A long gap in John's letters caused us to fear the Germans might avenge their defeats by punishing our PoWs. Mother's response was to throw herself even more frantically into Red Cross efforts, and she was out at yet another fundraiser in Westbury Town Hall.

'I can't even remember what it felt like to be at

peace,' I said, taking a long gulp of the cold, sharp drink from my pint glass. We'd opened a flagon of homemade apple wine that seemed to have turned into exceptionally potent, explosively fizzy cider.

'Oh, I remember you,' Gwen said, the freckles merging sweetly across her nose and forehead as she squinted into the low sun. 'That first day at the mill. Fresh faced little thing. All legs and arms, forever flicking your new hairstyle. Didn't think you'd stick it for more than a day or two.'

'I only saw it as a stopgap. Couldn't figure out what else to do,' I said, embarrassed at the memory of my youthful naïvety. 'Apart from nursing or teaching, there didn't seem to be much choice.'

'Proved you wrong, didn't we? You've done so well.'

'Thanks largely to you,' I said, putting my hand into hers.

She squeezed it back. 'Now look at us,' she started, and then stopped mid-sentence, listening. 'What the hell's that?'

'Motorbike? The Morgan? Robbie?'

'Too loud,' she said.

We listened for a second or two more.

The noise stopped suddenly and in that moment we both realised what it was. 'Oh hell, Doodlebug,' I shouted, throwing down my glass and standing up, grabbing her hand and starting to run towards the house. 'Into the cellar, quick.'

We ran through the conservatory, wrenched open the door and tumbled down the cellar stairs, falling into a heap at the bottom, just as the blast shook the foundations of the house. We held our breath as that horribly familiar symphony of glass and shrapnel, like triangles and timpani, seemed to fall all round. Like the tube station in London, that last night with Stefan, I thought. But the cellar was still intact. The door at the top of the stairs had slammed shut, but it was still on its hinges.

'Bloody hell, that was close,' I said. 'You all right?'

I felt Gwen's body shaking and thought she was laughing with relief. But then she sat up, and in the half dark of the cellar I caught the glint of tears on her cheeks.

'Gwen? We're okay. We're safe.' I pulled out a grubby handkerchief and offered it to her.

'For a moment I thought that was it,' she said, in a cracked voice, wiping her eyes and blowing her nose. 'I might have lost you.'

'We might both have been lost, you ninny,' I said, laughing with relief. 'But we're both still here.'

She turned and hugged me again, tighter than ever this time, and whispered into my hair, 'I couldn't bear to lose you, Lily. I do love you, you know.'

'You're the best friend I've ever had,' I said, kissing her cheek.

There were voices from the top of the stairs. 'Mrs Grace, Miss Lily, are you there?'

'Come on, we've got to find out what's happened,' I said, pulling myself out of her arms. We stood up, dusted ourselves down and climbed the stairs on shaky legs. As we emerged into the eerily bright evening sunshine, crunching through the broken glass now covering the conservatory floor, we saw Bert with a couple of other men at the door, all looking shocked and dishevelled.

'Thank goodness you're okay, Miss Lily,' he said. He was panting slightly and I could smell the beer on his breath. They must have run here from the pub up the road.

'We're both all right,' I said, 'we managed to get into the cellar in time, and Mother's out at the Town Hall.' I turned to look at the house. It seemed to have escaped major damage. 'Where did the bomb land? Is anyone hurt?'

'No one hurt that I know of,' Bert said grimly. 'But you need to come and see where it landed, Miss Lily.'

The kitchen garden was untouched but when we emerged into the yard it became shockingly obvious how close the V1 had landed. Through clouds of dust we could see clearly that where the finishing room used to be was now just a crater, surrounded by broken rubble. The walls, roof and every scrap of equipment and roll of silk in the finishing room had been dismembered and scattered around the yard, as if they'd been though a giant threshing machine.

'Bloody hell. Must have been a direct hit.' I felt curiously unshocked, but as we walked down the yard my knees went to jelly and I started to sway.

'Steady there,' Gwen said, putting her arm round my waist. I took deep breaths, trying to comprehend what had happened. Such devastation, just yards from where Gwen and I had been sheltering. Another very close call. A hat trick, after that fateful day at Cheapside and the raid the night before Stefan left. I'd lived through all three.

'Could someone fetch Mother from the Town Hall?' I said. 'She'll be desperate to know we're safe.'

'Shall I go?' Gwen said.

'No, I need you here please,' I said. 'Someone else?'

Bert kicked at the remains of a broken vat. 'Don't look like there's much to salvage there, Miss Lily,' he muttered gloomily.

'Are you sure no one was in the building?' Gwen said.

He nodded. 'Not in the mill, neither,' he said. 'Afternoon shift clocked off two hours ago.

The mill seemed to be relatively intact, but shards of glass hung like bunting of glittering diamonds on the criss-cross tape in every one of the windows. Bert pulled out a set of keys and unlocked the door. As we walked cautiously through each section the extent of the damage became horribly clear: flying glass had been hurled like a million knives slicing through every piece of woven cloth, pirns and hanks of yarn in the weaving, warping and throwing sheds.

'Sod's law, isn't it,' Gwen said, as we looked across the weaving shed from the steps, trying to comprehend the extent of the destruction. 'If the blackout blinds had still been in place they'd have caught most of this.'

'It'll take months to sort out,' I said, feeling very close to tears.

Gwen nodded. We both understood what a mammoth task was ahead, even after the windows were repaired, to restock with raw, throw, wind, re-warp and get the looms weaving again.

News travelled quickly. Within a few minutes dozens of people — neighbours, workers and their families — appeared, and a major clear-up began. Every broom and dustpan was deployed for sweeping, every pair of protective gloves issued to people removing broken glass from the windows, every pirn bin emptied to become make-shift dustbins, every available hammer employed fitting temporary boards at the windows to make the building safe. In the middle of all this activity Mother arrived, with tears of relief in her eyes as she found us. 'What can I do to help, girls?'

'Cups of tea for the troops?' I said.

'Wilco. Coming right up,' she replied, and headed off to the canteen.

Long after darkness had fallen, I called all the helpers together.

'A thousand thanks for everything you've done tonight, you have all been wonderful,' I said. 'Tomorrow's Sunday, and we all deserve a day of rest. On Monday the hard work starts again. Good night, and God bless you all.'

'Let's call it a day too shall we, Gwen? Mother's gone back to get supper.'

As we started back to the house she said quietly, 'You were incredible this evening, Lily. You reminded me so much of Harold. They looked at you with such respect.'

'That's the nicest thing anyone's said to me in a long time,' I said, giving her a hug. 'We make such a good pair, you and me. I could never have done these things without you.'

Gwen kissed me tenderly on the cheek and we went indoors.

I hadn't heard from Vera for weeks and then, one evening, there was a telephone call from her mother.

'Please come when you can, dear,' she said. 'She's home for a few days and says she wants to see you.'

Why hadn't Vera telephoned me herself? When I pressed her mother for more, she just said, 'She's just got herself in a bit of a pickle. Nervous exhaustion, they call it, I'll let Vera tell you more herself, dear.'

'Shall I come now?' I said, feeling a little nervous. I wasn't entirely sure whether Vera had really forgiven me after my outburst about John. Had I somehow contributed to her stress?

'As soon as you can,' she said.

Vera was sitting up in bed, her face even more pale than usual. As I walked in she said, 'Oh, Lily, I'm so glad you've come.' The childhood bedroom seemed hardly changed from the times we'd spent many giggly nights there together. Magazine pictures of horses and film stars still battled for space on the flowery wallpaper.

'What's all this about nervous exhaustion?' I said, sitting down on the bed, taking her hand. It was trembling.

'It's nothing. I just need a few good nights' sleep.'

'Have you been on night shifts?'

She shook her head. 'It's the V2s. Every bloody night, and you can't hear them coming. It's almost worse than the Blitz.' She started shaking with great sobs that made me feel helpless. 'Oh God, Lily, when is it going to end?'

'They're running scared, we just have to carry on for a few more months.' I tried to sound reassuring but wasn't even convincing myself.

'I can't go on,' she wailed. 'Every bed is full and if they don't die we just have to do our best to patch them up and send them out again. Firemen, police, ambulance drivers, factory workers. Just ordinary people trying to make the best of it. Most of them won't ever really recover. They're burned, or we've had to cut bits off to save their lives. Or their lungs are shot from inhaling smoke. The children are the worst. Whatever did they do to deserve this? But every day we have to put on a brave face and pretend it will all be hunky dory. What else can we do?'

She pressed her head into the pillow, thin shoulders juddering. I stroked her hair, trying to calm her.

A little later, when her mother had brought tea, I said, 'I'm so sorry, Vera, I hope I didn't make things worse, having that little paddy with you and Mother over dinner.'

'Don't be silly,' she said, smiling for the first time. 'That's long forgotten. We all knew why you were upset, but it's difficult to know what to do for the best.'

A few days later she had recovered sufficiently to come for tea at The Chestnuts. 'Don't worry,' I told her when she arrived, 'Mother's bursting to tell you about the latest parcel she's getting ready for John. You can talk all you like about him, I really don't mind any more. I'll go and

343

help Gwen get the tea ready.'

As I walked Vera home later she said, quite out of the blue, 'What's going on, Lily?'

'What do you mean, 'what's going on'? With whom?'

'Between you and Gwen.'

'Sorry, I don't know what you mean,' I lied, my stomach knotting.

'The way she looks at you, when you're talking. The way she smiles at you. She worships you. You can't have missed it. There is something going on.'

'There's nothing going on,' I repeated, too sharply. I knew exactly what she was talking about; Gwen's easy intimacy, the pecks on the cheek, the touch on my arm, the hand on my knee. As we'd brought the tea into the drawing room, Gwen had put her hand round my waist.

'Lily?' Vera paused, 'You're not?'

'Not what?' I snapped.

We faced each other in the road, both struggling for words. She spoke first, in a low, quiet voice. 'I suspected she was, you know, one of those. But you, Lily?'

I shook my head. 'I don't understand what you are talking about. Honestly.' Vera's face was blank with disbelief. 'We're just friends.'

'How could you?' she shrieked. 'What about Stefan? Just a few months after he's been reported missing? The love of your life, you said. Whatever are you thinking of?'

'No,' I shouted, my voice resounding down the empty road. 'You've got the wrong end of the stick completely.' I grabbed her by the shoulders, looking directly into her face. 'Listen to me. Can't you understand? Nothing's happening. *Nothing*.'

She looked down at her feet and started to tremble. 'Oh, Lily, I'm so sorry,' she said, in a wobbly voice. 'It's this bloody stress again. I overreact to everything these days. That's why they sent me home. Can't seem to keep things in perspective at all. I should never have said those things.'

'It's all right,' I said, but it wasn't. My legs gave way beneath me, and I sat down suddenly on the grass verge, put my head on my knees. Vera sat down beside me.

'It's just,' I started.

'Just what?'

'I miss him so much it hurts. I can't bear it,' I whimpered. 'My world's fallen apart and Gwen's holding me together. She's a good woman, Vera, so kind, so generous, so strong, always there. I don't know what I would do without her.'

'But, Lily, can't you see what she feels about you? She doesn't want comfort. She's thinking of you in a different way.'

I shook my head, miserably.

Just a few evenings before, as I soaked my aching limbs in the bath with my mind in a kind of reverie, there had been a knock on the bathroom door.

'Come in, door's open,' I called, assuming it was Mother.

Gwen came in, clearly naked under her dressing gown, and sat on the toilet seat. We had never been coy with each other, often parading around in bras and suspenders without thinking, but the way she looked at me now was unnerving. It was too intimate. I felt vulnerable. Then I was thrown completely off guard when she said, suddenly, 'Can I get in with you?' For a moment I thought she was joking, but the smile in her eyes was deadly serious and her implication perfectly clear.

'Oh, Gwen,' I said, sitting up and starting to pull my towel towards me, to cover up my breasts. 'I'm sorry, I'm just getting out.'

Her eyes hooded with disappointment and my stomach knotted as I realised that, unwittingly, I had led her on and now, somehow, I had to disentangle myself without hurting her.

She nodded but didn't say another word as I got out of the bath and slipped away to my room. I waited nervously for her usual knock on the door, but she did not appear again, nor the next night. In a way it was a relief, because I didn't need her nightly comfort so much these days. I was sleeping so much better now. Nothing further was said, and I was relieved when our easy friendship had started to resume. I'd thought nothing more about it, till now.

Walking back from Vera's house I realised that she was right. My craving for consolation had turned into an unhealthy dependency, and I had been taking a terrible risk with Gwen's affections. I must find the courage to talk to her, I thought, to make sure we were both clear where we stood.

A couple of days passed and my resolve wavered. I struggled to imagine how the conversation would go, what I could say without hurting her feelings irrevocably. It was too risky, she was so important to me. I couldn't imagine life without her. The right moment never seemed to come up. And then it was too late.

⋆ ⋆ ⋆

'Miss Lily, there's a man in the visitors' room, says he'd like to speak to Mrs Holmes.'

'Did he give his name?'

'Sorry, I forgot to ask him.' My secretary looked down at the floor, embarrassed by her omission.

'Uniform?'

'No, civvies.'

'Tell him I'll be there in a few moments. Get him a cup of something while he's waiting.'

Cold callers were rare these days. A sliver of absurd hope pierced my carefully constructed defences. It was three months since the telegram, yet I'd had no official confirmation of Stefan's fate. Could this stranger be about to tell me he was alive, after all?

Despite the grey suit, it was clear the young man had seen recent military service: the sallow complexion, a thin face too worn for his years, the brutal haircut parted like a white scar slicing across his head. He held his shoulders stiffly as he stood and formally shook my hand. The left sleeve hung emptily at his side.

'Mrs Holmes? Peter Newman. Thank you for seeing me.' The very faintest hint of an accent; not German, but Polish perhaps?

'Sit down, please,' I said, trying to keep my voice steady. The visitors' room felt incongruous and impersonal. Should I invite him to the house instead, I wondered? No, I'd rather face this without Mother around.

'Mr Newman. How can I help you?'

He smiled, showing sadly crooked teeth, reached for a small khaki canvas bag, just like the parachute bag Robbie had brought to the mill that day, and put it onto the table. I took a deep breath, steeling myself for what he was about to show me.

'I was a good friend of your husband, Steve,' he said, deftly unbuckling the strap with his one hand and reaching into the bag. Steve. Even now the name sounded unfamiliar. 'He was a very courageous man. A wonderful friend. This is for you.'

I observed, in a detached kind of way, that my hands were trembling as I took the envelope with Stefan's curly handwriting on it: *To my darling Lily*. I knew exactly what this was — the letter the troops were all told to write before going to the front line.

'Thank you,' I said quietly, 'Do you mind if I read this later?'

'Of course,' he said. 'In this bag there are some of his effects we thought you might like to have. I will leave it with you.' His effects. What a strange English phrase this foreigner had learned.

There was a pause and I wondered what to say next. I still felt curiously calm. Everything was now clear. 'From your use of the past tense, I take it you're telling me he's dead?' I asked. 'I still haven't had any official confirmation.' My voice sounded flat and unfamiliar, as if someone else were saying these terrible things.

He looked a bit surprised, and nodded slowly. 'I'm afraid so, Mrs Holmes. I am so sorry. I didn't realise you hadn't heard. Would you like a cigarette?' He fumbled in his pocket with his one hand and with fascinating dexterity pulled out a packet of cigarettes and flipped it open, offered me one, then took one in his mouth, took out a Zippo and lit them both.

The familiar feel of a cigarette in my fingers and the long pull of smoke gave me courage. 'Can you tell me how he died?'

His eyes were down, deliberately not meeting mine. 'They told me to say it was the result of enemy action.' The room fell very quiet. No distant rumble of looms or voices on the stairs. He looked up. 'I want to be honest with you, Mrs Holmes. It wasn't really like that. He did not die in the heat of battle, but what he did was just as brave, perhaps more so.'

I followed his gaze to the door. It was ajar. I got up and closed it, my limbs working automatically. When I sat down again he took a deep breath. 'Mrs Holmes, what I am about to tell you is still an official secret, so you must promise not to repeat it to anyone.'

'Go on,' I said, surprising myself with my apparent composure.

'Steve and me and ten others were being dropped behind enemy lines in France,' he started, looking down again, perhaps afraid of the pain he was about to cause. My head went

349

into a spin. Being dropped? By parachute? I knew he'd been on a dangerous mission but this sounded so much braver, and so much more terrifying than any of the scenarios I'd imagined.

'I didn't know he'd joined the paratroopers,' I managed to croak.

'It doesn't matter what organisation we were working for, all you need to know is that we were going there to help stiffen up the resistance.'

' 'Stiffen up'?'

'Get them organised, you know, ready for D-Day. As I said, it doesn't matter.' He looked up at me, checking my response.

'Go on,' I said again, 'Please. I am okay.'

'It was dark and noisy, and bloody scary in that plane,' he said. 'We knew we'd be trying to avoid the flak at the coast, then jumping into enemy territory in the dark, not really sure what we'd find when we got there.' He paused, as if experiencing it all over again, took a deep breath and started again, talking quite quickly.

'Steve was so calm, so self-contained. Always the best person to have around in a fix like that. He knew exactly why he was there — settling the score, he used to call it. And in that plane he reminded me. It gave me courage. We had maps inside our jacket linings, printed on silk. He said you wove it, here at the mill?'

I nodded.

'He also sewed the threads from his tallith into the lining. As you probably know, he wasn't religious but he was going to say the prayer when he jumped, he said. You know it? *Shema Yisrael?* For his mother.'

'Hannah,' I said, with a shiver. Where was she now? Isaak and the little girls? How had they fared? I'd wanted to write to them when we got the telegram, but of course it was impossible.

Peter Newman was still talking. 'But this is what I most want to tell you, Mrs Holmes. When we got to the drop zone, we were all standing in line waiting to jump. I was right in front of Steve, close as this,' he held his hand a few inches from his face. 'So I could hear clearly what he was saying. He shouted 'Good luck chaps', and then, just before I jumped, I heard him whisper, 'I love you Lilymouse. Keep little Stevie safe for me.'' He looked up and smiled shyly at me. 'I thought it might comfort you to know this.'

I didn't even feel like crying.

'Those were his exact words, I can hear them in my ears even now and I thought, you lucky bastard, forgive my French, Mrs Holmes,' Peter Newman said.

I found myself smiling back at Peter Newman, calm and even happy, grateful to him for telling me about this beautiful moment, and at the thought of my precious boy sending his love across the sky.

He carried on, his words tumbling over themselves now, as if desperate to tell the story while he still had the strength. 'But then it went wrong. I landed on a rooftop and buggered my arm,' he waved his empty sleeve. 'Didn't get rescued for a couple of hours and by that time I assumed Steve and the radio ops had landed safely and gone into hiding. The Frenchies found their bodies. They must have died instantly. Still had harnesses and 'chutes on, they said. Christ, I was gutted.'

'They'd been shot?' At least it would have been a quick death.

'No, there were no gunshot wounds. It was a bit of a mystery at the time and when we got back the top brass couldn't tell us anything. ' Peter Newman shook his head, took a drag on his cigarette and stubbed it out viciously.

'They buried the boys secretly near the graveyard, and I got airlifted back home. Couldn't save the arm but at least I'm here.'

'Would you take me back there, one day, show me where they were buried?' I said, with a small sigh of something like relief. Even if I didn't know exactly how Stefan had died, I now knew that he had died honourably, doing something he felt passionately for, with men that he loved. When this was all over, I could visit his grave.

'Of course,' he said, picking up his empty coffee cup and peering into it with an unfocused gaze. 'It would be an honour, Mrs Holmes.'

'Can I get you some more coffee?'

'No, no thank you. You're very kind.'

We fell into silence for a moment. There was a question I had to ask, but I didn't really want to hear the answer. 'I know this might be difficult, but was it possible to find out . . . ' I faltered. 'Did he suffer any pain, do you think? Before he died?'

'Well, I did hear something, a bit later.'

'Please carry on,' I said. Every muscle was knotted with the tension of holding myself together, but I felt a kind of peace. There was nowhere else but this room, this man's voice, the gentle lilt of his accent.

'One day in the hospital I looked at the bed next to me and it was one of our lot, Giorgio we used to call him. He'd been leading one of the other teams. He landed on power lines and lost both his legs, poor bastard. Their radio ops was also killed on landing. When he got back to Blighty they told him another lad died that night. Same way. That made four of them.'

Peter Newman paused, searching for words. 'It seemed they'd come down far too quick. They'd all bought it, almost instantaneously, he said. They would not have felt any pain.'

The room started to sway, like a ship in a swell. I grabbed the table edge to steady myself.

'What do you mean, coming in 'too quick'? What went wrong?' This was so different from what I had expected. I could see them plummeting in the dark, hear the terrified screams. The rocking got worse, nausea rose in my throat.

Peter Newman seemed shaken by the memory of it all, but his voice was strong. 'We don't really know, Mrs Holmes.' He looked at me carefully. 'From what Giorgio was told, the drops were fine and the 'chutes opened okay. They just hit the ground too fast. These things happen. Perhaps we were too low, or it was something to do with the lines, or the packing, or the 'chutes themselves. Don't suppose we'll ever know.'

The 'chutes themselves. As his voice tailed off the little room stopped rocking and went cold and silent except for the phrase reverberating in my head, and then, all jangled up with it, the sound of Robbie's voice: *Get it wrong and . . .*

'Oh no,' I gasped as the realisation hit me like a punch in the stomach, 'not the parachutes.'

'Mrs Holmes?' Peter Newman peered at me, concerned now. 'Are you okay?'

I took a breath, forced my eyes open. The room was a blur. 'Yes, sorry, do go on.' I held myself tight, still gripping the edge of the table, as he started again.

'Not much more to tell I'm afraid. Before I leave I wanted to say,' he faltered and I tried to twist my lips into an encouraging smile. 'I heard so much about you from Steve, and I'm pleased we've met after all this time, but sorry it had to be in these circumstances.' He paused, started again. 'I'm not just saying this, but truly Steve was one of the finest men I've ever known.'

I did not say the words that were shaping themselves in my head like a demonic chant: *It was me. This fine man, your friend, my husband, and those other fine men died because of me. It was all my fault.*

Instead I heard myself politely thanking him for coming, then shook his hand and saw him out.

22

In many cultures, silk is used to wrap bodies before burial, as a mark of respect for the deceased. However among Jewish people it is forbidden to bury the dead in silk shrouds, or clothes embroidered with gold, as this is considered to be an expression of haughtiness and the destruction of useful property.
From The History of Silk, **by Harold Verner**

I watched Peter Newman walking away across the yard and through the gate, strong and alive in spite of his terrible injury. The world that had receded into insignificance in that little room was now bursting with sound and colour all around me, but I was utterly paralysed, unable to think of anything except the words he'd so casually let slip: *the 'chutes themselves.*

In the very spot where I now stood, outside the front door of the mill that evening in March two long years ago, I'd said 'yes'. That potent, fatal lie that allowed faulty silk to go through. Faulty silk makes faulty parachutes. Faulty parachutes cost lives. A single syllable, my word alone, probably caused the deaths of four men. What if, instead, I'd said a simple 'no'? A sweet and honourable truth, told with the courage to stand up to Robbie's bullying, admitting that the silk wasn't ready? Stefan and the others might still be alive. My boy would have come home to me, held me in his arms, grown old with me.

Instead he was rotting in a hidden grave, deep in foreign soil. Why had I been so weak, so unable to just tell the truth? And then, even worse, why had I been so deceptive, concealing my lie and never telling a soul.

Now I know the true meaning of retribution, I thought, as memories of those Old Testament illustrations in our family bible came swimming into my head. The screaming souls drawn irretrievably downwards into a pit of flames. The pain of guilt and not knowing felt like a thousand knives in my head. This truly was hellfire, and no less than I deserved.

It would be better to be dead than to live with this abyss of unanswerable questions. For a few mad moments I considered the options for killing myself. Lying on the railway line waiting for a train, or weighing my pockets with stones and falling into the river? Or perhaps jumping into one of those deep steaming cauldrons in the dye room? I could almost feel the scream of scalding flesh, the dark boiling liquid blistering my eyes. In fact, I welcomed the idea. Nothing could be worse than this agony of shame.

But it wasn't only my fault, that silk. The raw was poor quality; Bert was incompetent. And Gwen, where had she been at that critical moment? Not in the finishing room supervising Bert, as I'd specifically asked. No, she was elsewhere in the mill, sorting out some 'emergency'. She'd taken her eye off the ball. The blame was partly hers. She helped to kill Stefan.

The tea break klaxon sounded above my head, interrupting these crazy, nightmarish thoughts. I turned and went inside, surprised to find my limbs still functioning, and climbed the stairs to the office. I heard myself saying, 'Terrible headache.' No need to mime the pain. 'Going home. Any problems, ask Gwen.' The secretaries nodded sympathetically. Clearly I looked the part, too.

There was only one thing in my mind now: anaesthesia. I slipped across the yard, crept into the house, grabbed a full bottle of whisky from its hiding place in the cellar and ran up the stairs to my bedroom, ignoring Mother's call, 'Lily, is that you?'

I wedged a chair against the door and drew the curtains, hoping the darkness would help to bury my despair. The shame was excruciating, my anger burned like a fire and all I could think about was stopping the agony. I sat on the bed and started gulping straight from the bottle, retching as the fierce liquid seared my throat. After a while the pain began to recede. I became fascinated by the way the pattern on the curtains was swirling around. My thoughts retreated, and my eyelids began to close.

Much later I woke to hear Gwen knocking, trying the door handle. The chair didn't budge, I noticed with grim satisfaction. 'Lily, are you in there? Let me in, won't you?'

'Don' wan' see anyone,' I shouted, my head throbbing horribly with the effort.

She tried the door again. 'What's the matter, love? Please let me in.'

My head was spinning and I felt sick, furious to be woken and reminded of my wretchedness. 'Not your bloody love.' I heard myself screeching. 'Go away'.

There was a silence. She'd gone, but I knew she wouldn't give up that easily. I must have passed out again, because I woke to hear something heavy being applied to the door. With a horrible crunch of broken chair the door swung open and there she was, outlined against the light, holding what looked like a crowbar.

'For God's sake, Lily, why did you block the door?'

'Go 'way,' I groaned. 'Don't want anyone.'

I could see by her shadow in the doorway that she was hesitating. But she said again, 'No, Lily. What's going on? You've got to tell me.'

Her kindly persistence seemed to act as a catalyst, like Jekyll's potion, or the rising full moon for a werewolf. The fetid mixture of sadness and guilt, anger and intoxication turned me into some kind of deranged, enraged animal. Rationality slunk into the shadows.

'Tell you wha's going on,' I slurred, launching myself off the bed and trying to stand up, swaying like a sailor newly onshore. Holding onto the chest of drawers and attempting to square my shoulders, I heard a stream of crazy language coming out of my mouth. It was my voice, but I had no idea where the words were coming from, and neither the will nor the power to stop them. Relinquishing responsibility felt deliciously sweet.

'The silk, parachute silk. Bert buggered up

when Mrs So Ruddy Important was oh so busy somewhere else. Tha's what killed Stefan. Three others besides. Fucking faulty parachute silk.' I enunciated these last four words clearly and the alliteration felt good, so I said them again. 'Fucking faulty parachute silk.'

She closed the door behind her. 'Stop shouting, you'll wake Grace,' she said, quietly. 'You're drunk.'

'Very perspi-spict-atious of you.'

'Sit down,' she said, more forcefully now. 'I'll get you a coffee.'

'No,' I shouted, swaying dangerously. 'Don' want bloody coffee. Don' want anything. Go away.'

'I haven't a clue what you're talking about. Calm down and try to explain what you mean.' Even through my booze-blurred senses I could tell she was losing patience.

'Tell you wha' I mean,' I said, peering at her in the dimness, struggling to stay upright. My tongue felt too big for my mouth. 'A man came, today. Friend of Stefan. Said they all jumped out of a plane. Over France. Fucking faulty parachute didn' work.'

The silence was so profound for a moment I thought I'd gone deaf. Then she moved towards me.

'Oh my darling Lily. Why didn't you come and tell me?'

I held up my hands to ward her off, almost losing my balance. 'Don' bloody darling me,' I snarled. 'Don' come near me you, you . . . ' Drunk as I was, I managed to stifle the word, but

359

she knew what I'd been about to say and backed away, her face luminous in the darkened room.

'But the parachute might not have worked for lots of reasons. How can you say it's anyone's fault?'

'Telling you now!' I heard my shout reverberate in the room.

'What faulty silk, anyway?' she said, quietly persevering. 'We didn't sell any faulty silk.' She paused, and then her face contorted with the shock of comprehension. 'For Chrissake, Lily, not those rolls, that afternoon?' she hissed.

'When you were s'posed to be there, Gwen. Making sure.'

'But I *told* you those two rolls were faulty. You didn't let Robbie take them, did you?' She was bellowing now, her eyes glittering in the gleam slipping through the gap in the curtains.

'He wanted twenny rolls. We promised twenny.' It came out as a snarl.

'You *didn't tell* him?' Her voice thin and incredulous, 'You didn't say *anything?*'

'Course I didn' bloody tell him. He'd've closed us down.'

Some vague sense of reason in my addled mind suggested the argument was deeply flawed, and confused me. My anger was starting to dissipate and I felt numb and deeply weary. I wanted to close my eyes for ever.

'Jus' go away. Wanna sleep.'

Before I'd even registered that she'd left the room I became aware that the door was closed and the room had fallen dark again. I was still standing, holding onto the chest of drawers. I crawled back to bed and fell into dreamless unconsciousness.

Early next morning I woke with a fearsome headache and raging thirst, and went downstairs for water. The events of the previous day were like a horrible nightmare. I couldn't believe they'd happened.

But when I went into the kitchen there was a letter propped against an empty milk bottle, with my name on it. I sat down and, with my head throbbing and eyes swimming, read:

> *Lily.*
> *For the past few hours I have been walking, trying to make sense of what you seem to be accusing me of. I am so sorry about what you have learned about the way Stefan died. He was very dear to me, too. I don't know exactly what his friend told you, but with all the millions of parachutes being produced it seems against all odds that this accident could have been caused by Verners silk.*
>
> *I have no idea why you allowed Robbie to take those rolls, but you seem to suggest it was my fault. For any part I played in this, I am deeply sorry.*
>
> *I have gone to Mother's for a few days.*
> *Gwen*

She came back a week later, and I tried my hardest to make amends, but it was never the same. We still functioned, of course, went to work each day, ran the business, dealt with staff and customers. But I felt empty and devoid of emotion, as if my soul had been stolen. Once or twice she tried to talk to me, to console me. Each time I brushed her off. Mother sensed that things were wrong and questioned me a few times, but I refused to discuss anything. I barely knew how to explain it to myself.

The only sensation I felt with any certainty was guilt. It gnawed at me like a canker; guilt that pride had caused me to lie so disastrously, guilt that my lie had possibly caused the death of my husband, guilt that I had accused my closest friend of being somehow complicit in my own terrible, unforgiveable error.

I couldn't bring myself to read Stefan's farewell letter, or even to look inside the canvas bag of his 'effects'. They stayed where I had thrown them, in the corner of my room, until one day I couldn't bear to look at them any more. I gathered them up and stuffed them, unopened, into his old suitcase alongside the zippered writing case containing his photos and other family mementoes. A few days later, in a fit of anguish and guilt, I wrenched off my wedding band and his mother's engagement ring and put them into the red felt drawstring bag. This went into the suitcase too, along with the Hay Camp note, and the bundle of his letters and the wedding photographs I had so painstakingly pasted into an album. I locked the suitcase and pushed it to the back of the wardrobe in the spare room, so that nothing was left to remind me of my complicity in the death of the man I had loved so much.

As the weeks went by and deepened into a callously cold winter, my guilt congealed like the ice on the flooded water meadows. I became miserably, implacably angry with myself and with the world. The only remedy was to grin and bear it, to soldier on, get over it. The war went wearily on, as many thousands more perished with each tiny victory.

We kept the home fires flickering, a little feverishly. Oh, we tried, Gwen and me. For a while we pretended that everything was back to normal. But as her bitterness turned into sorrow, I felt worse for hurting her all over again. Slowly, it became clear to both of us that there was nothing she could do to alleviate my wretchedness, and she seemed to build a self-protective barrier against my more unpredictable moods. We learned just to coexist. We were friendly enough, but the trust had evaporated and we communicated only at the most superficial level.

★   ★   ★

At last spring came and news that Hitler was dead, and everyone felt sure that the Germans would now cave in. Within days we learned that a peace agreement was about to be signed, and our hopes lifted even further. On the morning of Tuesday 8th May it was announced that Churchill would address the nation on the radio at three o'clock. More than a hundred workers, many of them wearing red, white and blue, gathered in the works canteen with their husbands, wives and families, to listen. The atmosphere was strangely muted; people greeted each other with respectful handshakes and there was an expectant hush in the room, as if they could hardly believe that this moment was really about to arrive.

But as soon as the words 'unconditional surrender' came over the airwaves, their cheers raised the roof. People were laughing and weeping all at once, kissing anyone close by, while others shushed them, eager to hear the rest of the speech. The hubbub hushed as Churchill continued, paying tribute to the men and women who had laid down their lives for victory and those who had 'fought valiantly' on land, sea and in the air, and erupted again with whoops of joy as he ended: 'We must now devote all our strength and resources to the completion of our task, both at home and abroad. Advance Britannia.'

'Three cheers for Mr Churchill,' someone shouted.

'And the Royal Family,' another added, and as everyone hurrahed and cheered Gwen nudged my arm, and whispered, 'Your turn, Lily.' My head went into a spin. I had been so busy enjoying myself that I'd forgotten that people would expect me to make a speech. I certainly hadn't prepared anything.

What would Father say, I wondered, as I stepped up onto a chair, just as he had done that day he'd tried to scotch the sabotage rumours. Looking out over the crowd and waiting for the clapping to stop, the answer came: there was no need to emulate my father any more. All I had to do was simply be myself.

I took a deep breath, and started: 'This is truly wonderful news and I think Mr Churchill has said it all,' I began, and waited for the cheers to die down. 'It remains only for me to thank you from the bottom of my heart, you and your families, for so steadfastly supporting me and my family throughout these terrible long years, and for working so hard to produce the essential supplies which, I am certain, have significantly helped this country achieve the peace we have all longed for.'

As I paused for breath, there was a deep, resonant shout of, 'Hear, hear.' Even in those two words his voice was instantly recognisable; there at the back of the room, standing a head taller than most of the crowd and beaming broadly, was Robbie.

It threw me off my stride for a moment, but I was determined to continue. 'I know that many of us have loved ones who will not be coming home, and my heart goes out to you all. But we can also look forward to welcoming others who made it through. In particular, we are hoping to hear news from my brother John, before very long.'

After more cheers I carried on, 'So thank you all once again. I am sure you will want to go and celebrate with your friends, so we are closing the mill now and for tomorrow. We will reopen at eight on Thursday morning. I gather something's been planned on the Market Hill and at the town hall this afternoon' — I looked over to Mother, who nodded — 'so we look forward to seeing you all there.'

'Three cheers for Miss Lily,' came the shout, and there were more hurrahs and much applause as several strong men lifted me onto their shoulders and carried me high above the crowd, my face burning with a mixture of embarrassment and pride. When we came to the back of the room Robbie reached up for my hand and they let me gently down to the ground beside him.

He kissed me on the cheek. 'Well done,' he said. 'Your father would be proud.'

'Thank you,' I said, flushing all over again. I wasn't going to let him spoil this day of celebration. The tables had turned — I had faced the worst and there was nothing left to fear, certainly not Robbie. The future of the mill no longer depended on his contracts; I was in control once more.

'Isn't it a wonderful day?' he said. 'Would it be too much to ask whether I could join you and the family for the celebrations? I've brought a few bottles as a contribution.'

'I expect we'll be going into the town centre to enjoy the festivities later,' I said, too excited and elated to be bothered about why he'd turned up just now, 'but you are welcome to join us for a quick drink at The Chestnuts first.'

I sent him back with Mother and went to tidy up a few things in the office. By the time I got to the house the living room was crowded with people in loud, celebratory mood: Vera's parents and some other family friends, mother's Red Cross colleagues, a couple of senior managers from the mill and their families, invited by

Gwen. Robbie was making himself useful by pouring drinks.

'Where did all this come from?' I said, as he passed with a tray of generously filled champagne flutes and whisky tumblers.

'Best not to ask,' he said with a wink. 'Scottish relations can come in handy at times. And there's more in the car in case we need it.'

By the time we set off for the town centre I was already feeling a bit squiffy and needed to steady myself by holding Robbie's arm on one side, and Gwen's on the other. I had never seen such celebrations in Westbury before: the Market Hill was packed and the party in full festive swing. All the shops had been decorated with red, white and blue bunting, and after a speech by the Mayor from the town hall steps, a band started up in the square.

'Care to dance, Mrs Holmes?' Robbie said, holding out his hand in that courteous gesture that so reminded me of the day we'd first met, New Year's Eve six years before. Before all the threats and bullying, when I was simply Miss Lily Verner. Before Stefan.

I don't remember saying yes, but I found myself in Robbie's arms, happily waltzing and foxtrotting as though there had never been a moment's ill feeling between us. Gwen gave me a curious look, but next time I saw her she seemed to be engaged in conversation with a group of people and had stopped watching.

After a while, the band struck up some more jazzy numbers and Robbie swung me round until I complained of feeling giddy and a little sick. He guided me over to the steps of the grocery store and went off to find a glass of water. While I waited, my head spinning, the music changed to ragtime. It was Stefan's music: I was suddenly overwhelmed with an almost unbearable surge of sorrow. The last time I had heard this tune, he had been playing it, his beautiful fingers dancing over the keys of Mother's baby grand.

By the time Robbie returned I had abandoned myself to my misery and tears coursed down my cheeks, unchecked.

'Lily?' he said, looking at me with concern. 'Oh, my dear wee girl. I'm so sorry, it's obviously a bit much for you. We'd better get you home.'

I leaned on his arm gratefully as he steered me through the crowds and down the road to The Chestnuts. Once there, he made coffee and came to sit on the sofa with his arm around my shoulder. As I sipped the coffee and started to sober up, the reality of this strange situation came home to me.

'Feeling better now?' he asked. I nodded, but the truth was that I had begun to feel queasy all over again. Whatever was I doing, resting in the arms of a man I had once hated more than anyone in the world? Alcohol loosened my tongue, and the words popped out of my mouth without thinking. 'Robbie,' I said, 'why are you so being nice this evening?'

He laughed. 'What a curious question,' he said, stroking my hair. 'We are at peace. It's the best day we've had for years. Besides, I'm always nice, aren't I?'

'Not when you bullied me about the silk. Not

when you threatened to tell Father about Stefan,' I said, astonishing myself.

He sat up and looked at me with a hurt frown. 'You must be imagining things, little one,' he responded smoothly, stroking my hair, 'I don't recall threatening you with anything, ever.'

'And then Stefan and the boys were interned,' I persisted, looking directly back at him. 'Did you have anything to do with that?' At last, I didn't care what Robbie thought. The sense of freedom was glorious.

To his credit, he looked visibly shocked. 'For goodness sake Lily, I was hurt when you turned me down and if I said anything out of turn it was only because I was green-eyed with jealousy, but I'm not that vicious. The authorities had records of all enemy aliens. It was just routine.' His shoulders slouched. 'Whatever must you think of me?'

I really wanted to believe him. I turned away, trying not to show in my face that the nagging doubt was still there.

'My dear Lily,' he murmured, turning my face back towards him with a gentle finger. 'The war is over. Can't we forgive and forget? I'd like to think we could be friends in future.'

He leaned forward and for a split second I was afraid he might be about to try and kiss me, and wondered what I would do if he did. But just then, to my great relief, we heard laughter on the front step and the key in the front door. Mother and Gwen were back. Robbie pulled away to a respectable distance at the other end of the sofa. They came in and we all had another drink or two, talking about the celebrations, our joy that Europe was finally at peace and when John might be freed at last. I don't remember exactly how I managed to get upstairs but next morning I woke late, still in the dress I'd been wearing yesterday, and with a terrible hangover.

I climbed gingerly out of bed and manoeuvred my way downstairs, trying to avoid any sudden movements and keeping my head as steady as possible. On the kitchen table were two notes. One was from Robbie, thanking me for 'a very special evening' and saying that he looked forward to seeing me again very soon.

The other was an envelope, addressed to Mother and me. It was a short letter ending, simply, *Verners has been my world, and I will miss you all, but now the war is over, I must go to look after my mother. Forgive me for leaving without saying goodbye, I have never been good at partings. Thank you both, for everything. Gwen.*

She left no address.

23

Since the 1940s artificial fibres have replaced silk for many uses. But despite these remark-able advances there are still certain occasions for which nothing can replace a genuine silk for its lustre, warmth, weight, depth of colour and for its sheer, breathtaking beauty.
From *The History of Silk,* **by Harold Verner**

It is September, my least favourite month. The month of melancholy signs, of imminent endings: swallows like commas on television aerials, horse chestnut leaves yellowing and starting to fall, mellow evenings drawing in with a sharp chill. The month when both love and war were declared on the same day, nearly sixty years ago. The day that changed my life forever.

I feel increasingly frail and find myself wondering gloomily whether my health will hold out through another winter. Will I see the swallows return? The chestnuts bloom? Was his funeral only three months ago, and is it only two months since my dreams of starting a new life took such a sorry turn? I have trouble recalling my own name sometimes, but the memory of that morning is as clear as if it were yesterday. It was twenty-four hours until they found me, and they're still having trouble forgiving themselves.

'What if I hadn't called round that day, if you'd been stuck in bed for another night and day? You could have died,' Emily says, alarmingly.

Indeed I could.

It was the day after her parachute jump. I'd waited by the telephone in an agony of anxiety, and when she finally rang she gabbled so much with excitement that I couldn't understand a word she said. At least she'd landed safely, surviving without a scratch. I went to bed early, relieved that all was right with the world once more.

I woke to find myself lying on my back in bed like a stranded turtle, unable to turn over or get up. For a while I thought it was one of those dreams where your arms and legs refuse to work. I tried to wake up properly to thwart the dream, then opened my eyes and saw through the bedroom curtains that the sun was already high in the sky. I was already awake, and in a far worse nightmare: I couldn't move my right arm and leg. They were dead weights. My pulse pounded like a jack hammer. I can't have a heart attack now, I thought, feeling panicky. I am only eighty. There is so much more living to be done.

After a while my heart slowed and I started to think more rationally. It's probably just a momentary spasm — a touch of cramp perhaps, I reasoned. I tested my other limbs: my left arm and leg seemed to work and I could lift my head off the pillow. I struggled to sit up and managed to prop myself onto one arm. But when I attempted to push myself up fully I slipped, terrifyingly, halfway out of bed with my leg slumped on the floor. I was teetering on the balance. If I fell I would never be able to get up again.

With enormous effort I leaned over and with my good arm managed to haul the dead leg back onto the bed. It was utterly exhausting. As I lay back, shaking from the effort, trying to calm my racing heart, the full reality of my plight became clear: I was alone in the house and unable to get out of bed. I could be stuck there for hours, even days. I could be paralysed for good. If I was dying no one would find me till it was too late. I started to feel very sorry for myself, not an emotion in which I am accustomed to indulge.

I remember watching the cloud shadows travelling across my curtains with great speed. It must have been windy outside. I pulled myself together by trying to remember what day it was and spent a few moments going through what had become my weekly routine, if that is what you could call it. Emily's jump was on a Sunday, so it must now be Monday. No one was due to visit. I struggled some more to move my leaden limbs, but nothing happened.

After a while I started to get hungry and thirsty. And I wanted to urinate. Eighty's no age to become incontinent, I thought, as the pain in my bladder got worse.

I must have dozed off again, as the sun seemed to have moved around and there was a cool patch beneath my back. I realised with disgust that I had peed in my sleep. I started to weep with self-pity; this was too much to bear. Then the phone started to ring. At least someone was trying to get in touch with me. They will get concerned that I do not answer, and come to see what's happened, I thought. They will break the door down and rescue me.

The phone stopped for a few moments, then started again. The sound echoed through the empty house.

* * *

In the hospital they did lots of tests. 'I'm afraid it's a stroke,' the doctor said. 'But you're a lucky lady. You should be able to use your arm before too long and you may even be able to walk again if you do what the physio says.' I have been doing her fearsome exercises twice a day, and they seem to be working.

A stroke can have a silver lining. The family has moved into The Chestnuts to look after me. I can't get up the stairs, so I they have created what Emily calls my 'bedsit' in what used to be the dining room. The downstairs bathroom and toilet are close by, and with my stick I can hobble about. I can even get to the kitchen and make myself a cuppa. Life is not so bad, after all.

The house bustles again with the noise of family activities, Emily's younger brother and his friends sliding down the banisters, pop music blaring from the record player, the clatter of plates and the smell of cooking, the ringing of the telephone, the slam of the front door as they leave for work and school.

This morning Emily and her mother arrive together with my elevenses tray and a packet of Garibaldis.

'Dead fly biscuits, my favourite,' I say, to make Emily grimace. It works every time.

'How would you like to see my DVD?' she says, opening the packet while her mother pours. It seems an odd time to settle down for a film but I'm not complaining.

'I love going to the flicks,' I say.

'It's not a movie, it's a film of my parachute jump,' Emily says. 'The cameraman jumped beside me and took a film, to keep as a memento.'

My heart starts that skipping rhythm again. It's become so commonplace I take little notice. I reckon that while my heart's still beating, it proves I'm alive. But today it does seem a little more irregular than usual.

'Lily?' Louise has that concerned look. 'Are you okay?'

I take a deep breath, my usual trick when I need to pull myself together. 'Yes, darling, I'm fine,' I say, with only the slightest quaver.

'Have some tea.' She passes a mug. I'm glad we don't use cups and saucers any more. I can use two hands to steady a mug without looking too obvious.

Emily puts the DVD into its slot, and looks for the remote control.

'It just came today, I haven't seen it yet,' she says. 'To be honest I can't remember much, it was sooo scary. I'm sure I swore quite a bit, you'll have to forgive me.'

The music starts, loud and upbeat, and behind the titles is a tiny, flimsy aeroplane that seems hardly bigger than a crane fly. There is Emily, in

375

an oversized orange flying suit and cumbersome backpack, waving at us, and then climbing into the plane, and the door closing. There she is again with all the others, sitting silently in rows like fat orange pupae, as the plane takes off. We see it from the ground, climbing until it becomes a speck in the sky.

The film cuts back to inside the plane and the moment when Emily gets up from her seat and someone hooks her onto what she tells us is called a 'static wire.' For a heart-stopping moment she is outlined against the sky through the open door of the plane. Then she gives the camera the thumbs-up, a terrified smile beneath the goggles and she's gone, falling away towards the earth, shouting words we cannot make out.

The room feels superheated and I struggle to breathe the heavy air. The picture swims and blurs, I squeeze my eyes as tight as possible to shut it out, but I can't close my ears. The sound track is strident, painfully loud. Emily's shouts become distorted and then deepen, and I can hear his fear, and my own voice shouting back over the rushing wind, desperate to reach him.

Then there are arms around me, a warm hand holding my wrist, another stroking the hair back from my forehead, calming voices in my ear.

'Easy now, Lily. Deep breaths. Can you open your eyes? You're with us, safe in your room, look. Safe and sound. There now, you're fine.'

A little later I find myself lying on the bed, fully clothed, but wrapped warmly in my blanket. My radio is on quietly in the background tuned to my favourite World Service, and I can hear the slow comforting tick-tock of the grandfather clock in the hall. This, and the familiar smell of the wool blanket, lulls me, and I sleep.

★ ★ ★

Now it is teatime and Emily has brought me a poached egg on toast.

'How are you feeling, Gran?' she asks. 'Would you like something to eat?'

She puts the tray on the chest of drawers and helps me to sit up.

'I feel fine now, dear,' I say, telling the truth for once. I feel pretty good in fact. I wasn't the slightest bit hungry until she arrived, but the smell of melting butter on the toast makes my mouth water.

She gets out the bed table and opens its truncated legs, brings the food over and sets it down in front of me. Then she closes the door and pours the tea before sitting down in my armchair. She often stays to keep me company while I eat.

After a moment she says, 'I hope you don't mind me being nosy, but can I ask you something?'

I nod, my mouth full of egg and toast.

'This morning, when you had your funny turn, you know, in the middle of my DVD?'

I look at her blankly.

'You called out a name. You said, 'I'm so sorry, Stefan'. You said it a couple of times.'

This takes me by surprise, I cannot remember saying it. Tentatively, I test my reactions by repeating the name inside my head, *Stefan,*

Stefan, Stefan, until it starts to sound like a wave drawing back against the shingle. Best of all, blessed relief, the passing of time seems to have eased the guilt and sorrow. The memory feels strong and comforting, like a beautiful dream.

'Who's Stefan? And why are you sorry?' Emily persists.

I take another bite of egg and toast. Another sip of tea.

'So,' she says, 'are you going to tell me? You don't have to, of course,' she adds, carefully. 'But better out than in, as you always say.'

Her smile weakens me. I've started to pack up my life, sort out my affairs, organise my papers and the other collected ephemera of eighty years, but this is one piece of unfinished business I've tried to ignore; because I don't know how to deal with it.

I need to confess and ask for forgiveness, before I die, but the people to whom I owe my apologies are long gone. Except for Gwen, and I have no idea where she is, or even whether she is still alive. But now I can see a way forward and as if she's read my thoughts, Emily says, 'You can tell me, Gran. I can keep a secret, promise.'

The decision is made. I finish my last mouthful, and put down my knife and fork.

'Okay then,' I say. 'Are you sitting comfortably?'

She nods, nestling down into the little armchair next to my bed, and looking up expectantly.

So, not knowing how much I will tell, I make a start. 'One day, your great-uncle John came home and said he wanted to help some Jewish children get out of Nazi Germany . . . '

My granddaughter listens intently, without saying a word or moving a muscle, as I explain how I became a silk weaver, how Stefan and the boys came to work at the mill, how her uncle John went off to war, and her great-grandfather died trying to save someone in the rubble of the Blitz. How I found myself in charge of the mill, and the pressure of the contracts to supply wartime silk.

The teapot has gone cold by the time I get to the part about my lie, and I wonder whether I will be able to explain to her what I can barely admit to myself, let alone to anyone else. But the words pour out, as if my brain has been subconsciously rehearsing them for most of my life.

'It was a dreadful, terrible mistake,' I say. 'I have regretted it ever since.'

'I don't see why it was so terrible,' she says in a whisper. 'Everyone makes mistakes. You taught me that, Gran.'

'But this was much, much worse.'

'Why? No one got hurt, did they?'

So, with the sadness spilling out until it almost chokes me, I tell her about the telegram and the visit from Peter Newman. How I believed that Stefan died as the result of the faulty parachute silk I allowed through. And then I run out of words.

The room is silent for a moment. There are pools of tears in her brown eyes, and the crimson flush of her cheeks matches the dash of dye in her fringe.

'Oh my goodness, Gran,' she says quietly, 'Has this been haunting you all these years?' I nod and hand her a handkerchief. She wipes her face and sniffs a bit.

'I'm so sorry,' she says. 'No wonder you were so nervous about my jump.' More sniffling and throat clearing. 'I even made you watch the DVD.'

'You mustn't blame yourself. How were you to know?' I say, and we have a long hug. She sits down again and takes my hand.

'Look, Gran,' she says, in a matter-of-fact kind of way, 'do you realise you've been beating yourself up all these years over an accident which was probably nothing to do with what happened at the mill?'

'Perhaps,' I say, doubtfully. In all honesty, I don't know what to think any more.

'Did you ever try to find out what caused it?'

I remember now. 'After VE Day I wrote to the ministry but got the standard reply: official secrets and all that.'

'But that's more than sixty years ago, isn't it? Surely they would tell us now. Isn't there some-thing called the fifty-year rule? Or was it forty? I can look it up on the internet, find out who to write to.'

'I'm not so sure I really want to know, my darling, after so long,' I say, alarmed at the thought.

'But if it proved it wasn't the parachute that caused Stefan's death?' she says. 'Then it would clear your conscience after all these years.'

A band tightens painfully around my temples, the thought of learning the truth feels suddenly

380

terrifying. 'But suppose they confirm it *did?*'

She pauses and I can see there's a plan formulating in that clever little mind of hers. 'Did you ever tell anyone else? Grandpa?'

I shake my head. 'You are the first person I've ever told, and you will be the last,' I say firmly. 'Telling you has made me feel so much better, but I don't want to find out any more. Whether or not it caused the accident, letting that faulty silk through was a terrible thing and I'll never forgive myself.'

'Okay, I understand.' She looks pensive for a moment, and then she says, 'Have you got any photos of Stefan, Gran?'

I picture the old suitcase in its hiding place at the back of the spare room wardrobe, its hidden secrets safely locked away, and my resolve falters. Am I ready to open it again, I wonder? But then I think: if not now, then when? Never? Just leave it to my family to find it when I am gone? No, Stefan's life deserves more respect. It is time to recognise that loving him was an important part of who I am, and should be celebrated. My mind is made up. I take a deep breath and tell Emily to go and get the suitcase. She soon returns with it, triumphant.

'It's locked, Gran. Have you got a key?'

'In the little drawer, top right hand side of my desk,' I say, pointing, and in an instant the old leather case is on the table in front of me, and the key is in my hand. I'm flustered for a moment, recalling with perfect clarity the relief I felt when I closed it the last time, fifty-five years ago. Like closing a terrible chapter of my life, putting behind me that fatal error and my dreadful behaviour, so that I could stop thinking about it and move on.

Now, Emily is standing impatiently beside me. There is no going back.

The two brass catches unlock easily and flick open with a satisfying, good quality clunk. As I open the lid and cautiously lean it back onto its leather hinges a mixture of ancient smells wafts out — brown paper, raw silk, envelope gum, writing ink, rubber bands, photographers' chemicals — and with it a wave of memories.

Everything is untouched, and seems unmarked by the passing of half a century. On top of the khaki canvas bag is the letter, with my name in faded ink: *Mrs Lily Holmes*. I lift it up cautiously, turn it over. I can hear Emily holding her breath.

'Gran? It's still sealed. Haven't you read it? All these years?' she whispers beside me.

I can only shake my head.

'Shall we open it?'

I nod.

My dearest Lilymouse,
If you are reading this you will know that I didn't make it. I am so, so sorry. I could have refused this mission but I am sure you understand why I have to go. I owe it to us all, but particularly my family and our friends.

You have been my world, these past five years. From the second I first saw you I fell in love. Head over heels. With you I have experienced the most blissful moments of my life, and thinking about you and our future together has kept me going throughout all our times apart. I want to enjoy peace with you, see the world together as we promised, have lots more babies and grow old with you and our family around me.

My eyes are brimming with tears and my glasses are so misted up I cannot read any more. Emily gently takes the letter from me and reads the rest of it, her voice wobbly and cracked.

But if this is not to be, then all I can say is that I love you, Lily, with every part of my being and every cell of my body. This will never die and I hope you will remember it throughout your life. When he is old enough please tell our little one that his father loved him, very much.
For ever. S xxx

She puts down the letter carefully, and pulls me to her. For a long time we hold each other, sobbing quietly. Eventually she sits up, wipes her face with the back of her hand and takes a deep breath.

'Oh, Gran,' is all she says. 'What a beautiful letter.'

I nod, and try to shake myself back into this world again, feeling numb. I can't bring myself to talk about it, not immediately.

'How's about another cuppa?' I manage to croak.

While she's gone, I put the letter gently back into its envelope, give it a kiss and tuck it under my pillow where it will be safe and warm, for reading again later.

I take the khaki canvas bag out of the suitcase and my arthritic fingers manage to open, with only a slight struggle, its stiff canvas buckles. Inside I find his Pioneer Corps beret, a half-finished packet of Players and a Zippo lighter, a paper-back of Sherlock Holmes short stories called *The Last Bow*, and that familiar black leather writing case.

I unzip the case with a trembling hand. Tucked in to the pockets are a bundle of blue aerogrammes in my handwriting held together by a withered rubber band, and the buff envelope of photographs, one of me on our wedding day and the three smaller photos of his mother, father and sisters that Stefan first showed me in the tennis hut. They peer sadly out of the grainy black and white prints like faces from a history book.

Long after the war ended, Kurt wrote to tell me that he and Walter had gone back to Germany, only to discover that their parents, and grandparents, aunts and uncles had all perished in concentration camps, except for a cousin who had managed to get to America. The farm had been split up, the house was derelict. They had travelled north to Hamburg to trace the Hoffmann family, uncovering further grim news. Isaak had been taken first, and there seemed to be no record of him being seen ever again. Hannah, Anna and Else were taken to

Buchenwald and had managed to survive until an outbreak of typhoid swept through the camp, killing nearly half of its malnourished inmates. They perished within weeks of the end of the war.

I check all the pockets in the writing case and find, at last, the little shred of his tallith — the final symbol of his Jewishness.

Inside the suitcase is the green vellum-covered album, with a label in my girlish hand — *Our Wedding Day* — a bundle of his letters to me tied with a blue ribbon and the Hay Camp note, and underneath this is a single item of his clothing, the old brown leather jacket, the one he arrived in. I press it to my face and the leather still smells of him — the nutty aroma of raw silk mingled with tobacco. As I pull it out of the suitcase, something small and red falls out: it is the felt drawstring pouch containing my wedding and engagement rings.

As Emily comes back with the tea tray I hastily push the little pouch down the side of the bed. She sets the tray down and looks at me carefully.

'Mum's wondering what we've been doing in here all this time,' she says. 'She told me not to tire you out. So shall I leave you in peace now? We can talk about it some more tomorrow, or another time?'

'No, I'm not tired,' I lie. I feel safe with her now, confident that I can explore my memories further without anger and pain. The genie is out of the bottle now, I think, and that is fine. I don't need to put it back.

'If you're sure?' I nod, and she pours the tea.

'I've got so many questions, but I'll understand if you don't want to answer them,' she says.

'Ask away,' I say, feeling stronger with every
sip.

'I hardly dare ask, but what does he mean by
'our little one'? Were you pregnant?'

I nod, wondering why her eyebrows arch with
alarm.

'You're not going to tell me it's Dad?' she
blurts out.

'Oh, no,' I say hurriedly, realising how insensi-
tive I've been. 'Your dad is definitely Grandpa's
son. I got pregnant, but I had a miscarriage at
three months, after Stefan and I got caught in an
air raid. But I never got the chance to tell him.
Anyway, I found out that it wasn't a boy after all.
It was a little girl.'

'How dreadful. I'm so sorry, Gran,' Emily
says, 'I never knew.'

'Not many people did,' I say. 'I named her
Hannah, after his mother. I sometimes imagine
that if she'd lived, she'd have been a bit like you.'

'How like me?'

'Smart, sassy, independent. The way I used to
be.'

'I'm glad Dad is Grandpa's son, all the same,'
she says. 'It would've been a bit of a shock for
him to find out he was someone else's.'

We laugh together now, it feels so easy. The
memories have haunted me for so many years,
bottled up and painful, but I am starting to
understand that these experiences made me
what I am, and I must accept them. Acceptance.
Wasn't that the final stage of grieving Emily

talked about? At least I've stopped being angry. So perhaps I'm nearly there.

'Have you got a photo of Stefan?' she says.

My fingers fumble to undo the satin string ties of the wedding album and turn the heavy pages of tiny black and white prints that I so carefully mounted with small photo-corners. They were taken by Gwen with her Box Brownie — no official photographer for us, in that rushed wartime wedding.

'That's him,' I say, pointing.

'Wow. He's really fit,' she says, peering closer. 'So dark and mysterious-looking. I can see why you fell for him. And look at you in that gorgeous dress. You look like a film star. What's it made of? Raw silk?'

'Cream Shantung. The dress was made by your great-grandmother in just a couple of weeks.' I'm smiling now at the memories I've tried to deny, all these years.

'When I get married I'm going to have a dress made out of it too,' she says.

'And so you shall, my darling,' I say. 'I'm sure your dad will arrange it for you.'

'"Wedding of Sgt Stephen Holmes and Mrs Lily Holmes, 14th February 1944",' she reads. 'Stephen Holmes?'

'He had to change his name. His whole identity really. You know, because he was Jewish. It was too dangerous to be a Jew in Europe those days.'

'Oh,' she says, understanding. 'Have you seen that statue of the Jewish children at Liverpool Street station?'

'I went to see it once, but since then I've tried to avoid it — it's too sad,' I say.

She turns back to the album, 'What's the uniform?'

'Pioneer Corps — he'd just left it to join the other lot.'

'Did you ever find out what they were called?'

'I read an article about something called SOE — Special Operations Executive — a few years ago in the paper. They did undercover stuff like that. But Peter Newman never told me any details. It was top secret anyway.'

She shakes her head, and turns back to the photo. 'So that's Great-Auntie Vera. I recognise her. But who's this?'

It must have been one of the shots Mother took. We are all on a slant. Gwen is frowning at the camera and her hair is flying loose from its careless bun. Even in this small black and white print I can make out the freckles. What would I give to see them again.

'Gwen Collins,' I say, trying to sound more nonchalant than I feel. 'Used to work at Verners during the war.'

Emily looks up at me quizzically. 'She must have been a close friend, to come to your wedding?'

'She was,' I say. 'A very good friend. She was factory manager all through the war and she looked after my mother and me after Great-Grandpa Harold was killed.' I don't have the heart to say how she supported and comforted me, after Stefan died.

'What happened to her? Is she still alive?'

'I don't know,' I say truthfully. 'She left Westbury after the war and went off to live with her mother. We lost touch. I did try to find her but she didn't leave any address.'

'That's a shame,' Emily says mildly. 'She sounds like a great person.'

One of the best, I think. But treated shamefully by me.

After a while I put the album aside and take out the Hay Camp note. 'You might like to keep this,' I say, handing it to her. 'They printed their own currency in the Australian internment camp and he brought it back for me. Might be worth something these days, you never know.'

'Wow,' she says, examining the roughly printed words on the scruffy scrap of paper. 'I will keep it safe, thank you. But you know I'd never sell it, Gran. It's an heirloom.'

This is the moment. I reach down the side of the chair cushion and find the small red pouch. As I pass it to her, I can see Stefan's smile as he handed it to me that night, just as if he were in the room. She loosens the drawstring and gently shakes out the rings into her palm, with a small intake of breath. She holds the engagement ring up to the light and twists it so we can both see how the sapphires still twinkle their deep blueness, and how the pearls gleam, after all these years.

'Oh. It's beautiful. Are those pearls? And what are these blue stones? Can I try it on?' I nod and she slips it onto her finger.

'They're sapphires, and it was his mother's ring,' I say. 'He gave it to me when he proposed

389

on Christmas Eve 1943, after he'd got back from Australia. All of his family died, so it's very precious. The wedding ring isn't valuable, but I want you to keep them both. Look after them, and pass them on to your children to keep a little bit of him alive.'

For once, she is out of words and keeps her head bent, looking at the rings. After a moment she swallows and looks up, blinking back the tears, and leans to kiss my cheek.

'It's so special; I don't know what to say.'

'That's a first,' I say, and we laugh again.

24

*As one of the oldest branches of textile manu-
facture the British silk industry has inherited
traditional skills and craftsmanship, which have
been handed down through generations. But
despite its many setbacks, the industry today is
not only vigorously alive, but is marked by a
modern outlook and an alertness to new trends
and technologies which will surely stand it in
good stead for centuries to come.*

Last words of The History of Silk,
by Harold Verner

It is two weeks since my chat with Emily, and I
am more at peace with the world than I can
remember.

I have been re-reading all of Stefan's letters,
and mine to him. The young woman who wrote
them is a stranger to me now, with all her
desperate passions and wild flights of fantasy,
but I feel great affection for her. I have spent
hours studying all the photographs, even using
my magnifying glass, and find that the anger and
guilt have almost gone, and are replaced by
tender and sometimes even joyful memories. But
the photos of Gwen still make me mournful.
How could I have let someone who was so
important to me disappear without trace?

The only post I get these days is invitations to
funerals, so when Emily arrives with an envelope

my first response is to wonder who has died now.
She has a mischievous look, as if she knows who
the letter is from.

'I've got a confession to make,' she says,
settling into my armchair, still holding it.

'Is the letter for me?' I ask.

'Yes, but I need to explain.'

'Explain away, I'm not going anywhere.' What
madcap scheme is she up to now?

'When you showed me the photo album you
mentioned Gwen Collins.'

I nod, and my heart starts to thump.

'I googled her and found her name on a
website about Dorset artists. I emailed them for
her address.'

I am too astounded to ask what googled
means. 'Dear God, you've found her. You know
where she lives?'

She hands me the envelope. It's been opened,
and is addressed to Emily.

'Shall I read it?' I ask.

She nods.

2 Ledbury Cottages
Bingham's Houghton
Dorset

Dear Emily,
   *The secretary of Dorset Artists' Circle has
been in touch to say you contacted them on
behalf of your grandmother, asking about
Gwen Collins.*
   To answer your questions:
   Yes, Gwen is alive but is currently in

hospital. *It's not good news I'm afraid.*

*Yes, I am sure she remembers your grand-
mother. She told me about her job at
Verners and how she lived with Lily and
Grace during the war.*

*Finally, I really don't know whether she
would like to get in contact again. Lily was
very dear to Gwen at one time but, for some
reason she's never fully explained, they lost
touch and she didn't seem keen to talk about
it.*

*Sorry for the 'snail mail' but we are not
wired up (if that's the phrase).*

With best wishes
Catherine Ryan

'Gran?' Emily's voice seems to come from
somewhere far away. 'Are you cross with me for
not asking you first?'

I have waited so long for news of Gwen, anything.
Now I know she's still alive, the idea of seeing
her again, of asking for her forgiveness, seems
suddenly the most important thing in the world.
I clear my throat and manage to croak, 'Of course
not, my lovely. I'm thrilled you've found her.'

'But this Catherine person doesn't seem sure
it's a good idea to get in touch.'

The words jiggle on the page: *It's not good
news I'm afraid.* Time might be running out. I
don't care what Catherine Ryan thinks.

'How do you do this googling thing?' I ask.
'Would it find a telephone number?'

'I'll give it a try,' she says, getting up. 'Back in
a mo.'

We google, and we ring directory enquiries, but there are no numbers for G. Collins or C. Ryan at that address. Then clever-clogs Emily suggests we ring the nearest hospital, in Dorchester.

'They won't let me talk to her,' I say, losing my nerve.

'Worth a try?'

'Go on then,' I agree reluctantly. It is useless to resist when a Verner jaw juts like that.

She grabs the telephone and dials.

'Good afternoon, I was wondering if I could speak to a Miss Gwen Collins,' Emily says. 'I think she's a patient at your hospital.'

There is a voice at the other end and she punches the air with her fist and puts her hand over the mouthpiece, 'Bullseye! They're putting me through to the ward.'

After a long silence, she says, 'Hello. Is that the ward sister? . . . Do you have a Gwen Collins on your ward? Is there any chance I could speak to her? . . . Or Catherine Ryan . . . I'm a very close friend . . . Yes, practically related.'

I am transfixed by my granddaughter's chutzpah. I could never be so bold. After another agonising pause there's a voice at the other end.

Emily squeaks with surprise but quickly gathers her composure. 'Is that Catherine Ryan? This is Emily, Lily's granddaughter. You wrote to me?'

She points silently at the phone and then to me, suggesting I should take it. I shake my head and she says, 'Hold on a tick, I'll put you onto Gran.'

She hands the receiver to me. It feels as though I am taking a grenade packed with emotion that could explode at any moment. My hands shake so much I nearly drop it and my voice comes out awkward and tremulous. 'Miss Ryan? This is Lily. So sorry to trouble you,' I manage to say.

'I thought we might hear from you,' she says calmly, apparently unfazed. 'Your granddaughter's obviously a very determined young woman. But I'm sorry you can't speak to Gwen right now, she's gone to have a scan.' I detect a sing-song lilt to her voice, Irish perhaps?

'How is she?' I can hardly bear to hear the answer.

'She's rallied a bit today. If the scan's okay they might let her home.'

I struggle to find a way of asking the question. Finally I just say it straight. 'Miss Ryan, I am so pleased to have found you and I very much want to see Gwen again. Do you think she would agree?'

'Truthfully, I don't know,' she says. 'But when she's feeling a bit more with it, I'll ask her, shall I?'

'I don't want to put any pressure on her.'

'Even if she says yes, she'll be too unwell to travel, so you'd have to come to us. Could you manage that?'

'I'm sure I could persuade my son to drive me,' I say, crossing my fingers. Emily is nodding energetically. 'I'll give you my number and wait to hear from you, shall I?'

'That'd be grand,' she says.

It's been only three days but feels like months. The questions chase each other exhaustingly round my head. What's happening? Is Gwen home yet? How is she? Has Catherine mentioned me? Has she asked her? What if she says no?

In the meantime I have been working on the family.

'Are you crazy, Mum?' Simon says. 'You struggle to get to the loo on your own and you're talking about travelling all that way?'

'Don't be so rude to your mother,' Louise chides. 'But seriously, Lily, it's a long way. Five hours' drive at least. I'm sure your doctor wouldn't recommend it.'

'She's got to go, Mum. It's so important,' says my faithful granddaughter. I smile at her gratefully.

'I don't care what the doctor says,' I say firmly. 'If you won't drive me I'll take a taxi.'

At last, Catherine telephones. 'Gwen's back home,' she says. 'She's very weak but they've got the pain medication pretty much sorted. She would like to see you, Lily, very much. Can you come? Soon-ish?'

I feel tearful with relief. 'Would later this week do? Say Thursday or Friday?'

'Either,' she says.

'Thank you so much, Catherine. I do look forward to meeting you.'

'Please, call me Cath,' she says. 'See you soon.'

My son has caved in. He will drive and we will stay in a bed and breakfast overnight on the way, to break the journey. Emily's determined to come too and she's booked somewhere for the three of us, with a bedroom for me on the ground floor.

I feel foolishly nervous, as if it's a job interview. At night, I lie in bed rehearsing what I will say. During the day I unearth outfits unworn for years and exhaust myself trying them on.

'What do you think, blue or beige?' I ask Emily, holding the cardigans against me.

'Blue every time, Gran. Bin the beige,' she replies, with that wonderful conviction of the young.

My home hairdresser comes to smarten me up — my hair is still thick and straight, but all white now, of course. We take the photo album and Emily helps me wrap (with ribbon, no tricky sticky tape) a copy of the book.

As we draw up in the unpaved lane outside a small stone cottage — the middle in a row of three — a person I take to be Cath is standing in the porch. She's a younger woman, I guess in her late sixties, wearing a gardening apron over jeans and a T-shirt. She could be Gwen's sister, has the same sturdy build, pale skin with freckles, and streaks of ginger in unkempt greying curls.

The front garden is overgrown but there are a few splashes of late colour: lanky yellow roses and the last red blossoms at the top of tall hollyhock stems swaying in the breeze.

'You must be Cath,' I say from the open car window. She nods. 'Meet my son Simon and granddaughter Emily — she's the one who tracked you down.'

'So pleased to meet you all,' she says. 'Come on in.'

Emily and Simon support me as I shuffle up the gravel path with my sticks and when we reach the porch, she suggests I rest a moment. The wooden settle and my bones creak in unison.

'I'm trying to get on top of it all, without much success,' Cath says waving at the garden with a rueful smile, a bundle of bindweed still in her hand. 'I had this idea of smartening up for your visit, but it's a lost cause I'm afraid.'

'How is she?' I ask.

'Well, she's frail, as you'll see. But the pain medicine's working okay at the moment. She's really looking forward to this.'

The front doorway is so small Simon has to stoop and, inside, the ceilings are almost as low. The room smells of wood smoke. At first I think it's empty; a threadbare three-piece suite is set round a blackened brick fireplace and a low table laden with books and newspapers. On the walls are sketches and watercolour landscapes I assume to be Gwen's. No nudes, though.

'They're here, Gwen.' Cath leads our slow procession towards the other end of the room where a couple of high-backed winged armchairs are placed close to each other, facing away from us. Beyond these are French windows through which I can see another overgrown patch of greenery with fruit trees.

'Lily, is that you?' That voice, deep and smoky,

is so familiar the tears prickle behind my eyes. But as I shuffle round and come in sight of her, it's as if someone has played a trick on me. There, in one of the chairs, is not Gwen but a small crumpled person with hardly any hair, whose bones shine through shrivelled skin like a fledgling bird. She gazes at us, slightly bemused, as Emily guides me to another chair and helps me sit.

Cath offers to make tea and the others go with her, tactfully leaving us alone.

'Gwen?' The pale green eyes, huge in her shrunken face, slowly focus into that old intense look. Skeletal hands reach towards me. I am surprised to find them so warm, the grip so strong. I remember the deft way she manipulated tiny picking shears, how her fingers travelled across a warp, detecting broken threads just by the feel. And those hands softly on the back of my neck, stroking away my nightmares.

'Lily? Is it really you?' she says in that surprisingly robust voice.

I nod, unable to speak.

'I've been thinking about you so much lately,' she says. Fat pools of tears brim in the red-rimmed eyes.

'Me too,' I murmur and pass a handkerchief — I've brought two. After a bit, Cath returns with the tea tray and we are now both sobbing openly but laughing at ourselves too. Our hands are entwined like a lovers' knot, neither of us willing to let go.

'Would you look at the pair of you,' Cath says delightedly, setting down the tray. 'You seem to be getting on very well. We're going to take our tea into the garden. Leave you two to your memories. Can you serve yourselves? Shout if you need anything.'

By the time I finish pouring the tea my tears have dried and my voice is stronger. 'She's a lovely woman, Gwen.'

'I know,' she says fondly. 'We've been together thirty-five years. A long time. I'm very blessed.'

I sit back, take a deep breath. 'Gwen, there's something . . . ' I gasp with exasperation, struggling to recall the words I've rehearsed in my head so many times.

'It's all right,' she says. 'You don't have to say it.'

I'm determined not to falter, to say it properly.

'The way Cath supports you now, that's how you were for me back then. The warp to my weft. Remember? After VE Day I tried to find you, ask you to come back and see if we could start again. But you disappeared. No trace.'

'That's how I wanted it,' she mutters.

'I just felt so guilty I couldn't forgive myself. What I need to know now is,' she looks up at me sharply, wondering what I'm going to say, 'can you forgive me?'

She doesn't reply at once and I find myself holding my breath, fearful of how she'll respond.

Then she says, simply, 'You hurt me terribly. If I'd stayed any longer the bitterness would have been like this bloody cancer of mine, eating away at me. In the end, the best thing was just to try to cut it out. Brutal, I know, but for the best.'

She reaches forward and takes a sip of tea as I

listen to the swish of the pulse in my ears. I know she hasn't finished. She puts the cup down with a shaky hand and takes a moment to summon reserves of scarce strength.

'Mum was ill and at first it took all my energy to nurse her. When she died I fell into a black hole for a while. Eventually I pulled myself together and went to a counsellor. Cath and I met in the waiting room — she had this crazy idea she could be cured of women. Hah.' Gwen laughs in that familiar stagey way. 'We soon put paid to that. The therapist was rubbish, but Cath soon healed my depression.'

She pauses and smiles at the memories. 'As time went by I thought about you less and less, and after a while realised that I had forgiven you, after all. And now all I remember is how much I loved you.'

Her words fill the silent room and wrap themselves round me like a balm. My shoulders relax, the pains in my legs are easing. After a bit she squeezes my hand and the spell is broken. Before long we are cackling like a couple of crazy old witches over some long forgotten joke when the others come back from the garden.

'So who's this handsome young fellow?' Gwen says, peering up at him.

'The ninth generation of Verners,' I say. 'Don't you recognise the Huguenot genes?'

'Simon Merrison,' he says, bending to shake her bird-like hand in his great paw. 'Lily's son. Very pleased to meet you.' He sits down beside her, in the pool of sunshine filtering through the dusty panes of the French windows.

'And this is my granddaughter, Emily Merrison,' I say.

Gwen looks at her with that intense gaze I remember so well. 'What a beautiful girl. The image of your gran when she was your age, Emily.'

Emily blushes at the compliment, just as I used to.

'I recall a Merrison,' Gwen says, turning a quizzical gaze to me. 'Michael, wasn't it? Yarn merchant from the Midlands somewhere. The one with the curly hair. You married him in the end?'

I nod, tears pricking the back of my eyes as I recall the photos in the funeral slide show of that tall, confident young man with the almost violet eyes, who loved Battenburg cake.

'Good looking boy, I always thought. Didn't he go to Syria or someplace and send us back that troublesome yarn?' she says.

'He came to Westbury a few weeks after VE day and we got married in 1947,' I say, ignoring her mention of troublesome yarn. 'We were married for nearly fifty-three years — very happily.'

'My grandpa,' Emily says fondly. 'He was a lovely man.'

'The kindest man on earth,' I say. 'Absolutely the best husband anyone could have wished for.'

'I take it from the past tense that he's not alive?'

'He died earlier this year,' I say. 'But my son and his wife, and their two wonderful children have moved in with me to The Chestnuts. I'm a lucky woman.'

'Ah, The Chestnuts,' she sighs. 'I lived there too, you know, for a short time,' she says to Emily and Simon. 'Such a fine house. Those wonderful Constable views.'

'The views haven't changed,' he says. 'The house has central heating and a few other mod cons, but otherwise it's much as it was.'

'The tennis court?'

'That's gone I'm afraid. We needed space for more car parking.'

'And the kitchen garden? The smell of gooseberries warmed in the sun always takes me back.'

'Sorry, that too.'

She sighs wearily, and turns to me. 'And did brave brother John come home safely?'

'Yes, he did, but thin and looking terribly aged,' I say. 'He and Vera finally got married just before Christmas '45 which perked him up a bit, and he worked at the mill for a while. But he couldn't bear it. After all those years of being cooped up he was desperate for wide open spaces. He started volunteering for the local nature reserve, then got a full time job as a warden. Badly paid, but he loved it. Stayed there till he retired.'

'Is John still alive?' Gwen asks.

'No, he died five years ago. And Vera got dementia sadly, spent her last few years in a home. I couldn't manage looking after her myself.'

'By God, old age is not for the faint hearted,' she says, and we laugh in mutual sympathy.

'So you ended up running the mill single handed, after all?'

'You always said I had management potential.' Gwen smiles. 'You remembered.'

'Mum was an excellent managing director,' Simon says. 'Highly respected by everyone in the business.'

'You didn't believe me at first, did you?' she says drily. 'But you proved my point in the end.'

I take the photograph album out of my bag and we hand it around, exclaiming happily at shared memories. It is still hard to believe that somehow, wonderfully, I can face them without flinching, even welcome them. The ghosts have been outed, as Emily said the other day about a corrupt politician. It seems appropriate; they're better outed than in.

'How's business?' Gwen asks, handing back the album.

Simon tells her about the ups and downs of the past few decades: Rapier machines that have done away with shuttles and weave at twenty times the speed, the opening up of Chinese raw silk supplies, the decline of the tie and menswear trade, the royal wedding dresses they have woven. And the success of a new business; the silk furnishings trade, reintegrated into the firm in 1980 after splitting away in a Verner brothers' feud a century ago.

She listens intently but I can see the effort of fighting the pain is draining the animation from her face. We will have to leave soon and it is unbearable to contemplate. I know that I will never see her again.

Then Emily says, 'We forgot the book, Gran. It's in the car, I'll go and get it.'

She comes back and helps Gwen unwrap the parcel. On the book jacket is a black and white photograph of Father, standing proudly with one of the new power looms they had just installed in the late '20s, with Jim Williams beside him.

'How wonderful, I'd forgotten about Harold's book. How did you get it published?'

'Simon and I, we finished writing it together,' I say, 'Emily typed it into the computer and scanned all the photographs so we could get it printed as part of Verners' two hundred and fiftieth anniversary celebrations.'

She's turning the pages, looking at the photographs, touching the small samples of silk pasted into the index. But she has missed the frontispiece. I lean over to open it, and she reads out loud what I have written there: 'To Gwen, who taught me about warp and weft, and helped me through the dark times. See p. 122.' She turns to the page, and there is the photo of the two of us standing outside the double doors at the front of Old Mill, squinting into the sunshine. The caption reads: *Verners' wartime management team, Lily Verner and Gwen Collins in 1943.*

'I don't remember that being taken. What a pair of scruffs,' she says, laughing, showing it to Cath. 'Whatever was I doing in those dreadful turn-ups?' She closes the book and turns to me, more seriously, 'But we did the business, didn't we?'

'We definitely did the business. Thanks largely to you, we held it together and did the business.'

As we start to leave, Cath helps her to her feet

and I totter over to embrace her. I feel the bones beneath her skin, the frail arms that weakly hug me. When I put my lips to it her cheek feels like parchment, but is warm with life.

She whispers, 'I'm so glad you came. Of course I forgive you. I just hope you can forgive yourself.'

Because my throat is clogged with sadness, I just say, 'I love you.'

Epilogue

The girl pulls over a plastic chair and sits down, tucking her long legs under the hospital bed. The old woman's hands, brown mottled skin draped loosely over visible bones, are neatly arranged across her chest. As the girl takes one into her own hand she is surprised by its warmth. She looks intently into the inert grey face, its closed eyes, the slack lips moving with each shallow breath.

'Gran? Can you hear me? I've got two very important things to tell you. Are you listening?'

There is no response from the bed, but she carries on.

'First of all, you know Stefan's Hay Camp note you gave me? Dad took it to get it valued and it's worth thousands! Amazing. He says I should pay for Uni with it, but I'm going to keep it with the rings, to remember him by, like you said. And pass it on to my grandchildren. Now, this is the really important thing, so listen carefully.'

With her other hand the girl unfolds the heavy cream bond, with its neat print and official crest, and reads out loud:

Dear Miss Merrison
Your enquiry about the deaths of Sgt
Stephen Holmes and his colleagues on or
about 15th May 1944 has been passed to me

407

by the Office for Information.

I can confirm that Sgt Holmes, formerly of Royal Pioneer Corps, joined the Special Operations Executive in January 1944 and after a period of training, was one of twelve men selected for a mission to be parachuted into France as part of advance operations in preparation for the D-Day landings.

Regarding the accidents which killed Sgt Holmes and the other men that night, there is no evidence of what caused them. One possibility is that the plane's altimeter was faulty, causing the pilot to fly too low at the drop points. This could have resulted in a miscalculation in timing for pulling the rip-cords, and thus landing too fast.

However I can tell you that the parachutes used by paratroops such as the SOE operatives in 1944 were almost certainly not made of silk. By this point in the war, silk canopies were used only where cockpit space was very limited, i.e. for fighter pilots, but for all other purposes, such as dropping paratroops, equipment and supplies, parachutes of cotton and/or nylon had been in general use for some months.

I hope this information is of some use in your research.

The girl puts the letter down and looks into her grandmother's skeletal face. The eyes are still closed, sunk deep and purple in their sockets.

'You see? I was right. It wasn't your silk. Not your fault,' she whispers. 'Please, Gran? Please tell me you can hear me.'

The room is silent except for the sigh of the old woman's breathing, the hum of the heating pipes and the squeak of shoes on the linoleum outside.

And then the girl feels something. She cannot see them moving but the bony fingers press almost imperceptibly into her own.

Is she imagining it?

No, she dismisses the thought.

She is sure of it.

We do hope that you have enjoyed reading this large print book.

Did you know that all of our titles are available for purchase?

We publish a wide range of high quality large print books including:
Romances, Mysteries, Classics
General Fiction
Non Fiction and Westerns

Special interest titles available in large print are:
The Little Oxford Dictionary
Music Book
Song Book
Hymn Book
Service Book

Also available from us courtesy of Oxford University Press:
Young Readers' Dictionary
(large print edition)
Young Readers' Thesaurus
(large print edition)

For further information or a free brochure, please contact us at:
Ulverscroft Large Print Books Ltd.,
The Green, Bradgate Road, Anstey,
Leicester, LE7 7FU, England.
Tel: (00 44) **0116 236 4325**
Fax: (00 44) **0116 234 0205**

Other titles published by
The House of Ulverscroft:

TOBY'S ROOM

Pat Barker

Toby and Elinor, brother and sister, closest friends and confidants, are sharers of a dark secret, carried from the sweltering summer of 1912 into the battlefields of France and wartime London in 1917. When Toby is reported 'Missing, Believed Killed', another secret casts a lengthening shadow over Elinor's world: how exactly did Toby die — and why? Elinor's fellow art student, Kit Neville, recently returned from the war with his face destroyed, was there in the shell-hole when Toby met his fate, but he is in no mood to talk. Enlisting the help of former lover Paul Tarrant, Elinor determines to uncover the truth. Only then will she be able to finally close the door to Toby's room.

TEN THINGS I'VE LEARNT ABOUT LOVE

Sarah Butler

Alice has just returned to London from months of travelling abroad. She is late to hear the news that her father is dying, and returns to the family home only just in time to say goodbye. Daniel hasn't had a roof over his head for almost thirty years, but to him the city of London feels like home in a way that no bricks and mortar ever did. He spends every day searching for his daughter; the daughter he has never met. Until now . . .